I0778980

BLACK RAVIK
Return To Jeeapa

SCREENPLAY

Paul D. Escudero

WORKBOOK PRESS LLC
187 E Warm Springs Rd,
Suite B285 Las Vegas NV 89119 USA

Website: https://workbookpress.com/
Hotline: 1-888-818-4856
Email: admin@workbookpress.com

Ordering Information:

Quantity sales. Special discounts are available on quantity purchases by corporations, associations, and others. For details, contact the publisher at the address above.

Library of Congress Control Number:

ISBN-13:   978-1-965732-33-5 Paperback Version

REV. DATE: 03/25/2025

Black Ravik

Paul D. Escudero

EXT. DAY. SPACE PORT LOCATED IN THE MERGENKY CAPITAL CITY OF QUOM ON PLANET GWABA.

MUSIC DURING VOICEOVERS AND VANCES DEPARTURE:

[https://www.youtube.com/watch?v=1-kbEQmVgbc]
Bortkiewicz - Piano Concerto No 3

VOICE OVER

Departure and regret permeated the air as Vance and his family gathered at the space port located in the Mergenky capital city of Quom on what turned out to be a somber day.

None of them predicted what could happen so unexpectedly like this.

Kara, Vance's spouse and their two children who were very mature for their ages, patiently waited for those final moments as Vance's shuttle prepared for launch.

Vance and Kara's two children were born while traveling in space during the Andromeda Galaxy Mission aboard the Mergenky Space Federation Scout Class space craft MSFS-1.

Also, along for that past mission was Pilot Kwongab, Copilot Monachi, and their two children who also were born during the Andromeda mission creating two families in space.

This multi-year Andromeda Mission had just ended several years ago.

More than likely no other Mergenky will travel to Andromeda for generations if ever. The Andromeda Mission that resulted in two families starting in space and survived quite well thanks to planning and luck, but those experiences now influenced the complexities that now existed in their lives.

Kara resigned from the Mergenky Space Federation (MSF) immediately upon return from the Andromeda Mission because she had a family, she wanted to be close to, and the children to look after.

Vance on the other hand was like a fish out of water living in the domed city of Quom, the Mergenky capital. Vance therefore chose to remain in the service of the Mergenky Space Federation.

The experience of attempting to return Vance to Earth proved to be rather an unfortunate experience for him, that included no possibility of ever going back to Earth to live.

The opportunity to remain in the MSF gave Vance an outlet that would allow him to have a sense of achievement and experience more galactic adventures.

Vance's children were at the age now that Mergenky educational processes removed the children from the household and deposited them in Mergenky Learning Centers, where they were psychologically tested and determined what best fitted their futures.

The Mergenky Learning Centers then programmed the children to be highly successful in those professions. Vance's children had been home for a few days, excused from their Mergenky Learning Center classes to spend a brief period since their father was deploying to perform some serious activities on this upcoming mission.

Kara found refuge working in Mergenky Healing Centers after her children enrolled into a boarding school on the other side of the planet, and after the strange experiences during the Andromeda Mission, her work gave a sense of release especially with Vance departing for another assignment of which the details he could not divulge to his wife and children.

Vance's absence could extend 180 Mergenky days but would have plenty of time to unwind when he returned which would coincide with the children yearly break from the Mergenky Learning Centers allowing them to have some family time together.

Vance's immediate departure wasn't heart breaking, though Kara knew she would ultimately feel empty the minute Vance stepped aboard the transport shuttle that would take him up to MSS-21 Space Station where his ship was docked and due to depart the solar system in a few hours.

SPACE PORT
PUBLIC ANNOUNCEMENT
All passengers please proceed to Shuttle number 44
for immediate departure to MSS-21.

The announcement over the intercom suddenly added to everyone's melancholy which is unexpected for Mergenky. However, Vance's children were half human and had emotional characteristics.

Vance was suddenly regretting his decision to embark upon this adventure.

VANCE
Looks like it's time for me to go now.

KARA
Stay safe, wherever you go and don't worry about us, we'll be ok.

VOICE OVER
Kara had a strange premonition; she might not ever see Vance again. But their last few days together before Vance's departure were filled with loving affection and appreciation on many levels.

Kara and Vance had both survived the artificial intelligence disaster that Martha created during the Andromeda Mission.

And as a psychoanalyst as well as medical practitioner, Kara did everything to block those memories out of her mind.

Kara also applied neuro-electro-discontinuities to Vance so that he would put those memories far behind and focus only on the future.

Kara wasn't totally satisfied her treatments for Vance had completely worked, but the many days after the Andromeda Mission slowly evolved to a more tranquil environment.

Kara felt she had accomplished some of her objectives. She knew though, down deep inside many scars remained and would be impossible to fully heal.

The last hug was enduring and meaningful. Kara eventually came to cherish the way the departure occurred, not only for the sake of the kids who loved their father dearly.

But also, the way Vance seemed to touch Kara's inner fabric of her soul left indelible emotional marks.

Vance's gentle and kind words and the complexities of his human emotion were uncommon for Mergenky.

> *One last hug, totally uncharacteristic of the Mergenky which drew some gawkers, seemingly amused that such an emotional display in public. The nature of the departure set the stage for a fond memory that would transcend time.*
>
> *The kids were sad and bewildered, but they were fortunate their mother's profession knew how to treat them for this departure, which Kara hoped would become a lessor occurrence in the future.*

Vance looked Kara in the eyes.

VANCE
I love you, Kara.

Vance kissed Kara dutifully on her lips, then hugged the kids one more time, then bent down and grabbed his grip which contained a few personal items, then turned and walked up the ramp into the Shuttlecraft.

At the top of the ramp at the Shuttle's hatch, Vance turned waved at Kara and the Kids, and walked into the Shuttle and was guided to his seat by Artificial Intelligence (AI).

The blast shield came down in front of the visitor observation area. The clear *Glastic* panels were stronger than bullet proof glass and allowed observation of the Shuttle launch which occurred momentarily.

Civilian Shuttles were not allowed to have the Antimatter Magnetic Resonator Transformer (AMRT) magnetic drive systems, only the MSF military craft had them for security reasons.

Civilian transport appeared nothing like MSF had, but the main form of transport up to MSF-21 Space Station, was conventional *Civilian Transport Launch Vehicles* (CTLV) that had an artificial gravity machine and chemical rockets to get it up into orbit.

Thanks to the artificial gravity provided by the ship's machinery, huge rocket engines used on Earth were not needed on the Mergenky CTLV's.

Vance could not see outside the ship, there were no windows for him to look out. He knew his wife and kids were watching, and 180 days would be a long time, but it would be unlike his trip to Earth and the Andromeda Mission that took many years.

The G-forces were very mild even though acceleration was high because the anti-gravity machinery protected them from the force that would otherwise require a pressure suit. The flight up to the space station was a mere 20 minutes prior to docking.

<u>EXT. CGI. SPACE. SHUTTLE SPACE CRAFT LANDING AT SPACE STATION SS-21. (15 SECONDS)</u>

Fully under robotic control and precision, the transport CTLV slipped into the landing pad area of the huge circular space station.

Mergenky Space Station 21 (MSS-21), rotated in a fashion to give long term occupants some gravity like sensation due to the centrifugal force and the space station's gravity inducer that allowed people to walk around the extremely large circular space station as if in moderate gravity field.

All the inhabitable areas of MSS-21 were located on the giant hub approximately 6.28 miles in circumference, one would almost think looked like a lit-up bicycle tire from a distance. The inner support struts just like on a bicycle extended to the center where the power plant, artificial gravity machinery, water reservoirs, air tanks, and recycling equipment existed.

MSS-21's magnetic grippers which utilized electro-magnets on the space station landing pad areas as well as on the Shuttle landing gear frames, worked similar in fashion to Maglev Trains on Earth which provided additional breaking and a gentle landing.

MSS-21's service traversers existed that mated to the side of the shuttle pressure hull seal and door which only had to move a few inches to mate properly to the hull of the ship, establish airtight grip with the transition chamber then properly pressurize.

<u>INT. SPACE. CTLV SHUTTLE CABIN</u>

Within a minute when all the signals indicated safe to depart the Shuttle craft, the passengers were allowed to stand and take their personal articles with them.

<u>INT. SPACE. CTLV SHUTTLE PRESSURE LOCK</u>

As soon as they all were inside the pressure lock, the door to access to the Shuttle was closed and the pressure lock sealed and protected from any possible rapid air decompression.

<u>INT. SPACE. CTLV SHUTTLE DECONTAMINATION ROOM</u>

The CTLV shuttle passengers all then were guided through a door into a decontamination room where one by one they went into what appeared as private dressing rooms where they were required to undress, put their Mergenky space attire on, which for Vance was an MSF flight uniform delivered to him via an automatic door mechanism.

Vance was instructed to take all his personal objects and clothes and deposit them in the same container his flight suit came out of, where they would be decontaminated and returned to him.

After Vance dressed and received his personal articles back, he pressed the exit switch indicator next to the exit door which opened into another airlock and shut behind him as he entered. The air in this compartment was exchanged rather quickly with air that had something of a scent to it.

<u>INT. SPACE. MSS-21 SPACE STATION MAIN COORIDOR</u>

Moments later the exit door opened to this decontamination lock, and he was suddenly inside the MSS-21 Mergenky Space Station.

Vance had been informed by Mergenky Space Federation (MSF) staff on Gwaba:

MSF STAFF

An MSF CRUISER 34 (MSFC-34) crew member will meet you at the arrival gate on MSS-21 and escort you through security to MSFC-34.

VOICE OVER

For this mission, Vance was appointed as the Navigator for MSFC-34.

In the time Vance had on the Mergenky Scout Class Ship MSF S-1 traveling to and from the Andromeda Galaxy, with Martha's extensive training sessions between her evil episodes, Vance had achieved an expertise in flying Mergenky craft exceeded almost all MSF-pilots.

Certifications to Vance's hours of piloting the S-1 including manual flight, were preserved, and given to MSF despite the fact they had to COLD-START Martha when she became evil and out of control.

If it were not for the fact Vance was not Mergenky but from Earth, considered a backwards planet, he'd be at least the Co-Pilot and Executive Officer for this mission as recommended by Kwongab, his former pilot and good friend.

However, Vance looked at the Mergenky Cruiser's Navigator assignment as a considerable privilege. He was also assigned to perform special operations during this priority deployment.

Though knowing it would lead to a lot of sleepless periods, Vance nevertheless was somewhat enthralled to be chosen to go on such a high priority secret mission, though parts of it left him with a degree of trepidation.

Some jealousy and resulting comments by the cruiser's crewmembers who learned an Earth person would be navigating them on this mission made it all the way to Mergenky MSF Headquarters.

Kwongab hearing some of the rumors, requested in advance of Vance's deployment to the ship to visit MSF CRUISER 34_and talk with the crew of nearly 50 people on the large Cruiser.

Kwongab would not be going with them but wanted to make sure Vance received all the support and due respect he earned over the years on missions for MSF.

<u>INT. MOORED AT MSS-21. MSF CRUISER 34 CREWS LOUNGE</u>

As the crew crowded into the crew's lounge barely large enough to hold them all at once, which was the case for an all-hands meeting, Commander Kwongab walked to the front of the room with the ship's Captain, Koasa.

The room was suddenly quiet as the unexpected visit from one of the legends of the MSF brought special meaning and importance to the mission they would be undertaking.

Captain Koasa, the cruiser's commanding officer was given the nod by the Executive Officer meaning it was time for his remarks.

MSF-34 CAPTAIN KOASA

Crew, I know everyone is ready to embark upon this vital mission and your training is complete and you all know what is expected of you, and if you think I brought Commander Kwongab one of our most experienced pilots in MSF here to give you a pep talk or any tactical and strategic information, that's not why he's here.

Kwongab looked around the room and started getting a feel for everyone present.

MSF-34 CAPTAIN KOASA

Because of the nature of our business, we have high surveillance on all of you, not only in your training environment, but also in the conduct of your everyday lives since the future and safety of the Mergenky people rests so heavily on your actions, we can't leave to chance certain situations and thus must be ever vigilant.

Kwongab started using his telepathic neural expansion abilities on crew members close to him to get a read out on how they felt about the situation.

MSF-34 CAPTAIN KOASA

We are missing one of our crew members, Commander Vance the new Navigator, who was detained at MSF headquarters for special briefings required for our mission and will be here in a short while.

Our distinguished visitor is here to say a few words about Commander Vance which he hopes will be useful for you in helping you adjust to a non Mergenky Officer assigned to a high position such as ship's Navigator.

Kwongab with his special neural expansion telepathic ability, that neither crew nor their Captain knew existed now worked on the crew, reading their minds, and indoctrinating them in ways they didn't understand, but knew there was more needed to help make Vance's transition to the cohesive team streamlined and efficient.

The captain nodded at Kwongab who already knew what he was thinking, *time to proceed.*

COMMANDER KWONGAB

Greetings fellow Mergenky Space Federation Members. It's a privilege to be here to see you off on your mission.

For your own security I do not know the details of your mission and assignment, as it should be, but I know there is always an element of risk in what you will be doing simply traveling long distance in space.

This is not new to us as I know there are a few of you who participated in the Jeeapa Conflict, many years ago. So, you already know how violent and terrifying situations can get out there when facing the likes of the Anarchie and others.

Kwongab looked around the crew's lounge and randomly selected individuals to get a feel for how they were responding. He knew some of them were excited to meet one of publicized pilots of the Jeeapa War.

COMMANDER KWONGAB
My main reason to be here and it may seem totally unprecedented, and it truly is because of the extraordinary events that were bestowed upon me as well as your new crew member, Commander Vance, who has been assigned as Navigator for this mission.

I know it might seem rather incredible we would suddenly have an Earth Person as a Navigator on one of our top-of-the-line Mergenky Cruisers, a person from what is perceived as an inferior planet.

But as I take the time to give you a brief history of the Navigator Commander Vance, you will understand why he was picked ahead of many Mergenky well qualified for the job. I hope to make that point momentarily.

Kwongab did spot some negativity in an individual but continued searching the crowd as he continued with his remarks.

COMMANDER KWONGAB
We must venture back in time and discuss what has occurred that made Commander Vance such an ideal choice to be MSFC-34's Navigator.

Kwongab looked onto the crew and could see curiosity in everyone's face. Much about Vance they didn't know and would soon learn. This hand-picked crew was the best that MSF had to offer, but Kwongab thought a little tweaking would help Vance establish his presence when he reported aboard later in the day.

COMMANDER KWONGAB
My first contact with Vance was nearly 20 years ago when I abducted him from his home on planet Earth.

Kwongab could see the surprise in a lot of faces.

COMMANDER KWONGAB
Unfortunately, my Scout Class Ship had a delamination of the cloaking field during the recharging of the AMRT and we were suddenly exposed to a nearby home where Earth Person Vance was enjoying himself out in his back yard.

I had no option but to bring him aboard my ship to avoid a C5 covenant violation.

As punishment for my failure as a Scout Pilot to avoid detection from Earth Terrestrials, I was ordered to make Vance a crew member of my ship and take him with me until further notice.

Not long after this abduction of Vance happened that resulted in him being a crew member, the Anarchie decided to invade Jeeapa, and the war was on.

In probing the crew's mind, Kwongab discovered most of them were curious about the story and their real emotions were not quite exposed.

COMMANDER KWONGAB
Vance learned quickly, and was an integral part of the crew, and during one of our extremely dangerous missions where the odds were against us, Vance suggested a strategy that we utilized that made the difference and we survived.

Kwongab looked around the room. He wanted to see their body language when he informed them of the outcome.

COMMANDER KWONGAB
Our small scouting force of five Scout class ships was able to delay the Anarchie just long enough to where reserves from MSF were able to do a surprise attack on Anarchie flanks which turned the battle.

Kwongab knew some of the crew members were aware of what happened on Jeeapa, they just didn't know who was involved. This revelation intrigued them.

> **COMMANDER KWONGAB**
> Because of Vance's extraordinary personality, the MSF decided later we could return Vance to Earth, and he had promised to not divulge to his planet we had been there.

Now the stares grew quite intense.

> **COMMANDER KWONGAB**
> Our mission to the Andromeda Galaxy coincided with travel past the Gamulin area and the decision by MSF was to return Vance to Earth where we believed he would best live out his life.
>
> During that attempt to return Vance, our cloaking field failed us one more time and Vance was exposed.
>
> It quickly became clear to Vance as well as to us that he could not remain on Earth. We offered Vance to take him with us on the Andromeda Mission, which he agreed to go.
>
> The Andromeda mission lasted many years.

Kwongab stated then looked out into the audience and probed the minds of those closest to him. It appeared the crew was taking in the information with all sincerity.

The transcendental quality of Kwongab's mind probing seemed to stir a few crew members that reciprocated by expanding their thought processes and imagery Kwongab planted in their minds to enhance the impressions.

> **COMMANDER KWONGAB**
> During that long mission, Vance slowly qualified as pilot.
>
> During some of the space battles we found ourselves forced into, Vance piloted the Scout while I operated the laser weapons.
>
> We had several close calls and Vance's success in routine training paid off as he skillfully piloted us while we successfully engaged enemy combatants.

Kwongab could sense some of the crew members were responding favorably to these comments and his neuro expansion telepathic implants.

COMMANDER KWONGAB

While in the Andromeda Galaxy we visited a dozen worlds and were forced into a half dozen space encounters including a war between two worlds.

There were hundreds of space craft involved with advanced weapons.

Vance was an integral component of those missions.

Upon return to Gwaba, MSF analyzed all the training data, and mission data and evaluated Vance as a highly successful pilot as he proved himself under fire. Vance is a certified MSF pilot though he's your Navigator.

Part of Vance's tasks from time to time was to navigate us to our destinations. In essence he has about 20 years' experience in piloting and navigating in much further destinations and more vast scenarios than most MSF Pilots and Navigators do in their entire careers.

Kwongab remained quiet intentionally for a long moment to give the crew time to reflect on what he just said and to probe more crew members.

COMMANDER KWONGAB

I'm here today to ask you all to give Commander Vance a fair working environment and support him.

Vance will not let you down.

Vance's the type that will willingly give up his life for your well-being. He proved that when he was severely wounded with poisonous arrows on one of the planets during the Andromeda Mission.

Without having a doctor on the ship, Vance would not have made it home alive and came close to dying as it was.

The crew thought they were daydreaming the encounter, but Kwongab was telepathically inserting the visuals and the sounds that occurred during Vances encounter and wounds caused by poisonous arrows.

COMMANDER KWONGAB
I would also like to add, we encountered an Anarchie
Battleship in the Andromeda Galaxy, and were lucky
the Anarchie had stripped down the Battleship to get
there, otherwise we might not have made it back.

We had a battle with that Anarchie Battleship. Vance
skillfully manually flew the Scout Class Ship, and we
prevailed against that Anarchie Battleship.

Kwongab further applied his neural expansion abilities on crew members close to him,
as he knew he could only do a few in the limited time he had.

Kwongab got some indications he was successful in indoctrinating some crew
members and hopefully it would make Vance's trip a lot easier and reduce the effects
of the jealousy that circulated in rumors. Those rumors were obviously manifested by
individuals that were envious and disturbed that an Earth Man would be elevated to
such high levels of authority and responsibility.

COMMANDER KWONGAB
Captain Koasa, I want to thank you for giving me the
opportunity to address your crew.

CAPTAIN KOASA
Commander Kwongab, it's a pleasure having you
aboard my ship. Many of the maneuvers and strategies
we'll employ came from your patrol reports.

We'll try our best to emulate what you have done in
the past and hopefully that will lead to a successful
mission.

COMMANDER KWONGAB
Thank you, Captain Koasa, I must depart now as I
have some urgent matters to attend, and you obviously
need to complete your pre-underway checks.

CAPTAIN KOASA
Commander Kwongab, let me escort you off the ship.

Captain Koasa then gestured to head for the passageway that would lead them to a
turbo lift then to the ship's exit back into MSS-21 aboard a CTLV.

VOICEOVER

Kwongab did not want Vance to see him there nor discover what he had just done. But under the circumstances he felt that based on the rumors he heard, and the neural expansion telepathic investigation of crew members showed results that convinced him it was well worth the effort.

Kwongab didn't have to go through decontamination like Vance did off the Shuttle since all MSF ships were always in a state of decontamination.

Kwongab walked through MSS-21 and made his way to the operations center where he was cleared to go in and humbly waited to watch the new Mergenky Cruiser MSFC-34 depart for its mission.

After MSFC-34 departed, Kwongab would take a CTLV shuttle down to Gwaba and resume his life as a mentor and instructor for MSF pilots who were in Command School ready to take over a ship.

***

BLACK RAVIK

<u>INT. SPACE. MERGENCKY SPACE STATION 21 MAIN CONCORSE</u>

VOICE OVER

Vance was not expecting a green skinned person to meet him on MSS-21. There were a few green skinned people in the MSF because their planet Frăctŏng had been in the Alliance for several thousand years.

The Frăctŏngians like the Mergenky had been assaulted by the Anarchie in an aggressive and persistent manner.

The Frăctŏngians (pronounced FRAC TONE GIAINS) simply had to side with the Mergenky who were benevolent and peaceful or face the reoccurring Anarchie onslaught.

Mergenky protection was not always consistent or effective and the Jeeapa debacle added to their uncertainty.

*The Frăctŏngians knew poor help from the Mergenky
was still a lot better than no help facing future Anarchie
threats, even though these threats seemed to diminish
in the many years since the Jeeapa Campaign ended.*

The green skin Frăctŏngian Lieutenant Shănguāngdēng (pronounced Shan Guang Dung) looked humanoid except for the green skin and red hair set her off as rather peculiar looks.

As part of the MSF Alliance, Lieutenant Shănguāngdēng was detailed to MSS-21 before she became a crew member of MSFC-34 and was often used to help coordinate a lot of MSF people coming and going to make sure they quickly and efficiently got transferred from their CTLV Shuttles to waiting ships due to depart. However today, Lieutenant Shănguāngdēng would escort Vance to the MSF Cruiser MSFC-34 which she too was scheduled to depart on as well as a weapons operator.

Lieutenant Shănguāngdēng a weapons expert also doubled as a translator. There was a good chance that during this mission they could end up at Frăctŏng.

Lieutenant Shănguāngdēng stood by the airlock and having looked at Commander Vance's portfolio, easily recognized him from his MSF profile photographs she had just viewed on her personal communicator data terminal.

LIEUTENANT SHĂNGUĀNGDĒNG
Commander Vance, I'm Lieutenant Shănguāngdēng
here to escort you to MSFC-34 which is waiting for
you for our departure.

VANCE
(In perfect Gwaba/Mergenky dialect.)
Thanks, I appreciate that, Lieutenant Shănguāngdēng.

LIEUTENANT SHĂNGUĀNGDĒNG
How was your CTLV Shuttle flight, Commander Vance?

VANCE
Shănguāngdēng, everything was fine except having to
say goodbye to my wife and children.

LIEUTENANT SHĂNGUĀNGDĒNG
I'm sorry to hear about that. But you know that MSF
prefers to have crew members who are not in family
status.

VANCE
Yes, and for good reasons.

Vance was not totally unfamiliar with MSS-21 since he had departed and arrived here before, but the huge structure can be difficult to find departure gates, and having a knowledgeable person help navigate to the right location can save a lot of time.

Luckily, Vance and Lieutenant Shǎnguāngdēng were not far from the MSF Cruiser MSFC-34 and in five minutes were reporting aboard. Vance knew his way around the Cruiser and walked to the Bridge where he expected to meet Captain Koasa.

<u>INT. SPACE DOCK MOORING. MSF CRUISER MSFC-34</u>

Lieutenant Shǎnguāngdēng followed Vance to the Control Room/Bridge as she was part of the maneuvering watch, manning a sensor station and fired lasers if required. She then introduced Vance.

LIEUTENANT SHǍNGUĀNGDĒNG
Captain Koasa, may I introduce you to our Navigator
Commander Vance.

VANCE
Captain Koasa, reporting as required and ready to
assume my duties.

CAPTAIN KOASA
Welcome aboard Commander Vance. I'm looking
forward to working with you on this mission.

VANCE
Thank you, sir, I am ready for the mission.

CAPTAIN KOASA
Have you checked into your quarters yet?

VANCE
Not yet, Captain.

CAPTAIN KOASA
Lieutenant Shǎnguāngdēng will you please escort
Commander Vance to his Space Cabin and show
where his living quarters will be for the mission.

LIEUTENANT SHĂNGUĀNGDĒNG
Certainly sir

Shănguāngdēng then turned towards Vance.

LIEUTENANT SHĂNGUĀNGDĒNG
Please follow me, Commander Vance.

The Navigator's Space Cabin was not far from the Bridge. Just like the Captain and his Executive Officer, he needed to be able to get on the bridge with short delays.

30 feet after the bridge was Vance's Space Cabin. It was not cramped but it wasn't nearly as robust as the old Scout rooms Vance experienced.

LIEUTENANT SHĂNGUĀNGDĒNG
This is your Space Cabin, Commander Vance.

VANCE

Thank you, I'll get settled in briefly and meet you back on the bridge.

LIEUTENANT SHĂNGUĀNGDĒNG
We'll be waiting.

Lieutenant Shănguāngdēng then turned and walked back to the bridge.

Vance's room had a standard MSF terminal, full Phototronic Neural Network (PNN) capability and looked comfortable, but almost cramped. His gel sleeping container looked very similar to the one he had on the Scout.

VOICEOVER
*Vance knew his old pal Martha was gone, and these
Mergenky Cruisers were set up entirely differently.
He felt it would never be the same without the PNN
Artificial Intelligence manifestation of Martha.*

*Vance sat his Grip down on the little work stand. He
would not be spending much time here over the next 24
hours as he needed to navigate MSFC-34 to a couple
destinations.*

*As part of their mission Vance remotely downloaded
to the MSFC-34's Phototronic Neural Network (PNN)
required Navigation vectors while he was getting final
briefings at MSF Headquarters.*

After stowing his small number of personal items into storage bins, Vance then proceeded to the bridge where the last of the pre-voyage checks were being completed.

CAPTAIN KOASA
Are you all set to go, Commander Vance?

VANCE
Yes, Captain, I have the flight plan loaded in PNN, we
are all ready to go when you give the order.

CAPTAIN KOASA
Very well, Commander Vance. We'll launch at
14:00:00 GSTH.

The Bridge was manned and ready. Vance noticed Lieutenant Shǎnguāngdēng was sitting at a console which had sensor displays and weapons controls. No doubt she would play an integral part in their activities.

Other MSF personnel were at consoles monitoring the MSF Cruiser's status of several items including engineering parameters of the AMRT and other propulsion related equipment's.

MSS-21 provided Cruiser MSFC-34 sensor readings of all the nearby space so that when the Mergenky Cruiser MSFC-34 undocked, it's navigation and collision avoidance system had any craft that might be a risk to collision programmed into the navigation algorithms to ensure they would avoid any possible collisions and leave the solar system unmolested. Once Cruiser MSFC-34 ventured a few Kilometers away from MSS-21, their own sensors would keep them safe.

The ship's Captain of an MSF Cruiser often did not appear on the bridge during a maneuvering watch as he was usually busy in his Space Cabin reading his operational orders, and often in planning meetings either with the ship's Engineer, Weapon's Officer, or in certain circumstances his Intelligence Officer who was the only person besides himself to get certain restricted information.

Today however, knowing a very distinguished guest was up in the operations center on MSS-21 to see them off, Captain Koasa put all those meetings and tasks away for a while and remained on the MSFC-34's Bridge.

MUSIC FOR THE LAUNCH OF THE MISSION:

https://www.youtube.com/watch?v=E8kYVo9usSI

Yuja Wang plays Prokofiev Piano Concerto No. 1 in D-flat major, Op. 10

When 14:00:00 GSTH finally arrived a brief while later, the automatic sequencing began.

PNN in full control of the AMRT's had propulsion power immediately available for maneuvering. Artificial gravity was online and life aboard the Cruiser was as expected for these trained professionals all knowing they were embarking on a critical mission that would take them a long distance away from Mergenky home world Gwaba for an extended period. All the crew knew this would most likely be a very challenging underway on MSF Cruiser MSFC-34.

<u>EXT. CGI. SPACE. MERGENKY CRUISER MSFC-34 LAUNCHING FROM THE SPACE STATION. 45 SECONDS.</u>

The electromagnetic grippers were rephrased into repulser's. A subtle movement started the undocking in a linear acceleration starting from inches per second that in less than a minute was approaching feet per second.

Vance observing the Navigation plot with the sensor overlays, from infrared, ultraviolet, as well as neutrino scanners that acted like a radar providing range information had anything possibly that would be a factor in their course vectors calculated, plotted, as well as mitigated. Course vectors and steerage adjusted as necessary by PNN.

Back in the "Cowboy" days when Vance was flying in the Andromeda Galaxy in manual mode, he would have had no issues manually steering the Cruiser away from MSS-21 and into deep space far from the Mergenky Space Station.

However, in the Mergenky society that expects automation, the Cruiser slid away from the space station in full autopilot. All Vance could do during the maneuvering period, while moving away from MSS-21 is verify the vectors matched the flight plan he loaded.

Vance would never be authorized by the Cruiser Captain Koasa to undock in manual mode. Vance knew he was capable of piloting the Mergenky Cruiser vice the PNN that was doing it now.

Unlike the Mergenky Scout Class ship Vance traveled around the galaxy and to the Andromeda, the Mergenky Cruiser MSFC-34 did not have a space telescope. There would be no planetary observations, nor the accommodations Kwongab made for him.

This mission would be a new experience for the crew that was substantially larger than the crew size on the Mergenky Scout S-1. However, the Mergenky Cruiser's crew worked in shifts, so unless they were at battle stations or a casualty, only 1/3rd of them would be seen at any given time.

Unlike the Mergenky Scout S-1 which could remain in autopilot for long periods of time due to the extensive automation it had, the Mergenky Cruiser MSFC-34 had a control room personnel complement that performed functions in the control room. Those crew members remained until they were relieved at the end of their shift by the next section because they were a space warship and had a different mission. They could also unexpectedly come across an Anarchie War Spaceship with unknown intentions.

VOICE OVER

For the next 12 hours, Vance would be ever vigilant in the control room observing the fully automated travel and validating they traveled exactly in the direction and at the speed he specified in the flight plan.

The Control room had numerous scanner displays giving them a full 360-degree view at all elevations, and awareness of any possible approaching objects that might be a problem for them, which they might need to maneuver to avoid.

Unlike the Gamulin Solar System where Vance came from, there were no asteroid belts to penetrate.

Leaving Gwaba was straight forward, just point to empty space in the direction you wanted to go and increase speed. There were many directions to go in that would avoid any other planets in the solar system, so the navigation in this part of the mission was quite simple compared to where they would be going.

When the MSFC-34 traveled a good distance away from MSS-21, the captain announced:

CAPTAIN KOASA

I'll be in my Space Cabin, don't hesitate to call for me
if needed.

Captain Koasa then walked out of the control room and a short distance to his Space Cabin where he would go over records and meet with various officers on the Cruiser for planning purposes and voyage milestones.

As the day progressed, Vance caught glances of Lieutenant Shǎnguāngdēng who looked at him a dozen times or more. There might have been some slight curiosity. It stands to reason that a native of Frǎctǒng would be curious of another outsider like Vance navigating an MSF Cruiser and was by itself considered most bizarre and the least likely thing to ever happen on a Mergenky Cruiser. However, Vance felt secure in his role.

Lieutenant Shǎnguāngdēng's smile was infectious, and her personality appeared pleasant and non-assuming. No doubt she was a very intelligent person, with the special gift of being a successful translator for one of the more crucial languages in the Alliance.

VOICE OVER

Vance had no idea where his new-found self-assurance came from, but he knew he could do his job well.

In Vance's recent meetings with Kwongab at MSF headquarters during the past few days, Vance unknowingly underwent a significant amount of neural expansion telepathic subtle indoctrination from Kwongab.

In what appeared to just be a friendly encounter with Kwongab, his once mission partner to the Andromeda Galaxy, Vance was telepathically conditioned to help build psychological strengths to cope with the rigors of an MSF Cruiser Navigator assignment.

Kwongab knew the seriousness of the mission and it would take all of Vance's efforts to keep the Cruiser safe by carefully navigating it through a lot of tough places.

The amount of responsibility bestowed upon Vance could easily crush the average Mergenky.

However, Vance was not like the average Mergenky. Vance's life experiences as well as Kwongab's neural expansion telepathic techniques prepared Vance by supplanting a significant amount of new critical thinking ability.

Kwongab hoped his mental tampering might help Vance cope when he got in a tight spot that Kwongab feared was most likely to occur.

Kwongab didn't like seeing his best friend go out in harm's way like this, but recent events called for action and their reaction time had no flexibility, hence General Kahn picked the best man for the first deployment of Black Ravik, Vance's real purpose being onboard.

FLASHBACK:
General Kahn in a private meeting explained to Kwongab why Vance was picked to deploy Black Ravik on its first mission:

GENERAL KAHN
Vance has more recent combat experience than most Mergenky Navigators, and he certainly had significantly more Navigational experiences during the very long Andromeda Galaxy mission.

COMMANDER KWONGAB
General Kahn, I agree, and I was in a privileged position to see Vance perform when we got into a couple tight squeezes. Without his help, I'm not sure we would have made it back.

***

The MSF Cruiser MSFC-34 steadily sped up as the AMRT's hummed their magic while the matter to anti-matter reactions released huge amounts of energy directly into propulsion coils producing magnetic grip, allowed huge, sustained acceleration that would take Cruiser MSFC-34 out of the solar system in about 12 hours at conservative speeds.

Once outside the Solar System in deep space, Captain Koasa returned to the bridge. Only a few of the crew knew what they would be accomplishing next.

CAPTAIN KOASA
Commander Vance, are you ready to test the new Shuttle craft?

COMMANDER VANCE
Captain, I'm ready whenever you want to commence.

CAPTAIN KOASA
I think now would be an excellent time. We might as well make determinations of satisfactory performance before we get too far away from Gwaba in case the craft needs some tweaking.

COMMANDER VANCE
The ship is in fully automatic navigation mode in accordance with our flight plan.

CAPTAIN KOASA
What if something happens to you and you cannot make it back to the Cruiser?

COMMANDER VANCE
In the event of a problem with the Shuttle and I can't make it back to the ship, all necessary navigation vectors are programmed in.

CAPTAIN KOASA
I assume PNN can get us back to MSS-21 with those vectors.

COMMANDER VANCE
Affirmative Captain Koasa. Also, I understand that Lieutenant Shǎnguāngdēng will be the acting navigator in my absence.

CAPTAIN KOASA
Very well commander, gather your crew and report to the Shuttle in preparation for launch.

VANCE
On my way Captain.

The ship's Phototronic Neural Network (PNN) Personality Erica monitoring the conversation, already programmed with crew members listed as part of the BLACK RAVIK away team, immediately notified all members to report to the Shuttle in preparation for launch. Vance understood that would happen and as he approached the Shuttle Bay, the Artificial Intelligence Erica informed Vance:

ERICA
Commander Vance, all the BLACK RAVIK crew members scheduled for this test flight have been notified and are on the way to the shuttle.

A three-dimensional holograph of the Cruiser and the Shuttle were suddenly presented near Captain Koasa in the Cruiser's control room where he could visually monitor the progress of the shuttle launch. As part of the pre-mission briefs, Captain Koasa already had a plan laid out as to the shuttle launch sequence and the tests they wanted to do.

VOICEOVER

This was a new type of Shuttle. The Shuttle essentially had a miniature Antimatter Magnetic Resonator Transformer (AMRT) installed as part of the BLACK RAVIK modification.

The miniature AMRT power plant was not installed for power density function of the prime mover, but the power was required for the cloaking device Black Ravik.

The propulsion capability was only marginally better than previous Shuttles. Whereas stealth was the highly desired feature designed in an increasingly more hostile galactic situation arising.

INTEL had recently reported the Anarchie had recovered from their previous stinging defeat at Jeeapa and appeared to be planning for another showdown.

In some circles of the Mergenky Intel, fear was starting to grow that Anarchie would one day soon reach out and become a menace towards the Mergenky again.

Captain Koasa felt concern that there were several destinations this Shuttle might be needed during this mission to allow the away team to arrive undetected, which their lives may depend, or worse yet avoid a covenant violation by exposure to the Gamulins in the sector of space that included planet Earth.

In a few minutes Vance reported from the Shuttle:

VANCE

Captain Koasa, all team members are present in the shuttle, and we are all ready for the launch sequence, all systems indicate [No Defects Detected] (NDD).

CAPTAIN KOASA

Very well Shuttle, standby.

Captain Koasa looked at the chronometer and said:

CAPTAIN KOASA

PNN, on my mark commenced Shuttle launch sequence.

ERICA
Standing by.

The personality of the AI personality was named Erica, but MSF personnel simply conversed with it as PNN.

CAPTAIN KOASA
Mark.

ERICA
Shuttle Launch Sequence in progress.

Erica's voice announced crisp and articulated. The bridge party watched with wonder of why they were testing a standard device carried throughout the fleet. For security reasons they had not been exposed to *Black Ravik*, the super-secret Shuttle cloaking capability.

Watching the animated scale model 3D holograph of the MSF Cruiser, Captain Koasa observed a computer-generated replica that had so much detail and resolution, it looked like the real thing, just in miniature.

EXT. CGI. SHUTTLE LAUNCH FROM MERGNKY CRUISER MSFC-34 (15 SECONDS).

The Shuttle Bay hatches slowly opened swinging 120 degrees so it would be away from the Shuttle when it launched. Additionally, on the animated 3D holograph, a tabulated text area stated each action taking place such as hatch opening.

Once the interlocks closed which made it safe to proceed to the next phase, the Cruiser's Shuttle repulser's energized and slowly put up a magnetic field that pushed against the electromagnets mounted in the Shuttle lander feet.

Even though these lander feet were not very large, they were very strong, built from Spactron 300 and had very strong computer controlled electromagnets installed on them.

In the past 150 years Spactron 300 remained the most advanced metal in this area of the Milky Way Galaxy.

Spactron 300 metal was lighter than aluminum and stronger than steel, it had incredible properties. And only Mergenky had the secret process to manufacture Spactron 300 metals as well as efficiently cut and drill through Spactron 300 by altering its mechanical impedance through vibration.

The Shuttle started moving in the total vacuum of space vertically out of the Shuttle Bay inches per second and soon increased to feet per second.

As to not interfere with the artificial gravity of the Cruiser, the Shuttle artificial gravity would not be energized until they were at least several hundred meters away from the Cruiser. The Shuttle maneuvered per the test plan on a geometry to validate the radar cross section in its fully cloaked mode that would soon be tested.

The Shuttle applied forward direction propulsion and slowly moved out in front of the Cruiser where it slowed down to match speeds with the Mergenky Cruiser about 500 meters directly in front of Cruiser MSFC-34.

<u>EXT. CGI. SHUTTLE MANUVERING IN FRONT OF MERGNKY CRUISER-34 (15 SECONDS).</u>

All the visual and radar scanners were plotting the presence of the Shuttle exactly the way experienced in operating the fleet's Shuttles. Once the Shuttle was in the proper Geometry ready to perform its maneuvers, Mergenky Cruiser MSFC-34's PNN Erica was notified via scrambled communications.

Captain Koasa walked over to the sensor operators and stood right behind Lieutenant Shănguāngdēng.

CAPTAIN KOASA
Lieutenant Shănguāngdēng I understand you are one
of the best sensor operators in the MSF?

LIEUTENANT SHĂNGUĀNGDĒNG
Thank you for your kind words captain, but I think I'm
rather ordinary and typical of a sensor operator.

CAPTAIN KOASA
Lieutenant Shănguāngdēng the MSF says otherwise
on your fitness report. That's why I explicitly asked
for you to go on this mission.

LIEUTENANT SHĂNGUĀNGDĒNG
Well, I'm very glad to be going on this voyage,
Captain.

CAPTAIN KOASA
That's good, because before we are all done, your
services will be highly valued. But for now, we'll
discover why I wanted someone of your caliber on the
sensors as we commence this test.

LIEUTENANT SHĂNGUĀNGDĒNG
Alright. Captain, I'm ready to do my part.

CAPTAIN KOASA
Excellent, let's begin.

The captain then walked back to the conning deck which was elevated a few feet above the sensor operators in front of him where he had a full 360 multi-elevation view of the space around him.

INT. SPACE. MERGENCKY CRUISER C34 CONTROL ROOM/BRIDGE.

BACKGROUND MUSIC FOR THIS SEGMENT:

https://www.youtube.com/watch?v=mF8oTzXoyts

Prokofiev: Symphony No. 7

The Cruiser's Bridge essentially appeared to Captain Koasa as if he were inside a three-dimensional globe with transparency so that he could observe the control room and especially the sensor operators for moments of exigencies that might manifest in the rigors of space travel, and ostensibly even space combat.

This Mergenky Cruiser with little warning could very well experience; space combat; especially since Intelligence Reports started to paint a picture that was straining a few nerves back on Mergenky home world planet Gwaba.

VOICEOVER
Captain Koasa felt glad that the public had experienced a few good years without the turmoil of the nature witnessed on Jeeapa. In the long period since, the Jeeapa Dome City had been repaired and restored to its previous luster.

Sadly, the public thought the peace dividend would last forever. Unfortunately, they could not compute the depths of which arrogant and greedy individuals would go. People had their price as well as their agenda.

The Anarchie took the Jeeapa debacle just as badly as the Russians had with the Americans during the Cuban Missile Crisis. The similarities were that in due course, their leader was deposed by members of their intelligence communities. The aftermath was an eventual arms race.

VOICEOVER

Part of this mission was to ascertain whether Mergenky INTEL Reports could substantiate the Anarchie may have discovered a source of Blue Diamonds in the Gamulin Solar System.

Hence another good reason to bring Vance along so that his linguistics skills would help the Black Ravik Away Team find evidence.

MSF needed such information before General Kahn approached the civilian leadership to plead for urgent requisitions of materials needed to resurrect the fleet from the results of many years of neglectful peace dividends on ridiculous social programs while the fleet rotted.

If Mergenky INTEL was right in their Anarchie estimates, the MSF could very well get caught with their pants down again like during the Jeeapa War..

Captain Koasa and other senior officers were not too happy about future security prospects just by observing the behavior of the Anarchie by secret Scout Missions, one of which Commander Kwongab recently completed in total secrecy observing Space Trials of new classes of Anarchie Space Fleet Battleships.

FLASHBACK:

<u>INT. MSF HEADQUARTERS, GENERAL KAHN'S CONFERENCE ROOM.</u>

GENERAL KAHN'S
TECHNOLOGY ADVISOR

Analysts had concluded that if Anarchie finally were able to obtain the most needed material to reconstitute their once proud fleet; blue diamonds for the laser optics, that would be bad news to MSF.

GENERAL KAHN'S
DEPUTY COMMANDER

More powerful lasers will allow Anarchie Fleets to deploy more intense lasers on a target with the deadly consequences that MSF has previously enjoyed a qualitative edge.

GENERAL KAHN

If INTEL was right for a change, and not going after another wild goose chase concerning th Anarchie which they often got accused of, obtaining a large quantity of those blue diamonds would be a game changer.

GENERAL KAHN'S
TECHNOLOGY ADVISOR

With new focusing techniques and pulsed power obtained with the ever-expanding universe of power electronics, all the Anarchie need is a quantity of blue diamonds to create arrays that focus light that would approach the power spectrum density of our MSF thirty-inch lasers.

GENERAL KAHN

Anarchie deploying larger lasers means that in future slugfests, the MSF might have to change our tactics and not be able to continue employing what is starting to appear as obsolete methods.

GENERAL KAHN'S
TECHNOLOGY ADVISOR

The battle space will get increasingly more complicated and complex if INTEL estimates have merit.

GENERAL KAHN'S
DEPUTY COMMANDER

Even with the help of PNN to target and control our MSF lasers, Anarchie always make up for qualitative differences by using more quantitative operations.

GENERAL KAHN'S
TECHNOLOGY ADVISOR

Due to Anarchie non-secular society, that is a lot easier for them to implement than what the MSF would have to do to counter it.

GENERAL KAHN

However, the first thing was first. MSF needs to get evidence without tipping off the Anarchie we discovered their acquisitions in case this problem

was a lot bigger than what both planners and the Intel
Community estimated.

INT SPACE MSFC-34 CONTROL ROOM.

The key to determining whether Anarchie obtained blue diamonds was right in front of
Captain Koasa on his three-dimensional scanner globe that surrounded Captain Koasa
now on the mission to find out: BLACK RAVIK.

EXT. CGI. SPACE. SCANNER VISION OF THE SHUTTLE IN FRONT OF THE
MERGENKY CRUISER C34 ON TACTICAL SURVILANCE DISPLAYS. 15
seconds.

INT SPACE MSFC-34 CONTROL ROOM.

> LIEUTENANT SHĂNGUĀNGDĒNG
> Captain, the scanners have no problem painting an
> image of the Shuttle in front of us. Optical and Pulsed
> Wavelength Trackers have a good lock on target.

> CAPTAIN KOASA
> Very well Lieutenant Shănguāngdēng.

The picture derived from multiple wavelengths created a highly detailed image that
was not only photographic quality, but the perfection of the image showed zero flaws.

> CAPTAIN KOASA
> Shuttle, commence phase one.

INT SPACE. BLACK RAVIK SHUTTLE.

> VANCE
> MS (a.k.a. Mother Ship), Understand, commence
> phase one.

INT SPACE MSFC-34 CONTROL ROOM.

Captain Koasa walked out of the surveillance sphere over directly behind Lieutenant
Shănguāngdēng where he watched her track the Shuttle with the Black Ravik
modification currently disabled.

> CAPTAIN KOASA
> Lieutenant Shănguāngdēng it appears you exhibited
> no difficulty in observing the Shuttle and your Optical

and Pulsed Wavelength Trackers have a good lock on
target.

LIEUTENANT SHǍNGUĀNGDĒNG
Yes Captain. The shuttle is continuously illuminated
by various wavelengths providing a very high-
resolution image, that will not lose much fidelity even
at much longer ranges. Optical and Pulsed Wavelength
Trackers holding solid.

CAPTAIN KOASA
Thanks to the neutrino and ultraviolet pulses, I see
there is no smearing or distortion on your display due
to Doppler or excessive range rates encountered by the
maneuver the shuttle is now executing.

LIEUTENANT SHǍNGUĀNGDĒNG
That's an odd maneuver what the Shuttle is performing.

CAPTAIN KOASA
You only think that because it's a relatively small ship.
If it was much larger you would have no issue figuring
out what the Navigator Commander Vance is doing.

Lieutenant Shǎnguāngdēng stared at her holographic screens and did not determine the
maneuver and looked puzzled.

Captain Koasa realized Lieutenant Shǎnguāngdēng would be very disappointed soon
when he informed her Vance was performing a Capmoc-Drulyenslv maneuver in
accordance with the test plan.

LIEUTENANT SHǍNGUĀNGDĒNG
Alright Captain, I'm embarrassed to admit I have not
figured it out yet, but I can see it's an intricate pattern
created by the maneuvers.

CAPTAIN KOASA
Lieutenant Shǎnguāngdēng, the Shuttle is on the first
leg of the Capmoc-Drulyenslv maneuver.

LIEUTENANT SHǍNGUĀNGDĒNG
Now that you have mentioned it, it all makes sense. It
seemed so clever; I missed the obvious.

CAPTAIN KOASA
Lieutenant Shǎnguāngdēng don't feel bad. In recent
years due to fleet tempo our proficiency has decayed.

The public now has the mindset that our peace dividend will last forever, and we no
longer train with the vigor and enthusiasm we did when the Anarchie were at our
doorstep and attacked Jeeapa.

LIEUTENANT SHǍNGUĀNGDĒNG
I understand Captain, and I feel slightly embarrassed
I missed a classical maneuver such as a Capmoc-
Drulyenslv maneuver.

CAPTAIN KOASA
Lieutenant Shǎnguāngdēng, you will have plenty of
time during this voyage to home in your skills.

LIEUTENANT SHǍNGUĀNGDĒNG
Are we going to perform training simulations during
this mission?

CAPTAIN KOASA
Yes, we'll do some simulations, but we will also do
the real mission, and if we get caught performing our
mission, we'll be tested to our limits, I'm sure.

INT SPACE. BLACK RAVIK SHUTTLE.

In a few minutes, Vance reported:

VANCE
MS, this is the Shuttle, complete all maneuvers, ready
for phase 2.

INT SPACE MSFC-34 CONTROL ROOM.

CAPTAIN KOASA
Shuttle, proceed with phase 2.

INT SPACE. BLACK RAVIK SHUTTLE.

VANCE
Commencing phase 2.

Aboard the Shuttle, Vance directed his co-pilot:

VANCE
Energize *Black Ravik.*

The co-pilot lifted the switch guard and turned on Black Ravik mode.

<u>INT SPACE MSFC-34 CONTROL ROOM.</u>

At that point in time Lieutenant Shǎnguāngdēng reported:

LIEUTENANT SHǍNGUĀNGDĒNG
Captain, the Shuttle just disappeared, something might
be wrong with our scanners!

CAPTAIN KOASA
Lieutenant Shǎnguāngdēng , the scanners are working
just fine. I want you to see if you can find the Shuttle.
Apply all your tricks. Pull the signals out of the mud.
I want you to spare nothing, you have permission to
use all the Special Pulses and Wavelengths (SP&W).

VOICEOVER
*SP&W was reserved for wartime only. Under normal
conditions it was never allowed in peacetime and from
time to time they were modified in the event the enemy
discovered the pulse type or if a spy provided that
information to them.*

*The Mergenky had traitors (spies) in the past working
for Anarchie. How any Mergenky could possibly sell
out to Anarchie seemed almost illogical. How any
Mergenky could willingly help the most vile and evil
beings in the galaxy just did not make sense.*

*MSF psychiatrists had worked hard on the traitors
that they caught to try to figure out what drove them
to spy for the Anarchie. In some cases, it was simply
the thrill of spying. In other cases, it was political in
nature and done to embarrass the administration or to
make it appear inept to force political change.*

Lieutenant Shǎnguāngdēng was doing her best. She pulled all the energy out of her
soul in attempting to regain contact, but nothing worked, including visual.

Lieutenant Shǎnguāngdēng was aware of cloaking devices on the Scouts and a few other special craft, but she had never seen, heard, or witnessed a Shuttle cloaked in her military experience, nor had anyone else on the ship.

Vance was not going to announce the code word *Black Ravik* over radio or neutrino communication links for fear of interception, especially if there was a spy back on Gwaba who might have informed the Anarchie of their departure.

Even though they had done modified baffle clearing and they did not detect anyone trailing the Mergenky Cruiser, the possibilities existed a loose trailer could be back behind them at considerable distance using passive monitoring of the ion trail that high-speed transiting craft made in space by hitting the very few hydrogen atoms and releasing energy in the process.

Anyone listening to an ion trail would think they were listening to certain marine life back on planet Earth if they had sonic detectors. The collisions noise with hydrogen atoms happened at about the same rate as the biologics communicated under water. Snapping shrimp is a good example.

Vance programmed the Shuttle to make the exact maneuvers recorded in Shuttle PNN memory made during Phase-1. The Shuttle's scanners had no problems detecting the MSF Cruiser. During the debrief for Captain Koasa, Vance would show Captain Koasa these results.

<u>INT SPACE. BLACK RAVIK SHUTTLE.</u>

Moments later as Lieutenant Shǎnguāngdēng sat feeling slightly dejected for her failure to detect and track the Shuttle, Vance ordered his co-pilot, deactivate *Black Ravik.*

Suddenly the Shuttle reappeared directly in front of the MSF Cruiser and Vance simultaneously reported:

> VANCE
> Completed Phase 2 maneuvers, ready to redock the
> Shuttle.

INT SPACE MSFC-34 CONTROL ROOM.

> CAPTAIN KOASA
> Redock the Shuttle.

<u>INT SPACE. BLACK RAVIK SHUTTLE.</u>

> VANCE
> Commencing redocking.

Vance turned to his co-pilot as he selected docking maneuver on the control panel.

VANCE

Back in the Cowboy Days, when I was in the Andromeda Galaxy, Commander Kwongab would have allowed me to manually dock the Shuttle.

SHUTTLE CO-PILOT

What's the cowboy days?

VANCE

That's what we call back in the old days when I lived on Planet Earth in the Gamulin sector, probably before you were in the MSF.

CO-PILOT

I see, is that some type of colloquialism?

VANCE

In a way it is, when we get time, I'll tell you about Planet Earth.

CO-PILOT

Yea I would like to hear about Planet Earth.

<u>EXT. CGI. SPACE. SHUTTLE FLYING BACK AND LANDING IN THE SHUTTLE BAY OF THE CRUISER 15 SECONDS.</u>

The PNN in the MSF Cruiser and the PNN in the Shuttle would communicate vectors to each other and carefully guide the Shuttle back to the Shuttle Bay where it softly touched down on the landing pad.

In the last 3 seconds the Shuttle was traveling at centimeters per second by magnetic tug that precisely controlled the velocity. Vance's Cowboy Maneuver would have most likely resulted in a slight bump they all would have felt.

<u>INT. SPACE. SHUTTLE. AWAITING SHUTTLE BAY PRESURIZATION ALLOWING A-TEAM TO EXIT THE SHUTTLE (DURING VANCE'S STATEMENT BELOW).</u>

As the hatches for the Shuttle Bay were closing and getting ready to pressurize the compartment so that crew members could exit the Shuttle Bay, Vance reminded all of them:

VANCE
Team remembers, Black Ravik is classified higher
than security clearances for the Crew of the Cruiser
MSFC-34, do not discuss *Black Ravik* with anyone.
Our lives may eventually depend on keeping this big
secret.

Soon the Shuttle Bay was pressurized and as soon as it passed a 14 PSI test, artificial intelligence on the shuttle annunciated via the intercom:

ARTIFICIAL INTELLIGENCE
It is now safe to exit the Shuttle.

Vance pressed the EXIT button and the Shuttle's PNN determined the interlocks were closed and safe to proceed, then opened the Shuttle door, which the away team then exited.

INT. SPACE. CRUISER MFSC-34 PASSAGEWAY.

As soon as Vance entered the hallway leading towards the Control Room, Erica, the personification of Artificial Intelligence that transcended Martha in many ways suddenly appeared in a 3D holograph.

ERICA
Commander Vance, Captain Koasa has requested you
report to his Space Cabin.

VANCE
On my way.

Erica's image then disappeared as it faded into millions of little squares quickly in three seconds.

INT. SPACE. CAPTAIN KOASA'S STATE ROOM.

Erica's image then reappeared in the Captain's Space Cabin where she informed him:

ERICA
Captain Koasa, Vance is proceeding to your stateroom
as requested.

CAPTAIN KOASA
Thank you.

ERICA
Captain Koasa, you are most welcome.

While Vance was walking towards the Captains Space Cabin, the PNN in the Shuttle craft downloaded all the reconnaissance scan images and video to the ship's PNN and holographic images of video as well as sensor displays would be available for them during the debrief.

As soon as Vance arrived at the captain's door, as prearranged, Erica appeared just inside as the door hissed under pneumatic control which could also be manually opened in an emergency.

ERICA
Captain Koasa is waiting for you, please enter.

Vance walked into the luxurious Captain's Space Cabin that had substantial room for something that would be of critical dimensions for travel through space and in combat.

Captain Koasa sitting at his desk, looking at some files on a clear projector that provided 3D visualizations as well as 2D formats for specified types of information or pictures or video, looked up.

CAPTAIN KOASA
Welcome back Commander Vance, please have a seat.

VANCE
Thank you.

CAPTAIN KOASA
Vance let's look at your Shuttle sensor data.

VANCE
Yes, I would like to see how it appeared.

Captain Koasa directed PNN:

CAPTAIN KOASA
Playback all the Shuttle sensor data.

Immediately a holograph appeared that was quite complex, almost the sphere the captain experiences in the control room. For an untrained or person not exposed to the Mergenky technology, one could easily get the notion they were standing in a spherical space and looking everywhere at once.

The resulting imagery from the shuttle's sensors were clear and compelling.

VANCE
The shuttle observed the Cruiser 100% of the time
as the shuttle performed the two Capmoc-Drulyenslv
maneuvers.

There essentially was no difference between phase 1 and phase 2 as far as Vance's ability to observe MSFC-34, which was reassuring and proved the cloaking field operated truly one way as designed. Black Ravik did not prevent the shuttle's ability to observe and if necessary, defend themselves. Even though the fire power of a Shuttle was minimal, the away team's only recourse was to attempt to outrun an enemy.

CAPTAIN KOASA
Now let's look at the replay of the Cruiser's scanners
for the same Black Ravik Capmoc-Drulyenslv
maneuvers.

VANCE
This should be interesting.

CAPTAIN KOASA
PNN playback the sensor data from the Cruiser during
the same periods spanning phase 1 and phase 2.

During phase-1 there were no issues tracking the Shuttle, it was clear and in high fidelity.

PNN then showed the results of the CO-PILOT energizing Black Ravik and the subsequent immediate change in imagery.

CAPTAIN KOASA
As soon as you energized the Shuttle's Black Ravik,
the shuttle disappeared as planned.

Vance seemed in awe as he watched the replay of MSFC-34 sensor data.

CAPTAIN KOASA
In real time, you vanished. PNN is doing some
temporal averaging to see if they can get a sniff of the
data they acquired.

VANCE
How long will that take.

CAPTAIN KOASA
Not sure, let's ask Erica.

The PNN personality Erica always eavesdropping on the crew to anticipate questions or requests immediately responded:

ERICA
Captain Koasa, the neutrino temporal analyzer has already processed 50% of the ensembles acquired during Commander Vance's Capmoc-Drulyenslv maneuver during phase-2 geometries. Video presentation and instrumented fractals will be available in 30 seconds.

VOICE OVER
As promised 30 seconds later a new Holograph appeared and only a blurred like image appeared with what appeared about 95% of the image eliminated.

One would never guess it was a ship and because it was ensemble averages, it could not be done real time and by the time an enemy got a look, it was too late as the Shuttle would be long gone by the time they got it processed.

CAPTAIN KOASA
Well, there you go, looks rather amazing what we accomplished.

VANCE
Certainly was.

CAPTAIN KOASA
The reason why I called you in for a private talk is I want to go over phase-3 with you as I do not want to wait until we reach Earth to fully test the shuttle's capability with the away team.

VANCE
That's understandable.

CAPTAIN KOASA
I've decided since the Frăctŏng planet is just a couple days away at our present velocity, we could do a test there.

VANCE
And where precisely would we go and what would we want to discover?

CAPTAIN KOASA
Why not break into their MSF Academy?

VANCE
Why would we want to do that, they have some serious security there.

CAPTAIN KOASA
Precisely the point, a very hard target to really check your away team. At least it's a friendly planet and we can explain our presence.

VANCE
What would be our response if we got caught.

CAPTAIN KOASA
That's why I've decided to send Lieutenant Shǎnguāngdēng with you for that very reason. She'll be the translator and spokesperson for the MSF.

VANCE
Does Lieutenant Shǎnguāngdēng know about Black Ravik?

CAPTAIN KOASA
As sensor operator she already observed you disappearing with the use of *Black Ravik*. She knows you can do it; she just doesn't know anything about the *Black Ravik* technology.

VANCE
Is she cleared?

CAPTAIN KOASA
Lieutenant Shǎnguāngdēng will get a partial briefing just like your other crew members, they don't have the need to know about the internal workings of the machine.

VANCE

As you wish Captain, I'm here to support you with my upmost ability.

CAPTAIN KOASA

Vance, I know that, and I appreciate that you are dedicated to the mission and am glad to have you aboard my ship.

VANCE

Thanks Captain.

CAPTAIN KOASA

Why don't you go get a bite to eat, then we'll meet on the bridge and look at the navigation vectors you are going to have to lay down to get us there.

VANCE

Give me about 20 minutes sir.

CAPTAIN KOASA

Take your time, have a good meal. I'll wait for you. We got a couple days to prepare.

The captain nodded at Vance who then stood up and walked out of his Space Cabin and walked smartly to the crew's lounge.

<u>INT. SPACE. CRUISER MFSC-34 CREW'S LOUNGE.</u>

Vance went up to a food machine and ordered his meal.

The automated system utilized essentially 3D food printing by taking basic substances and synthesized proportions in well tasting and nutritious servings. A tray with all Vance's food requests soon appeared which he then took to an empty table.

Vance could not help but notice a few crew members staring at him and the typical unemotional Mergenky did not have the social skills of an Earth Person or the mannerisms that manifested a friendly and cohesive working relationship.

There was nothing unusual about the Mergenky Cruiser Crew Members and it was not a personal snub, it was simply the way Mergenky were, to which Vance had grown accustomed.

Vance was one third the way through his meal, following the captain's advice and slowly eating and enjoying and savoring the taste, which fully emulated some of his favorites he was able to get programmed into the food processors.

Suddenly, Lieutenant Shǎnguāngdēng walked into the lounge went over to the food ordering console and read in her order. She was eating a standard MSF meal, designed more for brain power and physical stamina. Thus, her order appeared on a tray in less than a minute. She grabbed her food tray and quickly noticed Vance eating alone and walked to his table.

LIEUTENANT SHĂNGUĀNGDĒNG
May I join you?

VANCE
Yes, please have a seat.

LIEUTENANT SHĂNGUĀNGDĒNG
Did you enjoy your Shuttle ride?

VANCE
Definitely. I've always liked playing with new toys
and MSF is always creating new toys.

LIEUTENANT SHĂNGUĀNGDĒNG
It sure seems that way.

VANCE
You had a long watch.

LIEUTENANT SHĂNGUĀNGDĒNG
Well so did you.

VANCE
That's expected from the navigator.

Lieutenant Shǎnguāngdēng responded in a degree of unfavorable opinion of Navigators.

LIEUTENANT SHĂNGUĀNGDĒNG
On the ships I've been on in the past, the Navigator
usually enters the flight plan in the PNN then spends
the rest of the voyage in his Space Cabin amusing
himself.

Vance had a flashback as Lieutenant Shǎnguāngdēng's comment brought back memories of the Canoon and the Lar he experienced during the past Andromeda Galaxy Mission.

VANCE

When I was on the Andromeda Mission, we met an alien race where the Navigator spent most of his time on the Bridge and usually died an early death from lack of sleep.

LIEUTENANT SHĂNGUĀNGDĒNG

Are you done for the day, or do you have more to do?

VANCE

After I finish my meal, I'm going to meet with the captain and go over future operations. How about yourself?

LIEUTENANT SHĂNGUĀNGDĒNG

My shift is over, I was going to go relax and perhaps get some sleep to build up some stamina for the mission.

VANCE

Well, enjoy your time off, we may get busy real soon.

LIEUTENANT SHĂNGUĀNGDĒNG

Do you know something we don't know?

VANCE

Well even if I did, it would not be appropriate for me to discuss something with you that I'm not authorized to divulge to anyone not designated to be the recipient of that information.

LIEUTENANT SHĂNGUĀNGDĒNG

Well, I understand that.

VANCE

Tell me a little about your planet, I've never been there.

LIEUTENANT SHĂNGUĀNGDĒNG

Frăctŏng is more like Earth than Gwaba. The personalities I'm told are far more like Earth people than the Mergenky.

VANCE

When I traveled to the Andromeda Galaxy, I saw several different kinds of people, but never anyone green such as you.

LIEUTENANT SHǍNGUĀNGDĒNG

Our green skin goes back millions of years. The physiology is not well understood, and our diet is not too dissimilar from the Mergenky who have skin coloring almost the same as you.

Vance didn't take long to finish eating and stated:

VANCE

I need to go back to the bridge now, my day is not done.

LIEUTENANT SHǍNGUĀNGDĒNG

I'll see you sometime later when I get back up on my watch.

Vance then stood and took his food tray over to the disposal and recycling console that took all materials and reprocessed them to an extent allowing them to spend a longer time in space. Just like 3D Printing of their food, 3D recycling took care of all refuse and the Spactron 300 metallic utensils they used while eating.

Vance proceeded to the bridge/control room, which was a relatively short walk, where he found Captain Koasa patiently waiting for him.

<u>INT. SPACE. CRUISER MSFC-34 BRIDGE/CONTROL ROOM.</u>

CAPTAIN KOASA
Enjoy your meal?

VANCE
Yes, was as good as expected.

CAPTAIN KOASA
No problem with lack of Earth Cuisine?

VANCE
Not really, I've gotten used to MSF meals.

CAPTAIN KOASA

That's good to know. Alright, let's go over your navigation vectors and let's see how we need to modify our schedule.

VOICE OVER

All Vance had to do is say, "Navigation Plot."

As a result, PNN suspended a 3D holograph near him which showed their MSFC-34 Cruiser position in space scaled to show the Mergenky solar system including the planet Gwaba and nearby space.

Colorized vector lines showing ships trajectory and its wake reminiscent of bygone era of maps and charts.

Vance having been trained on the "knobology" and the man machine interface concepts knew he could raise his hands into the holograph and systematically squeeze it which would change the range scale automatically.

Successive squeezing of the holograph created a new holograph that suddenly brought additional solar systems into the view with suspended labels on the stars and the planets, plotted precisely where they existed now.

Even though all the imagery was real time animation, it appeared as if someone was observing through a space telescope.

One of the solar systems that now appeared happened to be the Frăctŏng system, and Lieutenant Shănguāngdēng's home world. The next test phase of the super Shuttle was to land on a planet unobserved. Doing the test on an Alliance or partnership planet allowed an element of security.

VANCE

Here's our current track plotted with the blue line and the red line is the proposed change to transit towards Frăctŏng to exercise phase 3.

CAPTAIN KOASA
The chart looks appropriate.

Captain Koasa stated then ordered:

CAPTAIN KOASA
PNN send the updates the Navigator has made and inform MSF of our new track and expected times.

Within a moment PNN Erica's voice reported:

ERICA
Captain Koasa, MSF has received our updated navigation coordinates and plan.

CAPTAIN KOASA
Commander Vance, I think it's time we call together your Away Team and the new translator for a meeting and start working on the penetration plan for phase 3.

VANCE
Understand Captain.

CAPTAIN KOASA
PNN, contact all Shuttle crew members assigned to the *Black Ravik* mission and have them report to the Captain's Space Cabin for a meeting. Also request Lt. Lieutenant Shǎnguāngdēng presence at the meeting.

Moments later PNN reported via Erica's voice and sudden 3D appearance.

ERICA
Captain Koasa, all Shuttle personnel, and Lieutenant Shǎnguāngdēng have been notified to attend the meeting in your Space Cabin.

CAPTAIN KOASA
Understood, thank you.

ERICA
You are welcome, captain.

In a few minutes all those required to attend slowly filed in and as each approached the outer door, Erica met them and escorted them into the captain's outer room/office.

Captain Koasa's inner office which had his entertainment center and gel tube for sleeping and recreation was not accessible to the crew.

The outer room which was the *de facto* chairman of the board's business office often was used for meetings when top security was necessary.

Once inside the room and the entrance door shut and sealed, scanners looked continuously for bugs, illegal electronics, or other devices that might be useful in espionage or sabotage. Had such an effort took place, it's highly doubtful the device would have made it past all of Erica's sophisticated snooping abilities.

With Lieutenant Shǎnguāngdēng present, there was not enough chairs so one person had to stand. That didn't seem to bother one of the MSF Shuttle team members who probably enjoyed standing since they spent a lot of time sitting in the control room.

CAPTAIN KOASA

> Everyone in the room except for Lieutenant Shǎnguāngdēng have been previously cleared for *Black Ravik*.
>
> As of now Lieutenant Shǎnguāngdēng is provisionally cleared and will soon be briefed by the security manager of her requirements.

When Captain Koasa determined everyone required was present, he began his discussion points.

CAPTAIN KOASA

> Let me remind all of you, none of you are to ever discuss *Black Ravik* with anyone without my permission. And it's not likely I would give it.

C.U. OF THE *BLACK RAVIK* SHUTTLE CREW SEQUENTIALLY DURING CAPTAIN KOASA'S REMARKS.

Captain Koasa predicted possible questions and before anyone could ask them quickly explained:

CAPTAIN KOASA

> *For* you who were on the Shuttle, you didn't know Lieutenant Shǎnguāngdēng was the sensor operator and observed you disappearing when Vance ordered *Black Ravik* energized.

Captain Koasa looked around the room and observed most of the faces showing signs of curiosity.

CAPTAIN KOASA
Exactly how *Black Ravik* works is not a need to know
for any of us. And for security reasons, nobody on
this mission will know the *Black Ravik* principles of
operation, just that it works and makes the Shuttle
invisible.

Captain Koasa nodded at Vance that gave him the notion to stand and get ready to do his presentation.

CAPTAIN KOASA
Now onto the next phase of our mission, I'm going
to have the Navigator, Commander Vance lay out our
change of plans.

Vance stood up and walked over next to a holographic projector area next to one of the walls.

VANCE
PNN put up our intended track to Frăctŏng on a
navigation holograph.

Suddenly a holograph showing the overall track from Gwaba to Frăctŏng materialized. The high-resolution graphic appeared highly in detail and would look exactly like a telescope observation from the angle taken.

A highly bright thin red line depicting the Mergenky Cruiser vectors towards the planet Frăctŏng was superimposed on the holograph which crew members intuitively knew was the alternate course of which they would take to get to Frăctŏng.

The red vector line branched off the main blue line those crewmembers familiar with the Navigation Voyage Vector System (NVVS) understood was the new track laid down by the Navigator.

None of the away team sitting in the room were expecting this track. As far as they knew they were heading straight for the Gamulin Solar System. Even though they were highly curious and rather astonished they withheld their curiosity and patiently absorbed the briefing that unfolded.

VANCE
As you can see the original blue track on the VNVS
goes off the screen to our original destination you were
trained for. What you see now is an additional red trace
going to Frăctŏng where we will do additional tests for
our new *Black Ravik* capability.

There was a mix of astonishment as well as surprise on the faces of the Shuttle crew and Lieutenant Shǎnguāngdēng

VANCE
Nobody on Frăctŏng knows we are coming, and ideally, we'll arrive at our destination, do some reconnaissance for practice, then return to the ship and continue our mission.

Silence permeated the room as this unexpected divergence from the original plan gave them a subtle reminder that some of them learned in the Jeeapa War, in the MSF expect the unexpected.

VANCE
Any Questions?

LIEUTENANT SHǍNGUĀNGDĒNG
Any reason why we can't stop in Frăctŏng for a social visit since it's one of the Alliance worlds?

CAPTAIN KOASA
We don't want anything to ostensibly delay or impede the mission plus the security level is extremely high.

BLACK RAVIK MEMBER
Why do we need to do this additional test?

CAPTAIN KOASA
I realize we are taking great risk just flying the Shuttle down to Frăctŏng and back. However, we are only doing this as an 11th hour test because of previous C5 covenant violations on Earth, by our best pilots, we want to make sure the technology is solid and avoid a repeat.

BLACK RAVIK TEAM MEMBER
Why did you choose Frăctŏng to do additional tests?

CAPTAIN KOASA
For a variety of reasons, first and foremost it is the closest alliance planet to our original track to the Gamulin System. Thus, it's not out of our way, so we do not lose that much time doing this last test at Frăctŏng.

LIEUTENANT SHĂNGUĀNGDĒNG
Am I going to be the sensor operator during the Shuttle deployment down to Frăctŏng?

CAPTAIN KOASA
Lieutenant Shănguāngdēng, for the Frăctŏng landing, you will replace Lieutenant Salizrek on the Shuttle, as the Shuttle sensor's operator. Lieutenant Salizrek, who is a qualified Cruiser Class sensor operator will replace you on the watch bill as the sensor operator.

LIEUTENANT SHĂNGUĀNGDĒNG
May I ask why I've been reassigned to ride the shuttle?

CAPTAIN KOASA
You are being sent along as a translator just in case we run into difficulties.

LIEUTENANT SHĂNGUĀNGDĒNG
What about when we get to the Gamulin System?

CAPTAIN KOASA
We will swap you back to sensor operator on the Cruiser and Lieutenant Salizrek will deploy with the Shuttle down to Earth.

LIEUTENANT SHĂNGUĀNGDĒNG
Any reason why I can't go to Earth since I'm the sensor operator for the landing on Frăctŏng?

CAPTAIN KOASA
We want you on the Cruiser while in Gamulin Space. You are our number one Sensor operator, and the biggest concern is the risk to the ship.

LIEUTENANT SHĂNGUĀNGDĒNG
Why is all this necessary?

CAPTAIN KOASA
The Shuttle and crew are expendable. The loss of the Cruiser would be a serious loss of capability in a period of uncertainty.

LIEUTENANT SHĂNGUĀNGDĒNG
Understand all.

CAPTAIN KOASA

For today's briefing we are only going to go over the
Frăctŏng phase. A separate planning meeting for the
Gamulin portion will be held later as we approach that
solar system.

Soon, call signs, egress plans, exit strategy in the event the unthinkable happens and a
few other details were fully discussed.

CAPTAIN KOASA

In case anyone forgets any aspect of the mission, PNN
will keep you fully informed and reminded at critical
moments to make sure compliance and execution on
schedules were maintained.

As the MSF Cruiser slowly made its way to Frăctŏng, all the details were hammered
out and by the time they arrived in orbit in a cloaked profile, everyone knew exactly
what they were doing.

INT. SPACE. MSF OPERATOINS CENTER ON MSS-21.

Kwongab was in a conference room at the operations center on MSS-21 when he first
gleaned some of the details of what was in store for Mergenky Cruiser MSFC-34.

When Mergenky Cruiser MFSC-34 slowly left the near space sensor range, it was time
for Kwongab to go back to the surface of the planet and resume his work grooming the
prospective commanding officers for a fleet that was slowly decaying into a deplorable
state due to complacency created by the false sense of security that erupted in the years
since Jeeapa.

Kwongab walked out of the OPSCON down a hallway, took an elevator down several
floors where he got on the MSS-21 narrow gauge tube train that went completely
around the large 6.28-mile-long circular space station. At the Shuttle area, he got off
the tube train and went to a Shuttle that was ready to board for a return trip to the
planet's surface.

It was all in a day's work, by the normal end of shift, Kwongab was back on the planet,
taking one of Quom's tube trains to the 2-mile-tall high rise building he lived in.

INT. DAY. DOME CITY QUOM ON MERGENKY PLANET GWABA.

VOICEOVER

Monachi had not resigned from MSF, her children
were taken away shortly after they returned

from Andromeda and put in the Juéduìhuīhuáng (pronounced Jewa Duay Hway Hwong) Foundation, Center for Advanced Learning, a very prestigious institution.

What enabled Monachi's children's admission to the Juéduìhuīhuáng Foundation Center for Advanced Learning was partly due to Martha's constant education of the children. But also, the children were very close to the robots they received as gifts from the Larian World located in the Andromeda Galaxy. These robots acted as constant teachers during the Andromeda Mission.

With the children eager to learn and being trapped aboard the Scout Class Ship with nowhere to go, the robots spoon fed them vast knowledge.

Thanks to Martha's radio link to the robots, all the ship's data banks were available for that educational purpose.

At first it was sad when the children left as they were being taken away by Mergenky officials, for the special education program, but Monachi knew it would propel them in their life statures by a whole quantum.

Education-wise Monachi and Kwongab's children were already at least 10 years ahead of their peers.

As part of the internal education process on Mergenky Space Craft, individuals receiving training were granted certifications as they completed courses, and their progress was cataloged and registered for credits.

In essence Kwongab's children had completed all their education requirements by the time they returned from the Andromeda Mission.

Monachi would be alarmed as well as possibly weep if she discovered the essence of the special government program that her children would be placed in high-risk situations in the future.

Monachi's gifted children's lives would be surrounded by espionage and cloak and dagger events.

Unfortunately, the galaxy wasn't peaceful, the government was simply pragmatic and took the best and brightest and put them where they suited society and provided the most benefit.

In the first visit home after their mid-term examinations, the children had changed to the point Monachi was alarmed.

Monachi knew something wasn't right. For many years Monachi and Kwongab had both agreed and insisted upon that neither of them would use the neural expansion telepathic ability on each other or the children.

Monachi was slowly reaching the point she could not resist doing it to discover what was really going on with her children who were unmistakably going through a psychological transcendence of some sort.

Kwongab arrived home just in time to save her from breaking her vow to not do neural telepathic examination of her children.

Life would go on and she would just restrain herself until the need arose to go beyond that point of no return, and she knew that once she did, Kwongab could discover it if he too violated his own oath and used neural expansion telepathy on her and discovered she had probed the children's minds.

The evening was pleasant, as the family was all back together again, and enjoying every precious moment. Kwongab took his family to the Gwaba Great Canyon that evening for dinner and some entertainment.

In the morning, the kids remained at home, they had the two surviving Larian robots to enjoy again. There were two other Larian robots previously for a total of four initially who perished in an unfortunate sabotage incident during the Ponarian campaign around the final period of the Andromeda Mission.

The Larian robots rarely had the opportunity to leave the residence with Monachi and Kwongab who was always busy with MSF affairs. Now that the kids were back for a couple weeks break, they could all go out and see some of the sights and take it all in.

The children were very happy to be back with their robot friends whom they terribly missed while staying at the *Juéduìhuīhuáng Foundation Center for Advanced Learning*.

***

<u>INT. DAY. MSF HEADQUARTERS.</u>

While Monachi was in her program manager's office dealing with the intricate fabric of MSF logistics nightmares, Kwongab went back to the training community where he was suddenly between classes because the last PCO class just graduated, meaning they were now command capable and had the proper licenses to command an MSF spaceship of any size or class.

Kwongab sitting in his office looking at the calendar thinking the timing was impeccable, kids were home for a short break, his PCO class just graduated, and even though Monachi would have her head up to alligators in work, at least he could spend some quality time with the kids.

Then suddenly General Kahn walked into his office and upset the applecart.

GENERAL KAHN
Good morning, CommanderKwongab.

COMMANDER KWONGAB
Good morning, General Kahn.

GENERAL KAHN
I was advised about your personal situation, kids home
on vacation and a few other items, but there have been
some developments that have come to my attention,
and I've decided we need to undertake an urgent
mission.

COMMANDER KWONGAB
And what is it you expect me to do General?

GENERAL KAHN
Commander Kwongab, your old ship, S-1 just finished
a space docking refit. It has a full crew ready to go,
trained and provisioned. Its CO just graduated from
your PCO class this week. I'm sure he's a good CO,
but the mission I have in mind may be too much for a
green commander.

Kwongab was suddenly alarmed as this conversation was quickly moving into another *New Mission* arena, which he was not poised to undertake considering his family situation.

COMMANDER KWONGAB

General Kahn, I was hoping to have some down time and be with my family for a few days since my kids are home during their school break.

GENERAL KAHN

Kwongab, I'm sorry to put you into this situation, but it must be done.

COMMANDER KWONGAB

General Kahn is there any reason why it must be me, there are other pilots available.

GENERAL KAHN

Kwongab, we need to send a seasoned pilot on this mission, and without stripping one of our experienced pilots off another Scout, the only seasoned pilot with proficiency to conduct such a mission that's available is you.

COMMANDER KWONGAB
How long will this mission take?

GENERAL KAHN

I know this is not going to sit well with you and you have already sacrificed quite a bit for the MSF, but worst-case estimates are about two months.

COMMANDER KWONGAB
I suppose I do not have any other options.

GENERAL KAHN
Under the circumstances, no you do not.

Kwongab knew he had crossed over the point of no return. MSF had plans for him, especially if what Mergenky Intel was suggesting, *a resurgence of possible Anarchie aggression.*

Unlike most of the Mergenky that had enjoyed almost

a long period of peace dividend, Kwongab had spent most of those years in and going to and from the Andromeda Galaxy and a few special operations.

Kwongab was looking forward to a few years of down time, and perhaps a squadron commander's job or on the General's staff for planning.

COMMANDER KWONGAB
Just where do you intend, I take S-1 and when do you expect me to leave?

GENERAL KAHN
This is an urgent matter, I'll get into the details in a minute, but we'll give you time to go home. We are sending Monachi home as well to spend the rest of the day with you and your children.

COMMANDER KWONGAB
Seems like urgent matters always find me.

GENERAL KAHN
It comes with the territory. The best always pays the steepest price. S-1 will pick you up at the Quom space port this evening.

COMMANDER KWONGAB
What's so urgent that I must leave tonight?

GENERAL KAHN
You are to then do a high-speed transit to Frăctŏng where you will find MSFC-34 doing a test of its new *Black Ravik* Shuttle.

COMMANDER KWONGAB
Interesting.

GENERAL KAHN
You will go in cloaked and shadow MSFC-34. After it completes its *Black Ravik* test, it will be heading to the Gamulin Star System where it will be doing a reconnaissance on planet Earth to discover if Anarchie has recently been there.

COMMANDER KWONGAB
Why am I shadowing MSFC-34 to Earth?

GENERAL KAHN
In Case they run into an Anarchie ambush, we hope that you can help them escape or warn them in time.

FRĂCTŎNG BOUND
Monachi appeared slightly alarmed when she was suddenly called into her boss' office, which was a rare occurrence. It usually meant there was a logistics disaster somewhere she would have to unsnarl.

MONACHI
Yes, sir, what can I do for you?

MSF LOGISTICS COMMANDER
I don't know how to put this to you, so I'll just be blunt. I've been ordered to send you home for the rest of the day so you can be with your husband for a few hours.

MONACHI
What's this all about?

MSF LOGISTICS COMMANDER
I'm sorry to have to inform you, your spouse Commander Kwongab is deploying this evening on an urgent mission for MSF.

Monachi was mildly stunned, but at the same time she knew they were warned it would be best if they resigned from MSF because of stresses placed on family members.

MONACHI
I see.

MSF LOGISTICS COMMANDER
We'll manage ok here without you today. Go spend some quality time with your spouse, and if you need some time off tomorrow, I'll understand.

MONACHI
Thank you, sir, for your consideration under the circumstances.

Monachi obtained her personal items and left MSF headquarters and hopped on the tube train and quickly made her way home.

The kids were just discussing with the robots what to do today. A walk was planned and just before they were about to leave, Monachi arrived home suddenly.

CRYSTAL

Mother, you are home kind of early.

MONACHI

I was given the rest of the day off.

CRYSTAL

Is something wrong?

Crystal, the oldest child, looked slightly alarmed knowing her mother didn't look happy.

MONACHI

It's your father. He's suddenly getting deployed this evening, without much warning. He should be arriving home any minute now so we can spend some time with him. I'm going to change my clothes, then we'll talk about what we want to do.

Shortly after Monachi changed out of her MSF uniform and into civilian clothes, Kwongab returned. He didn't look happy, either.

KWONGAB

How's everyone today?

CRYSTAL

Not so good.

KWONGAB

Why?

Kwongab recognized the mood shift immediately upon entry, there was a sense of drudgery and no doubt the kids already knew he was being sent on a high priority mission that was just due to commence.

CRYSTAL

Mom said you were being called away, going somewhere later today.

KWONGAB
Yes unfortunately, I must go, but we have the day and time to have a nice meal together.

Monachi didn't look so happy.

MONACHI
Why do they need to send you?

KWONGAB
I know I've done a good job of teaching my student and the new pilot Commander Gōngniúgǒu (pronounced Gong nyo go) on S-1 and I feel he is probably more than capable of handling the mission.

MONACHI
Then why do they think they need to send you?

KWONGAB
MSF is somewhat particular in how they want to handle high priority missions.

MONACHI
They always apply the heavy hand of reasoning.

KWONGAB
Well, that's partly for good cause and partly from lessons learned from sending out neophytes when they should have sent the *"Pros from Dover"* in the first place.

MONACHI
I've never heard that phrase before, where did you pick up that slogan?

KWONGAB
Vance taught me that.

MONACHI
Whatever the case may be, Kwongab, I know you were looking forward to spending some quality time with your children.

KWONGAB
Yes, I missed them terribly while they were off at
school all the way on the other side of the planet at the
distinguished learning center.

Monachi dressed very pretty, the kids looked good as well.

As they were getting ready to leave the residence one of the Larian robots, Charles,
spoke.

CHARLES
Kwongab, would it be possible for us to accompany
you?

Kwongab wasn't in the mood for the two robots tagging along, but Monachi knew how
close the kids were to the robots intervened before Kwongab could reply.

MONACHI
Yes, we would love you to come with us, Charles.

Kwongab and Monachi could and often conversed with neural expansion so they
could communicate without anyone else knowing especially in front of the kids. Now
was such another time.

<u>C.U. ALTERNATING BETWEEN KWONGAB AND MONACHI DURING THE
TELEPATHIC EXCHANGE. THE TIMING ON EACH C.U. OCCURS WHILE THE
PERSON IS TELEPATHICALLY SPEAKING, ALMOST LIKE VOICEOVER.</u>

KWONGAB
(Telepathically)
Why did you invite the robots along?

MONACHI
(Telepathically)
They are the children's best friends.

KWONGAB
(Telepathically)
They're just robots.

MONACHI
(Telepathically)
That's how you see them, but that's not how the kids
feel about them.

KWONGAB
(Telepathically)
I don't understand why.

MONACHI
(Telepathically)
When we were traveling in the Andromeda Galaxy
and we had all those issues with Martha and some of
the aliens, we could not devote as much time towards
the children as we should have.

KWONGAB
(Telepathically)
What does that have to do with it?

MONACHI
(Telepathically)
The robots took up the slack. Our children are
doing well, thanks to these robots who achieved a
considerable accomplishment with all they taught the
children.

KWONGAB
(Telepathically)
I suppose they might be a good distraction today in
view of my sudden departure.

MONACHI
(Telepathically)
Of course, they are. The children will be sad as soon as
you leave, the robots will help them get over it.

With that Kwongab nodded to Monachi and soon the entire family, two robots included
proceeded to the elevator of a 2-mile-tall building with an excellent view down to the
surface where they easily got on a tube train that took them to an entertainment center,
where they could combine recreation with a meal later and be able to get back on the
tube train easily to escort their father to the space port.

<u>INT. EVENING. DOME CITY QUOM ENTRTAINMENT CENTER.</u>

Kwongab's children didn't enjoy the entertainment center, and the food later just
wasn't palatable since everyone seemed to lose their appetite because of the sadness
permeating out of the knowledge Kwongab would soon depart them.

The two robots conversed via their *radio control interfaces*, which meant nobody knew when they were talking to each other.

NOTE TO CINEMATOGRAPHER:

Robot Charlie communicated to Robot John using his *radio control interface.* This is also handled like VOICEOVER or TELEPATHICALLY conversations.

ROBOT CHARLES
(Radio Control Interface)
Everyone seems subdued.

Robot John replied to Robot Charlie on his *radio control interface.*

ROBOT JOHN
(Radio Control Interface)
Charlie, it's apparent that Kwongab's departure has upset Crystal and Clausevoig.

ROBOT CHARLES
(Radio Control Interface)
The children were looking forward to spending time with their dad.

ROBOT JOHN
(Radio Control Interface)
They have not been together much since they returned from Andromeda.

ROBOT CHARLES
(Radio Control Interface)
Their school break is certainly ruined now.

ROBOT JOHN
(Radio Control Interface)
They will enjoy staying with us. We'll make their time interesting.

ROBOT CHARLES
(Radio Control Interface)
Yea, just like we did on the Mergenky Scout.

The two Robots learned a lot from Martha and since they had complete unobstructed access to much of the Mergenky Scout S-1 PNN files during the second half of their Andromeda Galaxy mission.

The two Larian Robots developed an extensive understanding of the Mergenky civilization. And now that most of the days, while the children were gone and Kwongab and Monachi away at work, they had free access to all the communications and data terminals in the residence.

Since they could read via their *radio control interface*, they were constantly learning and had acquired an acute understanding of the Mergenky nuances. In the coming weeks they would once again fill the role of surrogate parents as galactic events more and more consumed Kwongab and Monachi's time.

EXT. EVENING. GWABA SPACE PORT

MUSIC FOR THIS SCENE:

https://www.youtube.com/watch?v=7qqrIusxVAI

Prokofiev: Romeo and Juliet Suite

VOICE OVER
At the prescribed time Kwongab and his family arrived at the space port. Kwongab walked through the security checkpoint and an MSF representative was there and led him to a landing pad area.

From behind the blast protection which wasn't needed with the Scout which had AMRT propulsion, Monachi and the children and the robots observed Kwongab's departure.

It was a rare occasion when an MSF ship appeared on the surface of the planet. The main reason was to pick up Kwongab, but the atmospheric transition also gave them an opportunity to test some of their vital circuitry recently overhauled and reconditioned.

In some ways Monachi and the kids were happy to see their old home again, but at the same time glad they were not on it fearing what Martha could possibly do to them if she were ever restored.

EXT. CGI. EVENING MERGENKY SCOUT S-1 ARRIVES AT THE LANDING PAD AREA 10 SECONDS.

VOICE OVER
The ship didn't touch down, it didn't need to. As soon

> *as the ship was directly overhead the MSF employee stepped aside suddenly a tendril came down and Kwongab was suddenly foisted up into the craft which then started flying up into the sky, accelerating as it went.*

EXT. CGI. EVENING. MERGENKY SCOUT S-1 DEPARTING AND HEADING OUT INTO SPACE. 10 SECONDS.

> *Within a minute S-1 was no longer visible as it quickly left the solar system and was making tremendous speed that few ships other than the Scout could manage to perform.*

The family then turned and went back to the tube train and were taken to their home where they got off. The children would spend their school break with the two robots as Monachi would be back at work the next day untangling the snarl of 20 years of deferred maintenance that left MSF logistics in a deplorable condition.

To get Mergenky Scout S-1 operational for the current mission they had to cannibalize a lot of parts from Scout S-5, rendering it inoperable and undeployable for any time in the foreseeable future.

***

INT. DAY. MERGENKY SCOUT S-1 PASSAGEWAY THEN CONTROL ROOM

The pilot Gōngniúgǒu on Mergenky Scout S-1 was demoted to assistant pilot upon Commander Kwongab's arrival to Scout S-1.

Kwongab knew the Mergenky Scout S-1 very well after living years on it during the Jeeapa War, and later Andromeda Mission, had no problem quickly finding his way to the bridge.

Commander Gōngniúgǒu his former student just a week ago was not the least happy that such an arrangement could manifest, but he would accept the fact only on the merits of the Pilot's reputation and incredible history.

Kwongab looked at the Navigation plot and turned to Gōngniúgǒu.

COMMANDER KWONGAB
Since we are clear of Gwaba and orbiting traffic, I suggest we go to your Space Cabin where I can brief you as to what we will be doing.

GŌNGNIÚGǑU
This way Commander.

Commander Gōngniúgǒu led Commander Kwongab from the bridge to the short distance to Gōngniúgǒu's Space Cabin which he had not been asked to vacate, nor did Kwongab intend to do so.

<u>INT. SPACE. MERGENKY SCOUT S-1 PILOT'S SPACE CABIN.</u>

They walked into Kwongab's old residence aboard S-1, where Kwongab lived so many years and experienced a vast number of experiences. Not much had changed since he departed, it was all standard Mergenky furnishings, though well maintained.

In the privacy of the pilot's Space Cabin, Kwongab started the conversation.

> COMMANDER KWONGAB
> Commander Gōngniúgǒu, you will retain command of this ship. I am along as an advisor. General Kahn wanted me to relieve you, but I explained to him I fully certified you for command and have no reservations of you commanding this vessel.

> COMMANDER GŌNGNIÚGǑU
> That's rather interesting, Commander Kwongab.

> COMMANDER KWONGAB
> You will discover in your communications from MSF that you will receive momentarily, I am authorized to change your operational orders as conditions exist at the time may preclude certain actions intended or respond and react to threats, we encounter during on our tasking.

Commander Gōngniúgǒu very coy in his mannerisms nodded and remained silent.

> COMMANDER KWONGAB
> By now you know our abrupt deployment has some high priority, as the unprecedented manner of our departure included sending the Scout S-1 to the planet's surface to pick me up.

Commander Gōngniúgǒu nodded and carefully analyzed what Kwongab next stated.

> COMMANDER KWONGAB
> Commander Gōngniúgǒu your primary mission hasn't changed, we are an arm of the INTEL community, and

our primary mission is scouting, and we are the eyes and ears for the fleet in long range reconnaissance.

COMMANDER GŌNGNIÚGǑU
What exactly are we going to be doing Commader Kwongab?

COMMANDER KWONGAB
The Scout S-1 will be trailing Mergenky Cruiser MSFC-34 on its current mission. Our main reason is to observe and if they get into trouble such as an unexpected encounter with the Anarchie to either give them advance warning of an approaching force or if they get caught up in lethal combat to do whatever we can to help them escape.

COMMANDER GŌNGNIÚGǑU
The Anarchie have not been in this area of space in over 20 years, why would they come this way now?

COMMANDER KWONGAB
I'll get into that in a minute.

COMMANDER GŌNGNIÚGǑU
Alright sir.

COMMANDER KWONGAB
Initially, MSFC-34 will be doing a test of a modified Shuttle on the planet Frăctŏng in about 12 hours from now. At the completion of that test, which is the last milestone before they continue their assignment, they will proceed to the Gamulin sector. We'll be following them and observing them.

COMMANDER GŌNGNIÚGǑU
You mean planet Earth that is under Galactic Quarantine.

COMMANDER KWONGAB
That's correct.

COMMANDER GŌNGNIÚGǑU
Why are they going to Earth?

COMMANDER KWONGAB
That is compartmentalized information, but I will tell you it is a fact-finding trip, and based on INTEL reports, it's possible to run across Anarchie in the Gamulin sector.

COMMANDER GŌNGNIÚGǑU
Commander Kwongab, are the Anarchie are violating Earth's Galactic Quarantine?

COMMANDER KWONGAB
Mergenky Intelligence thinks that's the case.

COMMANDER GŌNGNIÚGǑU
How are we going to proceed?

COMMANDER KWONGAB
I want you to lay course to Frăctŏng. We must arrive fully cloaked and if we are lucky, we'll detect MSFC-34 and possibly observe its Shuttle operation.

COMMANDER GŌNGNIÚGǑU
I would think that shouldn't take too long or be much of a challenge.

COMMANDER KWONGAB
At the conclusion of the special shuttle test if it's successful like we anticipate, they will then immediately head to the Gamulin Sector.

COMMANDER GŌNGNIÚGǑU
So, the plan is, we'll then trail them to that destination doing reconnaissance?

COMMANDER KWONGAB
Yes, that's correct. We'll let them get a head start so that they do not detect our ion wake from high-speed transit.

COMMANDER GŌNGNIÚGǑU
When can I inform the crew.

COMMANDER KWONGAB
That's up to you, but I recommend you and your Navigator lay out your tracks before you do so. I'd

like your Navigator to brief me when he completes inserting all the navigation vectors in PNN.

COMMANDER GŌNGNIÚGŎU
One last question Commander Kwongab. Do you wish to move into this Space Cabin?

COMMANDER KWONGAB
No, that will not be necessary, in fact I prefer you to stay here so you are close to the bridge. I'll take one of the Space Cabins nearby.

COMMANDER GŌNGNIÚGŎU
There is an empty Space Cabin next to the Navigator.

COMMANDER KWONGAB
Great, that will work just fine.

VOICE OVER
For some reason, Commander Gōngniúgŏu felt reassured and comfortable with his PCO instructor, Commander Kwongab on board.

Commander Gōngniúgŏu didn't quite understand why he felt so pleasant, but he didn't know Kwongab had utilized his neural expansion mental telepathy to modify his thoughts and implant new path forward ideas.

Commander Gōngniúgŏu had a "type A" personality in his fitness reports that indicated he could be a bulldog.

If there was going to be any type of confrontation between the ship's CO and a "rider," it was completely mitigated by sending Kwongab.

That may have been one factor in General Kahn's decision in sending Kwongab in the first place.

The Scout now sped up to speeds it had not seen since the Andromeda Mission as it darted out into space like a hot sirocco with every intention of arriving at Frăctŏng ahead of MSFC-34 fully cloaked and observe their test and then the MSFC-34 departure.

FRĂCTŎNG AND THE GAMULIN'S

<u>INT. SPACE. MERGENCKY CRUISER MFSC-34</u>

Vance was afforded a few hours of rest prior to reporting to the bridge to navigate the MSF Cruiser to the stationary orbital location directly above the MSF Academy on Frăctŏng.

Due to the large separation and distances between Alliance planets, several MSF academies were located on a half-dozen worlds so that students did not have to be transported long distances for their training. This allowed students to visit their families during short breaks several times a year and was viewed as a morale builder.

The Mergenky Space Federation Academy was a post graduate school that trained Mergenky and Alliance World Cadets as well. All candidates completed their normal education and professional studies prior to joining MSF.

The Academies did not waste precious time in teaching general education since all students were pre-certified as obtaining those credentials, and MSF could then concentrate on specifically the military training. The Academy was only two years long and resulted in an advanced degree in Space Warfare and Exploitation.

VOICEOVER
The decision to land at the Frăctŏng MSF Academy would test Black Ravik and the Away Team's capabilities to the most extreme since the level of security there was considerably higher than what they would find on Earth.

If they screwed up there would be no penalty since Frăctŏng was a friendly Alliance planet, and they had an interpreter who was an MSF officer as part of the away team to resolve any issues that transpired during the event.

Just like on Earth, this Frăctŏng landing required extensive INTEL gathering to pick the right building and defeat all the security measures.

Vance was suddenly awakened by a PNN Erica clone, which is like Martha on Mergenky Scout S-1, an electromagnetic and electrostatic manifestation of the next generation robotics.

ERICA
Vance, it's time for you to attend navigation matters on the Bridge.

VOICEOVER

Vance was a little groggy from slight sleep deprivation, so Erica gave him a slight jolt of biofeedback to stimulate him and arouse him into awakening so that he could immediately function as would be the case if the captain decided to announce Man Battle Stations.

Vance slid out of the liquid gel ampoule like container he slept in and was helped dry by Erica, not too dissimilar to the way Martha helped him on the Mergenky Scout S-1.

Vance put on his flight suit, then reported to the Bridge where the captain had just arrived moments before as they were now in the approach lanes to the planet.

EXT. CGI. SPACE. MSFC-34 APPROACHING THE PLANET FRĂCTŎNG. 10 SECONDS.

Normally space craft would sail past the space buoys that identified all approaching inbound craft and get authorization to enter orbit at specified locations. Like many other Alliance planets, Frăctŏng required stationary orbits to minimize confusion and better enable tracking all space craft anchored in space.

Today MSFC-34 arrived cloaked and from a direction of least likely probability of detection. One of the most secure locations on the planet was also one of the most vulnerable from space.

INT. SPACE. MSFC-34 CONTROL ROOM/BRIDGE.

There was not much chit chat going on in the MSFC-34 Control Room/Bridge as everyone was up to their most professional mannerisms. The captain nodded at Vance who went right to work on the navigation pane where he manipulated the vectors and tweaked the navigation problem ever slightly.

The closer the MFSC-34 got to the planet, the better granularity of the navigation grids and more precise maneuvering was permitted.

Vance could not use ILS or any other navigation aids because that would trigger an intrusion alarm since they did not pass into the planet access channel buoy system where they would have been identified. An automated ILS system would take over ship's controls and precisely place them at a specific geo-synchronous orbit.

With the P-points all laid in by Vance, streaming vectors were flowing on the navigation holograph. These little streaming radial strobes were a length representing velocity. The faster the ship went the longer the strobes were painted on the holographic display.

As MSFC-34 slowed down and approached a geosynchronous orbit, the streaming strobes shrank down to slowly blinking dots. As soon as the ship reached lock on the geosynchronous orbit the dot became solid and a blinking circle surrounding the dot indicated anchored in space. Unless the ship maneuvered, it would stay in perfect alignment with a P-point on a planet at a fixed distance and angle.

VANCE
Captain, we are space anchored.

CAPTAIN KOASA
Very well Vance, muster your away team and man the
Shuttle.

VANCE
On my way, captain.

Simultaneously, those Away Team members not assigned to the maneuvering watch waiting or resting in their Space Cabins were notified by the PNN personality Erica to proceed to the Shuttle for launch. Everyone on the away team was ready, just waiting for their orders.

<u>INT. SPACE. BLACK RAVIK EQUIPPED SHUTTLE</u>

In a few minutes everyone was seated in the Shuttle, strapped in and Vance reported:

VANCE
Bridge this is the Shuttle, Away Team members are
all present, systems status indicates [No Defects
Detected] (NDD) and fully functional. Ready to
commence shuttle launch sequence.

Captain Koasa looked at the Shuttle Launch holographic display that included chronometer readouts calibrated to GSTH and saw he was within the launch basket time constraints, then ordered,

CAPTAIN KOASA
Shuttle commence launch sequence.

SPLIT SCREEN EXT. CGI VIEW OF SHUTTLE LAUNCH ON ONE SIDE AND SHUTTLE LAUNCH HOLOGRAPHIC DISPLAY IN THE CONTROL ROOM ON THE OTHER SIDE.

EXT. CGI. SPACE. ANNIMATED VIEW OF MSFC-34 SHUTTLE LAUNCH. 15 SECONDS.

INT. SPACE. MSFC-34 CONTROL ROOM/BRIDGE. COINSIDING WITH EXTERIOR SHOT ON SPLIT SCREEN

Captain Koasa observed the 3D animated holograph of the Cruiser MSF C-34 launching the Black Ravik equipped Shuttle.

What Captain Koasa did not know is at a safe distance away, Commanders Kwongab and Gōngniúgǒu also watched a similar sight on their super-secret neutrino scanner display.

Additionally, the space telescope on the Scout provided direct video feed of the visible light spectrum display of the Black Ravik equipped Shuttle launch sequence.

SPIT SCREEN

EXT. CGI. SPACE MERGENKY SCOUT S-1 MONITORING MFSC-34 SHUTTLE LAUNCH.

AND

SCOUT S-1 CONTROL ROOM SIMULTANEOUSLY.

> SCOUT S-1 SENSOR OPERATOR
> The Cruiser MSF C-34 Shuttle hatches opened.

A moment later:

> SCOUT S-1 SENSOR OPERATOR
> The Black Ravik equipped Shuttle emerged, flew approximately 1000 meters away from Cruiser MSF C-34 then disappeared on the space telescope display.

> COMMANDER KWONGAB
> However, the image on the neutrino scanner still painted the Shuttle in high resolution.

> COMMANDER GŌNGNIÚGǑU
> I sure hope the Anarchie do not have anything like this neutrino scanner.

> COMMANDER KWONGAB
> Intel indicates they do not have the technology yet,

but we fear it's only a matter of time before they will obtain such technology.

COMMANDER GŌNGNIÚGǑU
Should we follow the shuttle to the planet?

COMMANDER KWONGAB
Yes, that's why we are here.

As the invisible Shuttle proceeded to the planet surface right on target, towards building 137, MSF Academy administration building the trailing cloaked Scout closely followed it at a safe distance. Timing of arrival coincided in the evening as it was expected most of the administrative personnel were gone for the day.

<u>EXT. NIGHT. FRĂCTǑNG MSF ACADEMY.</u>

The Shuttle came right down and landed on the lawn directly in front of building 137. In Vance's possession was a picture of MSFC-34 they would leave on the CO's desk as a calling card.

VOICEOVER

Upon arrival the first thing they would have to do is restrain the security personnel. Since this was perceived as peace time, the guards were not trigger happy or expecting any visitors.

The Black Ravik Away Team dressed as cadets in their disguise quickly approached the building. They had about 15 minutes to complete the job before security rovers would come by and check the watch in the building.

The security staff were not expecting any students this time of day and were confused when the students entered the building. Before they could think of anything, the two security guards were lying face down on the floor semi- unconscious and cuffed at the arms behind their back and their legs.

Having memorized the building layout, Vance's Black Ravik Away Team quickly made their way to the 2nd floor and found the locked CO's door. Nobody was present on the 2nd deck.

*Using an unscrambler device, the CO's locked door
was quickly opened, though an intruder alarm had to
be quickly deactivated. That would be the tough part,
but they had with them a former safe cracker who had
all the latest gizmos used in defeating intruder alert
systems. Once disarmed they breathed slightly better.*

Vance placed the beautiful 11 by 17-inch, framed picture, of MSFC-34 on the CO's desk.

VANCE
Ok team we are done here, time to get back to the
Shuttle.

The team soon piled back into the Shuttle and launched.

EXT. CGI. NIGHT. BLACK RAVIK EQUIPPED SHUTTLE LEAVING AS SHOWN
ON SCOUT S-1 NEUTRINO SCANNER WITH KWONGAB AND COMMANDER
GŌNGNIÚGǑU OBSERVING IN SCOUT S-1 CONTROL ROOM. 15 SECONDS.

INT. NIGHT. BLACK RAVIK EQUIPPED SHUTTLE.

Lieutenant Shǎnguāngdēng sat in one of the four forward seats of the Shuttle next to Vance operating the Shuttle's Sensors.

VANCE
Where do you live on this planet?

Lieutenant Shǎnguāngdēng pointed at the reconnaissance map.

LIEUTENANT SHǍNGUĀNGDĒNG
Right around this residential area.

VANCE
Would you like to make a quick visit there?

LIEUTENANT SHǍNGUĀNGDĒNG
Sure, but how can we do that?

VANCE
We'll just buzz over there quickly. We are way ahead
of schedule.

With absolute radio silence people, up on MSFC-34 had no idea what the Shuttle was doing. Vance felt this would be additional check to verify the integrity of their cloaking ability flew the Shuttle to the area Lieutenant Shǎnguāngdēng indicated.

As they got closer the zoom feature of the electronic map allowed them to see more precisely Lieutenant Shǎnguāngdēng's parent's residence.

Unlike Quom, the Frǎctǒng city of Mǎnyuè had areas like Earth that were pleasantly populated and not the super high density.

Lieutenant Shǎnguāngdēng's parents' home had a lawn out front that was more than sufficient to land on. Though her parents might not be too happy in the morning when they saw the imprint left behind by the heavy Shuttle.

The Shuttle landed at Lieutenant Shǎnguāngdēng's parents' home on the front lawn.

VANCE
I'll give you 5 minutes to go say hello to your parents
then we must leave.

LIEUTENANT SHǍNGUĀNGDĒNG
I really appreciate this.

VANCE
No problem.

Lieutenant Shǎnguāngdēng got out of the Shuttle walked up to the family home front door and pressed a *Guest Arrival Button*, which operated like Earthly doorbells. A moment later, her father opened the door and to his great surprise and delight was his daughter wearing a strange looking MSF uniform!

LIEUTENANT SHǍNGUĀNGDĒNG'S FATHER
Oh my, what are you doing here!

LIEUTENANT SHǍNGUĀNGDĒNG
I only have 5 minutes, I'm on a secret mission and the
MSF craft is parked out front nearby I must leave on.

A moment later Shǎnguāngdēng's mother and a sibling appeared, and they were all hugs and smiles. The conversation was very brief, but the enjoyment was extensive.

Unlike Mergenky, the Frǎctǒng were slightly emotional people. From inside the Shuttle, Vance observed the home coming and became slightly emotional himself observing the brief meeting on the doorstep of the home. He was not the only person watching with great interest. Vance and his fellow Black Ravik Away Team did not know they had someone also watching.

About 100 feet above them offset about 50 meters was the Mergenky Scout S-1 fully cloaked and already registered 2 data points that would be of interest to MSF.

It would not result in cancelation of the mission, but it would provide ample warning to the Black Ravik Away Team. During the brief minutes of entry and egress from the Shuttle, they created moments of vulnerability. If there were sensitive scanners nearby, merely opening the door to the shuttle for entry would give up some of their stealth. Within a brief amount of time MSF and MSFC-34 would be duly informed.

Vance might otherwise be disciplined for taking Lieutenant Shǎnguāngdēng on a joy ride to see her family, but it was a blessing in disguise as it gave a 2nd opportunity to double check the findings of the vulnerability, Vance exposed in the process of doing this nice deed.

Suddenly the concern for the lack of stealth in such vulnerable moments transcended the transgression of altering the flight plan for a quick joy ride.

Lieutenant Shǎnguāngdēng walked into the home for a few minutes looked around and had some small talk with the family.

SHǍNGUĀNGDĒNG'S MOTHER
How are things at MSF?

LIEUTENANT SHǍNGUĀNGDĒNG
Everything is fine, I'm assigned to a Cruiser and love
my job.

SHǍNGUĀNGDĒNG'S FATHER
What do you do on the Cruiser?

LIEUTENANT SHǍNGUĀNGDĒNG
I'm a sensors and weapons officer.

SHǍNGUĀNGDĒNG'S MOTHER
Why did you come here?

LIEUTENANT SHǍNGUĀNGDĒNG
I can't tell you what that's about, just that a nice man
who oversees our Away Team decided he could give
me a few minutes to visit you.

SHǍNGUĀNGDĒNG'S MOTHER
That's very nice of him.

LIEUTENANT SHĂNGUĀNGDĒNG
It certainly is. Otherwise, I could not see you in probably for a couple more years.

SHĂNGUĀNGDĒNG'S MOTHER
Well, we are glad he allowed you this precious time.

LIEUTENANT SHĂNGUĀNGDĒNG
So am I, but I must now go, he only gave me 5 minutes.

SHĂNGUĀNGDĒNG'S MOTHER
We understand dear and tell him we sincerely appreciate what he did for you."

LIEUTENANT SHĂNGUĀNGDĒNG
I will.

The family walked out the front door with Lieutenant Shănguāngdēng who walked out to the lawn where in the dull light of night lights around the house, they could see nothing!

Shănguāngdēng's mother asked her father:

SHĂNGUĀNGDĒNG'S MOTHER
Where is she going?

Suddenly Lieutenant Shănguāngdēng's family saw something like a door open with a few internal sources of light exposing the fact something was there!

VOICE OVER
That observation did not escape Kwongab who also noted with great anxiety the extent of the compromise of position.

<u>INT. NIGHT. SCOUT S-1 CONTROL ROOM.</u>

COMMANDER KWONGAB
The shuttle operators must shut down all internal sources of lights before they open the shuttle door in the future.

COMMANDER GŌNGNIÚGŎU
This might also compel them to do a special light check before they proceed with the remainder of the mission.

INT. NIGHT. BLACK RAVIK EQUIPPED SHUTTLE.
VOICE OVER

Once Lieutenant Shǎnguāngdēng was inside the Shuttle, seated and buckled in, they went airborne with little or no sound that could be heard.

All Lieutenant Shǎnguāngdēng's family knew is their daughter simply vanished into what was probably some type of secret MSF craft. It almost seemed spooky.

INT. NIGHT. SCOUT S-1 CONTROL ROOM.

Kwongab knew the Black Ravik Shuttle would be launching momentarily and suggested:

COMMANDER KWONGAB
Commander Gōngniúgǒu, I recommend you open the area to the Shuttle to give them wide berth.

COMMANDER GŌNGNIÚGǑU
Concur, Commander Kwongab. PNN please take us two hundred meters away from the Shuttle.

The automatic flight controls of the Scout responded immediately, and it moved as required while maintaining vigilance on the Shuttle to make sure there would not be any possibility of collision.

As expected, the Shuttle launched and went vertical, heading back to its mother ship Cruiser MSFC-34.

INT. SPACE. CRUISER MSFC-34

As soon as the Shuttle docked and Vance exited the shuttle when prompted to do so, Erica informed Vance:

ERICA
Commander Vance, please report to the Captain's Space Cabin for a special briefing.

Vance went directly to the Space Cabin where the captain was waiting.

CAPTAIN KOASA
Welcome back Commander, we have a few things to go over.

COMMANDER VANCE
Yes sir.

CAPTAIN KOASA
Commander, I was not informed that we would have a visiting spacecraft observing this test until they sent a report just now. Under the circumstances it's probably fortunate MSF did.

VOICE OVER
Vance was suddenly elevated not only in anxiety, but the sudden awareness of outside visibility alarmed him on several levels, especially since he just did a cowboy style joyride that MSF probably frowned upon.

Captain Koasa didn't seem perturbed but did express some concern justified under the circumstances since the event exposed some inherent weakness they never planned on.

CAPTAIN KOASA
Commander Vance, when you took Lieutenant Shǎnguāngdēng to her parents' home for that brief stop over the observing craft was able to see inside the Shuttle due to the internal lighting.

COMMANDER VANCE
That is an aspect of *Black Ravik* that was never contemplated or discussed.

CAPTAIN KOASA
For all future night operations, we need to come up with a system to shut down all light emitting devices in the Shuttle to prevent inadvertent exposure.

VANCE
What about the electronic footprint?

CAPTAIN KOASA
Unfortunately, that too is also a problem area, but there is not much we can do about it.

COMMANDER VANCE
Does this mean the mission to Earth is canceled?

CAPTAIN KOASA

No, but it means you must be aware you have a lot
more risk than you previously were aware of.

COMMANDER VANCE

Why doesn't MSF cancel the mission so we can work
out the bugs?

CAPTAIN KOASA

Commander Vance there are a few things going on that
Mergenky Intelligence Agency has advised General
Kahn I'm not authorized to divulge to you.

But I can tell you it's becoming increasingly important that we complete this mission
even if the risk is much greater.

COMMANDER VANCE

So, it's a go even though we know we now have some
vulnerabilities?

CAPTAIN KOASA

Yes, we are now heading to the Gamulin system. The
vectors you have laid out for the navigation system are
already moving us in that direction. We are currently
increasing speed and will soon be in a high-speed
transit.

Vance knowing there was a good possibility he might get a lecture on his recent
Cowboy style joy ride to Lieutenant Shǎnguāngdēng parents' home figured now would
be as good a time to address it and get it behind them.

COMMANDER VANCE
Anything else you wish to discuss Captain?

CAPTAIN KOASA

After you get some rest, we'll have a planning meeting
and come up with internal lighting procedures, and we
may want to do some in-flight tests during our transit
to test our ability to mitigate some of these deficiencies
we discovered on your planet visit.

COMMANDER VANCE
How can we test them in space?

CAPTAIN KOASA

The Shuttle is fully automated, we can have PNN
deploy the Shuttle, move it out in front of us, open the
door and test our lighting system.

COMMANDER VANCE

You don't want a person onboard during the test?

CAPTAIN KOASA

We could have asked for a volunteer; the person
would have to put on a spacesuit since we'll have to
depressurize the Shuttle when we open the door.

COMMANDER VANCE

I certainly would volunteer.

CAPTAIN KOASA

Not a bad idea, and I think it might be a good idea
to have your sensor's operator with you for training
purposes, do dry run on whatever fixes we come up
with.

COMMANDER VANCE

I am ready to do the checks.

CAPTAIN KOASA

Get some rest and in say 6 hours GSTH, we'll meet
and put together our plan then execute it.

COMMANDER VANCE

Understand Captain. I would prefer that Lieutenant
Shǎnguāngdēng be the sensor operator when we
transit down to Earth's surface.

CAPTAIN KOASA

Any reason why Lieutenant Salizrek will not fulfill
that requirement?

COMMANDER VANCE

Lieutenant Salizrek didn't train with us on the Frăctŏng
mission, I think he missed out on some critical aspects
that Lieutenant Shǎnguāngdēng knows how to handle.

CAPTAIN KOASA
Very well Commander Vance, Lieutenant
Shǎnguāngdēng will replace Lieutenant Salizrek
for the Earth Mission on the Black Ravik. Carry on
Commander Vance.

Vance stood and walked out of the Captain's Space Cabin and walked down the hallway towards his Space Cabin and suddenly felt some hunger and decided to stop in the crew's lounge and get a bite to eat.

Lieutenant Shǎnguāngdēng followed Vance to the lounge and just as he was sitting down with his plate from the food synthesizer 3D printer, Lieutenant Shǎnguāngdēng approached Vance.

LIEUTENANT SHǍNGUĀNGDĒNG
Commander Vance, I really want to thank you for what
you did for me. It would probably be a couple more
years before I could visit my family.

COMMANDER VANCE
No problem.

LIEUTENANT SHǍNGUĀNGDĒNG
I hope you didn't get into trouble taking me to my
parents' home.

COMMANDER VANCE
No trouble at all, in fact it revealed some of our
weaknesses which we'll need to work out. I have a
meeting with the captain in about six hours to go over
the plan on how we are going to fix the issues. You
may be invited to the meeting.

LIEUTENANT SHǍNGUĀNGDĒNG
Anything I can do to help.

COMMANDER VANCE
Thank you, I appreciate that.

LIEUTENANT SHǍNGUĀNGDĒNG
May I join you for a meal?

Vance noting Lieutenant Shǎnguāngdēng had not yet obtained a meal from the food synthesizer 3D printer, responded:

COMMANDER VANCE
Sure, please have a seat when you are ready.

Lieutenant Shǎnguāngdēng walked over and pressed a couple buttons on the food synthesizer and was soon rewarded with a tray and food ingredients she requested. Moments later she was seated across from Vance who was enjoying his Mergenky modified meal.

LIEUTENANT SHǍNGUĀNGDĒNG
So now that we have completed this test of the shuttle will we continue to our major assignment?

COMMANDER VANCE
Yes, it looks that way, however we have some changes we need to make and test before we get there.

LIEUTENANT SHǍNGUĀNGDĒNG
When is all that going to begin?

COMMANDER VANCE
The captain is going to give us a rest period, then we'll be called into a planning meeting to come up with some work arounds for issues that were discovered in our visit to your planet.

LIEUTENANT SHǍNGUĀNGDĒNG
I guess that means after this meal, I should get some sleep instead of reading.

COMMANDER VANCE
I highly recommend it because I doubt that we'll get a lot of sleep after today.

LIEUTENANT SHǍNGUĀNGDĒNG
Are we transiting at a fast speed?

COMMANDER VANCE
Yes, and to a velocity I fear we could be leaving behind an ion trail that some other craft might detect and shadow us.

LIEUTENANT SHǍNGUĀNGDĒNG
How would we know?

VANCE

I've put a few Capmoc-Drulyenslv maneuvers in our voyage management algorithms. It will delay us a bit but if someone was trailing our ion trail at high velocity, the unexpected Capmoc-Drulyenslv maneuvers coupled with some emergency stops will make the chaser suddenly the 'chasee.'

LIEUTENANT SHǍNGUĀNGDĒNG

Doesn't an emergency stop before a Capmoc-Drulyenslv maneuver create a somewhat risky posture?

VANCE

If it's an Anarchie Battleship, it does make us a sitting duck for a kinetic weapon, but we'd at least get off an emergency distress message before we are all killed.

INT. SPACE. MERGENKY SCOUT S-1 CONTROL ROOM/BRIDGE.

On Mergenky Scout S-1, Pilot Gōngniúgǒu came to the Bridge and found Kwongab there intently monitoring the situation.

COMMANDER GŌNGNIÚGǑU

Commander Kwongab, shouldn't you take a rest period? We are transiting and clearly have MSFC-34 on our scanners as we trail them at a comfortable distance.

COMMANDER KWONGAB

Commander Gōngniúgǒu, yes, they are too easy to track, that's the problem. Their ion wake is almost as bright as a flashlight in a dark room.

COMMANDER GŌNGNIÚGǑU

Commander Kwongab, do you not think we are relatively safe here, out in deep space far from any solar system?

COMMANDER KWONGAB

Under normal circumstances you would be right, but the closer we get to Earth the higher the probability we might stumble across an Anarchie Battleship or an Anarchie Fleet formation.

COMMANDER GŌNGNIÚGǑU
Well, we could always outrun them.

COMMANDER KWONGAB
That's true, but MSFC-34 does not have the same speed advantage that we have with the Scout S-1. If MSFC-34 is intercepted at the wrong angle, she would be helpless as far as out running the Anarchie. We must be able to intervene.

COMMANDER GŌNGNIÚGǑU
So that's what this is about.

KWONGAB
I don't follow you.

COMMANDER GŌNGNIÚGǑU
MSF probably doesn't think I have the visceral fortitude to fully engage the Anarchie, should such an encounter take place.

COMMANDER KWONGAB
I would not say that, in fact, I do not think MSF is as concerned as I am.

COMMANDER GŌNGNIÚGǑU
And precisely what is your concern?

COMMANDER KWONGAB
I'm mostly concerned about chance encounters. We have good sensors and normally under the circumstances we could easily avoid the Anarchie.

COMMANDER GŌNGNIÚGǑU
Then what's the problem?

COMMANDER KWONGAB
If the Anarchie are on an unpredictable course and speed, not even knowing we are in this vicinity of space, there is a high probability they would detect MSFC-34's ion wakes and set up for a kill shot.

COMMANDER GŌNGNIÚGǑU
I see your point. We wouldn't have much reaction time to present ourselves in a way to distract them enough to withhold such an attack.

COMMANDER KWONGAB
Correct. All we need is a few moments, our sudden appearance, using decoys and dirtying up the electromagnetic domain, we would probably inhibit the first strike and give MSFC-34 enough time to maneuver.

COMMANDER GŌNGNIÚGǑU
What do you think MSFC-34 will do to mitigate such a disaster?

COMMANDER KWONGAB
Since Commander Vance was hand-picked to be the Navigator, I would bet in the due course of a short period we'll see a Capmoc-Drulyenslv maneuver and possibly an emergency stops just before so we'll overtake them and expose ourselves.

COMMANDER GŌNGNIÚGǑU
How will we know Commander Vance is commencing such a series of maneuvers?

COMMANDER KWONGAB
I recommend you inform PNN that if the MSFC-34's ion wake suddenly changes to slow the Scout and make an immediate hard right or left and reverse course. If the Navigator, Commander Vance maneuvers like I expect we'll soon observe him on our upper scanners as he starts the first leg of the Capmoc-Drulyenslv maneuver.

COMMANDER GŌNGNIÚGǑU
PNN, did you understand Commander Kwongab's instructions.

Martha's voice responded:

MARTHA (PNN)
Yes, Commander Gōngniúgǒu, I'm instructed to

do an emergency course reversal if MSFC-34's ion wake suddenly declines and monitor MSFC-34 which should be easily detected on the upper scanners as the ship does its first leg of the Capmoc-Drulyenslv maneuver.

COMMANDER GŌNGNIÚGǑU
That's correct PNN.

Commander Gōngniúgǒu turned towards Kwongab and asked a question he didn't know why he was asking, that was initiated via Kwongabs telepathic manipulations.

COMMANDER GŌNGNIÚGǑU
Commander Kwongab, what should we do when he starts leg #2 of the Capmoc-Drulyenslv maneuver?

COMMANDER KWONGAB
Good question: because this second maneuver could place us in jeopardy of being detected which would cause MSFC-34 to do further checks that might cause them to lose their stealth.

COMMANDER GŌNGNIÚGǑU
Anything we can do to prevent counter detection?

COMMANDER KWONGAB
If we make a 45-degree course change on the I – J plane, we would still be opening the range at the same time regain contact on our side scanners which offer the highest resolution and better tracking.

COMMANDER GŌNGNIÚGǑU
What will that accomplish for us?

COMMANDER KWONGAB
Once Vance's done with the 2nd leg and starts the 3rd and final leg of the Capmoc-Drulyenslv maneuver, we'll know which way he is heading before he returns to course and our new course would then be in the opposite direction he's heading, most likely a perpendicular course to his original track.

COMMANDER GŌNGNIÚGǑU
PNN, did you understand all of Commander Kwongab's

instructions for all the possible maneuvers that MSFC-34 could make, and how we should respond?

Martha's voice responded seemingly shriller than before.
MARTHA (PNN)
Commander Gōngniúgǒu, I'm well versed in the Capmoc-Drulyenslv maneuver and will take all appropriate actions to avoid counter detection.

COMMANDER GŌNGNIÚGǑU
Commander Kwongab, what should we do if we think they detected us and are getting ready to commence IFF checks? [IFF: Identification friend or foe]

COMMANDER KWONGAB
Any IFF communications are risky because if there were a trailer, it would expose the fact we have some sort of coordinated activity going on and that would raise the specter of clandestine like responses. So, our choice of method must be also the weakest one which has the least amount of long-range detection.

COMMANDER GŌNGNIÚGǑU
What do you suggest?

COMMANDER KWONGAB
I think we have no choice but to utilize the tangramization ability of the war reserve ultra-violet system. But I would caution you to only use it once or twice maximum.

COMMANDER GŌNGNIÚGǑU
Its minimal probability of detection is pretty good, but it's not proven the Anarchie haven't built something to intercept it.

COMMANDER KWONGAB
True, but thanks to the Tangramization scheme and the special encryption provided for their mission, in case they had to do an IFF, any Tangramized information we sent will be useless to any enemy.

COMMANDER GŌNGNIÚGǑU
Understand all.

Kwongab's neural expansion telepathic influence on Commander Gōngniúgǒu was starting to pay dividends as he appeared to become more cooperative vice the earlier almost outburst to a confrontation.

> COMMANDER GŌNGNIÚGǑU
> PNN, if we get any indication MSFC-34 has detected us and starts overtly scanning us, send an immediate Tangramized IFF via the war reserve ultra-violet system.

> MARTHA (PNN)
> Commander Gōngniúgǒu, the Tangramized IFF replay sequence has been loaded into a communication buffer for the ultra-violet system and ready to transmit if required.

> COMMANDER GŌNGNIÚGǑU
> PNN, I would like you to inform me just before you transmit in case I decide to delay.

Martha's voice was clear and concise, seemingly with almost an edge to it.

> MARTHA (PNN)
> Commander Gōngniúgǒu, understand, inform you before transmitting the ultra-violet IFF signals to get your concurrence,"

> COMMANDER GŌNGNIÚGǑU
> Looks like things are well in order, I'm going back to my Space Cabin Commander Kwongab. I suggest you take some time off and relax as well.

> COMMANDER KWONGAB
> Thanks Commander Gōngniúgǒu, I'd prefer to be on the bridge for a while, I'm curious to see how the Navigator on MSFC-34 performs, since I trained him over a 12-year period.

Commander Gōngniúgǒu responded in a positive manner taking new interest in this situation.

> COMMANDER GŌNGNIÚGǑU
> Maybe I should wait and observe a little myself.

COMMANDER KWONGAB
Yes, you should stay and watch, this might get interesting."

COMMANDER GŌNGNIÚGǑU
I bet it will.

COMMANDER KWONGAB
Commander Gōngniúgǒu, have you ever done a Capmoc-Drulyenslv maneuver?

COMMANDER GŌNGNIÚGǑU
Only in the trainer's sir.

COMMANDER KWONGAB
A bird's eye of one being done by a trailing vessel is quite an experience.

COMMANDER GŌNGNIÚGǑU
I imagine it is. How long do you think it will be before MSFC-34 performs a Capmoc-Drulyenslv maneuver?

COMMANDER KWONGAB
Good question. The idea is to be fully unpredictable when you do it.

EXT. CGI. SPACE MSFC-34 COMMENCES A CAPMOC-DRULYENSLV MANEUVER 15 SECONDS

INT. SPACE. MERGENCKY SCOUT S-1 CONTROL ROOM/BRIDGE

It did not take long before the ghostly voice of Martha reported:

MARTHA
Ion wake of MSFC-34 is decreasing, possible emergency stop. Commencing course reversal.

Looks like you didn't have long to wait long Captain Kwongab.

COMMANDER KWONGAB
Indeed.

VOICE OVER
The sensor operator on MSFC-34 had about 5 seconds

he could have nailed the Mergenky Scout S-1, but because of lack of experience and the appreciation of the critical nature of the timing, the Mergenky Scout completed the course reversal, slowing in the process and eliminating any possible ion trail that might have been detectable.

Had the Mergenky Scout S-1 continued their course and speed with just a few more seconds to spare they would have been illuminated and easily detected and tracked by MSFC-34.

Vance hadn't quite ascertained the level of vigilance decrement the backup sensor operator exhibited. He certainly did not have the charisma and drive that Lieutenant Shǎnguāngdēng exhibited who would not be back on watch in the control room for at least another 6 hours.

Kwongab stated the statistics he knew to be the cornerstone of the emphasis in employing such space warfare tactics.

COMMANDER KWONGAB

Quite often during the first leg of the Capmoc-Drulyenslv maneuver, a ship detects a trailer.

COMMANDER GŌNGNIÚGǑU
Very interesting.

COMMANDER KWONGAB

Each maneuver afterwards only nets at best 25% detection because the trailer would have also maneuvered by now to avoid counter detection.

Moments later well into the event Kwongab made the observation:

COMMANDER KWONGAB

True to form, Vance had programmed MSFC-34 PNN a high quality Capmoc-Drulyenslv maneuver.

In some ways Kwongab was glad they were not counter detected, but also somewhat disappointed Vances Capmoc-Drulyenslv maneuver didn't counter detect them. What Kwongab didn't know was the B-team sensor operator at the present time operated the sensors, not the A-team that would be on later.

With no detections of trailers, as soon as the 3rd leg of the Capmoc-Drulyenslv maneuver was complete, MSFC-34 returned to base course with everyone satisfied they had not detected a trailing spacecraft.

COMMANDER GŌNGNIÚGǑU
Well Commander Kwongab, your timely maneuver worked out well, they don't know we are trailing them.

Observing the ion trail behind the Cruiser growing in intensity with the high speed obtained in the transit, Kwongab understood Mergenky Scout S-1 sadly had not been detected by the Cruiser.

Soon Kwongab was alone on an empty bridge after Commander Gōngniúgǒu left except for a sensor operator Kwongab requested remain fully manned until after they departed Earth on the return leg from the mission.

***

CHARLES
The two robots unpacked Kwongab's children's school backpacks so they would have ample time to do some review work and work on any assignments required for completion by the time they returned to school.

VOICE OVER
Today Robot John escorted the children to an entertainment center where numerous kids from Quom were taken by their parents to do fun games and participate in group activities, which could be a Mergenky sport or a simulator or other device. Robot Charles was left behind doing the work of a domestic engineer.

With robot efficiency, Charles didn't take long to complete all the domestic chores and was now faced with free time.

As an inquisitive robot, Charles wondered what kind of curriculum the children were taking at the Juéduìhuīhuáng Center for Advanced Study on the other side of the planet. Charles wasn't spying on the children, just curious as to what they were learning.

Charles first opened Clausevoig data carriage and started taking observations of what it contained. There was very little to do with academics in the back-pack contents. It was almost 100% related to espionage and spying.

Charles was utterly stunned!

With his photographic robotic memory, Charles could record images of most of the documents very efficiently.

Charles then put everything exactly in the order he found it.

Charles then opened Crystal's backpack and scanned her documents. She too was also not learning academics. Almost all the contents of Crystal's study guides and data carriages were also about espionage.

Charles had plenty of Mergenky data cartridges, a very super compact way to store information which allowed him to study the Mergenky civilization at great speed.

Even though Charles was not humanoid, his vast computational power and artificial intelligence allowed him to analyze the impact and consequences of Mergenky/human activity as well, if not better, than a Mergenky, Earth Person, or even super sensitive Anarchie.

Charles had grown fond of Monachi during the Andromeda Galaxy mission and viewed her with great admiration.

Monachi arrived home before her children and the robot John returned. This gave Charles an opportunity to inform Monachi about something he knew would become very unpleasant for her.

CHARLES
Hello Monachi, how was your day.

MONACHI
Fine Charles, thank you for asking.

CHARLES
Monachi, maybe this might not be the best time to bring this up especially since Kwongab just departed which no doubt has added some anxiety to your already stressed world.

Monachi, who admired Charles for his spot on demeaner took him very seriously every time she conversed with Charles. He was like an extra eye in the back of her head to help her cope with the ever increasingly complex world she lived in.

The way Charles laid the foundation for what he would next tell her caused Monachi to raise her antenna up and dropped every other concern for the moment and focused on every word Charles said.

MONACHI
Go ahead Charles, you might as well get the bad news
out quick so I can deal with it.

CHARLES
Monachi, do you know much about the school your
children are attending?

MONACHI
It's an advanced school, I assume they are doing
graduate level work.

CHARLES
Yes, your children are doing that. But do you know the
subject matter they are becoming masters at?

MONACHI
No, I thought it was a general education.

CHARLES
It is a general education into espionage.

MONACHI
What are you saying?

CHARLES
The government is training your kids to be spies.

Monachi knew this was no sort of joke because it was not Charles style. He was as straight a shooter as there could be. So, she took it all seriously and in fact she suddenly trembled as she realized the significance of it.

MONACHI
How did you find this out?

CHARLES
When I unpacked their school back-packs, I was

curious and looked at their course books which I have in memory and can display for you at a data terminal.

MONACHI
Yes, show me some of what you found.

Charles walked over to the nearest data terminal and via his *radio control interface* energized it and started feeding some of the more interesting portions he copied. The more he showed, the more distressed Monachi got.

Monachi had to cope with this revelation about her kids alone since her husband Kwongab was far away and would not be back home before the kids were taken back to school by a special government representative, charged with transporting the extra-achievers to the *Juéduìhuīhuáng Foundation*.

The last thing in the world Monachi wanted for her kids was to become Mergenky Spies, who had a life expectancy of five years if they were deployed.

Monachi was suddenly as sad as she had been during the darkest days of the Martha episode when their lives almost came to a crushing end. She didn't mind having smart kids, she just wanted them to have normal lives and not be involved in MSF or any other dangerous government entity.

***

ANARCHIE AND EARTH

VOICE OVER
The Anarchie had a problem, because of their physical appearance they could not openly operate on planet Earth. They needed a surrogate. It was a complex problem to solve. They approached it from many angles, trying kidnappings, abductions, and bribery.

Even before the Anarchie Ponarian expedition returned, the Anarchie had already begun executing their backup plan.

Thanks to Anarchie lucky interception of Larians visiting Earth in 1947 around the time of the Roswell crash, they were on the inside track to a new source of blue diamonds.

After Anarchie humiliating loss at Jeeapa, revenge became the Anarchie watchword.

In accordance with the disarmament agreement, most of their fleet was deactivated. That did not disturb the Anarchie all that much because they were secretly building a newer fleet with much better propulsion and new troop transports with the ability to deliver far greater the number of Anarchieborgs than the poorly executed plan at Jeeapa did.

In the review of the disaster at Jeeapa, the Anarchie concluded they came within a day and just a few Anarchieborgs short of taking out the Jeeapa DOME which was all that was needed to finally secure a vast source of blue diamonds which meant their heavy battleships could be fitted out with much larger and more devastating lasers.

The Anarchie Fleet would then match the Mergenky in the ability to deliver devastating laser fire from space craft that would make planetary conquest more certain.

Larger lasers on their Space Battleships would afford the Anarchie the ability to finally wipe out their chief rivals in this part of the galaxy, the Mergenky.

Once the Mergenky were out of the way, the Alliance would crumble, and the Anarchie Empire could spread out with no constraints.

Finally, the Anarchie were able to put together a string of events that ultimately led them to obtain a surrogate from the Russian Mafia who also was a member of the FSB [KGB].

INT. SPACE. ANARCHIE BATTLESHIP OFFICER STATEROOM.

VOICEOVER

The Anarchie finally kidnapped and abducted the right couple.

The husband, fearing what the Anarchie could do to his wife after watching a demonstration just for him with another abductee, knew he had to cooperate. He had a friend who was a mid-level guy in the Russian

Mafia, with connections to the diamond businesses Johannesburg, South Africa.

The Russian mafia sometimes dealt with diamonds and gold when they purchased certain toys or informants.

Just like the CIA's motto "Cash in Advance," the FSB [KGB] motto was "Kash After Killing.

Working through the surrogate Pytor Ilyich Beria, the Anarchie were able to get a good assessment on Blue Diamonds that could be acquired through one exclusive South African mine.

<u>INT. DAY. SAFE HOUSE NEAR SOUTH AFRICAN MINE.</u>

PYTOR ILYICH BERIA
(FSB (KGB) Agent and *Surrogate)*
Normally South African Mines would not be willing to sell so many diamonds for fear of destroying the price support built on scarcity.

ANARCHIE NEGOTIATOR
It's not for jewelry, it's for military hardware application and we only want uncut diamonds.

After being informed of the purpose, the South African Diamond miners started looking at the diamond sales differently.

ANARCHIE NEGOTIATOR
We have plenty to barter with, including precious metals such as gold and platinum and silver.

PYTOR ILYICH BERIA
(FSB (KGB) Agent and *Surrogate)*
We can get large sums of cash for the sale of precious metals and INTEL.

ANARCHIE NEGOTIATOR
We can easily get INTEL since no computer network on Earth is safe from Anarchie computer hackers.

Just like when the Mergenky had done 20 years before, the Anarchie siphoned off vast amounts of Earth's Internet information including precious INTEL easily sold to China, Iran, North Korea, and other interested parties.

The deals were done. The shipments were taken out to a very sparsely populated area of South Africa by the Russian Mafia.

<u>EXT. DAY. SOUTH AFRICAN DESERT AREA.</u>

VOICE OVER
The FSB (KGB) agent Pytor Ilyich Beria's Russian Mafia friend had no way of knowing he was dealing with Aliens. Pytor Ilyich Beria just wanted his wife back before she went totally crazy.

Pytor Ilyich Beria's wife was having a bad time staying on the Anarchie Battleship with the constant threat of an Anarchie coitus in case her husband failed and the extreme pain she would endure as she witnessed one of the abductees go through.

The final and largest shipment of uncut blue diamonds and the payment in precious metals, mainly pure gold, platinum, cash, and American KG98A Crypto codes was planned and staged in a baron area approximately 40 miles away from the nearest town close to Johannesburg.

The FSB [KGB] man's Russian Mafia friend brought along a dozen Russian Mafia men, fully armed.

RUSSIAN MAFIA LEADER
My men decided that they have enough fire power to take back the diamonds as well as keep the cash, precious metals, and CRYPTO codes from the '*customer.*'

Pytor Ilyich Beria pleaded with his mafia friend.

PYTOR ILYICH BERIA
Don't be stupid, you don't have enough fire power. They can easily kill you and your men.

The Anarchie would most likely have simply paid for the diamonds and left to avoid any observation they had been there in the event a galactic tribunal charged them with violating the Earth Quarantine.

Since the tribunal represented not only the Mergenky Alliance, but a dozen others, in a combined manner, they could wipe out the Anarchie without much effort. Therefore, there was some incentives to get the material and get off the planet before they were caught dealing with Earth Men.

Pytor Ilyich Beria was highly frightened when he dealt with the Anarchie for the first time, but as reality set in, he knew these were probably beings he did not want to screw with.

Pytor Ilyich Beria in almost a panic advised his Russian Mafia friend.

PYTOR ILYICH BERIA
Just do the trade and get the hell away from here.

RUSSIAN MAFIA LEADER
No, we are going to take their money and valuables
and keep the diamonds.

Pytor Ilyich Beria knew he was in a bad fix; this was not going to turn out well.

Observing from above the Anarchie saw the shooting begin as the Russian Mobsters killed Pytor Ilyich Beria and his friend. The transaction was obviously failing and the Anarchie negotiators were way behind schedule. They had no choice but to take stern measures to the double crossers.

The Russian mobsters didn't see it coming, soon their cars were getting hit and some blew up and some rolled over. In the span of about one minute none of the vehicles was operable, with wounded and mostly dying men laying on the side of the road.

The Anarchie came down swiftly and quickly inspected the vehicles and discovered the blue diamonds were in 2 of them.

ANARCHIE SPECIAL OPS ANARCHIEBORG
What do we do with cash and precious metals?

ANARCHIE NEGOTIATOR
Take it all, we can't leave any clues behind.

ANARCHIE SPECIAL OPS ANARCHIEBORG
What about these wounded Earthmen?

ANARCHIE NEGOTIATOR
Kill them and place them in the planetary lander, we'll
dispose of their bodies in space.

Very quickly the Anarchie cleaned up the area. As they departed, they placed their high-powered lasers on the vehicles and tore them to shreds.

ANARCHIE SPECIAL OPS ANARCHIEBORG
The local authorities would never be able to figure out
what happened here.

ANARCHIE NEGOTIATOR
What do we do with the man's wife on the ship?

ANARCHIE CAPTAIN
We'll take her with us, we can't leave her behind.

The Anarchie then left the planet and soon were out in deep space. Their fleet would soon have a new lease on life as the number of blue diamonds they obtained would be sufficient to fully equip many Anarchie Battleships with new laser optics.

The tide was rolling in on Mergenky laser superiority. *Revenge at Jeeapa* was just a short time away. This time it would be done right because the PEACE DIVIDEND MERGENKY let their guard down and were too arrogant to consider the feasibility of a rejuvenated Anarchie force.

*****

ERICA, BLACK RAVIK, AND THE ULTIMATE TEST
Vance had been resting well in gel container when Erica
awakened him with some slight jolt of biofeedback.

ERICA
Commander Vance, you requested to be awakened in
six hours.

VANCE
Oh yea, thanks.

ERICA
Commander Vance, the Captain asked me to inform
you to contact him when you are dressed and ready
to attend a planning meeting with him and your Black
Ravik Shuttle Crew to resolve deficiencies.

VANCE
I would like to get something to drink and maybe a
snack in the crews lounge first, do I have enough time?

ERICA
Yes, Commander Vance. Captain Koasa wants you

to be fully rested and ready to engage in Black Ravik
Shuttle activities. Let me know when you are ready to
see him, and I will inform him.

VANCE
Thank you.

Vance was quickly dressed and went to the crew's lounge where he acquired a serving
of Jovian Nectar, which for Mergenky is their form of orange juice loaded with vitamin
C and other nutrients. It also acted as an energy drink and worked better than caffeine
in coffee.

Soon Vance was ready for action, well rested, fed, fully alert and acuity above normal,
was poised to go see the captain.

VANCE
Erica, please contact the Captain, I'm ready to meet
with him.

ERICA
Commander Vance, the Captain has been notified,
stand by for instructions.

In a moment Erica's 3D holograph directed Vance:

ERICA
Commander Vance, please report to the Captain's
Space Cabin.

Vance didn't have far to walk, and the door was opened just as he arrived.

Shortly after Vance arrived and took a seat next to the captain, other Black Ravik Away
Team members arrived. After all those invited took their chairs, the discussion started
on how to modify the Shuttle to prevent outsiders from detecting light escaping the
Shuttle.

Vance came up with some novel ideas.

VANCE
Put a shade over all the monitors, they didn't need to
be so bright.

CAPTAIN KOASA
Good idea Vance, but before we discuss any other
ideas, I have something I must inform all of you about.

Suddenly there was great focus on the captain's every word.

CAPTAIN KOASA

I received a secret communique from MSF and decided it's time to level with you Black Ravik Away Team members.

Tension was now growing in all of those attending the meeting.

CAPTAIN KOASA

MSF wanted to make sure we covered all the bases in the *Black Ravik* design and therefore sent an MSF Scout out to monitor our mission on Frăctŏng.

After the Shuttle went invisible with the cloaking device, they could still see us with their new neutrino sniffer.

CREW MEMBER
Do the Anarchie have a neutrino sniffer?

CAPTAIN KOASA

We do not know if Anarchie have managed to design and build a neutrino sensor, but I wanted all of you to know there is some risk and it's not all well-known.

2ND CREW MEMBER
When the Shuttle is deployed would be a bad time to discover the Anarchie had such a device.

CAPTAIN KOASA
The Shuttle mission is still an all-voluntary assignment, if you wish to be dismissed from it let me know and we'll reassign you.

None of them requested reassignment. After a brief period where nobody had anything further to add the captain continued his discussion about light mitigation.

CAPTAIN KOASA
In a few minutes we'll try some of the suggestions you all made to reduce the light fingerprint and test it on another Shuttle flight.

LIEUTENANT SHĂNGUĀNGDĒNG
Will we slow down for the test?

CAPTAIN KOASA

Navigator when are we scheduled to make our next
Capmoc-Drulyenslv maneuver?

VANCE

PNN, could you give us how much time lapse before
the next scheduled Capmoc-Drulyenslv maneuver?

Erica's voice then responded without her holograph appearing, which was the new
MSF protocol to minimize the chances for another Martha event.

ERICA

Commander Vance, the next Capmoc-Drulyenslv
maneuver is scheduled to commence in 17 minutes
GSTH.

The captain then interjected.

CAPTAIN KOASA

Instead of speeding up after the Capmoc-Drulyenslv
maneuver, we'll just drift in space on our last course
before we return to base course and deploy the Shuttle
to do more checks.

CREWMEMBER

Captain, what checks will be done?

Commander Vance will fly the Shuttle out in front of the ship and open the Shuttle
doors so we can check light mitigation efforts.

VANCE

Understand Captain.

LIEUTENANT SHĂNGUĀNGDĒNG

Captain, may I also go with Commander Vance?

CAPTAIN KOASA

Do you think you can add positively to what he's
doing?

LIEUTENANT SHĂNGUĀNGDĒNG

Yes captain, by having a second person on board,
Commander Vance can concentrate on the light
mitigation, and I'll be able to determine if it
compromises the sensor management.

CAPTAIN KOASA
Excellent idea Lieutenant Shǎnguāngdēng, yes suit up as well and support the Shuttle flight and sensor deployments. The rest of the team remain aboard the ship, we do not need you on the Shuttle for this test phase.

LIEUTENANT SHǍNGUĀNGDĒNG
Yes, sir.

CAPTAIN KOASA
Lieutenant Shǎnguāngdēng and Vance we have just enough time before we slow down for you to get suited up so the Shuttle can be depressurized and the door opened and launched without delaying us, so we'll secure this meeting now and reconvene again after the test flight.

The team stood up and everyone exited the Captains Space Cabin.

In the ready room next to the Shuttle Bay space suits were prepositioned in the event crew members needed them for unknown exigencies. It was everyone's horror thinking that one day they might have to dawn one of those suits for loss of pressurization event in deep space.

To get into these spacesuits, they had to remove their crew uniforms first. The normal space uniform would not let them be comfortable and had to be removed first. Lieutenant Shǎnguāngdēng eagerly disrobed and put her space suit on. She did not think much about Vance looking at her body, but he was curious, he had never seen a nude green woman before.

There was some appealing nature in it, but he understood especially after the Andromeda Mission episode where Monachi had to use him to conquer Martha, he would never want to fool around with another woman including a PNN with the electromagnetic and electrostatic capabilities Martha exhibited for his pleasure.

No sooner than they were in the Shuttle than the ship was in the middle of a Capmoc-Drulyenslv maneuver. By now after several of these maneuvers, the trailing S-1 had developed a very good reaction time because the MSF Cruiser PNN was not doing enough random courses and had become too predictable.

<u>INT. SPACE. MERGENKY SCOUT S-1 CONTROL ROOM.</u>

Kwongab developed a critique on MSFC-34's Capmoc-Drulyenslv maneuvers performed and sent it to MSF who then analyzed the contents and forwarded the comments to Captain Koasa on MSFC-34 in special Neutrino Transmission Communiques before they approached planet Earth for the mission.

Kwongab was not too concerned because the S-1 was acting as a rear guard and while MSFC-34 was doing the Capmoc-Drulyenslv maneuver, the Scout S-1 started performing a modified Frazgrandopf which they could afford to do knowing MSFC-34 would catch any ship that was trailing if it got too sloppy.

A Frazgrandopf was a 2-maneuver clearing tactic designed for wolf packs when a frontal unit was doing a Capmoc-Drulyenslv maneuver. The Frazgrandopf allowed the rear guard to concentrate directly behind for a loose trailer.

Kwongab watching the MSF Cruiser and suddenly said:

> KWONGAB
> That's rather peculiar, they're not returning to base course like they usually do.

> COMMANDER GŌNGNIÚGǑU
> I wonder if they're having some kind of equipment issues.

Kwongab watched intently and the special neutrino sensors were in many ways like night vision, it lit up the Cruiser as if it were in broad daylight, with full fidelity and detail of the hull. The neutrino sensors had low probability of detection. Unless the MSFC-34 sensor operators were carefully monitoring for it then it would go unnoticed, especially if an operator was undergoing a vigilance decrement syndrome (VDS).

Kwongab suddenly said now fearing a disaster of some kind was commencing that was putting the crew into a lifeboat scenario. If so, it was very handy to have the Scout nearby to rescue them.

<u>SPLIT SCREEN</u>

EXT. CGI. SPACE. MSFC-34 SHUTTLE DEPLOYMENT AND TEST LEFT SIDE.

INT. SPACE. MERGENKY SCOUT S-1 CONTROL ROOM/BRIDGE RIGHT SIDE.

> COMMANDER KWONGAB
> They are opening the hatch for their Shuttle!

> COMMANDER GŌNGNIÚGǑU
> The shuttle has deployed.

The shuttle slowly moved out in front of the Cruiser and stopped directly in front of it a few hundred yards.

COMMANDER KWONGAB
I'm curious what they are doing!

COMMANDER GŌNGNIÚGǑU
They are maintaining radio silence; whatever it is they
are doing was obviously scripted.

Kwongab manipulated the holograph with his hands to resize the image and focused directly on the Shuttle with ample magnification afforded by the space telescope.

COMMANDER KWONGAB
They just opened the hatch on the Shuttle.

COMMANDER GŌNGNIÚGǑU
This is strange.

COMMANDER KWONGAB
The hatch was shut soon afterwards.

COMMANDER GŌNGNIÚGǑU
It's been open again!

COMMANDER KWONGAB
Martha do an analysis of the Shuttle and tell what
differences are occurring each time they open the
hatch!

MARTHA
Performing analysis.

Kwongab could not help but feel some psychological tremors by the sound of Martha's voice. Even though it had been a few years since the Andromeda Galaxy Mission, the memories of the drama with Martha would be permanent. He almost wished he didn't have to hear Martha's voice.

MSF fixed the bug that allowed Martha's AI to get out of control and become a menace to individuals on the mission.

For some of the former crew members, there was just too much pent-up emotion and Kara for example would never step foot aboard a Scout Class ship again. She also would not be happy if MSF ever sent Vance on a Scout class ship as well.

In a few moments Martha reported her analysis.

MARTHA
Commander Kwongab, the changes in the Shuttle craft between door openings is the internal light appears to be diminished each time.

COMMANDER KWONGAB
What are they doing?

MARTHA
It appears the people in the shuttle are purposely reducing internal light sources.

COMMANDER GŌNGNIÚGǑU
Light mitigation in the event their cloaking field insufficiently handles the task, like we reported to MSF.

COMMANDER KWONGAB
That must be it. They are working on fixing the deficiencies we reported to MSF.

COMMANDER GŌNGNIÚGǑU
We'll know soon. If they think they fixed it, they will redock the Shuttle and continue their way.

A few moments later Martha reported:

MARTHA
The Shuttle door stopped opening and closing.

COMMANDER KWONGAB
They must be completed with their "*fix*."

MARTHA
The Shuttle is maneuvering.

COMMANDER KWONGAB
Yes, and the Shuttle Bay hatches are opening, probably for a docking maneuver.

<u>EXT. CGI. SPACE. BLACK RAVIK SHUTTLE DOCKING ON THE MERGENKY CRUISER. 15 SECONDS.</u>

<u>INT. SPACE. MERGENKY SCOUT S-1 CONTROL ROOM.</u>

A few moments later the Shuttle docked, the hatches shut, and Martha reported:

> MARTHA
> The MSF Cruiser C-34 is increasing speed and changing course.

> COMMANDER KWONGAB
> They're probably continuing base course towards Earth.

LIEUTENANT SHĂNGUĀNGDĒNG AND OTHER MATTERS

As soon as the Shuttle docked, Erica's voice was produced in the Shuttle and stated:

> ERICA
> Vance, as soon as you change out of your space suits,
> you and Lieutenant Shănguāngdēng are requested in
> the CO's Space Cabin.

> VANCE
> Understand.

The two exited the Shuttle and went back into the ready room and changed out of their spacesuits and into their crew member uniforms.

This time Lieutenant Shănguāngdēng noticed Vance looking at her in an inquisitive manner. She felt an inner happiness because she like most Frăctŏng women had a sixth sense that told them when a man was enjoying their bodies, which they as a society had developed for pre-copulation stages when partners got romantic proclivity.

The fact this Earth person had positive reaction to her green skin made her increasingly happy. But she also knew she was at a vulnerable age where Frăctŏng women started reacting to their hormones which often manifested a sense of attraction and at the same time could release large amounts of pheromones causing unpredictable consequences.

Hence, like all good Frăctŏng mothers, Lieutenant Shănguāngdēng's mother taught how to minimize the pheromone explosion and keep out of trouble.

Frăctŏng people were very xenophobic, so any possibility of inter-racial or humanoidism would not be well received at home. Nothing would ever become of a relationship between her and Vance, but she was uplifted by her senses that she knew meant he appreciated what he looked at and if the circumstances were different, more would follow.

After they put on their crew uniforms, they proceeded promptly together to the Captain's Space Cabin where he was patiently waiting for them.

Erica's holograph welcomed them just as the door opened and they went inside the outer office.

ERICA
Please enter,

Sitting in front of Captain Koasa, the conversation began inquisitively by Vance.

VANCE
How did it work out?

CAPTAIN KOASA

It worked out well, the last two attempts were all acceptable. Were the sensors still useable?

LIEUTENANT SHĂNGUĀNGDĒNG

Yes. However the very last attempt was very difficult, the one we did just prior was far more easily to manipulate sensors and controls and use in a tough situation.

CAPTAIN KOASA

That's the one we'll use since it achieved what we want. Please provide me a detailed report later of exactly the series of efforts you made and then we'll get together and overlay your comments on the sensor readings.

VANCE

I am interested in observing the video replay of what exactly what you saw from the ship.

CAPTAIN KOASA
PNN perform the replay of the Shuttle test.

Soon the entire sequence of hatch openings was shown, and much like Captain Koasa articulated, was quite evident and the 2nd to last was more than acceptable and would be far easier for Lieutenant Shănguāngdēng to do in a real-life scenario.

At the end of the replay, it was quite clear they had produced a viable work around, and under the circumstances they were probably well advised to have done it before they ventured further in this mission as the galactic situation was changing increasingly daily.

The INTEL community had advised the Mergenky leadership, but the political situation at home was evolving back to pre-Jeeapa days where neglect and deferred maintenance was now the watchword of the once illustrious fleet that had repelled the Anarchie onslaught at Jeeapa.

Had that Anarchie pincer movement been successful, it would have allowed them to fully invade the Mergenky domain and wreck 100's of thousands of years of development and ingenuity a proud society had built.

Just like Stanley Baldwin followed by Neville Chamberlain who through negligence cost the British their Empire, in just a few years after the Jeeapa debacle, the Mergenky opposition party took control of the government and did not delay in redirecting financial assets that should have been directed at spare parts and critical maintenance of the fleet into seemingly nonsensical wasteful spending on what on Earth would be described as pork barrel politics. The Quid Pro Quo was enormous.

Now that Mergenky INTEL had indicators the peace dividend spending should come to an abrupt halt and serious attention to the MSF fleet be exercised.

Instead Mergenky INTEL was muzzled and anyone thinking of leaking the real situation to the public would quickly be disposed of.

Just like Stanley Baldwin muzzled Churchill in Great Britain, General Kahn was put in a similar situation.

As the Leader of the Mergenky Government was getting ready to start his last year in office before the next election which he would be leaving because of term limit restrictions, merely wanted to kick the can down the road and let the next administration deal with the Anarchie.

There seemed to be a strong correlation between Mergenky and Gamulin Earth politics of the Stanley Baldwin era.

***

<u>EXT. CGI. SPACE. MSFC-34 APPROACHING EARTH. 15 SECONDS.</u>

Music for this segment:

[https://www.youtube.com/watch?v=dt1VAv-4U3w]

Martin Scherber - Metamorphosis Symphony No. 2

VOICEOVER

In due time MSFC-34 approached Earth. Vance could not help but feel emotions.

Vance never expected to ever have an opportunity to go back to Earth under any circumstances.

Doctor Kara would probably become upset if she knew Vance's destination was Earth, especially if something bad happened and he found himself marooned on Earth.

MISSION TO EARTH

MSFC-34 didn't have a space telescope like the Scout, but nevertheless, MSFC-34 had the standard Cruiser scanners both visual light and extended wavelengths.

As the navigation vectors started building on an ever-expanding planet they were approaching, Vance could feel that strange sensation in his throat. He could not reconcile the feeling as anything other than the desire to go home to planet Earth.

The Mergenky MSFC-34 Cruiser Crew would be on their toes now, being very careful, because if INTEL was accurate in their reports and warnings, there was a high probability the Anarchie were likely somewhere in nearby space.

MSFC-34 had two more Capmoc-Drulyenslv maneuvers planned before they slipped into geosynchronous orbit. That's when they received their secret communique from MSF headquarters.

It was CO's eyes-only level of correspondence. After the Captain read the message PNN was due to destroy it when he said:

CAPTAIN KOASA

I want Commander Vance to look at it prior to destruction.

Erica's voice cautioned Captain Koasa:

ERICA

Captain Koasa, this level of correspondence is above Commander Vance's clearance level.

CAPTAIN KOASA

I've decided to make a command decision and grant

Commander Vance access to this information so that he can re-plan all remaining Capmoc-Drulyenslv maneuvers to fulfill the intent and the MSF critique.

CAPTAIN KOASA
Captain Koasa, your decision is noted in the ship's deck logs, and I must advise you that MSF requires justification of your action in writing as soon as you can break radio silence.

CAPTAIN KOASA
Very well, PNN, please request Commander Vance to my Space Cabin for consultations, and prepare to show him this report.

Moments later Commander Vance appeared, and the captain said:

CAPTAIN KOASA
Commander Vance, please sit down. PNN please replay the MSF report to Commander Vance.

MSF REPORT
AUDIO REPORT
WITH VIDEO OVERLAYS.
Discrepancy to address for Kaptain Koasa: MSFC-34 repeated geometries performed during the Capmoc-Drulyenslv maneuvers and failed to detect the MSF Scout class ship that trailed the Cruiser from Frăctŏng to the Gamulin Sector and Planet Earth.

<u>SPLIT SCREEN</u>

<u>EXT. CGI. SPACE. ANIMATION BASED ON ACTUAL REAL TIME GALAXY POSITIONING COEFFICIENTS. MSFC-34 ON LEFT SIDE PERFORMING CAPMOC-DRULYENSLV MANEUVERS. MSFS-1 TRAILING AND PERFORMING COUNTER DETECTION AVOIDANCE MANEUVERS ON THE RIGHT SIDE. (30 SECONDS).</u>

COMMANDER VANCE
The MSF Critique was a stinging endorsement to my failures.

CAPTAIN KOASA
The MSF report also means something obvious and

troubling such as, we were being followed. Every one
of our moves is under severe scrutiny.

As Vance did some soul searching, the only plausible explanation was someone along
the lines of Kwongab was shadowing their MSF Cruiser, probably with a Scout Class
ship, like MSFS-1.

VOICEOVER (VANCE)
THOUGHT
Is Kwongab somewhere nearby?

VANCE

I have no excuses, but I left it up to PNN to randomize
course selections during the maneuvers. That mistake
was mine and mine only, it will never happen
again. I will give PNN new instructions and better
randomization.

The next two Capmoc-Drulyenslv maneuvers were totally random like they should
have been in the first place. Vance was standing behind Lieutenant Shǎnguāngdēng
then on watch as sensors operator and intently watched to analyze the previously
uncleared baffle area and just when he thought it was clear, there was a slight anomaly.

VANCE
That sensor anomaly must be them.

LIEUTENANT SHǍNGUĀNGDĒNG
Who?

VANCE
The MSF spacecraft that's trailing us.

LIEUTENANT SHǍNGUĀNGDĒNG
How do you know that?

VANCE

Well, I could definitively see some delamination of
their cloaking field a very week visual exists.

LIEUTENANT SHǍNGUĀNGDĒNG

Now the mystery exists why they were sent to follow
us?

VANCE
There is probably more to the story than they wish to
share with us for security reasons, which means we are
in a dangerous area now.

Cruiser MSFC-34 was on its last leg of the transit, within the solar system and at the present velocity, they were a day away from obtaining a geostationary orbit around Planet Earth.

Vance and his entire *Black Ravik Away Team* were given a rest break because descending to the planet and the work down there could easily eat up three or four days with little or no sleep.

Mergenky battle enhancers would be provided to them. They lasted about 12 hours before the next dosage was needed to keep that extra alert status. The drug developed years ago during the Jeeapa Battle helped troops cope with severe stress and sleep deprivation.

The following day, the *Black Ravik Away Team* was suited up and they were soon underway in the Black Ravik equipped shuttle.

***

EXT. SPACE. MSFS-1 SCOUT CONTROL ROOM.

From a distance Kwongab watched the mission unfold with the Scout's space telescope. Soon after the Shuttle launch sequence, the Shuttle went invisible as it headed for Earth.

Scout MSFS-1 was currently situated in orbit synchronized to the dark side of the planet. The Cruiser also cloaked had no option but to stay directly over South Africa, where the diamond dealers had their offices in a suburb of Johannesburg, South Africa.

Using hacking principles derived from Earth studies the Mergenky crew on MSFC-34 spent time searching for clues and breadcrumbs left behind in the 'cloud' or server farms storing information about blue diamonds.

There were only a few companies on the planet that had blue diamonds for sale and every one of them was located within 30 miles of Johannesburg, South Africa.

The Shuttle touched down in the dark, away from any dwellings and ostensibly any eyewitnesses. With the MSFC-43 on board 3D printing capability, the Mergenky were able to produce clothing that matched current style and trends of people living in Johannesburg.

The Black Ravik Away Team deployed on the modified Black Ravik Shuttle were limited to eight people for this mission. The Black Ravik Shuttle could easily hold 35 for emergency evacuation, but the life span in space would be short lived.

The Escape Pod, another means of getting safely off the ship in a disaster could easily accommodate 40 if they could get inside soon enough to escape a ship in trouble.

The hatch for the Escape Pod could be blown by controls inside the pod in the even the ship lost power. Since the pod and hatch actuators were battery powered, the controls to emergency open the Escape Pod Bay Hatches were always available after the arming sequence was entered to make sure an inadvertent launch did not occur unless required.

Lieutenant Shǎnguāngdēng and three other *Black Ravik Away Team* members would remain on the Shuttle, including a pilot/navigator, a weapons system operator, a winch operator to hoist members up to the Shuttle in the event they could not land due to hostile conditions, and Lieutenant Shǎnguāngdēng operated all the sensors and communications if required.

Thanks to previous clandestine missions to Earth, the *Black Ravik Away Team* also had I-phones built on Earth but modified by Mergenky scientists to include special capability.

 Thanks to Mergenky advanced computational abilities, the cell phones had pirated accounts and were service ready to avoid getting caught with a Mergenky communicator in the event something went awry.

Commander Vance and three MSF Special Ops men left the Black Ravik Shuttle after it landed in an obscure location out of sight, could speak English.

During the past couple years, since arriving back from the Andromeda Mission, Commander Vance had tutored a dozen students in English as MSF forecast a future need to interface with planet Earth should the need occur.

Three of those eager MSF Special Ops English learners were now with Commandeer Vance as they walked from the Shuttle to a nearby road where they would walk towards Johannesburg and call for an Uber or a Lift driver out in front of a residence located about one half mile from where they exited the Black Ravik Shuttle.

VOICEOVER

Over the past several years, Mergenky Intel fearing Anarchie movement towards Earth had done surveillance on the planet and recorded much of the microwave signals around the planet and Satellite signals. Much of this was easy to decode.

Mergenky now had a fundamental understanding of planet Earth. They feared the Anarchie, who also was an advanced civilization, may have explored Earth in a likewise manner.

Mergenky Intelligence Agency, one of the best in the Galaxy, had to go about getting some information, the old fashion way: abductions.

Abducting Earth people was not too different than what happens on Earth. North Koreans abducting Japanese to teach their spies. Chinese abducting a variety of people for various purposes, and the Russians as well as the CIA often did it the easy way with "Cash in Advance," though the Russians were usually not quite as generous.

After some recent abductions carried out by Mergenky Intelligence Agency, the Mergenky Clandestine missions were successful at obtaining identity and items such as driver's licenses, credit cards, etc. The Mergenky were able to establish bona fide accounts and produce forged identification that would allow Commander Vance and his *Black Ravik Away Team* to travel unmolested throughout South Africa.

Within 30 minutes of arrival, the four were getting into an Uber taxi like car, heading for a hotel they would check in and use as an operation base for up to 72 hours.

Making appointments from the hotel and using it as a base gave the *Black Ravik Away Team* tremendous flexibility. The *Black Ravik Away Team* kept a low profile and were soon busy chasing down leads.

On board the MSF Cruiser MSFC-34 cloaked and orbiting Earth, internet exploration was going on to attempt to get clues as to which company possibly had some recent sales that would be a red flag for possible Anarchie involvement.

The novel communications that accompanied this mission was simply to use the existing cell phone infrastructure. By the time the telecom companies figured out they had been hacked and services provided for free, the Mergenky would be long gone. Plus, who would ever think the hackers were from outer space?

As soon as the Mergenky *Black Ravik Away Team* landed on Planet Earth, the cell phones provided to the *Mergenky Black Ravik Shuttle Crew* to communicate with the *Mergenky Away Team* were tested verifying they had good reception where they were parked. Unless someone came upon them, there would be no need to move the Shuttle.

The Shuttle had more than half the seats removed which was easily reconfigurable making it essentially an oversized enclosed *flying pickup truck* that could haul a significant amount of equipment if necessary.

Unlike previous Shuttle's this super-modified *Black Ravik* Shuttle with a miniature

AMRT had plenty of horsepower for the cloaking device and the anti-gravity device. Habitability was installed in the spare room created when half the seats were removed for this mission. There were several bunks and a chemical refuse remover.

If necessary, the Shuttle could simply lift off fly a short distance and dump overboard all refuse, which most likely would occur before they went back to the mothership.

Based on neutrino CHIRT (Critical Highspeed Randomized Tangramized) burst messages sent from the Mergenky Cruiser down to the Shuttle more INTEL was expected.

CRUISER MSFC-34
CHIRT MESSAGE
Five companies are identified as one of the probable companies possibly involved with the Anarchie and further analysis is being done including paper trails via internet links.

BLACK RAVIK SHUTTLE
CHIRT MESSAGE
Awaiting information.

VOICEOVER
Within 12 hours after landing, Vance and the Black Ravik Away Team were heading out to make a cold call on one of the diamond companies identified in a Mergenky Intel CHIRT message.

The four men wearing off the rack business suits purchased with recent abductee's credit cards approached the receptionist.

RECEPTIONIST
May I help you?

VANCE
Yes, we would like to talk with Mr. Blake.

RECEPTIONIST
May I tell Mr. Blake what this is about?

VANCE
We are diamond buyers from New York City, and we received a recommendation to consult him

on supplying some materials we are interested in purchasing.

RECEPTIONIST
One moment please.

Jasper Blake was fretting over his cashflow situation when the receptionist buzzed him.

RECEPTIONIST
Mr. Blake, you have some visitors in the lobby.

JASPER BLAKE
Who are they and what do they want?

RECEPTIONIST
They are diamond buyers from New York City and want to discuss purchasing materials.

Jasper then looked at the surveillance video on his computer terminal and saw they were well dressed men and thought, *this might get interesting.*

JASPER BLAKE
I'll be right out there.

Jasper Blake needed a few fast sales because his cash burn was getting out of control. Sinking another shaft down to work a new vein was getting expensive because of special requirements of operating down a mile below ground. Environmental controls and habitability were becoming costly.

The men were standing and waiting as Jasper came through a door into the lobby and approached the men. The lobby was empty except for the receptionist and there was plenty of room to hold a discussion, so there was no point in taking them back to the conference room.

JASPER BLAKE
Good morning. I'm Jasper Blake. What can I do for you guys?

COMMANDER VANCE
Hello, I'm Vance and these are my associates, and we are buyers from New York City and wanted to reach out to you and explore the possibility of purchasing some of your materials."

JASPER BLAKE
What precisely are you looking for?

COMMANDER VANCE
Uncut diamonds.

JASPER BLAKE
I see. Any particular diamond size or type?

COMMANDER VANCE
We want them at least 2 carrots, and we prefer the blue
diamonds because of our blue diamond products have
sold well in NYC.

JASPER BLAKE
We have a few blue diamonds, but if you want large
quantities, I'm sorry I can't help you out.

COMMANDER VANCE
Would you recommend another firm then?

JASPER BLAKE
The only other company I know of that had large
quantities of blue diamonds, recently sold almost all
their holdings, and I doubt they have much product
left to sell.

COMMANDER VANCE
Which company is that?

JASPER BLAKE
Consolidated Diamonds.

COMMANDER VANCE
What about DeBeers?

JASPER BLAKE
DeBeers have a lot of diamonds, but as far as I know
Consolidated is the only company that ever-found blue
diamonds in any significant amount.

COMMANDER VANCE
Well thanks for the tip, you have been very helpful.

Companies in America would not help each other with customers the way you seem to.

JASPER BLAKE
Even though we may be competing companies, if they have products we don't have, I don't mind sending customers to them. They do the same for us.

COMMANDER VANCE
Thanks for your time. I think we will contact Consolidated Diamonds.

JASPER BLAKE
Sorry I could not help you.

Vance didn't take long to get them out of the lobby and back into the car waiting for them outside.

VANCE
Take us back to our hotel please.

LIMO DRIVER
Right away sir.

***

Back at the hotel, they sent a cell phone text message to the Shuttle which was then sent up to the MSF Cruiser via a CHIRT burst transmission reporting their findings.

In a short while the Black Ravik Shuttle received a CHIRT message from Mergenky Cruiser MSFC-34.

CLOSE UP.

EXT. CGI. SPACE. MSFC-34 CONTROL ROOM. CHIRT MESSAGE ON HOLOGRAPHIC DISPLAY.

CRUISER MSFC-34
CHIRT MESSAGE
Researchers on the mission support staff are focused on Consolidated Diamonds. A total data mining of Consolidated Diamonds is underway. We are finding out as much information about Consolidated Diamonds as possible.

Vance knew this investigation included hacking their Consolidated Diamonds computer networks and intercepting communications.

<u>IND. DAY. BLACK RAVIK SHUTTLE CREW COMPARTMENT.</u>

BLACK RAVIK SHUTTLE
CHIRT MESSAGE
Understand all. Waiting for information.

Vance was sitting in the hotel room thinking about his next move and contacting Consolidated when he was looking at a newspaper and watching the TV.

TV REPORTER
Police have just discovered from a report by a rancher
of four SUV's found destroyed and all occupants
missing.

Eyewitnesses claim there were no bullet holes in
the automobiles or any possible explosive device to
cause the cars to explode. Police refuse to make any
comments.

Suddenly the hair on the back of Vance's head stood up.

Vance quickly texted a status report to the Shuttle that was rebroadcast up to the MSF Cruiser via a CHIRT burst transmission where further analysis could be made.

Vance also asked the question:

BLACK RAVIK SHUTTLE
CHIRT MESSAGE
Would it be advisable to take the Shuttle over to the
area of the four blown up cars and see if it appeared to
have lethal damage that could only be inflicted by an
advance race such as the Anarchie use? [Commander
Vance sends].

Vance was soon notified via CHIRT burst transmission:

CRUISER MSFC-34
CHIRT MESSAGE
Commander Vance, go ahead and fly over to the area
of the blown-up cars but if there was law enforcement
probing the area, do not land or get near the cars.
[Captain Koasa sends.]

BLACK RAVIK SHUTTLE
CHIRT MESSAGE
Understand all, we are on our way.
[Commander Vance sends].

Vance got near enough to take video and pictures and beam them up to the mother ship and beamed the imagery up to MSFC-34 via CHIRT attachment.

Soon Captain Koasa informed Vance via CHIRT:

CRUISER MSFC-34
CHIRT MESSAGE
Since the automobiles have no bullet holes or shrapnel damage, it's unlikely domestic earth technology was used to destroy the four cars.
[Captain Koasa sends.]

BLACK RAVIK SHUTTLE
CHIRT MESSAGE
Any forensics you can derive from the images?
[Commander Vance requests].

Almost as if MSFC-34 anticipated Vances question an answer immediately returned.

CRUISER MSFC-34
CHIRT MESSAGE
Photographic analysis of 27 distinct areas in the photographs show metal distortion that could only be inflicted by intense laser strikes. There is no evidence Earth has produced lasers capable of inflicting that type of damage to steel framed automobiles. The conclusion drawn is extraterrestrials attacked the cars and destroyed them.
[Science officer R. V. Tiāncái sends.]

Vance responded to the report via shuttle CHIRT message and replied:

BLACK RAVIK SHUTTLE
CHIRT MESSAGE
That's exactly what the *Away Team* thought. It's most likely the Anarchie had their hands involved in this attack and may still be in the area. Recommend extreme caution aboard MSFC-34.
[Commander Vance sends].

LIEUTENANT SHĂNGUĀNGDĒNG
Now it's just a matter of trying to figure out just who
was involved with the Anarchie and what transactions
occurred.

COMMADERR VANCE
We need to get to Consolidated Diamonds and find out
if they just sold a large quantity of blue diamonds to
a customer.

LIEUTENANT SHĂNGUĀNGDĒNG
How will we get them to tell us that information?

VANCE
I don't know yet, but I wish Commander Kwongab was
here. He seemed to always be able to get information
out of people.

Vance and the Black Ravik Away Team made it back to their hotel where they would attempt getting a meeting with Consolidated Diamonds and from there figure out who and how they would extract the information from.

Vance and the Mergenky were not the only ones in town seeking to discover what happened to the Russian mobsters.

The KGB (FSB) was also searching for answers, and they went right to Consolidated for a confrontation and a face to face.

Per Vance's instructions, since they now had faith in the quality of the Shuttle cloaking device, he ordered Lieutenant Shănguāngdēng to hover over Consolidated Diamonds offices and watch everyone coming and going. Men in suits arrived and were inside the building for a while and to everyone's surprise, they tracked those men heading back to Vance's Hotel. The stage was set for some discovery!

Unknown to Vance and the crew of the Cruiser MSFC-34 and the Mergenky Scout S-1 had been busy, silently observing all the goings on including intercepting communications.

Scout MSFS1 followed the Russian Mobsters back to the hotel as well. Because of the growing concern a transaction might have already happened and the Anarchie eliminated any possible eyewitnesses, Captain Koasa sent a special neutrino modulated message to MSF headquarters, advising them what they knew. MSF immediately sent a message back to Kwongab on MSFS-1. That message was also copied to Captain Koasa on MSFC-34 so that he could also read the contents.

Captain Koasa now knew certainly he was not the only MSF ship orbiting Earth. Another MSF spacecraft was nearby, and Captain Koasa knew who it was, but not why.

<u>INT. SPACE. MERGENKY SCOUT MSFS-1 CONTROL ROOM.</u>

The Scout was instrumental in intercepting the Russian mob communications and soon had a complete picture of what went on. On the Mergenky Scout MSFS-1 Bridge the conversation followed these developing revelations.

> COMMANDER GŌNGNIÚGǑU
> The Russian Mob provided the couriers for the blue
> diamonds but had never met the customer and are now
> out for blood.

They believe the customer ran off with the diamonds and the cash and took their men someplace and disposed of them.

> COMMANDER KWONGAB
> Based on the police investigation of the destroyed four
> automobiles, it is a recent event which means we have
> just missed the Anarchie.

> COMMANDER GŌNGNIÚGǑU
> We have figured out who the customer was, and they
> apparently are long gone with the diamonds. Why then
> should we stay?

> COMMANDER KWONGAB
> We will wait on Earth until MSFC-34 returns to
> Gwaba.

> COMMANDER GŌNGNIÚGǑU
> We might as well leave, MSFC-34 is no longer in
> danger with the Anarchie gone.

> COMMANDER KWONGAB
> We have no way of knowing they have completely left
> this solar system; they could still be out there and a
> threat. We need to wait and leave with MSFC-34 just
> in case.

Kwongab realized Gōngniúgǒu's impatience was showing in questioning their reason for remaining.

<u>INT. DAY. HOTEL ROOM. JOHONESBURG, SOUTH AFRICA.</u>

In the morning Vance and three away team members armed with concealed laser pistols were ready to go to Consolidated Diamonds and made an appointment with Wes Moore.

Luck was on the Mergenky side, when calling on the phone to make the appointment.

> WES MOORE
> Hello, Consolidated Diamonds.

> COMMANDER VANCE
> Wes Moore?

> WES MOORE
> Yes. How can I help you?

> COMMANDER VANCE
> Mr. Moore, my team and I visited Jasper Blake, and he didn't have sufficient products to sale, he suggested we contact you.

> WES MOORE
> How soon are you looking to make a purchase?

> COMMANDER VANCE
> We flew in from New York, we'd like to make the deal while we are here and carry some of the product with us back to New York, where our customers eagerly wait.

> WES MOORE
> Well, let me look at my calendar and get back to you when I can meet you. Where are you staying?

> VANCE
> We are at the Peach Hotel.

> WES MOORE
> Do you have a cell phone number I can call in case you are out.

> VANCE
> Yes.

Vance then gave him the cell phone number.

WES MOORE
Okay, I will talk to you soon.

Wes Moore then hung up and immediately called Jasper Blake whom he knew well.

WES MOORE
Jasper?

JASPER BLAKE
Yes.

WES MOORE
This is Wes Moore from Consolidated Diamonds.

JASPER BLAKE
Hello Wes, what's up?

WES MOORE
Hey, I had a guy contact me who wants to purchase some of our products and said you recommended he contact me, a gentleman by the name of Vance.

JASPER BLAKE
Oh yes, I met with him but unfortunately, we didn't have what he needed.

WES MOORE
What's he looking for?

JASPER BLAKE
They want only blue diamonds.

WES MOORE
Why is that? A lot of Jewelry designers do not like them. What are they using them for?

JASPER BLAKE
Well, he didn't say exactly, but the impression I got is it was some sort of industrial purpose.

WES MOORE
That sounds interesting.

JASPER BLAKE
Also, very peculiar was they did not want any precut diamonds. They wanted only the rough ones.

WES MOORE
I'll be God damned.

JASPER BLAKE
Why?

WES MOORE
We just had another customer requesting the same exact product.

JASPER BLAKE
No kidding.

WES MOORE
Yea, we cleaned up in lucrative sales.

JASPER BLAKE
How so?

WES MOORE
We made our entire year's profit quota with that one purchase.

JASPER BLAKE
Oh really, when did you do that?

WES MOORE
Just a couple days ago.

JASPER BLAKE
Wes, are you going to give me a little kick back for finder's fee?

WES MOORE
Tell you what, meet me over at Black Angus after work and I'll buy you a nice stiff drink.

JASPER BLAKE
That's the least you could do to steer the work your way.

WES MOORE
See you later.

JASPER BLAKE
Bye.

Wes Moore called Vance back right away.

VANCE
Hello.

WES MOORE
Vance?

VANCE
Yea.

WES MOORE
Hello, this is Wes Moore. We talked a few minutes ago, about a meeting.

VANCE
Yes, did you figure out when you can meet?

WES MOORE
Good news, a customer I was planning on meeting today canceled and I have time available now, if you can get over here right away.

VANCE
Sure, no problem, we'll be right there.

Vance was using a Limo Driver recommended by the hotel and was soon in route with the three other Mergenky *Black Ravik Away Team* members to Consolidated Diamonds.

The almost completely glass front of the building was handy to watch potential wholesale customers arrive. You can determine a lot about a customer based on their transportation.

The stretch limo helped to convey a sense of probable stature. Another simple method in the diamond trade was no product moved prior to payment. However, the company did not want to spin their wheels unless a true buyer appeared.

Easily observable from his office, Wes Moore observed the four men arriving, all dressed like executives in expensive suits. It all looked legitimate. They would check their credentials within five minutes of their arrival, the truth would come out one way or the other.

Vance approached the receptionist.

RECEPTIONIST
May I help you?

VANCE
My name is Vance, and I have an appointment with
Mr. Wes Moore.

RECEPTIONIST
One moment please.

The reception dialed Wes Moore's' phone and Vance could hear her talk.

RECEPTIONIST
I'll let him know.

The reception then hung up and announced:

RECEPTIONIST
Mr. Moore will be right out. Would you like coffee
while you wait?

VANCE
No that will not be necessary.

Within a minute Wes Moore arrived and approached the four men.

WES MOORE
Hello, are you Vance?

VANCE
Yes, that's me.

WES MOORE
Greetings Vance, I'm Wes Moore, we talked on the
phone, why don't we go to our conference room, and
we can talk there.

Vance and the men followed Wes to the conference room and soon they were sitting at a long table and began their discussions.

                    WES MOORE
So, tell me Vance what kind of product are you looking for?

                    VANCE
We are looking for something that is slightly unusual for a special customer who has a need for the equipment they manufacture. We need blue diamonds, at least 2 carrots in size and up to 5 carrots would be preferable.

                    WES MOORE
You are right, those diamonds are kind of rare.

Wes Moore lied as Mergenky INTEL said otherwise.

                    WES MOORE
How many diamonds are you looking to obtain?

                    VANCE
Well, this is just phase one of their development. Once they get to phase three, we expect to quadruple the amount.

                    WES MOORE
And how many is that?

                    VANCE
This is all in strict confidentiality.

                    WES MOORE
Of course.

                    VANCE
We want 4,000 diamonds in the initial transaction all uncut.

                    WES MOORE
Why uncut?

                    VANCE
The customer has their own milling machines and

wants to convert them for their purposes they claim produce the most accurate geometries possible.

Wes suddenly felt spooked. This was almost the same exact story he heard from his most recent customer just last week. Something was going on. There was big money to be made because if someone knew what industrial process required this many blue diamonds would be one hell of a future investment if you only knew now what it was all about.

WES MOORE

I'm sure we can provide the product, it's just a matter of determining exactly when we can fill the order. Are there any provisions to ship partial product count over say a 3-month period?

VANCE

I'm sure that can be arranged, but no doubt the customer wants the product as fast as you can deliver it.

WES MOORE

I know we can deliver all required diamonds in a 3-month period.

VANCE

Do you have any track record that explicitly shows blue diamonds over such a period?

WES MOORE

Yes. I do, we just delivered 8,000 blue diamonds in the 2 to 5 carrot range over the past 2 months.

VANCE

Do you have anything that shows that such as an invoice?

WES MOORE

I do and if you give me a minute I'll grab a copy, but I'll have to redact the client's name for privacy reasons.

VANCE
Sure, I want to look at that.

WES MOORE
Be right back, make yourselves comfortable.

The Mergenky were shrewd and smart and expected to be bugged in almost any place they visited; therefore, they all played the game from the time they arrived until they left. With all the surveillance on them, nobody ever caught on.

A document like what Wes brought two minutes later could not be conjured up that quickly from a fake. This had to be the real thing. Even though Wes redacted the name, whether intentional or not, enough of it was left where a sophisticated person could get enough off the document to recreate the name. They now had a lead to who purchased the diamonds.

So did the police because the name of the company that leased 3 of the cars recently blown up matched the invoice. Vance instantly recalled the name of the company whom the police were attempting to track down that was in this morning's paper. Unfortunately, when it was all finally pieced together, nobody could ever find the link between the Anarchie and the missing men.

Vance left his business card with Wes.

VANCE
I will call New York, and they will send you a purchase
order shortly for the diamonds.

WES MOORE
Let's get together after we get the purchase order,
perhaps we could have dinner if you got the time.

Vance lied.
VANCE

Yes, I would like that.

Wes, true to his word, went out for happy hour knowing he had just earned another gigantic bonus and provided all the liquids and spirits Jasper Blake desired for steering the business his way.

Vance did not bother checking out of the hotel. He had the Limo driver drop them off at a prearranged spot and after the Limo was gone and nobody appeared around them, the Shuttle door opened which broke some of the cloaking field and the four members of the Black Ravik Away Team got aboard and were soon deposited back on the MSF Cruiser with the knowledge that this part of the mission was over.

VOICEOVER
Commander Vance would probably have enjoyed a
quick visit to southern California, but he knew MSFC-

34 had critical information that needed to get back to MSF right away and their services were no longer needed here on earth.

The sad news was that Anarchie spies had already been to Earth and received the blue diamonds.

Now it was only a matter of time before MSF would face Anarchie once again in a bitter struggle as the peace dividend was now quickly eroding. With the mission milestones now complete, MSFC-34 found what they came looking for, and it was time to leave.

Soon the police were visiting the hotel and Consolidated Diamonds. The mystery just got steeper as the people who did not check out of their hotel rooms were people, they eventually discovered on missing persons lists.

Vance did benefit in one regard to the trip, thanks to the ship downloading a lot of internet files to study, Vance was given the privilege of learning how Earth and America had changed since his departure years ago.

However, to some extent there was a slight emotional sensation of seeing Earth one more time. Vance knew down in his heart he would one day want to visit Earth again, if not relocate to it.

DEPLOYMENT TO JEEAPA

The journey back to Gwaba was sooner than they planned. But the information brought back was far more severe than they anticipated at MSF headquarters.

<u>INT. SPACE. MSF SPACE STATION MSS-21</u>

General Kahn was at MSS-21 right at the terminal that MSFC-34 docked. Several of his staff were with him.

As soon as Captain Koasa and Vance exited the ship General Kahn met them.

GENERAL KAHN
Welcome back Captain Koasa, and Commander Vance.

CAPTAIN KOASA
Thank you General.

Captain Koasa then slightly bowed, and Vance followed a similar stance.

GENERAL KAHN
We decided to do the debriefing here on MSS-21 and we'll explain why during the debrief.

CAPTAIN KOASA
Understand General.

GENERAL KAHN
This way Captain.

VOICEOVER
General Kahn led the group. They did not have to go very far as the offices were only 100 feet away through a security barrier.

While they were walking to the offices, the Cruiser's PNN downloaded the patrol report to MSF. By the time they reached the conference room, the information was ready to be used during the debriefing.

The key players were seated at the long table, lesser ranked individuals were in chairs against the wall facing the table and chairs. General Kahn was at the head of the table with Captain Koasa on his right and Commander Vance on his left.

Once inside the MSF offices, staff members there provided drinks which a few of the MSF crew members accepted and offered snacks which everyone declined.

The official Mission Report had already been illustrated and voiced over.

All the presenters had to do was play the presentation and holographs and video images that were suspended in front of them.

About halfway through the debrief one of General Kahn's assistants walked over and whispered in his ear:

GENERAL KAHN'S ASSISTANT
(whisper)
General Kahn, Commander Kwongab is in the waiting
room.

GENERAL KAHN
Send him in. Does he have a group with him?

GENERAL KAHN'S ASSISTANT
Yes, four other crew members.

General nodded and the assistant momentarily left the room and shortly Kwongab, Commander Gōngniúgǒu, and three other officers came in and found chairs and sat down and observed the ongoing presentation.

Much of it, Kwongab already knew about since he was performing a close trail on MSFC-34 to make sure he could help it egress should they come upon a surprise and unexpected intercept of an Anarchie fleet.

The recap of the mission didn't take long, but General Kahn knew the significance of it.

GENERAL KAHN
Now all we need to do is figure out the time it will take
Anarchie to modify those blue diamonds and put them
in laser optics.

CAPTAIN KOASA
This will not end well, it's now just a matter of
time before we have our next confrontation, and the
question is *where* will it be?

COMMANDER KWONGAB
General Kahn, you requested my presence.

GENERAL KAHN
Yes, Commander Kwongab, I thought it might be
useful if you gave the crew of the MSFC-34 a short
briefing on your mission.

Vance was highly curious and watched with great interest as Kwongab did a similar brief, a Mergenky standard protocol where the report was sent over via PNN and soon they were watching the Scout's report, which left them in utter astonishment to learn Kwongab's ship had been there with them the entire time.

COMMANDER KWONGAB
In summary, we concluded the Anarchie left planet Earth the day before we arrived.

GENERAL KAHN
So, what do you think Anarchies' next move will be?

COMMANDER KWONGAB
The Anarchie tend to never give up once they decide to do something so my guess is they will make another move on Jeeapa.

GENERAL KAHN
That seems rather foolish.

COMMANDER KWONGAB
Not really, when you start to think about the decay in our fleet readiness with the peace-dividend over the past 15 years. If they have a lot of new ships already built, they just wait for new more powerful laser optics.

GENERAL KAHN
I think part of their overall plan would be the time it takes them to use all those blue diamonds to build larger and more powerful lasers.

COMMANDER KWONGAB
If they can install more powerful lasers on their battleships, then they might think they could take Jeeapa. The last time they had insufficient men on the ground, next time will be different if they operate true to form with overwhelming strength in the beginning.

GENERAL KAHN
How will we get an indication that Jeeapa is their target?

COMMANDER KWONGAB
If they do their typical plan, they will soon be sending surveillance flights over Jeeapa identifying all the defensive positions.

GENERAL KAHN
There are not many Jeeapa defense installations left

because the public has been spoon fed the peace dividend crap; we can expect a lot of surprises.

GENERAL KAHN'S
CHIEF OF STAFF
Should the Anarchie manage to take Jeeapa, the Alliance would be threatened because they would have a key base to split the Alliance and take us apart in detail.

GENERAL KAHN
It's the key to their ability to move in this direction.

After a short pause:

GENERAL KAHN
Otherwise they have no means to expand the Anarchie Empire because they are essentially boxed in with the Lúmzhīnites (pronounced Lom-she-nites) and the Zǒng Huàidàn's (pronounced Song Who-way-duns).

GENERAL KAHN'S
CHIEF OF STAFF
From my understanding the Lúmzhīnites and the Zǒng Huàidàn's have a mutual defense pact and together have the firepower to stop any Anarchie incursion into their territories.

GENERAL KAHN
That brings up my next point.

General Kahn solemnly looked at Kwongab.

GENERAL KAHN
I'm sorry Commander Kwongab but I'm going to have to send you out right away on another assignment.

COMMANDER KWONGAB
What about my next class that is due to start soon?

GENERAL KAHN
I know if the situation was normal, you are our best PCO instructor that we would avoid sending you.

General Kahn had to deal with a lot of sensitive INTEL that was becoming alarming to him that and only known by less than a handful of top MSF officials he could not inform Kwongab because it was extremely sensitive. He now leveled with Kwongab.

GENERAL KAHN
As we have just discussed and you yourself theorized, Jeeapa is the most likely avenue of assault, I want you to make a Surveillance Mission to Jeeapa.

COMMANDER KWONGAB
What will I be doing?

GENERAL KAHN
I want you to monitor for Anarchie intrusions into Jeeapa space, then I want you to personally go down on the planet and look at the defense configurations and report back if they are not prepared to repel any moderate Anarchie assault.

COMMANDER KWONGAB
That may take a while.

GENERAL KAHN
I expect you will need to spend about 30 Mergenky days at Jeeapa doing on on-site inspection and then come back and give me a full report.

COMMANDER KWONGAB
Understand. If I run into situations, I think I need to report, it would be best I communicate in-situ vice waiting until I return.

GENERAL KAHN
Commander Kwongab, I've learned to trust your judgement after numerous events. If you think you need to inform me about something don't wait to report it. Send it in-situ as you stated. In your OP-ORDERS, I will attach a special Franking Authority in case you run into resistance.

VOICEOVER
General Kahn's last statement hit Kwongab hard as the Franking Authority gives him temporary rank

and privilege as General Kahn's special envoy, which meant he would be speaking for General Kahn and have significant authority.

KWONGAB

Do I have time to go down to the planet and see my family before I go?

GENERAL KAHN

I'm sorry, Commander Kwongab. Commander Gōngniúgǒu and you, will leave right after this meeting on Scout MSFS-1 and transit to Jeeapa.

COMMANDER VANCE

General Kahn, if possible, I would like to be transferred to MSFS-1 and go with Commander Kwongab.

GENERAL KAHN

Commander Vance, you are needed on MSFC-34 where you are essential for navigation, but also in the event we must send MSFC-34 to Jeeapa.

COMMANDER VANCE
Understand sir.

GENERAL KAHN

You had extensive experiences in the last Jeeapa conflict and during the Andromeda Mission.

I think you would be valuable to Captain Koasa so you must stay as crew member to MSFC-34 and be ready to be deployed.

Vance responded very grumbly.

COMMANDER VANCE

General Kahn, since my kids are back in school, I'm ready to go now I could leave with MSFS-1 immediately.

GENERAL KAHN

Vance, you may have to leave right away on MSFC-34, depending on what Commander Kwongab reports back from Jeeapa. I suspect you will soon be seeing all the action you want.

COMMANDER VANCE
Even so General Kahn, it's always desirable to fight with your best buddies.

GENERAL KAHN
Vance, I understand your enthusiasm as well as your comradery, but at the same time, we can't put all our best people on one ship, we must spread them across the fleet in our depleted numbers.

VANCE
Understand General Kahn.

GENERAL KAHN
Commander Vance your past missions were vast and quite unusual because of your assignment to the *Andromeda Mission.*

You are not only assigned to MSFC-34 to fulfill the role as the ship's Navigator, but you are also there to be the mentor of the next generation coming up and part with them some of your experiences.

VANCE
Understand sir, I will do what I'm required.

GENERAL KAHN
Good, and to make up for you having to deploy right when your children were home on school leave, I'm going to have MSF take you and Doctor Kara to their school for a brief visit. But after that, you very well may be deployed right away.

VANCE
Thank you, sir.

GENERAL KAHN
Ok gentlemen, we covered a lot of territory, the briefings were very timely and excellent. I'm going to adjourn this meeting.

You all need to get back to your ships to prepare for upcoming missions and your operational orders will be in your ship PNN's when you get back.

The attendees started leaving the room.

GENERAL KAHN
Commander Vance, I'm going to arrange that
transportation, come back in about 30 minutes GSTH
and I'll have the details worked out for you by then.

COMMANDER VANCE
General, I will be back in 30 minutes, I want to walk
Commander Kwongab to MSFS-1.

GENERAL KAHN
Sure, see you Vance when you get back.

Captain Koasa nodded at Vance as he was leaving the conference room knowing General Kahn had things lined up for him.

The men filed out of the room. There was no need to get on the space station tube train, they could walk to MSFS-1.

The mission debrief attendees and Vance seemed like they were in a subdued mood.

The rigors of space service, taking men away from families, which was one of the prime reasons why MSF preferred single people with no families for moments just like this. Single people did not need accommodations such as families did.

Commander Gōngniúgǒu was walking side by side with Kwongab and Vance. He seemed quiet and low-keyed, taking it all in stride. It wasn't his desire to have someone else come in and take over his ship.

It wasn't that Commander Gōngniúgǒu was humiliated because Kwongab was a legend and PCO instructor, but he wanted the opportunity to prove himself and didn't want Babysitten by the PCO instructor.

Little did Commander Gōngniúgǒu know Kwongab had even less of a desire to be there because he knew in his heart his services were more urgently needed in the next PCO class.

Because of the extraordinary change in national defense posture that was going to be forced upon the Mergenky, Kwongab did not spare the neural expansion. He went full speed ahead and probed both Vance and Gōngniúgǒu to understand precisely what they were thinking and to evaluate their emotional and logical states.

To Kwongab, Vance was not an issue, his heart, mind, and soul were all in the right place. But Gōngniúgǒu was going to be an issue.

Kwongab had to work on Commander Gōngniúgǒu so that he would scale down his anger and resentment. In the days to come they would need maximum cooperation and innovative methods to cope with what the Anarchie bestowed upon them.

KWONGAB
How's your kids doing, Vance?

VANCE
They're doing okay, enjoying the school they are attending. Wish I could have spent more time with them during their school break though.

KWONGAB
Sorry it didn't work out for you.

VANCE
No problem.

KWONGAB
How's Kara doing these days?

VANCE
She went to work in healing centers. She keeps busy.

KWONGAB
When we get back from Jeeapa, perhaps we can get together, I'm sure Monachi would like to visit with Kara.

VANCE
Sure, anytime, she's welcome.

It did not take long for the men to get to the air locks for MSFS-1. Vance felt strange being this close to MSFS-1 knowing Martha was on the other side of the air lock. Would she recognize him with her new programing?

Kwongab had used his neural expansion ability all throughout the short walk and sized Vance up and felt slightly flattered that Vance held him in such high esteem. Vance still did not know of Kwongab and Monachi's super ability to read other people's minds and plant ideas in them. Suddenly at the air lock it was time to part company.

KWONGAB
It was good seeing you again, Vance..

VANCE
Likewise, Kwongab.

KWONGAB
Look forward to seeing you again.

Kwongab then turned and followed Gōngniúgǒu into the 1st airlock as they were now going into the Mergenky Scout S-1 entry path and soon would be leaving MSS-21.

Adjacent to the airlock was a viewer window, Vance went to and watched MSFS-1 launch out into space.

VOICEOVER (VANCE)
THOUGHT
*MSFS-1 will be going into harm's way. This is nothing
new to Kwongab, but will his luck hold out?*

As Vance privately watched within moments Mergenky Scout S-1 slowly slid out of its docking cradle and moved out into empty space, and soon they were on their way to destiny. In a moment Mergenky Scout MSFS-1 was out of sight, probably traveling at huge velocities.

Vance turned and walked back to General Kahn's office where he suddenly met Lieutenant Shǎnguāngdēng who had been called to the office and while Vance was gone, General Kahn and Captain Koasa compared plans and ideas and came up with the perfect solution that would give them more experience in operating their Black Ravik.

CAPTAIN KOASA
Vance, MSF made arrangements and Lieutenant
Shǎnguāngdēng will shuttle you to Quom to pick up
Kara and take the two of you to the other side of the
planet to visit your children.

VANCE.
How will we get back?

CAPTAIN KOASA
Lieutenant Shǎnguāngdēng will then fly you and Kara
home before taking you back to our Cruiser.

VANCE
What's in store for us?

CAPTAIN KOASA
By the time you get back to MFSC-34 we should know
what our plans are.

Lieutenant Shǎnguāngdēng took Vance and Kara via the Black Ravik equipped shuttle to Xǔduō Héliú Zhīchéng [the city of many rivers pronounced: Sue-do-owe Heli-uwe Ja-chong].

Due to the highly classified *Black Ravik* capability, the Shuttle had to be always guarded. Lieutenant Shǎnguāngdēng had another crew member with her so they could switch out and go find a place to eat or take care of personal matters.

VOICEOVER
Lieutenant Shǎnguāngdēng also understood the significance of Vance visiting his children and spending a few hours with his wife.

It's the least Lieutenant Shǎnguāngdēng could do for Commander Vance for taking her to her family's home on Frǎctǒng.

Vance was pleased to see Kara. She looked healthy and beautiful and did not appear to have aged since he met her.

The kids were getting older and smarter, and their schooling was evident in their conduct which was sincere and respectful, plus they genuinely were very happy to see their father, with the bonus it got them out of class for more than half the day.

It seemed the time came too quickly when they had to return the children to their boarding school and take Kara back because she had a patient backlog at the healing center, where Mergenky who normally do not get ill, require significant medical attention when they do.

Vance hugged his kids, and sadly said goodbye to them. Kara sensed the wonderful love between Vance and his two children, and that added to her emotional bonds to him.

Kara regrettably had to let Vance go off again and do his duty.

If it were possible for Vance to do something else, she would prefer it, but for now, he was locked into MSF service and in an extraordinary twist, was promoted to Navigator on an MSF Cruiser.

As Navigator, that assignment almost certainly designated Vance for future command and PCO school himself.

It would be a lonely life for Kara, but she consoled herself knowing she helped a lot of people in the healing center and eventually Vance would leave MSF, and they could enjoy their golden years together.

Vance and Kara walked to the Shuttle on a landing pad on the top of the school building which allowed wealthy parents to easily bring their children to school and take them home. Half the school were boarding students, the other half were not and many of them went home in the evenings in this manner.

The Shuttle took off after everyone was inside and strapped in. It did not take long for it to get to the other side of the planet Gwaba and land on the Shuttle pad of the healing center.

The door to the Shuttle opened and Vance got out first, with Kara following. It was a somber moment, and Kara did everything she could to hide her sorrow including desperately holding back the tears.

If she knew what Vance had been through, and the briefing with General Kahn, she would be far more depressed, therefore it was good for Vance's mind he did not reveal the seriousness of the circumstances he now faced.

Kara and Vance embraced which seemed timeless, but Kara was having a problem holding back her emotions, so she broke the embrace.

KARA

You need to go to work. It was nice seeing you. I'll be
waiting for you to come home.

VANCE

I love you.

KARA

I love you too.

Vance released Kara smiled, then Vance turned around and walked a few steps and entered the Shuttle and the door immediately closed.

Kara then walked to the Healing Center Shuttle Access doors and went inside the building, holding back the tears and succeeded in not revealing the emotional state she was in. It seemed almost one of the saddest days of her life.

The Shuttle launched and went directly up into space. The Cruiser MSFC-34 had already undocked from MSS-21 and was waiting to receive the *Black Ravik* equipped Shuttle, then depart. Their new operational area would be in the space between Gwaba and Jeeapa.

<u>INT. CGI. SPACE. THE SHUTTLE APPROACHED MSFC-34 AND THE SHUTTLE BAY HATCHES OPENED AND THE SHUTTLE COCKED. 15 SECONDS.</u>

<u>INT. SPACE. MSFC-34 CONTROL ROOM</u>

Captain Koasa waiting patiently in the control room/bridge, observed the 3D holograph simulation of the Shuttle landing and then when the Shuttle Bay hatches were closed, he did the X eye movement to remove the holograph which was standard for Mergenky pilots and Captains, or current officer of the deck in charge of the Cruiser or a Scout Class vessel.

While Vance was still in the Shuttle, just after the hatches were shut and the 14-pound air test completed, Erica's voice suddenly stated:

ERICA
Fourteen-pound pressure test satisfactory. You may
exit the shuttle. Commander Vance, please report to
Captain Koasa's Space Cabin.

VANCE
Understand, on my way.

Vance turned to Lieutenant Shǎnguāngdēng as they were walking from the shuttle bay.

VANCE
Thank you for being patient and taking me to see my
family.

LIEUTENANT SHǍNGUĀNGDĒNG
It's the least I could do for you Commander Vance.

Vance knew that *Lieutenant Shǎnguāngdēng would be a friend in the future*. He was happy that she was such a positive person and dedicated.

Dutifully Vance continued to Captain Koasa's Space Cabin.

As Vance approached the Captain's Space Cabin door, it automatically opened, and Erica was inside waiting in a 3D holograph that looked like a real person. Thanks to electromagnetics and electrostatics, she would also feel real just like Martha did in the past.

Erica brought back fond memories of Martha who not only had terrorized the expedition to Andromeda, but with her affection towards Vance, provided a man machine interface for splendid euphoria unlike anything anyone could imagine.

If there was any consolation, Kara was happy that MSF Cruisers did not have a Martha on board which meant the fatal attraction was not possible.

Captain Koasa was waiting for Vance.

CAPTAIN KOASA
Welcome back Commander Vance. MSF sent me our operational orders within that past hour. I've endorsed them and forwarded them to you so you can chart our course and work out the Navigation Vectors for where we'll be operating.

VANCE
Understand sir.

CAPTAIN KOASA
I know you will put Capmoc-Drulyenslv maneuvers in our transit as well as during patrolling, but I want you to add Frazgrandopf maneuvers and randomly substitute them for Capmoc-Drulyenslv maneuvers.

VANCE
But sir, we do not have another ship in front of us which is considered a prerequisite for performing a Frazgrandopf maneuver.

CAPTAIN KOASA
Vance, if you check the guidelines, you will discover there is a new provision for using Frazgrandopf maneuvers in lieu of a Capmoc-Drulyenslv when traveling alone.

VANCE
Captain, I was not aware, and I thought I had all the recent updates.

CAPTAIN KOASA
This was a recent change designed by Commander Kwongab for periods of austerity like we are now in, where a second vessel is not available, to give an added measure of baffle clearing for ships like ours which have poor rear-view capability.

Vance feeling utterly embarrassed for not knowing a major modification in operational security protocols didn't know how to handle it other than say:

VANCE
I'll look up the procedures and make sure there isn't something else I missed."

CAPTAIN KOASA
Not to worry Vance, this change just came out while you were on the planet surface visiting your family. When you go to your Space Cabin you will see all that has arrived in your personal folders in PNN.

Vance was suddenly not feeling quite negative, responded:

VANCE
Thanks Captain, I will certainly go check my files and see the updates. Anything else you wanted to discuss?

CAPTAIN KOASA
Yes, there is one other thing. We could be forced into prolonged battle stations. Normally under such circumstances we split the day in half, I take the first half, and the Executive Officer takes the other half.

VANCE
Understand sir.

CAPTAIN KOASA
Vance, the XO, Commander Dàqiú (pronounced Da Chew) is a good administrator and excellent backup for me, but he doesn't have your battle experience from Jeeapa and Andromeda, which patrol reports I've read.

VANCE
That's understandable sir since there hasn't been much combat since the Jeeapa War.

CAPTAIN KOASA

Commander Vance, I want you to take the shift and be with Commander Dàqiú.

VANCE

Since I can't be on call because I'm standing watch, who will Navigate while I'm resting?

CAPTAIN KOASA

Lieutenant Shǎnguāngdēng will be the backup Navigator while you are in a rest period so we can maintain navigational effectiveness around the clock.

VANCE

I will do my best to assist XO Commander Dàqiú.

CAPTAIN KOASA

I know you will.

VANCE

Any chance we may end up using *Black Ravik* on this mission?

CAPTAIN KOASA

There is always a good possibility.

VANCE

In what roles would you anticipate?

CAPTAIN KOASA

As you know we provide assistance and deliver critical munitions to ground forces in trouble.

VANCE

So, if we get into a shooting war, *Black Ravik* could become a major player if we know the Anarchie have not managed to build a neutrino sniffer to find it like we can.

CAPTAIN KOASA

Commander Vance, I think so.

Captain Koasa nodded at Vance which was the clue he was dismissed. Vance went immediately to his Space Cabin and to a data terminal.

VANCE
PNN give me all my updated files and messages.

Soon Erica was spitting out new mail one by one, and buried among them was the new directives from MSF headquarters.

VANCE
PNN, when I'm on the bridge please advise me of these directives in the event it appears I'm not adhering to them.

ERICA
Commander Vance, you will be duly informed when required.

VANCE
Thank you.

ERICA
You are welcome, Commander Vance.

VOICEOVER (VANCE)
THOUGHT
There is something about Erica's voice that sets her apart from Martha. It wasn't as if it were sexier, it just seems more pleasant.

For the most part those who went on the Andromeda Mission would prefer to never see Martha again, but unfortunately Kwongab was currently on MSFS-1 heading to Jeeapa Space where he had no choice but to be exposed to Martha and her voice.

After studying all the new directives, Vance quickly ascertained, the only one he was unaware of prior to today was the requirement to intermix Capmoc-Drulyenslv with Frazgrandopf maneuvers when traveling alone such as they now did as an advance guard approaching Jeeapa.

In the days to come the fleet was ready for an exercise and would soon join them after all the logistics were worked out.

Meanwhile, MSFC-34 was cruising in harm's way totally dependent on themselves and Vance as well as Captain Koasa were hopeful the Anarchie did not unleash raw aggression until more fleet assets arrived.

***

NAKED JEEAPA DEFENSES

<u>INT. SPACE. MEREGENKY SCOUT MSFS-1 CONTROL ROOM AND BRIDGE.</u>

Meregenky Scout MSFS-1 was now orbiting Jeeapa probing the porous space defense system.

It didn't take long for Kwongab to determine the situation down on Jeeapa was totally unacceptable.

The sweet *peace dividend* time had lulled the Jeeapa defense establishment into a sad false sense of readiness. There was a strong correlation to what the Americans experienced prior to December 7, 1941.The inevitable was never considered.

Kwongab and Commander Gōngniúgǒu rotated watches on the Bridge, as Kwongab had earlier advised Commander Gōngniúgǒu:

COMMANDER KWONGAB
It's imperative that one of us remains on the bridge
until we sort all this out, because nobody else aboard
has real combat experience and trainers are not like
the real thing.

COMMANDER GŌNGNIÚGǑU
Understand, Commander Kwongab.

After several orbits around Jeeapa and a few hours later without any challenges or IFF requests from the planet, Kwongab just about seen enough but thought it was time to do the ultimate test and summoned Cdr. Gōngniúgǒu to the Bridge.

COMMANDER KWONGAB
PNN please have Commander Gōngniúgǒu come to
the bridge.

Martha (PNN)
Commander Kwongab, Commander Gōngniúgǒu has
been requested to the bridge.

Within a moment Commander Gōngniúgǒu appeared looking as if he just was awakened from a deep sleep.

COMMANDER GŌNGNIÚGǑU
Do we have any issues sir?

COMMANDER KWONGAB
Aside from defense measures porous, space defenses also appear ridiculously unimpressive.

COMMANDER GŌNGNIÚGǑU
What are the main issues you see, Commander Kwongab?

COMMANDER KWONGAB
Commander Gōngniúgǒu we have now made several orbits around Jeeapa and have not been contacted for any IFF requests. The space defense grid apparently has lapsed into a dysfunctional situation.

COMMANDER GŌNGNIÚGǑU
Are you going to report this to MSF Headquarters?

KWONGAB
Not quite yet. I've decided we need some more qualitative evidence since we'll essentially be putting a General *On Report*.

COMMANDER GŌNGNIÚGǑU
What do you have in mind?

COMMANDER KWONGAB
During the Andromeda Mission, we used the ability for our Shuttle and Escape Pod to take on an electronic cross section of a much larger ship, such as the Scout. It fooled the enemy into thinking we had more large ships than actual.

COMMANDER GŌNGNIÚGǑU
Is that a method you want to try here?

COMMANDER KWONGAB
Yes. I think if we do that again here and proceed towards Jeeapa's planet surface and record the event, that will demonstrate a total lapse of space defense.

COMMANDER GŌNGNIÚGǑU
Isn't that a bit risky, they might mistake us for an enemy and shoot us down.

COMMANDER KWONGAB
Not if they haven't even bothered to power up their systems and worse yet, what if none of them are working?

COMMANDER GŌNGNIÚGǑU
Well, that's the *peace dividend* for you, it's no longer expected to work.

COMMANDER KWONGAB
All throughout history Empires were destroyed because they let their guard down after major victories like we had on Jeeapa many years ago.

COMMANDER GŌNGNIÚGǑU
When do you propose to do this test?

COMMANDER KWONGAB
Right now.

Cdr. Gōngniúgǒu was suddenly alarmed, this mission was starting to evolve into something beyond his expectations. One thing he didn't like was surprises.

COMMANDER GŌNGNIÚGǑU
Who's going to fly the Shuttle and the Escape Pod?

COMMANDER KWONGAB
Have the Co-pilot/Navigator Lóngrén man the Escape Pod. You will command the Scout, and I will be in the Shuttle and fly it.

Kwongab then added to the plan when he said:

COMMANDER KWONGAB
PNN search your files and determine if you have the Andromeda Mission Results and verify you have the electronic imaging we did for the Shuttle and Escape Pod during the battles with the Ponarians.

Momentarily Martha's voice responded.

MARTHA
Commander Kwongab, yes, I have those files.

COMMANDER KWONGAB
PNN download those files into the Shuttle and Escape
Pod flight control systems and prepare to launch after
we get personnel aboard them for this mission.

MARTHA
Commander Kwongab, files are being transferred, will
be complete momentarily.

COMMANDER KWONGAB
Excellent, notify Co-pilot Lóngrén to man the Escape
Pod, we'll brief him when he gets there.

Lt. Commander Lóngrén was just finishing his drink in the crews lounge when
Martha's holograph appeared and stated:

MARTHA
Commander Lóngrén you are ordered to man the
Escape Pod. You will be briefed when you get there.

VOICEOVER
*It did not take Lt. Commander Lóngrén very long
to reach the Escape Pod, and since the ship's PNN
notifications were always subject to MSF scrutiny, he
knew it was a valid order from the chain of command.*

*Lt. Commander Lóngrén was slightly perplexed not
knowing anything about what was about to transpire,
and to do something with the Escape Pod other than
evacuating the ship was considered highly irregular.*

*But having Commander Kwongab on board taking
over as pilot was also extremely irregular!*

Lt. Commander Lóngrén reported in, and his holograph image popped up on monitoring
panel in the Mergenky Scout's control room.

LT. COMMANDER LÓNGRÉN
Bridge, this is Lt. Commander Lóngrén in the Escape
Pod, present and ready for operations.

Commander Gōngniúgǒu instantly observed the holograph and responded.

COMMANDER GŌNGNIÚGǑU
Escape pod, Commander Kwongab will be briefing
the mission shortly, stand by.

INT. DAY. MERGENKY SCOUT MSFS1 SHUTTLE.

It took Kwongab a while longer to arrive at the Shuttle Bay and get inside the Shuttle, and as soon as he was strapped in, he proceeded with the impromptu briefing.

> COMMANDER KWONGAB
> All stations, Commander Kwongab present in the Shuttle and ready for operations briefing.

> COMMANDER GŌNGNIÚGǑU
> Shuttle, this is Commander Gōngniúgǒu in the control room/bridge, please brief all stations the mission requirements.

Kwongab's holograph popped up in the Escape Pod and in the control room/bridge simultaneously.

> COMMANDER KWONGAB
> All stations this is Commander Kwongab speaking.

There was a short pause as PNN verified communications appeared in high fidelity at each location.

> COMMANDER KWONGAB
> We are going to do a simulated attack on Jeeapa. The Shuttle and the Escape Pod will have an electronic image of a larger ship the size of the Scout. I will lead the formation in the Shuttle, the Scout will follow me, and the Escape Pod will follow the Scout through all maneuvers, just as if we are Anarchie formations.

> COMMANDER GŌNGNIÚGǑU
> Commander Kwongab, how are we going to handle Jeeapa responses?

> COMMANDER KWONGAB
> I don't expect any IFF operations since the planet has yet to respond to our presence.

> COMMANDER GŌNGNIÚGǑU
> What do you have planned for this formation?

> COMMANDER KWONGAB
> We will level off at 3000 feet after our simulated attack

on the Jeeapa Dome, then proceed back into space, to make our reports and plan for a visit to the planet's surface afterwards.

COMMANDER GŌNGNIÚGǑU
How will each ship maneuver especially if it's cloudy where we operate?

COMMANDER KWONGAB
PNN will track my position in space using tactical sensors and the Scout and Escape Pod will be in autopilot under the Scout's PNN control which will always keep formation intact.

There was silence so Kwongab asked:

COMMANDER KWONGAB
Any questions?

COMMANDER GŌNGNIÚGǑU
Understand all.

LT. COMMANDER LÓNGRÉN
Flight plan confirmed loaded in Escape Pod PNN. Understand all. Escape Pod is ready for launch sequence.

<u>EXT. CGI. SPACE. MERGENKY SCOUT MSFS1 LAUNCHING SHUTTLE. 15 SECONDS.</u>

COMMANDER KWONGAB
Commander Gōngniúgǒu Launch the Shuttle and Escape Pod. Engage the electronic signatures.

<u>INT. CGI. SPACE. MERGENKY SCOUT MSFS1 CONTROL ROOM.</u>

VOICEOVER
Commander Gōngniúgǒu observing the holograph that just popped up in the Scout control room, saw the animated launch display proceeding.

PNN, recognizing Kwongab's authority as well as his command and presence in the shuttle immediately complied launching the shuttle.

The animation on the Scout's system status holograph showed the Shuttle Bay hatches opening on the control room holographic launch status display.

<u>C.U. CGI. SCOUT CONTROL ROOM SYSTEM STATUS HOLOGRAPH IMAGERY SHUTTLE LAUNCH. 20 SECONDS.</u>

The animation based on sensor readings showed the Shuttle slowly started moving out of the Bay, first inches per second, then transitioning to feet per second.

After it was clear of the Scout, Kwongab flew in manual control and enjoyed every minute of it.

Kwongab maneuvered the Shuttle out in front of the Scout forming the formation they would fly in.

At 1000 meters in front of the Scout the shuttle with an electronic signature would appear like a legitimate Anarchie Battleship, Kwongab locked the shuttle and Scout S-1 into CONVOY MODE where each vessel would be locked into vectors the Scout controlled while following Commander Kwongab in the shuttle.

COMMANDER KWONGAB

Ok, I'm in position now, begin launching the Escape Pod.

<u>*C.U. CGI. SCOUT MSFS-1 CONTROL ROOM SYSTEM STATUS HOLOGRAPH IMAGERY ESCAPE POD LAUNCH. 20 SECONDS.*</u>

Another holograph popped up similar to the Shuttle launch sequence holograph, and soon a similar string of events occurred, and the Escape Pod was launched clear of the Scout MSFS-1 and PNN positioned it 1000 meters behind the Scout and illuminated its electronic signature of an Anarchie Battleship.

VOICEOVER (KWONGAB)
THOUGHT

If the defense grid on the planet was turned on and paying attention, they would be just about to jump out of their underwear in fear, as three Anarchie Battleships unopposed could do irreparable damage.

Three Anarchie Battleships could wipe out the Domed City of Jeeapa in just moments that had only recently been fully restored from the previous Jeeapa War.

It was only in the past three years that the piles of destroyed military hulks were finally cleared up. There were no scars of the Jeeapa War left on the planet.

COMMANDER KWONGAB
We shall now proceed to the planet. PNN, give me appropriate vectors to Jeeapa City.

Jeeapa City was currently on the nighttime dark side of the planet; however, the dome was semi-lit up as Jeeapa City never slept.

Similar to Las Vegas on Earth, Jeeapa City had numerous establishments set up to make recreation and enjoyment for the numerous miners that worked on the Jeeapa diamond mining colony.

Jeeapa City was principally rich because it was the only place other than Earth or the Trouc planet in the Andromeda Galaxy that was known to have similar blue diamond's necessary for the laser optics of the huge lasers carried on Mergenky Cruisers and Scout class ships.

The planet Jeeapa initially appeared like a ball the size of a large moon until they approached closer, it grew in dimension. This far out in space no real landmarks could be identified. However, in the span of just a few minutes, they closed the range rather quickly.

VOICEOVER
Kwongab remained ever alert for an IFF challenge, none of which came. The planet had been caught flatly unprepared.

Jeeapa preparedness was a disaster of unmitigated proportions that would leave General Kahn in total exasperation.

At the high velocity the Mergenky craft could enter the atmosphere without burning up, which gave them one chief advantage over the Anarchie, but it was assumed in due time they would lose that advantage.

Under normal conditions atmospheric penetration

would wipe out all sensors. The Mergenky had a special neutrino imaging system that was not affected by the electrostatic buildup caused by the huge ion collisions at high velocity.

The surveillance systems colorization was temporally disturbed but black and white remained fully functional until the penetration was complete.

The vectors towards Jeeapa City were right on the mark, and as soon as the colorization returned to the surveillance video, Jeeapa City on the dark side of the planet showed up in perfect clarity.

Kwongab could see on his scanners the two other ships trailing him. The electronic signature the Escape Pod made was excellent, and all three ships appeared like Anarchie Battleships from the surface on a radar tracking system had they been turned on and operating. More disturbing is the Satellite warning system had not detected and reported their presence!

The 50 miles to Jeeapa City came rather quickly, and still not a single inquiry from the planet surface. The three ships then leveled off at 3000 feet and flew over the dome of Jeeapa City, clearing it by about 1000 feet and leaving behind three huge shock waves.

COMMANDER KWONGAB

Maneuver back out into space into our previous orbit, redock the Escape Pod first, and have the crew do the proper tie down and maintenance.

After Escape Pod tie down is complete, dock the shuttle.

Commander Gōngniúgǒu feeling somewhat exhilarated from the simulated attack responded enthusiastically.

COMMANDER GŌNGNIÚGǑU
Roger that Commander Kwongab.

It did not take them long to reach orbit and the Mergenky Scout MSFS-1 still did not get an IFF inquiry. The Escape Pod docked, followed by the Shuttle.

Kwongab ordered via PNN:

COMMANDER KWONGAB
Lt. Commander Lóngrén, meet me on the Bridge.

Soon the Pilot, Copilot and Kwongab were together on the Bridge conversing.

COMMANDER KWONGAB
We'll wait another 8 hours, then Lt. Commander Lóngrén and I will visit Jeeapa and meet with the Jeeapa Commander, General Zŭzhī Bùliáng (pronounced Zoo She Bu Li An). I'm going to my Space Cabin in a few minutes to file a report to MSF. It's not going to be a pleasant meeting.

COMMANDER GŌNGNIÚGŎU
Is there any reason why I can't go with you to Jeeapa City, Commander Kwongab?

COMMANDER KWONGAB
Commander Gōngniúgŏu, we need to leave the Scout in orbit since the planet defenses are doing a terrible job of defense and surveillance. You need to remain onboard to command the Scout.

COMMANDER GŌNGNIÚGŎU
I understand that sir.

COMMANDER KWONGAB
Under the circumstances I find it prudent to have the best qualified person such as yourself aboard the Scout to command especially if an exigency manifests.

COMMANDER GŌNGNIÚGŎU
Thank you, sir, for the compliment.

COMMANDER KWONGAB
I would feel better stuck on the planet knowing the Scout was in able hands.

COMMANDER GŌNGNIÚGŎU
I appreciate the level of confidence you have in me, Commander Kwongab.

COMMANDER KWONGAB
Commander Gōngniúgŏu you are fit for command, but you were also one of the best students at PCO school. You have a lot to offer MSF.

COMMANDER GŌNGNIÚGǑU
Thank you, sir.

COMMANDER KWONGAB
Commander Gōngniúgǒu, you are most welcome. I'm going to rest for a few hours after I send the report, I'll be ready to go.

Kwongab turned to Lt. Commander Lóngrén

COMMANDER KWONGAB
Commander Lóngrén you should get some rest, I expect it will be a long day for us.

Kwongab went back to his Space Cabin and did the unpleasant work of reporting the exercise he just accomplished and the results of the dismal failure of the planet's space defense. He knew General Kahn was not going to be pleased.

COMMANDER VOICEOVER
It didn't take long for Kwongab to piece together the report. The report appeared as a narrated briefing. Much of it was verbal with attachments from sensors of the Scout, Shuttle, and Escape Pod automatically recorded during the exercise.

Gwaba was not that far away, the neutrino message would be received by General Kahn in less than an hour.

In Kwongab's report, the bottom line provided recommendations including endorsement from General Kahn sent to Jeeapa Commander, Zǔzhī Bùliáng, noting Commander Kwongab's special Frankin.

Commander Kwongab requested that General Kahn's communique to fully authorize Kwongab to do a planetary onsite inspection of the defense grid assets including monitoring stations and maintenance records as well as current directives.

Kwongab also requested a meeting with the current Jeeapa Commander, Zǔzhī Bùliáng, whom he privately felt should probably be sent packing, though that would be a job for General Kahn himself to decide.

Two hours later, predictably the response from General Kahn came. It was not a pretty response to say the least.

Mergenky Scout MSFS-1's operational orders were changed. Due to General Kahn's absolute breakdown in trust for Jeeapa Commander Zǔzhī Bùliáng, Kwongab was ordered to do an immediate inspection and make on the spot recommendations.

As part of the inquiry, General Kahn reiterated to Jeeapa Commander Zǔzhī Bùliáng that Commander Kwongab was given franking orders which as a direct representative to General Kahn could legally override anything Jeeapa Commander Zǔzhī Bùliáng attempted. Hence, Kwongab had leverage.

VOICEOVER

General Kahn announced in his response, he would be visiting Jeeapa as soon as he could break away from issues he now was dealing with.

Because of security concerns, General Kahn, fearing possible intercepts of their communications could not elaborate what held him at Gwaba.

But Kwongab could easily estimate it had something to do with recent INTEL reports and the Earth's Blue Diamonds acquired by Anarchie Special Operations Task Force just complicated matters.

Interestingly, an hour after receiving General Kahn's response, the planet lit up.

IFF Interrogations and communications from the planet surface was as expected when the boss must give you a wakeup call.

Three hours after leaving behind a huge Sonic Boom on the domed City of Jeeapa, Mergenky Scout received their first IFF inquiry.

Four hours after the sonic boom, Mergenky Scout S-1 received a personal invite from General Zǔzhī Bùliáng.

Commander Gōngniúgǒu was on the bridge and received the communications video holograph of General Zǔzhī Bùliáng.

GENERAL ZǓZHĪ BÙLIÁNG

MSFS-1 this is General Zǔzhī Bùliáng, I would like to invite you to the planet surface for a meeting.

COMMANDER GŌNGNIÚGǑU

General Zǔzhī Bùliáng, this is Commander Gōngniúgǒu. I'm the pilot of MSFS-1.

We anticipated your reception. In approximately four hours we'll be sending visitors down to the planet's surface via shuttle.

GENERAL ZǓZHĪ BÙLIÁNG

I want the entire MSFS-1 crew down on the planet immediately.

COMMANDER GŌNGNIÚGǑU

General Zǔzhī Bùliáng, under directives from MSF our operational orders require us to remain in orbit around the planet.

You will be briefed on the Away Team when they arrive at your designated rendezvous point. Would you please send us the vectors to the location?

GENERAL ZǓZHĪ BÙLIÁNG

You should have them momentarily. Looking forward to your visit.

General Zǔzhī Bùliáng's holograph faded out. Commander Gōngniúgǒu was not going to wake Commander Kwongab or Lt. Commander Lóngrén because he knew they needed their rest for a very long day ahead.

COMMANDER GŌNGNIÚGǑU
(THOUGHT)

God help us if the Anarchie suddenly appeared.

INT. SPACE. MFSC-34 CONTROL ROOM.

General Kahn sent a separate communique to Captain Koasa on the MSFC-34 advising him that he would be soon visiting Jeeapa in the near future and while in Jeeapa space might take time to visit and inspect his Cruiser. Also noted was the need to be at the top vigil and during the visit he would provide a special briefing.

Captain Koasa displayed the communication holograph to Vance while the two were on the bridge together during a watch-to-watch turnover as planned.

CAPTAIN KOASA

What do you make of this Vance?

VANCE
I would say Jeeapa is probably in for big trouble if
General Kahn is coming this way.

CAPTAIN KOASA
My thoughts too.

Lieutenant Shǎnguāngdēng could not help but overhear the conversation since the two were standing right behind her on the console. After what she experienced on Earth in her support mission, finding the Anarchie had beat them to Earth and acquired a large assortment of blue diamonds, meant they were mobilizing, and the results would not be good.

LIEUTENANT SHǍNGUĀNGDĒNG
Sir, I have MSF Scout S-1 on surveillance sensors in
orbit around the planet.

CAPTAIN KOASA
Lieutenant Shǎnguāngdēng that's good you located
MSFS-1. Keep an eye on them and we must be
prepared, an attack could come from any direction.

LIEUTENANT SHǍNGUĀNGDĒNG
Understand sir.

CAPTAIN KOASA
Commander Vance let's look at the plotting table. I
want to set up a search plan based on Scout MSFS-1
orbiting Jeeapa.

VANCE
Alright sir.

CAPTAIN KOASA
We don't want to be pointing our most sensitive
sensors in the same direction the Scout is looking.
Therefore, as we track their orbit around the planet,
turn the ship to always be pointing at least 90 degrees
off the heading of the Scout. That will increase the
area we collectively search."

VANCE
Roger that.

CAPTAIN KOASA

Also, if we do have detections, without giving away our position, report to the Scout our calculated position of any possible ship.

VANCE

Does that include freighters and passenger transport spaceships?

CAPTAIN KOASA

Yes, just in case the Anarchie are using some type of decoy.

VANCE

Anarchie reconnaissance ships often use freighters to hide their positions while penetrating defense grids.

CAPTAIN KOASA

Exactly, and if we are in position to get a closeup, approach the ship, especially if its relative motion appears to be heading towards Jeeapa.

VANCE
Will do.

CAPTAIN KOASA

Fine, I'm going to get some rest now, be sure and read all General Kahn's comments and wake me if S-1 contacts us for any reason."

COMMANDER VANCE
Will do.

After the Captain left, Vance approached Lieutenant Shǎnguāngdēng.

COMMANDER VANCE

Lieutenant Shǎnguāngdēng, Are you part of the oncoming watch?

LIEUTENANT SHǍNGUĀNGDĒNG

Yes sir, Captain Koasa wanted me with you because he wants to personally monitor the other sensor operator.

COMMANDER VANCE
Captain Koasa privately told me he has complete
confidence in you. And so, do I.

LIEUTENANT SHĂNGUĀNGDĒNG
Thank you, sir.

COMMANDER VANCE
You are most welcome.

Vance looked at the sensor displays and determined it would be best he no longer distracted Lieutenant Shǎnguāngdēng as she had a vital role in keeping the ship safe.

Conversations on the bridge were few if any. Everyone knew what they had to perform and as the consummate professionals worked at nearly 100% efficiency, only conversing when it was appropriate and related to the task at hand. With the number of watch standers in the control room it could get noisy otherwise.

Vance walked back onto the Bridge conning area set up for a conning officer. In the middle of the conning stand, he would be surrounded by a globe of holographic sensor icons and contact status. Vance's chair swiveled and as he looked out of his semi-transparent holographic globe, he was the center of, it was as if he was looking out into space, with stars, nearby planets and ships that were magnified and superimposed on the fully enclosed spherical holograph.

One of the attributes of patrolling and performing Capmoc-Drulyenslv and Frazgrandopf maneuvers was the images on the globe took different true positions as the ship maneuvered and pointed a different direction. This was beneficial in that the conning officer did not get channel vision to specific contacts or sectors of space.

In a heightened state of alert, when it was known enemy ships were probably in nearby space a slow gentle roll was done so that conning officers did not have to move out of their chairs and only had to turn their heads and eyes to do a complete surveillance of the surrounding space within scanner range as affirmative backup to the sensor operators.

The way MSFS-1 and MSFC-34 were being handled, there was no chance of an Anarchie surprise attack on Jeeapa, however, with just the 2 ships there was no way they could repel an Anarchie invasion force.

MSFS-1 and MSFC-34 were now merely part of the early warning system. MSFC-34 could probably slow them down a bit, but to go slug fest with a couple dozen Anarchie Battleships, would not allow them to fare well or even survive. Sadly the "Peace Dividend" created 2 sacrificial lambs with MSFS-1 and MSFC-34.

Kwongab on MSFS-1 (often referred to as simply S-1) knew he had to get Jeeapa's defense grid back up and operating in a cohesive manner, *otherwise it would be like shooting ducks in a barrel for the Anarchie.*

<u>FLASHBACK</u>
In his previous discussions with General Kahn had stated:

GENERAL KAHN
Should the Anarchie succeed in taking over Jeeapa, and get complete access to blue diamond production, the evil Anarchie Empire would then be unstoppable.

COMMANDER KWONGAB
Which means this corner of the Milky Way would be unbearable for civilized societies.

General Kahn responded with a grim look on his face knowing the Earth people would have no way of defending themselves.

GENERAL KAHN
The same people on Earth who unknowingly sold the Anarchie blue diamonds would soon themselves become victims, as Earth would appear on the Anarchie plunder list.

COMMANDER KWONGAB
However, if the intergalactic community discovered Anarchie doing such an act, they might find themselves at risk.

GENERAL KAHN
But it would be too late for the Earth people, the Anarchie would no doubt lay waste to the planet before they were kicked off it.

***

JEEAPA PATROL

Meanwhile on MSFC-34, Commander Vance sat down in the conning officer's chair and slowly swiveled the Surveillance Holograph globe with a joystick device that allowed him to see all the surrounding space as the image panned and pointed a different direction.

The relative position of any ships or planets remained locked in relative position to own ship in their "true position" in space just like radars paint true bearings and ranges on displays.

Once Commander Vance standing the officer of the deck watch viewed a complete circle on the surveillance holograph globe and got a handle on everything he saw, he then asked PNN questions on what he didn't recognize.

Commander Vance then did what Kwongab had taught him during the Andromeda Mission when they were dealing with the Ponarians.

Vance commanded via eye movement on the Navigation holograph a slow 360 degree roll of the cruiser that would re-image the space display so that images that would appear at his feet that would be hard to see were suddenly at the height of his elbow as the view reoriented on the 3D ships center display that his chair was in the middle of.

It was moments like this that a major space combatant team had to be vigilant. Out of sheer boredom is usually when terror strikes as the unpredictability of aggression is not fully appreciated by neophytes who never experienced it before.

That is one of the key reasons why Captain Koasa wanted Vance on the bridge while he was sleeping.

Captain Koasa knew Vance was not one of those Neophytes and he understood the harsh reality of space warfare, where extreme velocities can cause convergence much quicker than people realize.

From initial detect to a showdown and shooting can virtually be in less than a minute when two craft are approaching each other on reciprocal courses. The combined speed often exceeds light speed. The other ship is up on your 6:00 o'clock [rear] just as the sensor operator realizes what they have and IFF does not register which then automatically evokes a trip wire.

***

GENERAL ZŬZHĪ BÙLIÁNG

<u>INT. SPACE. MERGENKY SCOUT MSFS-1. KWONGAB'S SPACE CABIN.</u>

Martha suddenly woke Kwongab at the specified time. He was a little groggy, so Martha gave him a little extra shot of biofeedback to get him moving.

MARTHA
Commander Kwongab, it's time to go down to the
planet and meet General Zŭzhī Bùliáng

COMMANDER KWONGAB
Alright thanks.

Kwongab got out of the blue gel he slept in like all the Mergenky aboard the Scout and Martha was there to assist him dry off and put on his uniform. He then proceeded to the bridge where he met Commander Gōngniúgǒu. Likewise, Lt. Commander Lóngrén was already there on the bridge reporting as PNN had directed.

COMMANDER KWONGAB
We are ready to proceed to the planet's surface. In the event of an emergency egress, you know what to do. If you can help MSFC-34, do so, but don't put the ship at risk.

COMMANDER GŌNGNIÚGǑU
Understand all, Commander Kwongab. Good luck on your visit to General Zǔzhī Bùliáng.

COMMANDER KWONGAB
Thanks, I just hope General Zǔzhī Bùliáng takes our constructive criticism positively and acts on it before it's too late.

COMMANDER GŌNGNIÚGǑU
Be careful, General Zǔzhī Bùliáng may feel you altered his career path.

COMMANDER KWONGAB
General Zǔzhī Bùliáng needs to be more concerned about the Anarchie than he does me because something tells me, he's going to have to deal with the Anarchie sooner than he realizes. We just proved that his defenses are ill-prepared.

COMMANDER GŌNGNIÚGǑU
True, but he's a vindictive prick so be careful.

COMMANDER KWONGAB
So, you have heard about his reputation.

COMMANDER GŌNGNIÚGǑU
Yes. I also served under him as well as a former Captain Duòluò de Tiānshǐ (pronounced Dual-law de

Tian-shi) on MSFC-16 whose career he cut short for lesser reasons.

COMMANDER KWONGAB
I'm a direct representative of General Kahn, whom I've had a lot of dealings within the past. General Zǔzhī Bùliáng is now at a disadvantage, the evidence we sent in our report is pretty damming.

COMMANDER GŌNGNIÚGǑU
Our spoofing Jeeapa was a sad testimony to what General Zǔzhī Bùliáng is doing as the commander here.

COMMANDER KWONGAB
General Zǔzhī Bùliáng doesn't have much he can defend.

COMMANDER GŌNGNIÚGǑU
General Zǔzhī Bùliáng got caught with his pants down because he is a poor commander.

COMMANDER KWONGAB
General Zǔzhī Bùliáng is like many others all sucked up into the *peace dividend* nonsense, who do not realize those days are now over.

COMMANDER GŌNGNIÚGǑU
Our new problems with Anarchie could be like the past such as the 100-year war 15 centuries ago.

COMMANDER KWONGAB
Lt. Commander Lóngrén and I are departing now.

Kwongab then nodded and walked off the bridge with Lt. Commander Lóngrén following at a short distance. In a few minutes they were strapped in the Shuttle and Kwongab ordered:

COMMANDER KWONGAB
Launch the Shuttle.

A holograph popped up in Mergenky Scout S-1 control room where Commander Gōngniúgǒu watched the scale model holograph simulation as the hatches opened and the Shuttle launched out in space with Kwongab taking full control in manual flight mode.

INT. CGI. SPACE. SHUTTLE. LAUNCH AND OPERATIONS TO JEEAPA SPACE PORT. (30 SECONDS SPLIT HALF LAUNCH AN HALF ARRIVAL AT JEEAPA)

VOICEOVER

On Kwongab's head's-up-display he could see the moving vectors that pointed to a specific area of the planet. All he had to do was follow the arrows and he would get to his destination in manual flight control or go to autopilot.

At their speed it didn't take long to get to the atmosphere penetration point.

There was some slight vibration, as expected and then suddenly the craft felt more stable as it transitioned into the atmosphere cooling down from almost 4,000 degrees skin temperature on the nose leaving behind a slight vapor trail of hot ionized gas.

The Shuttle descended almost vertically towards Jeeapa City. The moving vector arrows pointed to a glowing disk which was the city dome they could see from 50 miles directly above.

The moving vectors arrows on the heads-up display guided the shuttle crew towards an area offset from the dome which was Jeeapa City MSF space port.

Huge space-transports would come and go from these launch pads.

The moving vectors arrows which signified the velocity by length were green if they were proceeding at proper speed, calculated by PNN. As they got nearer their objective the arrows turned yellow, which was too fast.

Commander Kwongab slowed down otherwise PNN would do it for him

If the shuttle exceeded safe thresholds, the arrows turned red and automatic breaking occurred. If the shuttle went slower than required, the velocity vector arrows turned blue.

As the shuttle slowed the arrows grew shorter and green again, meaning prescribed speeds.

The Shuttle slowly came to the destination and landed on the landing pad designated for them.

Commander Kwongab opened the door to the Shuttle and got out with Lt. Commander Lóngrén following him.

Commander Kwongab walked along the yellow walkway signifying the exit and on the other side of the transparent blast shield for chemical rockets that used to be used. There stood General Zǔzhī Bùliáng and several of his staff officers.

COMMANDER KWONGAB
Greetings General Zǔzhī Bùliáng.

GENERAL ZǓZHĪ BÙLIÁNG
Welcome to Jeeapa, Captain Kwongab.

COMMANDER KWONGAB

Didn't think I'd be coming back this way any time soon.

GENERAL ZǓZHĪ BÙLIÁNG

Well conditions change. MSF must go where they are required. Follow me and I'll take you to my office where we can discuss your presence here.

VOICEOVER

General Zǔzhī Bùliáng's demeaner betrayed him. But worse yet he had no idea Kwongab had neural expansion telepathic ability and could read his mind.

By the time they reached General Zǔzhī Bùliáng's offices, Kwongab already knew to the extent the general was upset and had already started working on General Zǔzhī Bùliáng's mind to calm him down a few notches.

General Zǔzhī Bùliáng's staff knew he was near blowing a cork.

Nobody screws over a general such as General Zŭzhī Bùliáng without suffering some serious reprisals.

Kwongab thus would remain several steps ahead of General Zŭzhī Bùliáng, and had it been any other pilot, its likely General Zŭzhī Bùliáng would have crushed the person.

They were soon all seated at the General's conference table when the discussions commenced.

GENERAL ZŬZHĪ BÙLIÁNG
Commander Kwongab, what possessed you to zip past Jeeapa early this morning and cause that sonic boom that rattled a lot of people.

COMMANDER KWONGAB
General, I know your rank and privileges as such, but as a direct representative of General Kahn, I have my franking orders on me and I do not wish to have to use them on you, but I will if I must.

General Zŭzhī Bùliáng's knew Kwongab possessed those special credentials with him that effectively and temporarily made Kwongab outrank him. He suddenly calmed down a bit, with the help of Kwongab's neural expansion telepathic manipulations.

General Zŭzhī Bùliáng's staff officers, waiting to see the showdown and possible arrest of Kwongab were suddenly dismayed at the sudden changes. Proceedings were not progressing as General Zŭzhī Bùliáng's staff officers expected.

GENERAL ZŬZHĪ BÙLIÁNG
Why did you come here Commander Kwongab.

COMMANDER KWONGAB
General Kahn ordered me to visit here and check out your defenses, and in my franking documents, you will see I'm required to have unfretted access to your entire defense network and do an on-site analysis.

GENERAL ZŬZHĪ BÙLIÁNG
I will not allow you such access, you are not cleared.

COMMANDER KWONGAB
General, please do not force me to use my special franking orders, I'm sure you will quickly regret it.

GENERAL ZŬZHĪ BÙLIÁNG
Ok, what do you want?

COMMANDER KWONGAB
First before I get into that, is this room cleared for C5
level and is every one of your staff cleared?

GENERAL ZŬZHĪ BÙLIÁNG
No, only half are cleared at the C5 level. The room is
cleared for C5.

COMMANDER KWONGAB
General those who are not C5 cleared must now
leave because what we need to discuss contains C5
information.

Some of General Zŭzhī Bùliáng's closest members who gave him emotional support
were not C5 cleared and looked in great disbelief when General Zŭzhī Bùliáng stated:

GENERAL ZŬZHĪ BÙLIÁNG
Alright, those of you who are not C5 cleared, please
leave now.

Half the room stood up and left. PNN verified all the attendees that remained were C5
cleared, or they would be politely asked to leave.

As soon as the door was shut, and the air seal finished its soft hissing sound the blue
light above the door lit up and started flashing under PNN control.

The flashing blue light signifyed a C5 level discussion was in progress and none of the
discussion could never leave the room.

COMMANDER KWONGAB
General Zŭzhī Bùliáng, we just came from planet
Earth after a visit General Kahn sent us to find out
whether Anarchie had acquired blue diamonds for
their laser optics.

GENERAL ZŬZHĪ BÙLIÁNG
That's interesting. What did you find out?

COMMANDER KWONGAB
We arrived a day too late. The Anarchie received a
substantial shipment of blue diamonds and left.

GENERAL ZǓZHĪ BÙLIÁNG
What does that have to do with Jeeapa?

COMMANDER KWONGAB
General Zǔzhī Bùliáng, INTEL reports indicate the Anarchie have approximately 24 new battleships ready to deploy.

GENERAL ZǓZHĪ BÙLIÁNG
What is the significance of that?

COMMANDER KWONGAB
The only item missing on those new Anarchie Battleships is blue diamonds for larger laser optics. It appears they solved that necessity.

GENERAL ZǓZHĪ BÙLIÁNG
That will probably take a while to manufacture and implement.

COMMANDER KWONGAB
Our experts believe with Anarchie diamond cutter expertise, it will be only a week or two before they will be able to deploy those new battleships with deadly lasers.

GENERAL ZǓZHĪ BÙLIÁNG
Why is that such a big deal, we got a viable peace treaty with them.

COMMANDER KWONGAB
INTEL has discovered the Anarchie do not intend on complying with the treaty.

GENERAL ZǓZHĪ BÙLIÁNG
So, what's the bottom line?

COMMANDER KWONGAB
We anticipate they will attack Jeeapa, and you are in harm's way.

GENERAL ZǓZHĪ BÙLIÁNG
I'm not convinced we'll be attacked and I'm not going to complicate people's lives here by forcing them to

upgrade our defense posture from peacetime rules to wartime procedures.

COMMANDER KWONGAB
General Zǔzhī Bùliáng, it's not within your purview to determine what INTEL or orders from MSF you wish to follow.

GENERAL ZǓZHĪ BÙLIÁNG
What exactly are you implying Commander Kwongab?

COMMANDER KWONGAB
Based on this morning's exercise and operations we conducted, Jeeapa MSF Command demonstrated your defenses are inadequate to deal with a potential Anarchie attack.

GENERAL ZǓZHĪ BÙLIÁNG
Well, I don't believe one is coming any time soon.

COMMANDER KWONGAB
That's not your call.

GENERAL ZǓZHĪ BÙLIÁNG
So, what about it?

COMMANDER KWONGAB
Per my instructions from General Kahn, I will do the inspection and make recommendations to you.

GENERAL ZǓZHĪ BÙLIÁNG
I may choose to ignore your recommendations.

COMMANDER KWONGAB
For any of those recommendations you chose not to implement, I'm also advised to report immediately to General Kahn.

You need to be prepared to explain to General Kahn for failure to comply with the recommendations.

GENERAL ZǓZHĪ BÙLIÁNG
This is all a bunch of crap. You are just stirring people up over nonsense.

COMMANDER KWONGAB
Is that so?

GENERAL ZǓZHĪ BÙLIÁNG
Yes, it is.

COMMANDER KWONGAB
Fine, think what you want, but we'll first take a tour of
the *Five-Mile Oval.*

GENERAL ZǓZHĪ BÙLIÁNG
You can't.

COMMANDER KWONGAB
Why is that?

GENERAL ZǓZHĪ BÙLIÁNG
The *Five-Mile Oval* is shut down and sealed off.

COMMANDER KWONGAB
For what reason?

GENERAL ZǓZHĪ BÙLIÁNG
Because we do not need it.

COMMANDER KWONGAB
General, let me inform you now, Lt. Commander
Lóngrén is my *space warfare actuarial,* he is
assigned to endorse my recommendations to you.
He is also required to report directly to MSF any
recommendations I give you that you refuse to comply
with.

GENERAL ZǓZHĪ BÙLIÁNG
What's that going to do for you?

COMMANDER KWONGAB
It's more likely what it's going to do for you.

GENERAL ZǓZHĪ BÙLIÁNG
Such as?

COMMANDER KWONGAB
A free one-way trip to Gwaba where you will then be
spending most of your future time.

Suddenly fear gripped General Zǔzhī Bùliáng who now started to realize, this was
more than he ever imagined. He was now getting a significant dose of neural expansion
telepathic fusions by Kwongab which he had no means to know if it were his own
thoughts or mental telepathic *implants*.

One *thought implant* General Zǔzhī Bùliáng now pondered:

VOICEOVER (GENERAL ZǓZHĪ
BÙLIÁNG) THOUGHT
*Those franking rights Kwongab apparently has could
put me on the next transport to Gwaba after I leave
my command in a not so ceremonious departure, and
utter humiliation.*

Thanks partly to Kwongabs temporary franking credentials as well as Kwongab's
neural expansion telepathic manipulations of General Zǔzhī Bùliáng, the General was
suddenly starting to slowly come around.

COMMANDER KWONGAB
How long will it take you to unseal the *Five-Mile Oval*
and get it back up and operating?

GENERAL ZǓZHĪ BÙLIÁNG
Probably a few weeks.

COMMANDER KWONGAB
We may not have a few weeks; how can you expedite
it?

Right then General Zǔzhī Bùliáng looked at one of his subordinates.

GENERAL ZǓZHĪ BÙLIÁNG
Go get several staff members together and put together
a team to commence unsealing the *Five-Mile Oval* and
put it back in full operation with command center and
headquarters.

The MSF Commander that General Zǔzhī Bùliáng spoke to then stood, walked out the
door in a very somber manner.

Kwongab had been working on the MSF Commander psyche as well. He didn't know why but he suddenly knew the urgency.

COMMANDER KWONGAB
Why didn't your space defense system detect us this early in the morning?

GENERAL ZǓZHĪ BÙLIÁNG
It was turned off.

COMMANDER KWONGAB
You've got to be kidding.

GENERAL ZǓZHĪ BÙLIÁNG
We have peace time remember. There was no sense in leaving the *space defense system* turned on and operating with shift work when it was not going to provide any benefits. This base has not detected any hostile craft in 15 years.

COMMANDER KWONGAB
Next recommendation: Jeeapa's *Space Defense System* will be manned continuously. Any unexplained sightings are to be relayed to MSF headquarters immediately with no delay.

The general simply nodded without making an affirm response. Kwongab wasn't impressed with the general's attitude, but he nevertheless continued the neural expansion telepathic activity which the general was slowly starting to respond.

COMMANDER KWONGAB
Is the space defense system manned currently?

GENERAL ZǓZHĪ BÙLIÁNG
Yes, but we didn't plan for a night shift.

COMMANDER KWONGAB
Send half the people home and have the rest remain here working, the people you send home are to come back in 12 hours and keep operations around the clock.

GENERAL ZǓZHĪ BÙLIÁNG
Alright.

COMMANDER KWONGAB
Let's look at one of your operational centers. Where's
the nearest located?

GENERAL ZŬZHĪ BÙLIÁNG
Just down the hall.

COMMANDER KWONGAB
Good I want to make observations.

General Zŭzhī Bùliáng stood up.

GENERAL ZŬZHĪ BÙLIÁNG
Please follow me.

General Zŭzhī Bùliáng walked out the door with Commander Kwongab and Lt. Commander Lóngrén following down the hallway about 100 feet were double doors with a cypher lock on them.

General Zŭzhī Bùliáng keyed in a number. A pneumatic actuator then slid both doors sideways and the General led them into a very large room. It had consoles enough to be manned by 100 to 200 people. Only 20 of them were manned. Kwongab could see the misery in the operator's faces.

GENERAL ZŬZHĪ BÙLIÁNG
Surveillance operators, let me have your attention
please. This is Commander Kwongab from MSF
headquarters visiting us. He may ask you some
questions.

COMMANDER KWONGAB
How many more operators do you have?

GENERAL ZŬZHĪ BÙLIÁNG
We have all these people, the other half of them are
currently away on leave or other assignments.

KWONGAB
Such as?

GENERAL ZŬZHĪ BÙLIÁNG
Picking up trash and making the base more beautiful.

COMMANDER KWONGAB
Get all those surveillance operators back immediately.

General Zǔzhī Bùliáng started realizing Kwongab was giving him what they call an *MSF enema* in the business office could only simply nod in affirmation.

COMMANDER KWONGAB
Where is the rest of the Jeeapa MSF Detachment?

GENERAL ZǓZHĪ BÙLIÁNG
They're doing community relations and other tasks I
felt necessary.

COMMANDER KWONGAB
Get them back immediately. There may not be a
community left to have relations with, if an Anarchie
Battleship arrives undetected.

General Zǔzhī Bùliáng turned to another one of his close advisor staffers.

GENERAL ZǓZHĪ BÙLIÁNG
Recall all hands to their perspective divisions and tell
them to prepare for a special briefing on how we will
have to temporarily shift our focus in the interim.

As part of his franking rights, Kwongab had Lt. Commander Lóngrén carry a device with him that recorded all the conversations which were soon made available to General Kahn, who was getting even more concerned.

INTEL reports General Kahn just received were indicating he might be forced into action far sooner than he hoped or planned.

Just like Kwongab knew firsthand looking at a possible disaster in the making, it was going to be touch and go as far as being prepared in time for what would soon be perceived as a full invasion attempt. The trip wires were close at hand.

The Mergenky had a well-placed spy who would signal the trip wire: *loading troops on transports.*

The Mergenky Spy was none other than Anarchie Captain Esau had been converted by Kwongab years prior during the Andromeda Mission.

Anarchie Captain Esau was a true believer in the approach to peace and the current Anarchie administration was only interested in revenge and conquest as they only contained malice in their hearts.

Captain Esau knew it was only a matter of time before they would do the unthinkable and attack the Mergenky setting off a major war that would lead to vast destruction and deaths.

Captain Esau knew the minute Anarchie leaders threw the treaty away and planned for war, they opened the prospects of a lot of carnage and suffering to their home planet, as he knew the Mergenky were not going to take an attack lightly. Lessons learned from the Jeeapa war was not to do something stupid and try it again.

Kwongab soon was flying all over the planet in MSFS-1's Shuttle which he chose to utilize wherever he went.

Kwongab reported to General Kahn:

COMMANDER KWONAB
It is the same *Soup Sandwich* everywhere (military
term for FUBAR).

GENERAL KAHN
What's the bottom line?

KWONAB
Negligence, deferred maintenance, outright criminal
neglect. As bad as things are, at least we now have an
accounting.

Several days later just as Kwongab had toured the last facility he was informed:

GENERAL ZǓZHĪ BÙLIÁNG
We now have the *Five-Mile-Oval* back up and
operational. I'm shifting headquarters to the *Five-
Mile-Oval*.

As soon as the Jeeapa MSF forces started observing the drastic changes afoot, they realized something was probably about to occur.

Fear gripped some of the Jeeapa garrison personnel.

In many cases the Jeeapa Forces new concerns led to a striking appearance change. There now manifested a noticeable and shift from peace time mentality, to one that exemplified people wanting to ensure preparedness vice the former malaise.

Kwongab took General Zǔzhī Bùliáng's sudden offer to tour the *Five-Mile-Oval* with him. They rode the elevator down and got out. There were armed guards there and even though the place smelled musky, it was slowly coming back to life.

GENERAL ZǓZHĪ BÙLIÁNG
The maintenance contractor workers are quite happy
to get lots of tasking and profits restoring the center.

COMMANDER KWONGAB
*I wonder if it could all be back online in time before
Anarchie Assault Forces show up?*

Later that day, a VIP ship from Gwaba arrived.

Commander Kwongab and General Zǔzhī Bùliáng were sitting in the General's office
going over some of the recent details when the general was prompted.

JEEAPA MSF STAFF MEMBER
General Zǔzhī Bùliáng we have an inbound VIP,
recommend you come up to the space port to greet
him. He should be here in ten minutes.

GENERAL ZǓZHĪ BÙLIÁNG
Commander Kwongab that could be General Kahn.
Why don't you come up to the space port with me?

COMMANDER KWONGAB
It would be my pleasure, General Zǔzhī Bùliáng
Commander Kwongab followed General Zǔzhī Bùliáng to the elevator

then to the surface where his personal hovercraft waited which he and Kwongab got
and just before it sped off to the space port.

The hovercraft was the planets main surface transport because of lessons learned from
the Jeeapa war when most of the bridges were destroyed. Near the 10-minute mark,
they arrived at the space port to watch an MSF high speed executive craft land. Soon
the door opened and there stood General Kahn.

General Zǔzhī Bùliáng was not a stranger to General Kahn who was interested is
ascertaining the preparedness and give General Zǔzhī Bùliáng and update as to the
eventuality he faced. It was not going to be a pleasant meeting.

Under normal circumstances, General Kahn would have fired General Zǔzhī Bùliáng
on the spot, but Kwongab's reports on progress were uplifting and it looked like he
was responding well to the many recommendations Kwongab gave.

General Zǔzhī Bùliáng spoke then bowed:

GENERAL ZǓZHĪ BÙLIÁNG
Welcome to Jeeapa, General Kahn.

General Kahn responded almost forcing himself to be polite in front of General Zŭzhī Bùliáng's staff members.

GENERAL KAHN
Good to see you again General Zŭzhī Bùliáng.

General Zŭzhī Bùliáng smiled with the most politically correct face he could make under the circumstances.

GENERAL ZŬZHĪ BÙLIÁNG
Likewise, General Kahn.

This was an auspicious reunion for General Kahn who was approaching retirement, as Jeeapa was one of the major events in his career.

GENERAL KAHN
Let's go to your office where we can have a conversation.

GENERAL ZŬZHĪ BÙLIÁNG
That's exactly what I was thinking.

Soon they were down in the *Five-Mile-Oval*, which General Kahn remembered quite well and as before only C5 cleared people were present.

GENERAL ZŬZHĪ BÙLIÁNG
Tell us general Kahn, what is the latest update on Anarchie activity?

GENERAL KAHN
It's not looking good, as far as we know the Anarchie have not yet started loading troops on their transports, but we think that is any day now.

GENERAL ZŬZHĪ BÙLIÁNG
So, they are really going to do it, scrap the peace treaty and put their population at risk with another war?

GENERAL KAHN
INTEL sure is painting such a picture for us.

GENERAL ZŬZHĪ BÙLIÁNG
How soon will we know?

GENERAL KAHN
As soon as they start loading their troop transports,
then figure invasion is less than 5 days away and the
Anarchie troop transports land on Jeeapa.

Suddenly General Zǔzhī Bùliáng wasn't feeling bad about Kwongab's visit. Kwongab just prevented General Zǔzhī Bùliáng from being caught with his pants down. It would have been a painful humiliating defeat for the Mergenky.

VOICEOVER (GENERAL ZǓZHĪ
BÙLIÁNG) THOUGHT
*However, unless MSF can get a sizeable fleet in time to
defend the planet, Anarchie could do a lot of damage.
MSF made a terrible blunder for not wiping out
Anarchie 20 years ago when they could have easily
done it.*

The men left General Zǔzhī Bùliáng's office when it seemed the important discussion had conveyed what was necessary for this short visit. They then walked a bit along the *Five-Mile-Oval* looking it over, bringing back memories to General Kahn.

GENERAL KAHN
Anarchie came close to taking the *Five-Mile-Oval in
the Jeeapa war.*

Kwongab responded as he had been asked to come with the two Generals in case they needed to ask him any pertinent questions.

COMMANDER KWONGAB
It was the very last milestone they needed to achieve
to assure planetary conquest.

GENERAL KAHN
However, heroic performances from you Kwongab,
Vickie, and others changed history.

COMMANDER KWONGAB
Hopefully we will not have to go to the wire again
with the Anarchie.

GENERAL ZǓZHĪ BÙLIÁNG
The best plan is to keep the Anarchie off Jeeapa and
deal with them in space.

GENERAL KAHN

The Mergenky ground forces ranks were heavily depleted with the *peace dividend* and the false sense of security. A major ground battle on Jeeapa now would lead to disaster.

General Kahn then gave the Jeeapa Commander Zǔzhī Bùliáng a major jolt.

GENERAL KAHN

General Zǔzhī Bùliáng, MSF has decided you need some additional forces and capability here. I have a Logistician back on Gwaba working out the details. Men and material will start arriving in a few days from now.

GENERAL ZǓZHĪ BÙLIÁNG

If you are implying levels of materials and manpower, I think you are, we do not have the facility to receive all that.

GENERAL KAHN

Jeeapa's MSF space port which has seen better days will quickly be back in its former glory as the reinforcements arrive.

GENERAL ZǓZHĪ BÙLIÁNG

Just exactly how does this Logistician know exactly what I need here?

GENERAL KAHN

Well General, if you investigate the matter, you will discover that during the last Jeeapa battles, the 5-mile oval was completely full of men and equipment. It's essentially a ghost town now.

GENERAL ZǓZHĪ BÙLIÁNG

Perhaps those men and materials might be needed elsewhere?

GENERAL KAHN

We have good reason to believe Jeeapa will be the corridor of invasion. The Anarchie know that to leave Jeeapa in our hands would be inviting a flanking maneuver on them.

COMMANDER KWONGAB
The Anarchie know that once they take this planet as far as they are concerned, they will be able to take down the Mergenky space dominance slowly and systematically in this area and be able to threaten our existence.

GENERAL ZŬZHĪ BÙLIÁNG
Did we really gain anything from the peace dividend?

GENERAL KAHN
No. Pay me now or pay me later as they say.

General Zŭzhī Bùliáng then brought up the subject of the infusion of supply and troops.

GENERAL ZŬZHĪ BÙLIÁNG
Such a huge influx of troops will clog our transportation system and place a severe load on our power grid.

GENERAL KAHN
On the other hand, if Anarchie knocks out all your power plants, you will not have a power grid.

GENERAL ZŬZHĪ BÙLIÁNG
That's assuming they are coming.

GENERAL KAHN
We know their coming, it's just a matter of when.

GENERAL ZŬZHĪ BÙLIÁNG
Intel's not always right.

GENERAL KAHN
It only must be right one time in a case like this to make its value.

GENERAL ZŬZHĪ BÙLIÁNG
Well, it hasn't happened yet.

GENERAL KAHN
Nor have we stated precisely when, just that you must be prepared, and we have enough anecdotal information now to warrant preparedness.

GENERAL ZŬZHĪ BÙLIÁNG
What kind of coordination plan is there for the logistics
supply chain?

GENERAL KAHN
It's interesting that you asked that question because I
was just about to tell you that I've ordered the Logistics
Lead to come to Jeeapa right away and sit down with
us showing the current plan.

GENERAL ZŬZHĪ BÙLIÁNG
When is the Logistics Lead arriving?

GENERAL KAHN
She'll be here tomorrow, and I expect Commander
Kwongab will want to visit with her.

With that General Zŭzhī Bùliáng raised his eyebrows a bit, wondering what kind of
interesting scenario existed between the two.

Kwongab most emphatically knew he was long overdue to size up the current situation
in space near the planet where Mergenky Scout MSFS-1 was ordered to patrol.

KWONGAB
General Kahn, I need to get back to the Scout MSFS-
1 soon and check up on things and confer with
Commander Gōngniúgŏu on the current situation out
there.

GENERAL KAHN
Commander Kwongab, I'm sure Commander
Gōngniúgŏu has everything under control, I need your
input on some of the logistics items.

COMMANDER KWONGAB
Understand General but I want to make sure
Commander Gōngniúgŏu understands the situation at
Jeeapa is getting more critical.

GENERAL KAHN
Captain Kwongab, go ahead and make a quick trip to
Scout MSFS-1, then get back here right away. I want
you to be here in 24 GSTH to meet the supply chain
expert.

COMMANDER KWONGAB
All right General, I'll be back in 24 GSTH, but I would
like to leave now to give as much time as possible to
Commander Gōngniúgǒu and verify we are adequately
searching the inroads to this area of space.

GENERAL KAHN
Very well Commander Kwongab, you may now leave.
We'll see you tomorrow.

COMMANDER KWONGAB
Thank you, General Kahn.

Commander Kwongab and Lt. Commander Lóngrén departed the *Five-Mile Oval*
taking the elevator to the surface where they had a hovercraft waiting for them which
took them the short distance to the MSF space port that had been semi-abandoned until
just a few days ago.

Their Shuttle was there waiting for them which then took them back to the Mergenky
Scout MSFS-1.

<u>EXT. DAY. JEEAPA CITY MSF SPACE PORT. MSFS-1 SHUTTLE DEPARTING
AND HEADING OUT TO SPACE (15 SECONDS).</u>

In about twenty minutes the Shuttle arrived back to the Mergenky Scout MSFS-1.
In a short period of time the Shuttle Bay was pressurized and Kwongab departed the
shuttle with Lt. Commander Lóngrén and headed to the control room.

<u>INT. SPACE. MSFS-1 CONTROL ROOM.</u>

Kwongab wasted little time in getting to the Bridge where he knew he would find
Gōngniúgǒu diligently carrying out his assignments.

COMMANDER GŌNGNIÚGǑU
Welcome back Commander Kwongab.

COMMANDER KWONGAB
Thank you. I'll have to leave again in about 23 hours to
meet with a Logistics supply chain expert tomorrow.

COMMANDER GŌNGNIÚGǑU
Any possibility that you can leave Lt. Commander
Lóngrén here with me. It got kind of hectic at times
with the target intercept and analysis with inbound
traffic while the two of you were gone.

COMMANDER KWONGAB
Yes, I can leave him on the ship tomorrow as I don't expect to be on the planet much longer.

COMMANDER GŌNGNIÚGǑU
What's the latest on the planet?

COMMANDER KWONGAB
MSF is getting ready to move a lot of assets here. Something is up, they're not telling us all the details.

COMMANDER GŌNGNIÚGǑU
When large numbers of troops arrive on Jeeapa, the public will start to get concerned.

COMMANDER KWONGAB
That's going to start happening immediately.

COMMANDER GŌNGNIÚGǑU
Any talk of evacuating some of the population?

COMMANDER KWONGAB
Not yet, but I think forced evacuations are around the corner.

COMMANDER GŌNGNIÚGǑU
We have yet to spot any Anarchie incursions.

COMMANDER KWONGAB
Give them time.

COMMANDER GŌNGNIÚGǑU
Any other concerns or issues?

COMMANDER KWONGAB
Let's look at your search pattern. We may need to make it more random.

COMMANDER GŌNGNIÚGǑU
Why? There has not been a trace of any Anarchie.

COMMANDER KWONGAB
If they have developed sensors in the past 20 years

equal to ours that existed 20 years ago, they might be able to see the Scout. If you have been doing repetitive course geometries, they might have snuck past you.

COMMANDER GŌNGNIÚGǑU
I don't see how.

COMMANDER KWONGAB
PNN plot own ship's position for the past 72 hours.

Within 20 seconds a holograph showing a 3D view of the tracks of the courses the Scout took were plotted. In essence it looked like a bowl of spaghetti. Kwongab took his hands and expanded the holograph which took the spaghetti like appearance and spread it in range to almost 4 times the size of the original plot. They could now see the individual tracks well.

COMMANDER KWONGAB
PNN, apply a cloud pattern in areas least traveled and
highlight the cloud pattern in a light pastel color.

Soon an incredible image formed, it only took about 5 seconds for Commander Gōngniúgǒu to see the error in his ways. There were at least 5 or 6 clouds in multiple directions from Jeeapa where a penetration from an INTEL gathering ship might have occurred.

Commander Gōngniúgǒu suddenly felt humbled. Earlier negative emotions he had from Kwongab coming aboard and assuming command of his ship were quickly dissipating.

COMMANDER GŌNGNIÚGǑU
I never would have thought.

COMMANDER KWONGAB
Even with a randomized pattern you will still have
penetration cloud areas, but their density will be less,
and your probability of detection will go up 400%
based on the theory I've developed.

COMMANDER GŌNGNIÚGǑU
What if Anarchie had already been here?

COMMANDER KWONGAB
There is an excellent chance they have been here,
however if they are monitoring the shipping lanes

between Jeeapa and Gwaba and see the increased level of shipments starting in a couple days, they will attempt further penetrations to determine Jeeapa's disposition.

COMMANDER GŌNGNIÚGŎU
What can we do to improve our search?

COMMANDER KWONGAB
PNN, calculate a random pattern that will fill in some of the cloud patterns using my file *Randomization Search Patterns to Maximize Probability of Detection.*

Martha's voice immediately reported.

MARTHA
Commander Kwongab, I am processing the file, do you wish me to remove the existing holograph to view the new calculated display of Randomization Search Patterns?

COMMANDER KWONGAB
PNN, yes remove but preserve this holograph in the event we want to go back and re-examine it.

Immediately the former holograph disappeared, and a new one appeared. The course lines colorized based on Track Number were far more random than the previous holograph.

COMMANDER KWONGAB
PNN, overlay the cloud pattern on this holograph showing our weak spots.

The new image showed much sparser cloud patterns. It was intuitively obvious to Gōngniúgŏu this search plan would be significantly more effective.

COMMANDER GŌNGNIÚGŎU
Commander Kwongab, we'll initiate this search pattern immediately.

COMMANDER KWONGAB
Commander Gōngniúgŏu there is one other thing you now need to do.

COMMANDER GŌNGNIÚGŎU
Such as?

COMMANDER KWONGAB
I sincerely believe we have had Anarchie incursions we missed, but they will be back within two days or less. You need to essentially re-organize the watch standers to modified battle stations. They can't stay awake forever, and the probability of detection is high.

COMMANDER GŌNGNIÚGŎU
What's the policy of dealing with Anarchie detections if we encounter them?

COMMANDER KWONGAB
If it's a small ship without a lot of fire power, destroy it. But, if it's an Anarchie Battleship, run away and get distance from it, make reports to MSF, and avoid any damage to the Scout. We will need this vessel in the coming weeks if raw Anarchie aggression occurs.

VOICEOVER
Suddenly, Commander Gōngniúgŏu was not so assure of himself. An element of fear hit him as he calculated the probabilities.

Commander Gōngniúgŏu had no doubt Commander Kwongab was right on the mark and in his gut feeling, he'd most likely be facing combat within 48 hours with no assurance the Scout would be victorious.

Commander Gōngniúgŏu had to avoid a trap and be sure he was prepared to respond immediately and get out of harm's way to insure he got the critical message off to MSF concerning the Anarchie incursion if confronted.

Commander Gōngniúgŏu wasn't aware that Kwongab was working on his thoughts via neural expansion telepathy.

Not all of Commander Gōngniúgŏu thoughts were his own. They just seemed like they were his own ideas, as was the case of anyone who was treated to neural expansion telepathic implants.

COMMANDER KWONGAB
I'm going to my Space Cabin to get some rest, tomorrow will be a busy day. I will probably be in meetings with a Logistics Expert they are bringing in to show the logistics supply chain processes that have been evoked to prepare Jeeapa for a possible invasion.

COMMANDER GŌNGNIÚGǑU
With all the possibilities of an Archie incursion why would you be going back to Jeeapa?

COMMANDER KWONGAB
General Kahn asked me to attend the meeting with General Zǔzhī Bùliáng and the Logistics expert tomorrow.

COMMANDER GŌNGNIÚGǑU
Understand Commander Kwongab.

Kwongab left the control room heading for his space cabin.

COMMANDER GŌNGNIÚGǑU
Lt. Commander Lóngrén, I want you to get some rest as well and relieve me in 12 GSTH's.

Yes sir, Commander Gōngniúgǒu.

FINDING THE ANARCHIE

<u>INT. SPACE. MSFC-34 CONTROL ROOM.</u>

Commander Dàqiú (pronounced Daw Chew) XO of MSFC-34 was on the Bridge with Commander Vance early into their shift. They had been out seemingly *drilling holes in space* as the crews often described it, with the Cruiser for several days.

COMMANDER DÀQIÚ
This is quite a different experience for the crew. They're not used to patrolling space like this.

COMMANDER VANCE
Space travel is typically 99% boredom and 1% terror.

COMMANDER DÀQIÚ
I can imagine you had some long boring days traveling to Andromeda.

VANCE
The boredom was quickly overcome because we were monitoring the formation of a planet.

COMMANDER DÀQIÚ
How did you do that?

COMMANDER VANCE
As you know, the Scouts have a large space telescope and once we got into deep space, we could re-orientate the Scout to point the telescope to any direction we wanted. Since we were traveling above light speed, we were able to observe this planet develop much quicker than it really did.

COMMANDER DÀQIÚ
How long did you monitor the planet, and did you name it?

COMMANDER VANCE
Yes, we called it Crystal and we monitored it for a two-year period that corresponded to numerous years' time compressed.

COMMANDER DÀQIÚ
You didn't have modal distortion on the imagery?

COMMANDER VANCE
PNN was able to eliminate all modal distortion and temporal anomalies of the video recordings.

COMMANDER DÀQIÚ
Anything interesting about the planet's development?

COMMANDER VANCE
The planet was a barren desolate world with no sign of life on it. After several weeks of monitoring, we observed a large comet strike the planet.

COMMANDER DÀQIÚ
That must have been quite a sight!

COMMANDER VANCE
The very large comet was made up of mainly ice.

There was a huge heat from energy release when the comet struck the planet, and the results were obvious.

The ice melted from the heat energy caused from the impact, resulting in water forming on the planet and major weather patterns immediately began.

COMMANDER DÀQIÚ
I bet that was a sight.

VANCE
It was.

COMMANDER DÀQIÚ
Did the planet get covered with water from the comet?

COMMANDER VANCE

A large ocean was created, and after several months we started seeing the planet greening.

COMMANDER DÀQIÚ
Was it caused by plant life forming?

COMMANDER VANCE
Yes.

COMMANDER DÀQIÚ

How could that happen? A few months is not long enough for evolution.

COMMANDER VANCE

The theory we developed was that the huge ice ball that hit the planet may have been frozen oceans from a planet destroyed in a super nova or some other phenomena. Plant life was trapped in ice including seeds which then sprouted on the new planet.

COMMANDER DÀQIÚ

I can see that as possibly one of the ways that life spreads through the galaxy.

COMMANDER VANCE

Seems possible. Plus, we produced two years of recordings of the planet showing the development of a new planet environment.

COMMANDER DÀQIÚ
We do not have much out here to entertain the crew. I hope MSF has a relief for us so that we can have a little Rest & Relaxation.

COMMANDER VANCE
Maybe some time off on Jeeapa?

COMMANDER DÀQIÚ
I've not been there in 20 years. I bet it has changed quite a lot.

COMMANDER VANCE
It took them almost 20 years to remove all the scars of the war.

COMMANDER DÀQIÚ
Dome rebuilt?

COMMANDER VANCE
Oh yes, better than ever.

COMMANDER DÀQIÚ
Well maybe I'll ask the captain to arrange for a ship's visit to Jeeapa.

COMMANDER VANCE
You should do that. The crew would enjoy it.

COMMANDER DÀQIÚ
Most likely few or none of them have ever been to Jeeapa. Maybe going there and seeing first-hand the place we fought our last Anarchie War would make it all worthwhile.

Lieutenant Shǎnguāngdēng who could overhear the conversation since Commander Vance and Commander Dàqiú were a short distance away momentarily turned towards Vance and smiled. Vance didn't know what she meant by that. *Perhaps she was just being polite?*

Vance was glad Lieutenant Shǎnguāngdēng was the main sensor operator during his watch with the XO, Commander Dàqiú.

Lieutenant Shǎnguāngdēng was a well-oiled spirit who never indicated any lapse of alertness, attentiveness, or indicate any vigilance decrement.

Sensor operators after many days of continuous surveillance operations can develop tunnel vision and in some cases daydream.

VOICEOVER

The artificial intelligence backing sensor operators seemed fine but if they were in a high-speed transit, reaction time was critical to avoid disasters.

In some cases, alarms went off just as meteors passed within feet to the point the artificial gravity machines were slightly destabilized into an irregular wabbly shaking for a few seconds that everyone on the ship could feel.

But as Kwongab once said, "That shaking sensation is good because it reminds us, we are still alive!"

Some Captains decided to rely strictly on artificial intelligence. They could care less if one of the Mergenky operators were on the console.

However, a few who never fully accepted artificial intelligence included Captain Koasa, Kwongab, and Vance.

During the Jeeapa war many of those Cruisers who were primarily employing AI without human operators were the ones destroyed, whereas ships such as one Captain Koasa served on, that had a skipper who desired the Mergenky sensor operator element involvement, survived.

Ship captains depending exclusively on AI were often demolished because the Anarchie spies obtained copies of algorithms that could help them predict Mergenky ship movements and tactics.

The one element Anarchie could never overcome was the random element caused by Mergenky sensor operators creating unpredictability and complicated the space battlefield.

Erica made an announcement as the two men were engaged in their conversation out of boredom.

ERICA
Commander Dàqiú, it is time to perform a Capmoc-Drulyenslv maneuver.

COMMANDER DÀQIÚ
PNN, execute the Capmoc-Drulyenslv maneuver.

Vance sitting in the pilot's chair and Dàqiú standing behind Lieutenant Shǎnguāngdēng would soon see a different perspective of space as the horizon shifted based on the new courses.

It would be difficult to maintain the vigilance, but under the circumstances they had no choice. Vance could just about feel the tension in the air as he wholeheartedly believed the Anarchie were going to come back for revenge.

Erica's voice announced moments later:

ERICA
First leg of the Capmoc-Drulyenslv is complete, no observations of potential targets.

Lieutenant Shǎnguāngdēng observing sensor displays for possible signals or emanations coming from nearby space, reported:

LIEUTENANT SHǍNGUĀNGDĒNG
All clear.

ERICA
Commencing 2nd leg of the Capmoc-Drulyenslv.

The time seemed to hang on forever and finally the 3rd leg of the Capmoc-Drulyenslv maneuver was complete and Vance then stated:

COMMANDER VANCE
Recommend we perform a Frazgrandopf maneuver now.

COMMANDER DÀQIÚ
Excellent idea. PNN now commence a Frazgrandopf maneuver.

Halfway through the Frazgrandopf maneuver, Lieutenant Shǎnguāngdēng reported:

LIEUTENANT SHǍNGUĀNGDĒNG
I have energy readings from a very distant contact.

COMMANDER DÀQIÚ
Any estimation of range?

LIEUTENANT SHǍNGUĀNGDĒNG
It's most likely outside the solar system.

COMMANDER DÀQIÚ
Any chance it's a meteorite or space debris?

LIEUTENANT SHǍNGUĀNGDĒNG
No sir, it's leaving behind an ion wake that can only occur via some means of propulsion.

COMMANDER DÀQIÚ
Send your sensor readings to MSF on an ultra-secure channel.

LIEUTENANT SHǍNGUĀNGDĒNG
Right away sir.

Within minutes the sensor readings were encrypted in the ultra-secure packet and beamed to Jeeapa, the nearest Mergenky outpost. Within minutes they responded with receipt and response:

MERGENKY OUTPOST
(MESSAGE)
The sensor imagery has been forwarded to Gwaba via high-speed communications.

LIEUTENANT SHǍNGUĀNGDĒNG
The sensor imagery sent to MSF included spatial diagrams that gave three-dimensional probability visualization of approximate target locations.

COMMANDER VANCE
Due to time of travel and distance blurring data, very long distant energy detections are not an exact science.

COMMANDER DÀQIÚ
Approximations were the best possible measures, but clarification will become more prevalent during enlightenment through ongoing observations.

LIEUTENANT SHǍNGUĀNGDĒNG
When ranges get excessive, the resolution decays and hence such detections are only good for early warning.

COMMANDER DÀQIÚ
The potential target will have to be prosecuted in much closer ranges for classification and targeting.

INT. CGI. SPACE. MERGENKY SCOUT S-1 ORBITING JEEAPA 10 SECONDS.

INT. SPACE. MERGENKY SCOUT S-1 KWONGAB'S SPACE CABIN.

Kwongab was just about to start getting into his gel tube to rest when suddenly Martha appeared in her 3D holograph.

MARTHA (PNN)
Captain Kwongab, we just received an ultra-secure channel communication from MSF.

COMMANDER KWONGAB
Display it.

Kwongab proceeded to put his flight suit back on and walked out to the Bridge where Commander Gōngniúgǒu was already studying the MSF communique.

INT. SPACE. MERGENKY SCOUT S-1 CONTROL ROOM/BRIDGE.

COMMANDER GŌNGNIÚGǑU
Looks like MSFC-34 detected a possible Anarchie incursion.

COMMANDER KWONGAB
The first detect I was afraid we would soon see.

COMMANDER GŌNGNIÚGǑU
We've been tasked to investigate this possible Anarchie contact.

COMMANDER KWONGAB
Did you get any reports of what MSFC-34 tasked to do?

COMMANDER GŌNGNIÚGǑU
They have been ordered to remain in their patrol area.
MSFC-34 is essentially planetary guard now.

COMMANDER KWONGAB
How long would it take us to get to the area of the
Detects without putting out an ion wake we could be
tracked at?

PNN responded with Martha's classic voice.

MARTHA (PNN)
Maintaining ion-avoidance speeds will take seven
hours.

COMMANDER KWONGAB
Let's head in that direction, maintaining ion-avoidance
speeds at the best speed possible. Monitor the ion
detectors to make sure we don't dither into ion bursts.
Slow down as necessary to avoid ion emission.

COMMANDER GŌNGNIÚGǑU
Any counter measure maneuvers in route?

COMMANDER KWONGAB
I recommend you randomly perform a Capmoc-
Drulyenslv maneuver at least once every two hours.

COMMANDER GŌNGNIÚGǑU
How about detections along the way?

COMMANDER KWONGAB
If you get a sniff of something, perform a Frazgrandopf
clearing maneuver to make sure we are not being
followed and set up for an ambush.

GŌNGNIÚGǑU
Understand.

COMMANDER KWONGAB
I'm going to get some rest, wake me up in Five GSTH
(Gwaba Standard Time Hours).

Kwongab then walked off the bridge and back to his Space Cabin where he undressed and climbed into the gel ampulle sleeping device and was soon sound asleep with the help of the biofeedback controlled by PNN.

The crew members aboard Mergenky Scout MSFC -1 and MSFC-34 were now in a heightened state of alert and a new reality.

Very little motivating factors were required because the sensation of a realization live mortal combat was becoming more and more likely any day. These MSF crew members knew it was just time before the shooting started, especially if this was a reconnaissance vessel sent out in advance of the Anarchie fleet.

***

CAPTAIN ESAU INCIDENT

<u>INT. DAY. ANARCHIE CAPTAIN ESAU'S HOME, ANARCHIE CAPITAL CITY FĚICUÌCHÉNG.</u> *(pronounced: Fei-cui-cheung)*

VOICEOVER

Mergenky Intel then suffered one of the biggest catastrophes in many years. The Anarchie, who were excellent purveyors of counterintelligence operations had an excellent track record of discovering spies.

Mergenky Intelligence gathering failures on Anarchie Worlds made it seem almost impossible for them to have a well-placed spy operating in the Anarchie Empire.

Thanks to Commander Kwongab's efforts including neural expansion telepathic insertions, Mergenky Intel managed to recruit Anarchie Fleet Captain Esau to spy for them.

Captain Esau became anti-Anarchie-establishment because he didn't like the way the current Anarchie leader was taking his country.

Captain Esau chose to spy for the Mergenky out of philosophical reasons which Commander Kwongab enhanced through long term exposure and telepathic implants during a long period during the Andromeda Mission.

Captain Esau was sophisticated and knew when or if he had surveillance put on him.

Captain Esau's ability to transmit messages off Anarchie worlds was extremely painful and he finally discovered Anarchie Intelligence investigating him with great interest.

Captain Esau knew he had about one last chance for another transmission before he would be arrested and brutally dealt with.

Captain Esau thus waited patiently for the most propitious moment, when he knew for a fact, the Anarchie Military were pre-loading troops and supplies for an invasion to make that supreme sacrifice hoping it would shorten and minimize a future war.

When Captain Esau was tipped off that his best friend's son was shipping out the next day, he knew this was the tripwire. The Anarchie Jeeapa invasion and revenge war against the Mergenky was soon happening.

Rumors had gone around the Anarchie fleet had just received a key ingredient for new weapons that would 'even the playing field' with the Mergenky.

The Anarchie leader was now exhibiting fully arrogant and imperialistic moods. The Anarchie were growing restless in allowing the Mergenky to stand in their way of expansion and galactic hegemony.

Now was the time to deal with the Mergenky and to reverse the humiliating defeat at Jeeapa years prior that Anarchie leader's grieving father suffered.

Anarchie INTEL didn't know how Captain Esau was going to tip off the Mergenky or where and when, they just knew Captain Esau was most likely a spy and they intended to prevent him from broadcasting their fleet's departure.

Captain Esau self-imposed exile to his private residence. Captain Esau just didn't seem to go anywhere to raise suspicions, so it was going to be next to impossible to catch him in the act so that they could then force him into a double spy role.

Captain Esau was fully aware of Anarchie lust for employing double spies and had no doubt they would torture him into performing that role as well.

The neutrino burst transmission was sent three times one-minute apart. This was done to ensure Mergenky outposts would intercept the message and provide it to the Mergenky INTEL apparatus.

After the 3rd message was sent with indications transmission quality satisfactory, he reluctantly destroyed his special neutrino communications device immediately after transmitting the warning message that would be eventually known by future generations as 'Esau's Trip Wire.'

Captain Esau took the communications device, about the size of a large book, pulled out a special processor black box the size of a stick of gum and broke it into a dozen little pieces. Without the special processor, the device was useless junk.

Captain Esau lived on the cliffs overlooking a crocodile infested coastline of an inland waterway. Anyone falling in would be instantly attacked by the fifty-foot-long crocodiles.

Captain Esau took a chair and sat it next to the balcony, climbed up on the chair so he could get on the balcony. After swallowing some special pills that would help him lose consciousness quickly, he threw the communications set into the river and the remnants of the integrated circuit he broke into pieces.

<u>INT. DAY. CAPTAIN ESAU'S HOME. CAPTAIN ESAU'S JUMPs OFF THE BALCONY INTO THE RIVER BELOW. 20 SECONDS.</u>

VOICEOVER

With the fast-acting poisonous drugs Captain Esau swallowed just before he jumped, he knew he was not going to feel any pain soon.

As Captain Esau jumped, Anarchie Intel agents broke through his front door and were a mere twenty feet away watching him go over the balcony dropping fifty feet down into the fast-running river, and as expected, the hungry crocodiles soon went after him.

Captain Esau floated a while quickly dying. 50-foot-long Crocodiles entered the river and went after him. Soon crocodiles started tearing into this lifeless reptilian Captain who had quickly died from the poisons.

Captain Esau's body was never found.

***

<u>INT. DAY. MERGENKY JEEAPA HEADQUARTERS.</u>

Within 30 minutes, General Kahn read the message. The showdown was coming, and he was ill-prepared. His worst fears were now starting to grow.

Another slug fest on Jeeapa was about to begin and he was at least three months away from having a fleet he would feel comfortable repelling the Anarchie. Sending Kwongab to Jeeapa turned out to be rather auspicious now it seemed.

General Kahn wished he had General Zarkin back, but unfortunately that was not possible, and he was now stuck with General Zǔzhī Bùliáng as the Jeeapa Commander.

GENERAL KAHN
(THOUGHT)
*Perhaps this latest INTEL will help reshape General
Zǔzhī Bùliáng's thinking?*

ANARCHIE INVASION

<u>EXT. CGI. DAY. *EXOSKELETONS* AND *CRAWLERS* ANNIMATION SHOWN DURING THE FOLLOWING VOICEOVER.</u>

VOICEOVER

*The Anarchie proceeded with their invasion loadout
with ample vigor.*

*The space assault transports had to be systematically
combat loaded so that the most important and critical
elements requiring unloading first, had to be loaded
last. Hence, everything went aboard in reverse order.*

*The creature comfort equipment went on first and
would come out last.*

*Lessons learned from the first Jeeapa War; combat
loading could not be segregated.*

*If they put too much air defense equipment on one
transport that got wiped out before landing, they
would have a severe deficiency in air defense.*

The Anarchie troop and equipment transports therefore were all loaded with some of each item's including munitions, food, lubricants, fuel cells, habitability, engineer's equipment, and sustainability materials and equipment.

Crowded in the transports were also Anarchieborgs, a lot tougher and meaner than what landed years prior.

Anarchieborgs now had updated body armor with better sensors and communications equipment.

Another huge improvement was the night vision eye patches which mitigated immediate glare from exploding munitions or laser attacks.

Having witnessed the brilliance of the Mergenky portashields, the Anarchie copied them. Even though Anarchie portashields were not made with Spactron 300 metal that only the Mergenky possessed.

The Anarchie invented a new type of metal to build portashields that proved to be very effective in stopping blue lasers.

As far as protection from pyrotechnics, the Anarchie never could recruit enough living volunteers to properly conduct pyrotechnics testing.

All the Anarchie knew for sure is the very few volunteers and the objects they put under an Anarchie designed portashields was protected far better than without.

Portashields, Crawlers, and Exoskeleton's were a big game changer this time around in the objective of capturing Jeeapa.

Thanks to rapid development of portable power, the Exoskeleton's had a range of about triple standard ground force transport and even could move at 40 miles per hour on level ground or road networks when needed.

What Exoskeleton's did for Anarchie Ground Forces

was to allow them to move their forces abreast instead of in a long line of antiquated single file "bomb magnets," a term used by the infantry for ground-based troop transports.

The ground forces had the same criticism towards vertical lift because on a hot battlefield, especially with good laser targeting, vertical lift methods were almost suicidal. With recent developments, the closer they hug the ground, the more likely they would survive.

Maneuver and stealth were the most advantageous. Some of the smaller Exoskeleton's referred to by the ground forces as well as the Mergenky INTEL as Crawlers gave one the impression they were designed like a snake.

Crawlers were designed to only raise four feet above the ground with a two-foot-tall crew cabin and two-foot-tall leg like devices instead of wheels.

In addition to carrying Anarchieborgs to the front lines, Crawlers allowed delivery of munitions, food, medical supplies to front line troops and remained below laser targeting which at best was line of sight, and in practical terms less than 5,000 yards.

After depositing troops and materials those four-foot-tall Crawlers were easily converted to ambulances. They could be sent via remote control or manually controlled.

A string of Crawlers could be used which meant an entire platoon or company sized element could be positioned by these Crawler devices strung together in a trainlike formation.

Even though the optimum or comfortable crawler speed was less than 10 miles per hour, the last 10 miles up to the front lines was usually the most trepidatious as the hazards were magnified every mile closer to the front lines.

Because the energy packs and the motor functions

were spread across all Crawler carts and multiple 'legs,' the Crawler Exoskeleton's had significant built in survivability. Individual carts could be quickly removed from the string if sustained severe damage.

Quite often, only 80% of the original Crawlers made it to the front lines, while 20% had been disconnected and removed very hastily which normally took less than a minute thanks to the automation and networking of controls.

The other type of Exoskeleton's, Cargo Hauling Exoskeleton's were massive in size and in most cases except for the highly specialized assault types, not used near front lines.

Cargo Hauling Exoskeleton's were designed to promptly move large cargoes from the transport ships to the bivouac areas.

One Anarchie warrior operating the large Transport Exoskeleton, could move as much cargo as a surface vehicle and do it climb up tall hills and over rugged ground away from roads.

Anarchie Exoskeleton construction allowed them to cross rivers and ravines and navigate their way through forests following a tree cutter exoskeleton designed to fell a tree with a cut close to the ground and dropped sideways out of the path clearing a passage Exoskeletons could easily follow.

Some Anarchie Exoskeleton's were pathfinders and assisted engineers in building new road networks.

Since the bulk of the lift would be Exoskeleton or vertical lift, only a limited number of debris needed cleaned out of the way for the Exoskeleton's to be able to see their footing for safe navigation.

Then there were other types of Exoskeletons used the way Earth people used tanks, loaded with armaments and lasers were on front line duty providing the tip of the spear in an assault force.

These Fast Attack Exoskeletons made it extremely difficult for Mergenky ground forces to penetrate the front lines. And if that did occur, the Fast Attack Exoskeletons could retreat at 40 miles per hour making it hard for ground forces to kill one of these monsters.

The Anarchieborgs and the Fast Attack Exoskeleton's were the last to be put aboard the transports. One of the reasons why Captain Esau picked the timing to send that desperate communication is that it was standard Anarchie policy to load out the Anarchieborgs and the Exoskeleton's within 24 hours of launch.

They could not put them on board any sooner to departure, otherwise a lot of fighting and defections might occur as reality set in that many of them realized they would not come back alive.

The Anarchie commander for the Jeeapa invasion, General Hēishé (pronounced He Ish) stood on the observation platform on the glorious Launch Day.

VOICEOVER

Launch Day was designated for the auspicious day that Anarchie Empire was to once again regain its Imperial Power status.

The Anarchie were on their way to destiny and avenge the Jeeapa debacle of almost twenty years ago. The most humiliating setback in Anarchie History was going to be reversed.

The plan which General Hēishé knew would work included first taking Jeeapa to secure the only viable source of blue diamonds which would also deny the Mergenky replacement laser systems for future craft making a strategic shift in the balance of power projection.

A *feint* would be conducted towards the planet Frăctŏng which would cause great political upheaval in the Mergenky Alliance, effectively dividing their forces so that Anarchie Assault Vessels could take apart Jeeapa and turn it into an Anarchie outpost to be a staging base to conduct direct assault on Gwaba.

Once enough of the Mergenky forces were wiped out, that would enable the planet crushers to come in and annihilate Gwaba and remove the Mergenky as a viable force in the region.

EXT. CGI. DAY. ANARCHIE SPACE WARSHIPS AND TRANSPORT FORCE LAUNCH. (2 MINUTES DURING THE FOLLOWING VOICEOVER).

VOICEOVER

General Hēishé watched the simultaneous launch of the fleet.

Anarchie Intelligence Group (AIG) operatives had just reported Jeeapa was a sitting duck having returned from another scouting mission performed just before fleet launch.

The Anarchie AIG's intelligence report on Jeeapa showed they left air defenses off at night, had no patrolling MSF warships, and had virtually no means to repel an invasion.

Another interesting Anarchie development was thanks to help from one of their spies as well as several Reconnaissance Passovers, the surveillance craft reported there was no activity around the Five-Mile Oval and no electronics emanations indicating the command center had been completely shut down.

Anarchie AIG's intelligence summary:

Mergenky MSF no longer has an underground command center to cope with an invasion like they did 20 years ago.

***

EXT. CGI. DAY. JEEAPA SPACE PORT TRANSPORTS LANDING FERRYING MERGENKY TROOPS AND MATERIALS.

30 SECONDS DURING THE FOLLOWING VOICEOVER.

VOICEOVER

Providence was once again with the Mergenky. The Anarchie reconnaissance flew over the day before Kwongab performed his test and simulated Jeeapa attack per General Kahn's orders.

What the Anarchie didn't know is Jeeapa's MSF Five-Mile Oval Command Center was back in operation.

Even though it needed some work to re-establish its former glory, Jeeapa's MSF Five-Mile Oval Command Center was slowly coming back to full efficiency and already MSF personnel were streaming in as the once semi-abandoned MSF space port was now alive with activity.

While Kwongab was out on Mergenky Scout S-1 chasing an unknown craft that appeared to have penetrated Mergenky Alliance Space near Jeeapa, the Logistician General Kahn requested, arrived.

The Jeeapa Logistics coordinator came via special transport that was also ferrying troops in, including technicians especially sensor operators to fatten the watch bill to eliminate any lapses of vigilance.

General Kahn met the logistics officer, Commander Monachi at the rehabilitated Jeeapa MSF Space Port.

GENERAL KAHN
Good to see you, Commander Monachi.

MONACHI
Thank you, General Kahn.

GENERAL KAHN
I've scheduled a meeting in the *Five-Mile-Oval* in 30 minutes with General Zǔzhī Bùliáng. I assume you brought all your timelines and transport schedules.

MONACHI
Yes General, I have a complete presentation that I prepared for General Zǔzhī Bùliáng as well as for his Logisticians.

GENERAL KAHN
Great, let's get going, we need to get this mobilization underway, as I fear we may be running out of time.

MONACHI
I understand General, that's why you will see the arrival of 15 Cruisers and 4 Scouts in 2 hours to initiate a defense grid to at least slow down an invasion while we scramble the fleet.

GENERAL KAHN
It's too bad we can't get the fleet here today.

MONACHI
The exercise their doing off Frăctŏng is necessary
because most of them are either green or rusty.

GENERAL KAHN
That's why I'm considering putting you and Kwongab
on combat spaceships.

MONACHI
Kwongab is already on a ship.

GENERAL KAHN
Yes, but he assures me that Commander Gōngniúgǒu
is fully capable of handling Scout S-1. I'm wasting 2
good pilots on one ship. As soon as S-1 gets back from
their current assignment, I'm putting Kwongab on a
Cruiser as its Captain.

MONACHI
What about me?

GENERAL KAHN
You know the Scout's well; one of the four arriving
will be your ship. Since you made all the arrangements
for the four Scouts, I'll let you pick which one you
wish to command.

MONACHI
That's an easy choice.

GENERAL KAHN
It is?

MONACHI
Yes, I'll take MSFS-4. It has the weakest Pilot aboard
the four of them.

GENERAL KAHN
Alright, let's get down, do the briefing, then you can
meet your ship in two hours.

MONACHI

My children are still home from school break.

GENERAL KAHN

I'll make appropriate arrangements to send them back to school. Do they need any adult supervision now?

MONACHI

No, they're in good care of our two robots who will be the best guardians.

GENERAL KAHN

How will they get back to school?

MONACHI

The school always sends a driver to pick them up and take them back to school.

GENERAL KAHN

What about your two robots?

MONACHI

They are quite capable of taking care of themselves.

GENERAL KAHN

Do you have someone in your office who can fulfill your duties as the chief logistician for this operation?

MONACHI

Absolutely. We have six logistics experts, all working in the team. I'll communicate with them and assign one of them to be the *Officer in Charge* and to carry on without me.

GENERAL KAHN

As soon as I get back to Gwaba, I want to meet the person you chose and get a readout from them daily on what goes on. I'm reluctant to take you away from a serious logistics challenge, but like you said, the MSF Combat Crews are rusty or green.

MONACHI

Unfortunately, that's how it is.

GENERAL KAHN

No officers have the recent experience that you and Kwongab have. Aside from the fact that we need your fighting spirit, we also need your intuition and leadership skills because I think we'll be in combat a lot sooner than people realize.

MONACHI

General, I tend to agree with you, and you will be pleased to know, most of the logistics planning is complete.

GENERAL KAHN
Really?

MONACHI

It's now just a matter of execution and we have worked out several contingencies, to deal with uncertainty in the battlespace in case certain situations evolve that we didn't predict.

GENERAL KAHN

I'm sorry you are not able to meet Kwongab, he might not be back before you leave on S-4.

MONACHI

Under the circumstances, our personal lives will just have to be put aside for a while. We have some serious business to deal with the Anarchie.

GENERAL KAHN

If we get a breather period, the two of you can meet up.

MONACHI
Yes, General, I hope so.

In due time, Monachi and General Kahn were at the conference room and briefing General Zǔzhī Bùliáng whose demeaner had completely changed as he was reading the INTEL reports and saw the last transmission from Captain Esau.

General Kahn started the dialog as the briefing started.

GENERAL KAHN
An Anarchie attack is now not a matter of *if*, it's now a matter of *when*.

MONACHI
Fleet component arrivals and more logistics items were streaming in and the expected arrival of the 15 Cruisers and 4 Scouts could not have come at a more auspicious moment.

General Kahn acted as if he knew the obvious how they all now felt.

GENERAL KAHN
The pressure is mounting.

ANARCHIE FRĂCTŎNG FEINT
Kwongab and Gōngniúgŏu watched the energy readings on the possible Anarchie penetrator as the distance had been reduced during the few hours that Kwongab had rested.

COMMANDER KWONGAB
We are now a lot closer but not close enough to identify the vessel.

COMMANDER GŌNGNIÚGŎU
The only ship that would be heading on the course to the Anarchie home planet has to be Anarchie.

COMMANDER KWONGAB
There would be no reason for Mergenky or Alliance ships heading in that direction.

COMMANDER GŌNGNIÚGŎU
If it had been a diplomatic ship, we would have been duly informed.

COMMANDER KWONGAB
We are getting close enough to enemy territory that we must be careful we do not get sucked into an ambush. When was the last time you did a Capmoc-Drulyenslv maneuver?

COMMANDER GŌNGNIÚGǑU
About one and half hours ago.

KWONGAB
Let's slow down, do a Capmoc-Drulyenslv maneuver,
then drift on the final leg for a few minutes, then do a
Frazgrandopf maneuver.

COMMANDER GŌNGNIÚGǑU
What's your reason for this double maneuver now?

COMMANDER KWONGAB
We don't want to blunder into an ambush, and if we
have some Anarchie trailing us, we need to know,
because they could be setting up an ambush ahead of
us.

COMMANDER GŌNGNIÚGǑU
PNN, perform the maneuvers Commander Kwongab
just specified and report the start of each leg on the
maneuver.

Martha's voice boomed.

MARTHA
Ready to perform the maneuvers.

COMMANDER GŌNGNIÚGǑU
Commencing maneuvers.

Right after the Capmoc-Drulyenslv maneuver, PNN reported:

MARTHA
Picking up long distance ion trails, multiple ships.

COMMANDER GŌNGNIÚGǑU
This could be the ambush you were worried about.

COMMANDER KWONGAB
Or it could be they have finally launched the invasion.

COMMANDER GŌNGNIÚGǑU
What do you recommend for our next move is?

COMMANDER KWONGAB

We are not pressed for time yet, and we do not presently know their course, we need to reverse course with a Frazgrandopf maneuver and open a bit and try to establish a good course they are on.

COMMANDER GŌNGNIÚGǑU

It's most likely they are heading straight for Jeeapa, why don't we just speed up and leave them behind and warn Jeeapa?

COMMANDER KWONGAB

What if it's another location that needs warned?

COMMANDER GŌNGNIÚGǑU

It doesn't seem logical to attack any other location but Jeeapa, it's on the flank of any possible invasion route, plus it has 90% of all the known blue diamond reserves.

COMMANDER KWONGAB

For now, we'll plot them and see if we can establish a course than warn MSF as soon as we decide on their base course and possible Anarchie Fleet disposition.

COMMANDER GŌNGNIÚGǑU

Plotting is fully automatic; ranging can only be accomplished via extensive plots on the energy plumes.

COMMANDER KWONGAB

At PCO school we taught you to rely on Maximum Likelihood Estimations (MLE). But when I was on planet Earth, I discovered a technique Earth Militaries used and I'm still working out the glitches, but I plan to soon suggest MSF implement it as a backup method to MLE for situations like this.

COMMANDER GŌNGNIÚGǑU

What do the Earth people do for long distance ranging?

COMMANDER KWONGAB

Earth militaries developed this Target Motion Analysis

technique almost 100 years ago, called *Ekelund Ranging. Ekelund Ranging*

COMMANDER GŌNGNIÚGǑU
How does *Ekelund Ranging work?*

COMMANDER KWONGAB
PNN do you still have my *Ekelund Ranging* files from the Andromeda Mission?

MARTHA (PNN)
Commander Kwongab, I have all those Ekelund Ranging files archived.

COMMANDER KWONGAB
PNN, I want you to perform an *Ekelund Ranging* calculation on the energy detections we think are the Anarchie.

MARTHA (PNN)
Commander Kwongab, I have all the data points necessary for this leg of the *Ekelund Ranging* calculation. Recommend change course towards the energy cluster for the second leg required for the *Ekelund Ranging* calculation.

COMMANDER KWONGAB
PNN, change course as required for the *Ekelund Ranging* calculation.

MARTHA (PNN)
Commander Kwongab, changing course.

Kwongab knew from the Andromeda mission, Martha would come up with a good estimate he could work with.

COMMANDER KWONGAB
Thanks to speed and distance, PNN was able to come up with an estimation of target location and range.

COMMANDER GŌNGNIÚGǑU
Commander Kwongab, I have no experience and thus would not have a good handle on how trustworthy *Ekelund Ranging* calculations can be.

COMMANDER KWONGAB
PNN, continue with incremental *Ekelund Ranging* course changes and calculations. Start plotting estimated position on the NAV plot.

MARTHA (PNN)
Commander Kwongab, I'm currently plotting instantaneous *Ekelund Ranging* calculations. Would you like me to plot *Averaged and Interpolated Ekelund Ranging* as recommended in your *Ekelund training documents?*

COMMANDER KWONGAB
PNN, yes plot the *Averaged and Interpolated Ekelund Ranging* results with spatial positional locations overlays on the Navigation Holograph.

In a short time Kwongab made an astute observation:

COMMANDER KWONGAB
The Anarchie Fleet is leaving behind a considerable ion trail, yet they have not accelerated to extreme speeds.

COMMANDER GŌNGNIÚGǑU
That's rather unusual.

COMMANDER KWONGAB
Last time I saw something like this was twenty years ago.

COMMANDER GŌNGNIÚGǑU
What determination did you make out of it?

KWONGAB
It's a classical clue to multiple troop transports.

COMMANDER GŌNGNIÚGǑU
Please explain.

COMMANDER KWONGAB
Aside from it takes quite a bit more energy to accelerate, but since the transports are significantly

larger than other classes of ships, there is a greater cross section hitting hydrogen atoms and creating a larger ion wake even though they are not going as fast.

COMMANDER GŌNGNIÚGǑU
So, this is probably the invasion fleet.

COMMANDER KWONGAB
Most likely.

COMMANDER GŌNGNIÚGǑU
Shouldn't we break off surveillance and transit high speed back to Jeeapa to warn MSF?

COMMANDER KWONGAB
That's an excellent idea, but we still do not know where they are heading. We'll have to trail them for a while to determine their base course.

COMMANDER GŌNGNIÚGǑU
That's a good idea Commander Kwongab. I would expect Anarchie would do some zig zag maneuvers to throw off a potential trailer or a wolf pack.

Mergenky Scout S-1 followed Anarchie Fleet offset a good distance and after a couple hours Kwongab made another astute observation as the *Averaged and Interpolated Ekelund Ranging* results are indicating a compelling base course for the Anarchie.

COMMANDER KWONGAB
Even though Anarchie are doing a well-conceived zig-zag pattern, I believe I've determined their base course.

COMMANDER GŌNGNIÚGǑU
What's your course estimation Captain Kwongab?

COMMANDER KWONGAB
Their heading directly for planet Frăctŏng.

COMMANDER GŌNGNIÚGǑU
Captain Kwongab, that doesn't make sense.

COMMANDER KWONGAB
Sure, it does.

COMMANDER GŌNGNIÚGǑU
How so?

COMMANDER KWONGAB
It's one of two reasons: either they are going to attack the Alliance and make a few hands fold to cause political upheaval, or its simply a *feint*.

COMMANDER GŌNGNIÚGǑU
What do we do?

COMMANDER KWONGAB
At this point in time, I think the best plan is to continue following them, launch a messenger buoy, timed to give us some distance from it before it transmits, and make sure what the real plan is, in case this is just a feint.

COMMANDER GŌNGNIÚGǑU
How soon will we know?

COMMANDER KWONGAB
I think if this is a feint to Frăctŏng, we'll see the real main body of Jeeapa assault craft in about 12 hours.

COMMANDER GŌNGNIÚGǑU
That means both worlds would get hit simultaneously.

COMMANDER KWONGAB
Exactly. Thus, putting pressure on MSF to preserve one of the planets while letting the other fall victim of Anarchie aggression until we can put in place a viable defense.

COMMANDER GŌNGNIÚGǑU
When shall we launch the messenger buoy?

COMMANDER KWONGAB
I'd suggest we launch it now with a timed transmission of 30 minutes from now which should put a good distance between us the buoy when it transmits.

COMMANDER GŌNGNIÚGǑU
PNN, put together a summary report and load it into

message buoy and launch it with data transmission to
occur 30 minutes after launch.

MARTHA (PNN)

Commander Gōngniúgǒu , messenger buoy will be
launched momentarily. Transmission delay 30 minutes
as requested.

COMMANDER KWONGAB

I suggest we change course, put a little distance
between us and the Anarchie so that when they
investigate the messenger buoy, we'll be outside their
scanner range.

COMMANDER GŌNGNIÚGǑU
What course?

COMMANDER KWONGAB

I'm going to pick a course I recommend we take
that will facilitate *Ekelund Ranging* calculations on
the Anarchie Spaceships sent out to investigate the
messenger buoy.

COMMANDER GŌNGNIÚGǑU

Captain Kwongab, please enter the course vectors you
desire.

Commander Gōngniúgǒu simply watched Kwongab operating the Navigation
holograph. It seemed as if almost all this activity was strange to Commander
Gōngniúgǒu.

VOICEOVER

*Like many now in the ranks of the MSF they had never
tasted real war.*

*It was now starting to become quite apparent to
Gōngniúgǒu that simulators were not the real thing.*

*To taste real blood, sweat, and tears one learns to feel
the battlespace.*

The Navigation holograph with contact overlays slowly rotated as they changed course
and put the transiting Anarchie behind them on a opposite and somewhat perpendicular
course.

Kwongab watched the navigation vectors show the aspect change of the Mergenky Scout MSFS-1 relative to the transiting Anarchie.

> COMMANDER KWONGAB
> The course changes effectively put the Anarchie Fleet behind us, but the Anarchie home planet is our starboard side where the sensors are the most sensitive.

Commander Gōngniúgǒu replied as he responded to Kwongab's insights as well as the neural expansion telepathic influences.

> COMMANDER GŌNGNIÚGǑU
> Even though the Anarchie Fleet remains beyond scanner range, if their ships come this way their energy wake should show up on the scanners.

> COMMANDER KWONGAB
> That's what I'm counting on.

> COMMANDER GŌNGNIÚGǑU
> Anarchie home worlds are far out of scanner range what good is this maneuver?

> COMMANDER KWONGAB
> In due time we might spot the actual invasion force traveling behind this Fleet if it's a *feint*.

The Scout continued the reciprocal course and just before the messenger buoy was to broadcast Kwongab suggested:

> COMMANDER KWONGAB
> I recommend we change course on a parallel track to the Anarchie heading for Frăctŏng so that we can observe the buoy transmit the message to ensure it was successfully broadcasted.

> COMMANDER GŌNGNIÚGǑU
> I concur, PNN change course matching the Anarchie Fleet calculated course.

Predictably when the expected time lapsed, PNN reported:

> MARTHA (PNN)
> Receiving message from message buoy. Transmission validated.

COMMANDER GŌNGNIÚGǑU
In a few minutes, we should get some response from
MSF.

Kwongab announced after hearing Gōngniúgǒu and the PNN report.

COMMANDER KWONGAB
I hope we are not directed to Frăctŏng. This smells like
a *Feint* and if we do not remain here, we'll miss the
opportunity to warn Jeeapa.

As expected, the reply came promptly. MSF was reacting. General Kahn evidently
saw things the same way Kwongab did, and their orders were confirmed to stay in this
region of space and monitor possible Anarchie attacks towards Jeeapa.

GENERAL KAHN
(via tangramized message)
Experts looking at your sensor data conclude this force
is not large enough to sustain an invasion for more
than a few days, therefore it's been determined to be a
Feint, we expect the real attack to be Jeeapa. Remain
patrolling in the sector you are in and report any other
Anarchie activity when you can.

As expected in a while, PNN reported:

MARTHA (PNN)
Sensors have started detecting ion wakes that indicate
high speed transiting ships.

Gōngniúgǒu responded showing concern with a facial expression:

COMMANDER GŌNGNIÚGǑU
Most likely sent out to investigate the source of the
messenger buoy signals,

Kwongab stated as a matter of fact:

COMMANDER KWONGAB
We are far enough away the Anarchie should not be
able to detect us.

MARTHA (PNN)
Upon completion of the transmission, the messenger
buoy self-destructed.

This was part of normal operations to ensure enemies did not acquire the technology.

MARTHA (PNN)
Anarchie spacecrafts are performing a search pattern.

Martha then put up a surveillance holograph showing an intricate maze of Anarchie positions relative to the Scouts position.

MARTHA (PNN)
Receiving ultra-violet and infra-red sensor beams from the Anarchie warships, signal strength 2.5 from the scanner pulses.

COMMANDER KWONGAB
PNN, what's the estimated probability of detection threshold?

PNN replied with Martha' haunting voice:

MARTHA (PNN)
Current MSF INTEL guidelines suggest signal strength 3.5 is a possible counter detection with figure of merit 50%..

COMMANDER GŌNGNIÚGǑU
Captain Kwongab, what do you suggest if we start getting some 3.5 signal strength detections?

COMMANDER KWONGAB
Commander Gōngniúgǒu, I have a reasonable belief that even though this ship is over 20 years old, we can still coax enough speed out of it to outrun the Anarchie.

COMMANDER GŌNGNIÚGǑU
What do you recommend if we believe we are counter detected and they charge us for attack?

COMMANDER KWONGAB
Our only option then is to point to Jeeapa and proceed there sending warnings we are being chased and request help.

The sensor holograph showing the blasts of ultra-violet and infra-red emanating out of the Anarchie ships gave the 3D enclosure display that Kwongab stood in the middle of, quite an eerie look. To present the information to the pilot and copilot in a way to distinguish between contacts or targets, they were color coded on the inverted globe like display.

COMMANDER GŌNGNIÚGǑU
The different Anarchie ships transmitted at different times and different pulse types.

COMMANDER KWONGAB
Some of the radial strobes shown on the sensor holograph indicate search in a scan mode, whereas other pulses were phased pseudo random placement.

VOICEOVER
Once PNN identified the radiator it was given a unique color-coding resulting in a surreal projection that imparted fantastic situational awareness.

At the same time the psychological effects were clearly manifesting a reaction in the crew members in the control room.

COMMANDER KWONGAB
Some of Anarchie transmissions may have been counterproductive, but since the consequences of not promptly maneuvering with these tracking aids are rather severe.

COMMANDER GŌNGNIÚGǑU
What was the rationale for that design?

COMMANDER KWONGAB
The system designers and planners understood fundamentally the psychophysical interface and designed the human interface to provide an optimum survival rate. Simply put they gave up comfort for the sake of survival.

VOICEOVER
Watching the 3D surveillance holograph which had an early warning audio component was truly an inexplicable eerie experience.

One could possibly equate the sound to the personal psychology of a sonar operator on an American

*submarine out in the Pacific Ocean during the 1940's
with destroyer's active sonars approaching just before
they let loose depth charges when attempting to sink
the submarine, Bungo Pete style.*

The Scout was on a good course to put some distance to the Anarchie who were in a search pattern near the location of the messenger buoy which subsequently self-destructed to prevent the enemy from obtaining the technology. The messenger buoys were expendable and never reused.

MARTHA
Signal Strength 3.2 for radiator #3 indicated blue on the surveillance holograph.

VOICEOVER
*Kwongab was using his neural expansion telepathic
ability on Gōngniúgǒu attempting to calm him down.*

*Without Kwongab's presence Gōngniúgǒu would have
elected to do a high-speed escape. In doing so the
Scout would have given off an extensive ion wake.*

*Kwongab estimated the Anarchie would then be able to
set a trap, especially if they had assets in the direction
the Scout had to travel for safety. Classic ambushes
were arranged in this manner.*

COMMANDER KWONGAB
Our tripwire probably is signal strength 4.5 with relative motion of the enemy ships implying counter-detection and pursuit.

VOICEOVER
*The moments seemed like centuries as the entire
control room of the Mergenky Scout MSFS-1 was now
transfixed on the obnoxious screeching sounds from
the early warning detectors.*

COMMANDER KWONGAB
It was now up to the Anarchie to show their hand first.

COMMANDER GŌNGNIÚGǑU
The Scout was too far distant for laser weapons to be effective due to excessive targeting ranges unless they got a lucky shot.

COMMANDER KWONGAB
But to close the gap to within lethal range would not
require these Anarchie ships a lot of time.

VOICEOVER
*When that moment transpired where Kwongab decided
all the factors spelled out a tripwire, predicated his
next move.*

KWONGAB
If the Anarchie hit a tripwire, we'll have to make an
immediate decision and take evasive courses and
avoid going over light speed which would create such
a huge ion wake that every Anarchie ship in nearby
space would see us.

COMMANDER GŌNGNIÚGǑU
A tricky maneuver will be required to get out of harm's
way.

COMMANDER KWONGAB
But it is important to stay in this area because if the
Anarchie are doing merely a Feint towards Frăctŏng
means the real invasion force would be coming by
sometime soon, and that's the INTEL that MSF needs
now the most.

Within a few more minutes there were a couple color coded splotches of target intercept
data on the surveillance holograph. It was obvious the Anarchie were looking hard for
them. Kwongab and Gōngniúgǒu stood in the middle of the commander's inverted
sphere watching the intercepts.

COMMANDER GŌNGNIÚGǑU
Almost 180 degrees of intercepts now exist across the
azimuth of the inverted sphere.

COMMANDER KWONGAB
We need to keep at least one flank clear and free
of contacts or face being encircled and possibly
destroyed.

COMMANDER GŌNGNIÚGǑU
If that's the case, we have no choice but to continue
this opening course, which is towards Gwaba, even
though it's a great distance away.

COMMANDER KWONGAB
In a short while the Anarchie will be between us and
Jeeapa, which means the only way back to Jeeapa
would require a circular end around.

VOICEOVER
*With the ample amount of neural expansion applied
to Gōngniúgǒu, Kwongab now had a very good
assessment of the man and now knew why General
Kahn was completely justified in putting Kwongab
aboard Mergenky Scout S-1.*

*Gōngniúgǒu was too green of a pilot to face the
exigency they now faced, alone.*

*There had not been a shakedown cruise or a major
training period to get Mergenky Scout MSFS-1's
combat team in top fighting shape. But the crew was
learning fast.*

MARTHA (PNN)
Signal strength 3.5 for radiator #3, we are at the INTEL
prescribed level of possible counter detection.

Kwongab swallowed hard and intensely monitored the surveillance holograph very
closely looking for the very first clue they had been counter detected.

KWONGAB
There are no sudden high-speed maneuvers towards
us, which would be the case if they thought we were
here.

Gōngniúgǒu's stress was slowly rising to the point that had Kwongab not been in the
control room, he might have succumbed at this point to a foolish maneuver such as
attempting to haul-ass (military vernacular).

MARTHA
Signal strength is 3.8 for radiator #3.

KWONGAB
What is the signal strength of the other 3 top radiators?

MARTHA
Signal strength is 3.1 for radiators 1 and 5 and signal
strength is 3.0 for radiators 6 and 8.

Tension continued to build. Gōngniúgǒu felt Kwongab's actions were reckless and feared the worse for Mergenky Scout MSFS-1 and was just about to utter a diatribe in comments when PNN suddenly announced:

MARTHA
Signal strength has decreased to 3.4 for radiator #3,
contact appears to be manuevering away.

Even though Gōngniúgǒu was holding his silence, it didn't matter, Kwongab could read his mind with his extraordinary neural expansion telepathic ability. Therefore, Kwongab started inserting ideas into Gōngniúgǒu's thoughts through neural expansion telepathy.

Gōngniúgǒu thought he was asking himself the question, but it really was Kwongab manipulating him.

VOICEOVER (COMMANDER
GŌNGNIÚGǑU) THOUGHT
Would those Anarchie ultra-violet and infra-red
scanners have picked up our ion trail had we done a
quick acceleration? [To haul ass out of here]

Gōngniúgǒu had more questions in his mind as Kwongab continued the telepathic mental probing without his knowledge.

VOICEOVER (COMMANDER
GŌNGNIÚGǑU) THOUGHT
Could Anarchie have set a trap or an ambush for us
had we sped up and gave our position away with a
huge ion trail?

After a while Kwongab knew that he had diffused the situation that could have got ugly had the former Mergenky Scout MSFS-1 commander attempted to retake command of his ship.

VOICEOVER (KWONGAB)
THOUGHT
Would the crew have backed me? How would PNN
have reacted and responded? Would it be considered
a mutiny?

MARTHA
Signal strength for all radiators are decreasing and
relative motion has shifted based on wavelength of the
ultra-violet and infra-red frequency shifts.

KWONGAB

It is now clear this group of Anarchie ships did not
get a sniff of us and are moving back to base course to
guard the transports they are escorting.

Kwongab and Gōngniúgǒu watched the holograph intently and finally PNN reported.

MARTHA

The Anarchie escort vessels have turned away and are
now opening.

COMMANDER KWONGAB

The search for the source of the Message Buoy
transmission went on for a while, and when nothing
was detected it's obvious the Anarchie shifted course
to rejoin the fleet heading to Frăctŏng.

Gōngniúgǒu stated in a semi-diplomatic manner that was laced with a thin layer of
resentment but conflicting with admiration.

COMMANDER GŌNGNIÚGǑU

Captain Kwongab, this will either be the biggest
blunder you ever made, or it will be the most astute
and innovative plan ever enacted.

KWONGAB

Commander Gōngniúgǒu, I'll always be the first to
admit when I'm wrong. However, if I'm right, it still
can turn into a bloody mess on Jeeapa.

COMMANDER LESTER

Monachi was with General Kahn in his temporary
office in the *Five-Mile-Oval*, when Commander Lester
arrived after being summoned.

In the back of his mind, General Kahn wondered:

VOICEOVER (GENERAL
KAHN) THOUGHT

*Did Monachi pick Scout MSFS-4 specifically because
Commander Lester was the pilot and commander of
that vessel?*

Commander Lester had been the co-pilot on Mergenky Scout S-1 when they abducted

Vance from Earth. Commander Lester filed charges against Kwongab for a C-5 security violation, but Kwongab was exonerated during the trial.

In reality, the unauthorized exposure was caused by Commander Lester not paying attention to the AMRT charging sequence that led to the delamination of the cloaking field and the subsequent disclosure of the ship resulting in the need to abduct Vance to eliminate an eyewitness left behind.

VOICEOVER

Even though General Kahn thought the possibility existed that Monachi picked Mergenky Scout S-4 for revenge, commander Lester's performance was nowhere near exemplary.

Under the exigency of the ongoing Anarchie threat that was manifesting this mobilization, General Kahn really wanted Monachi a seasoned and qualified pilot on one of the Scout class ships.

Mergenky Scout MSFS-4 just happened to be the most convenient to put Monachi on.

VOICEOVER (GENERAL
KAHN) THOUGHT

Unlike Mergenky Scout S-1 where Kwongab could easily handle Gōngniúgǒu, Commander Lester's personality would make it hard for Monachi to deal with. Hence, it's best to remove him and give him a staff job.

In rebuilding the five-mile-oval support infrastructure, there were numerous gaping holes in the command composition. Commander Lester can plug one of those holes.

General Kahn knew Monachi was waiting outside his office in an adjacent room used as a reception room so that he could maintain privacy with the estimated large number of people that would be coming and going.

The receptionist, a fine looking Mergenky female receptionist Stephquerie notified General Kahn with her holograph suddenly appearing on the corner of his desk.

STEPHQUERIE
(receptionist),
General Kahn, Commander Lester has arrived.

GENERAL KAHN
Send Commander Lester in first then I'll have Monachi
come in later.

Commander Lester soon arrived in General Kahn's office.

GENERAL KAHN
Have a seat, Commander Lester.

Commander Lester sat down looking coy wondering, why he was suddenly ordered
to transit to Jeeapa and meet with General Kahn precisely at the time that MSF was
scrambling a fleet to shield Frăctŏng from an apparent Anarchie intrusion and possible
invasion attempt.

Commander Lester's body language exposed he was in suspense at the sudden
summons to Jeeapa.

COMMANDER LESTER
Good morning, General Kahn.

GENERAL KAHN
We don't have much time so I'm not going to beat
around the bush. I've decided to make some changes,
and I'm going to transfer you to my staff here on
Jeeapa.

COMMANDER LESTER
So that's what this was about?

GENERAL KAHN
Yes, it is.

COMMANDER LESTER
Did I do anything wrong or violate any rules to deserve
my loss of my command on MSFS-4?

GENERAL KAHN
Commander Lester, you are an average pilot, you've
not done anything wrong, but with the expected
invasion I need a liaison to ground forces on my staff
who has fleet experience.

COMMANDER LESTER
General Kahn, may I ask you why you picked me for

a staff job when you know I want to be the pilot on MSFS-4?

GENERAL KAHN
Commander Lester, the staff position you will fill must be a pilot who understands space liaison business. I've decided that since you are extremely well honed on procedures and go by the book every time, someone like you would best fit that liaison role.

COMMANDER LESTER
When am I to leave MSFS-4?

GENERAL KAHN
You are not going back to MSFS-4, you will remain here at Jeeapa.

I've already sent your orders including to your Executive Officer and Co-pilot to obtain all your personal items and bring them down to the planet on the Shuttle after Commander Monachi returns to S-4 to take command of it as pilot.

Commander Lester responded with hate in his heart for that woman.

COMMANDER LESTER
So that's why she's out in the waiting room?

GENERAL KAHN
Yes.

General Kahn stated then ordered his receptionist via a holographic communication:

GENERAL KAHN
Stephquerie, please ask Monachi to come into my office.

A moment later Monachi walked into General Kahn's office after the air powered doors opened for her.

MONACHI
Reporting as ordered sir.

GENERAL KAHN
Commander Monachi, please have a seat.

VOICEOVER

Monachi, who was one of the four Mergenky individuals to have received the neural expansion telepathic implants could read Commander Lester's mind and immediately felt the seething hate that radiated out of him.

The Earth mission when Vance was abducted and the later trial had left raw marks on Commander Lester and now being removed from command and replaced by Kwongab's spouse, added fuel to the fire!

GENERAL KAHN

PNN, the following orders are to be transmitted to MSFS-4 Scout: Monachie.014 is hereby designated as pilot and commander of MSFS-4. She will do a turnover with Commander Lester in my office, then proceed to MSFS-4 and take command with her new set of orders for the ship.

PNN

General Kahn. All orders are now being sent.

GENERAL KAHN

Commander Lester, is your Shuttle still at the temporary space port?

COMMANDER LESTER
Yes General.

GENERAL KAHN

Monachi, I want you to get the material condition of MSFS-4 from Commander Lester, then proceed on MSFS-4's Shuttle back to the ship.

COMMANDER MONACHI
Yes, General Kahn. What will my next mission be?

GENERAL KAHN

Monachi right now we are lacking eyes and ears in protecting Jeeapa's flanks.

We only have one Scout and one Cruiser between us and the Anarchie home world.

I'm sending you out into that region of space where you will be another set of eyes and ears, to patrol the area and act as the early warning and trip wire for us.

COMMANDER MONACHI
What would be my options if I came across Anarchie?

GENERAL KAHN
Your role is to detect and report. You don't have enough firepower to deal with the Anarchie.

COMMANDER MONACHI
What is my guidance for an Anarchie encounter?

GENERAL KAHN
All I expect you to do is make the reports and do your best to protect the ship and make sure it doesn't get destroyed.

COMMANDER MONACHI
Understand, sir.

GENERAL KAHN
I expect the Anarchie will be coming in large numbers. After we regroup from the Frăctŏng invasion that's in progress, more fleet assets will arrive here to help.

We may have to use you as a decoy, but your orders are scouting and to avoid combat unless you get boxed in and half to fight your way out of a trap for survival.

COMMANDER MONACHI
How soon will I know my op area?

GENERAL KAHN
Your mission is now being uploaded to Mergenky Scout MSFS-4 PNN. By the time you arrive on MSFS-4, I expect your Navigator will have all the vectors laid out for your operations.

Monachi and commander Lester went over the material condition of MSFS-4 and all the maintenance issues with the ship were noted. Monachi then said:

COMMANDER MONACHI
I relieve you.

All the formal turnover was recorded IAW MSF requirements in the event there was a future need for a board of inquiry, such as would be the case of a loss of the ship.

GENERAL KAHN
Good luck Commander Monachi.

COMMANDER MONACHI
Thank you, General Kahn.

Commander Monachi then bowed and left the office. In a brief period, Commander Monachi left the *Five-Mile-Oval*, and was transported to the surface of the planet, where she got on the hovercraft that took her to MSFS-4's Shuttle at the space port.

There were several Shuttles at the space port, but Monachi could easily spot the Mergenky Scout S-4 Shuttle because of the unique design.

A Shuttle pilot was there waiting for her, now fully expecting Commander Monachi as the crew had been instantly informed of the change of command, that shockingly came unexpectedly.

The Shuttle pilot met Monachi as she approached the Shuttle.

SHUTTLE PILOT
Good morning, Commander Monachi.

COMMANDER MONACHI
Good morning, are we ready to leave the planet?

SHUTTLE PILOT
Yes Commander. I just delivered, Commander Lester's
personal effects so no need to send a shuttle back.

Commander Monachi climbed into the Shuttle and the pilot followed her closing the door behind.

EXT. CGI. SPACE. SCOUT MSFS-4 SHUTTLE CRAFT LEAVING MSF JEEAPA SPACE PORT FLYING TO THE SCOUT. 15 SECONDS.

Within two minutes the Shuttle was airborne heading into space. In the Shuttle were a few supplies MSFS-4 requested which they carried.

The Shuttle traveled almost vertically. Jeeapa air defense controllers alerted Mergenky Scout MSFS-4 the Shuttle was airborne calculated an intercept course to get close for the Shuttle docking.

INT. SPACE. SCOUT MSFS-4 SHUTTLE CRAFT DOCKING. 15 SECONDS.

Looking out the Shuttle window, Commander Monachi could see Mergenky Scout MSFS-4 Shuttle Bay hatch open and soon they were docking.

INT. SPACE. SCOUT MSFS-4

As soon as the Shuttle hatch was shut and airtight, a 14-pound air test was done indicating no air leaks, then PNN actuated Shuttle door opening and the pilot got out first, stood to the side and waited as Commander Monachi got out of the shuttle.

Having served on Scout Class ships for almost 20 years, Monachi knew them well, but also knew there were deviations between ships as numerous upgrades and maintenance periods changed the internal layouts from time to time. Because of the possible differences she said to the Shuttle pilot:

MONACHI
I'll follow you to the control room, so I don't get lost.

The shuttle pilot eagerly complied with Monachi's wishes.

SHUTTLE PILOT
This way Commander Monachi.

The Shuttle Bay was not far from the bridge and MSFS-4 was laid out exactly like MSFS-1, so Commander Monachi was instantly familiar. Monachi dreaded seeing Martha again.

Soon to Commander Monachi's surprise, commander Lester had chosen a different MSF PNN personality for ships control and environment, "Shirley." Monachi would not have to be reminded of Martha, which suddenly made her feel a lot better with the assignment.

Commander Monachi was introduced to each member of the control room/bridge including the Executive Officer/Co-pilot Lt. Commander Jiǎodòushì (pronounced Geo-doshi) whom she quickly asked:

COMMANDER MONACHI
Do you have our new operation orders?

LT. COMMANDER JIǍODÒUSHÌ
(Executive Officer/Co-Pilot)
Yes Commander Monachi, our new mission we
received is laid out on the Navigation holograph.

VOICEOVER

The Navigator standing next to the Executive Officer/ Co-pilot Lt. Commander Jiǎodòushì *instantly displayed showing the large-scale 3D map and the light traces to their boundary and projected courses to get there.*

Superimposed on the 3D chart were also two other Mergenky operational areas they were to avoid preventing possible collisions or friendly fire accidents. She could instantly see S-1 which she knew her husband was on, and MSFC-34 which she knew Commander Vance was now a navigator and crew member.

MSFS-4 plotted track, and speeds were conservative to eliminate the possibility of an ion trail.

What Monachi didn't know was her operation area was precisely where the Anarchie had just vacated. She was lucky they were outside scanner range when S-4 arrived.

Meanwhile both MSFS-1 and MSFC-34 were alerted MSFS-4 was joining them and their associated operation area.

INT. SPACE. MSFS-1 CONTROL ROOM.

At some point Kwongab would have to interact with MSFS-4 which he wasn't looking forward to dealing with Commander Lester, since MSF had not informed him of the MSFS-4 change of command.

Kwongab assumed he would have to deal with Commander Lester again, and he felt the lingering feelings were not only raw, but Commander Lester's long-lasting grudge was not going to end any time soon.

VOICEOVER (COMMANDER
KWONGAB) THOUGHT

I know from neural expansion checks in the past, Commander Lester resented the fact that his experiences on MSFS-1 and the trial he caused by filing the C-5 charges against me somehow delayed his entry into PCO school. Commander Lester always felt I was responsible for delaying his career.

But now Commander Lester was undergoing another transformation. As Liaison to the *Ground Pounders* and *Surface Warfare*, his whole world was quickly changing.

VOICEOVER
The Ground Pounders did not relish dealing with a pencil neck geek who didn't have a clue about their business.

Commander Lester had very little direct ground support experience since Jeeapa was the last real war and had been almost 20 years prior.

Commander Lester was rusty and slightly incompetent. However, the same could be said for 90% of MSF.

INT. DAY. JEEAPA MSF HEADQUARTERS-FIVE MILE OVAL.

General Kahn, much like General Zarkin, was eligible for retirement and no longer needed to stay with MSF. But General Kahn's concern over the ongoing Anarchie resurgence led him to stay on until this next threat was mitigated. He was feeling his age now and just hoped he could handle the stress.

One thing he did do is reach out to General Zarkin and offered to bring him back into MSF and take command of the Five-Mile Oval again. General Zarkin declined the offer stating:

GENERAL ZARKIN
I thoroughly trained my replacement, General Zŭzhī Bùliáng.

But General Kahn knew that Zŭzhī Bùliáng had not embraced the notion he was living on borrowed time and when first presented with Anarchie threats, was slow to respond.

It wasn't so much Zŭzhī Bùliáng, as it was the entire MSF who had fell victim to *peace dividend mentality*, believing there was no possibility of another large conflict in their lifetimes.

In a way Zŭzhī Bùliáng was no different than Stanley Baldwin and Neville Chamberlain on Earth who had not reacted quick enough to Hitler's threats. Stanley Baldwin was overly conscious of rebuilding the British Empire's former pre-WW1 glory.

As such, Stanley Baldwin did not want precious funds diverted to defense spending as he was trying to coax the economy out of the post stock market crash and depression era, Great Britain helped cause by implementing the gold standard for international trade. This also happened at a time when America had retaliated with anti-trade and immigration policies of both Calvin Coolidge and Herbert Hoover.

Stanley Baldwin considered FDR a 'Stalin Lite' and socialist whom he detested to the point he refused to meet his envoy Harry Hopkins sent over ostensibly to avert another global war with the Germans. It was also well-known Stanley Baldwin hated Americans in general.

Too little too late, just like Stanley Baldwin and Neville Chamberlain, the Mergenky political culture that now existed wasn't keen on vast military expenditures that was obviously needed.

General Kahn, who stayed at MSF to do as much as he could to stave off draconian budget cuts, feared most of the elected officials running the government would soon discover the folly of their *peace dividend* when it no longer worked.

<u>INT. SPACE. MSFS-4 CONTROL ROOM.</u>

VOICEOVER

The crew of MSFS-4 appeared in a semi state of shock and bewilderment. Commander Lester had been the pilot for several years and just when they were starting to get used to his idiosyncrasies, he was plucked out and shipped off.

It didn't happen in MSF all too often in that manner. Usually, the ship was brought to the surface, at a space port depending on what home world the pilot or captain originated from and would be relieved with pomp and glorious circumstances including family members brought in to witness and enjoy the event.

Quite often pilots and captains went through magnificent change of command ceremonies at the end of their careers, however in the case of Kwongab it was for promotion, plus he had spent a much longer than usual time aboard as pilot, almost unprecedented, but his longevity as S-1 pilot was due to the fact he headed the Andromeda Mission.

VOICEOVER

Crew members didn't know Commander Monachi's history quickly learned it when they went to the ship's PNN information system on their data terminals and made an inquiry about Commander Monachi's MSF history.

Commander Monachi was the longest assigned Co-pilot in Mergenky history. She was also the highest decorated Co-pilot for her involvement in the Jeeapa war aboard Mergenky Scout S-1, and her role as Co-pilot for the entire Andromeda Mission.

Monachi's persona was uncanny.

The crew felt in a short period of time she knew everything about them and the Mergenky Scout S-4. It was if she had some sort of photographic memory.

Monachi seemed to be able to sense their moods and always say the right things one expected or hoped she would say in the manner at which she did.

Of course, none of the Crew knew Monachi had neural expansion telepathic ability.

Also, despite the fact Monachi had given natural childbirth to her two children, she still looked amazingly young for her age.

Having a close friend like Dr. Kara was quite a blessing since Dr. Kara was an expert on longevity and had special formulas and techniques to extend people's lives such as her mate Vance, but she also had a complete understanding of the control of hormones to delay all the aging enzymes and replenish natural testosterone in men and estrogen for women.

Monachi had high levels of testosterone developed in her ovaries and estrogen which combined all but stopped her aging hormones. Monachi's only negative side effects were increased desire for sex, which Kwongab increasingly seemed to be avoiding.

Perhaps it was a combination of her hormone levels, her education, her many experiences in the Jeeapa War and the Andromeda expedition, that caused her to give the impression to crew members she was all business and seemed to only need one or two hours sleep a day.

As one crewmember put it:

CREW MEMBER
Commander Monachi issues more orders in a day than
their former pilot Lester did in a week.

It did not take Mergenky Scout MSFS-4 crew members long to figure out they would most likely find Monachi on the Bridge observing and interacting with the crew. As was the case the Scout on station in their patrol area getting ready for the inevitable.

FRĂCTŎNG

VOICE OVER

The Anarchie knew they had to make a compelling demonstration at Frăctŏng to convince the Mergenky that Frăctŏng was the actual target.

The Mergenky focusing on Jeeapa were slightly out of position to prevent the initial Anarchie landings on Frăctŏng.

Several squadrons of Anarchie Landing Craft made it to planet's surface approximately 100 miles east of the domed City of Yŏngbùmián de Chéngshì (pronounced Yong-bu-me-an Da Chung-she) meaning: the city that never sleeps.

Anarchie INTEL had done their homework well studying the Frăctŏngians and knew their disposition well.

If the Anarchie assault force was able to knock out Yŏngbùmián de Chéngshì, all the planet's command and control would be disrupted. This added another dimension to the fighting.

It also gave the lackadaisical leadership on Gwaba the belief this was the invasion which led them to deny General Kahn assets for Jeeapa as they were convinced this was the big event.

While ships on Gwaba were getting urgently repaired and back fitted and readied for sortie, they were leaving and heading off to the new war in almost single file. The need and urgency were far greater than the capacity being demonstrated.

The shape of the ground forces was one notch below pitiful.

The results of this unexpected combat meant MSF space craft were faced with atmospheric air support missions of the caliber and dimensions never anticipated, left only a marginal force in space dealing with the Anarchie assault force.

The Anarchie ground forces had been secretly training and preparing for a decade. All new types of equipment and techniques have been evaluated and tested.

The Mergenky were only able to destroy a paltry few of the landers and the landing for most of the Anarchie, completed mostly unopposed even though Kwongab had given MSF ample warning to get the fleet in position to repel the Anarchie.

The worst part of the feint was Anarchie did such a fantastic job of fooling the Mergenky, it didn't take long to convince Mergenky political rank and file this was the main event.

<u>EXT. CGI. SPACE. ANARCHIE TRANSPORTS APPROACHING THE ALLIANCE PLANET *FRĂCTŎNG*. 15 SECONDS.</u>

<u>*EXT. CGI. FRĂCTŎNG.* ANARCHIE TRANSPORTS LANDING. 15 SECONDS.</u>

When the Anarchie Transports reached planet surface, doors swung open and the *Exoskeletons* carrying large amounts of items egressed quickly out of the huge spacecraft and followed by the *Crawlers*. These Anarchie assets moved swiftly out of the Transports and set up a spearhead formation.

Because of where Anarchie ground forces landed, they did not have to worry so much about Mergenky Alliance Forces blowing bridges to slow them or stop them.

***

Mergenky Alliance Forces deployed a rapid response team approximately 75 miles West of Yŏngbùmián de Chéngshì where they had the benefit of an escarpment that would give them some high ground overlooking the obvious Anarchie line of approach towards Yŏngbùmián de Chéngshì, but also almost sheer cliffs the Anarchie would expend vast energy crossing to flank or knock them out.

The Anarchieborgs developed a false sense of security since the landings were mostly unopposed and most of their equipment arrived unscathed, set up a base camp not far from the landing zone and a first bivouac area after traversing only ten miles.

None of the *Crawlers* or *Exoskeletons* were damaged though a few near misses did cause some consternation of a few Anarchie *Crawlers* riders.

Anarchie Scouts and Raiders preferred to advance on foot. They felt their four-foot-tall Exoskeleton crawlers were more useful in carrying extra food and equipment so they would not have to rely on building a base camp which could be disrupted should the Mergenky recoil and hit them hard.

By the Anarchie landing in the dark made it much more difficult for the Mergenky to deal with the invasion force.

The Anarchie Battleships sent were evenly split with a mixture of older laser technology and new capability thanks to the *Blue Diamonds* that Anarchie Special Forces obtained from Planet Earth.

The twenty Mergenky MSF Cruisers sent to deal with the Anarchie Invasion Force should have been enough to contain the immediate threat. However, the new Anarchie laser optics changed the entire dimension of space battles. Maneuver and tactics suddenly became manifest destiny. The old days of slugfest were not going to work.

Once the enemy was sited the Mergenky went at the Anarchie fleet protecting the transports and the troops on the ground. The area was cordoned off extremely well by the Anarchie.

It did not take long for the MSF Cruiser captains to send warnings to MSF that Anarchie Battleships possessed a more formidable offensive capability.

<u>EXT. CGI. SPACE. FIGHTING BETWEEN ANARCHIE BATTLESHIPS AND MERGENKY CRUISERS. (20 SECONDS)</u>

VOICEOVER
The intensity of fighting quickly focused all attention on Frăctŏng to the point General Kahn was getting requests to send the two Scouts MSFS1 and MSFS4 and Cruiser MSFC-34 to Frăctŏng which he resisted and was starting to take direct criticism from top Mergenky leadership for *not throwing all his eggs in one basket.*

Kwongab, Monachi, and Captain Koasa were all appraised of the Frăctŏng situation, but Kwongab had a sick feeling in his *gut this was a feint, and the real blow was just about to occur.*

VOICE OVER
The only thing that went right for the Mergenky on Frăctŏng was the fact the Anarchie were so overconfident they went into bivouac after traveling only ten miles.

The Anarchie did however send their Scouts and Raiders forward to clear the area head of them but come morning they had to go under camouflage sheets just a few miles short of the first out cropping's of the long escarpment that was quickly getting Mergenky and Alliance buildup.

The Anarchie had the disadvantage of being almost 100 feet below the Mergenky now digging in on top of the escarpment, and air defense batteries at Yŏngbùmián de Chéngshì prevented Anarchie overflights during the day to get a closer look of the disposition of the enemy that waited before them.

The first major ground battle of Frăctŏng was just a little more than 12 hours away. As soon as the sunset, the Anarchie would take down their camouflage and mount up and head due east to an area where the escarpment tapered off where they would have the easiest climb for their Crawlers and Exoskeletons. The Anarchie who had been awake for some hours, many out of fear of dying in space from a Mergenky assault took advantage of this period to catch up on their sleep.

VOICED OVER

The Mergenky did nothing to provoke the Anarchie into battle early as they were naturally reactive and not proactive despite history that called for a change of strategy.

The Mergenky Alliance leadership was faced with the age-old dilemma that just like in the wild animal world species did not change their appearances or mannerisms, nor would Anarchie.

The peace treaty was thus built on a false sense of euphoria which Mergenky believed, that since the Anarchie suffered a terrible defeat at Jeeapa years ago they would not be so aggressive in the future.

Internal Anarchie politics and warlike traits with thousands of years of imperialistic victories were not going to be changed simply by one singularity at the previous Jeeapa War defeat.

The Anarchie to some extent popularized the peace dividend mentality in Gwaba by showing a continuous reduction in arms and military size. When in fact in secret they were secretly doing something altogether different and far cleverer.

Thanks to Anarchie compartmentalization and harsh treatment of defectors and spies, they did a good job of obscuring their buildup and their intentions.

Anarchie diplomats were directed to be aloof and not argumentative and give the persona of cooperation and constructive engagement.

The shocking truth of their real plan of picking up where they left off and the conquest of Jeeapa just was not something the politicians at Quom would ever believe.

Mergenky INTEL did have one ace in their pocket, Captain Esau who warned them of a secret buildup. Unfortunately for Mergenky INTEL they could not take Captain Esau's information to Mergenky leaders without destroying the only real highly placed spy they had who was in position to hit the tripwire in the event the unlikely were to happen.

Mergenky INTEL was thus powerless to mitigate the disaster that now bestowed upon the MSF and in particular the Frăctŏngians if they could not stop the major force now just 90 miles from the Frăctŏngians capital city in Yŏngbùmián de Chéngshì, the nerve center of their Alliance forces.

VOICEOVER

A spy who wants to be remembered and not give his life away for something unimportant waits for the moment such as like the Anarchie invasion fleet departure to do that one remarkable act that would put him in the history books to be remembered.

Without Captain Esau's earlier warning, its likely both Yŏngbùmián de Chéngshì and Jeeapa would have been caught flat footed and taken out which would have accelerated the rate to which the Mergenky civilization would have crumbled.

Richard Sorge and Hotsumi Ozaki who paid for their success in spying with their lives during Earth's WW2 and were of that mold providing the most important

INTEL during the war, advising Stalin Japan had no intentions of attacking Russia which allowed Stalin to move 18 Divisions from Eastern Russia to Moscow to save it.

Americans had Morris Childs in the Kremlin for 29 years until 1982.

The Mergenky had Captain Esau.

Anarchie planners estimated that if they wiped out Gwaba's air defense, it would only take one Anarchie Battleship just one hour to annihilate their capital Quom. Based on past practices, the Anarchie were heartless and brutal and often employed a *Clausewitz like* "total war" and wiping out a society to put fear in the hearts and minds of future opponents.

Because of the humiliation the Mergenky handed the Anarchie at Jeeapa years prior, any Mergenky military commanders knew the Anarchie would give them no quarter. It would be wholesale slaughter unlike anything the Mergenky had ever witnessed.

Wise military commanders such as General Kahn knew they should have seriously damaged the Anarchie 20 years earlier to prevent this day, despite the liberals in charge of the government's attitudes. But now it was too late, and it would be touch and go as far as survival was concerned.

General Kahn had some INTEL that still gave indications that Jeeapa was the Anarchie ultimate target, and they would be arriving soon.

When pleas were sent out from Quom to strip the five-mile oval of troops to reposition them to Frăctŏng, they did not affect General Kahn's planning and his philosophy and viewpoint *that he was sitting at the epicenter of the upcoming second battle of Jeeapa.*

<u>INT. DAY. JEEAPA FIVE MILE OVAL UNDERGROUND COMMAND CENTER</u>

MSF HEADQUARTERS GWABA
(Tangramized Message)
General Kahn you have been summoned back to
Gwaba to meet with the Mergenky Leader.

General Kahn temporarily ignored the summons.

VOICEOVER
General Kahn knew he had to stay until the fighting started on Jeeapa because he didn't have confidence that General Zŭzhī Bùliáng believed that Jeeapa was

a target, nor would it be struck.

General Kahn realized however once the battle began, General Zŭzhī Bùliáng would conduct himself appropriately since his own life would be in jeopardy.

General Kahn would however prefer to stay on Jeeapa to see the battle through and perish, if necessary, should they lose.

Reports received in the five-mile oval were a little sketchy at first, but it didn't take long for General Kahn to realize the oncoming disaster that was now revealed in the incoming streaming reports.

Just about any other military commander would have succumbed to the political pressure, and abandoned Jeeapa and thrown all their eggs into one basket on Frăctŏng, leaving a wide-open corridor to Jeeapa.

The most disturbing news the past two hours was the report:

GENERAL KAHN'S CHIEF OF STAFF
We lost of four Cruisers with the loss of all crew members when the ships were destroyed in space near Frăctŏng.

GENERAL KAHN
Do we have any video recordings of the event?

GENERAL KAHN'S CHIEF OF STAFF
Yes, General.

GENERAL KAHN
I want to see what happened during that battle. PNN show me footage of the loss of the four cruisers.

<u>EXT. CGI. SPACE. FRĂCTŎNG SPACE BATTLES. (30 SECONDS DURING FOLLOWING VOICEOVER)..</u>

Music during this battle segment:

[https://www.youtube.com/watch?v=_ydKh38fN0U]

KURT ATTERBERG - SYMPHONY NO.8 IN E-MINOR, OP.48 STARTING AT 4:30 MARK. *With pyrotechnics overlays.*

VOICEOVER

Thanks to the elaborate video recording ability of PNN on Cruisers and Scouts, instantaneous space battle results sent to General Kahn and his INTEL analysts on Jeeapa within minutes of the actual action.

General Kahn was essentially looking at gun camera video and status reports these cruisers sent off as their hulls were breached and serious damage resulted in eventual loss of the ships.

The Mergenky Cruisers being damaged recorded various views of the actual combat ongoing as well as all the surviving ships that might have been close or at a safe distance.

Intelligence experts doing the replay just moments after the events quickly tallied up the score card.

This incredible space battle seemed like a high-tech supernatural phenomenon, that such a space battle could elicit.

The Mergenky who were not expected to show human emotion could not completely avoid it as the horrific detail exhibited the supreme sacrifice these four cruisers made.

<u>EXT. CGI. SPACE. FRĂCTŎNG SPACE BATTLES FLEET'S CONVEREGING HUNDRDS OF LASERS ATTACKING SIMULTANEOUSLY. 30 SECONDS</u>

<u>MUSIC DURING THIS BATTLE SEGMENT:</u>

[<u>https://www.youtube.com/watch?v=_ydKh38fN0U</u>]

KURT ATTERBERG - SYMPHONY NO.8 IN E-MINOR, OP.48 STARTING AT 21:48 MARK *With pyrotechnics overlays.*

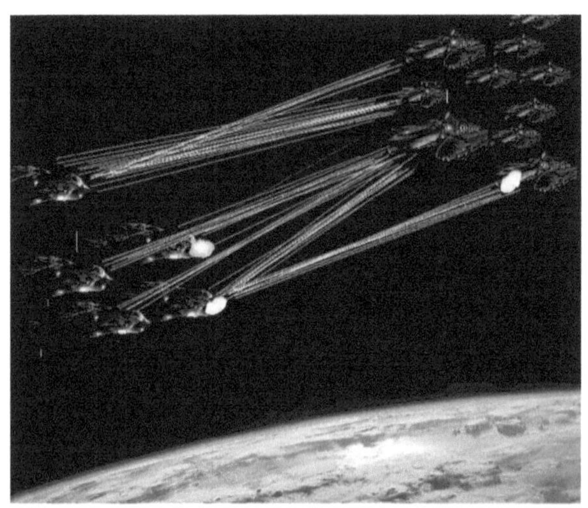

VOICE OVER

Watching the two fleets converge on the replay video created a sensation that any onlooker observing would have feeling of extraordinary thoughts as the Anarchie and Mergenky ships lit each other up with those multiple simultaneous intense laser strikes zipping back and forth.

The entire sides of ships took on a glaring bright surface, as multiple lasers hit home their lethal carnage.

As the sides of the ships cooked away and clouds of materials jettisoned out due to the pressure difference between the internal hull pressures and the vacuum of space, the highly ionized particles further energized by the intense laser energy gave off a shimmering that lasted briefly before the ship succumbed to its hemorrhages.

The first Mergenky Cruiser blew into a cloud of sparkling debris and gasses and a spontaneous super bright flash as the instantaneous energy release of the AMRT contents fully enveloped in a witch's brew of gases created by the plasma like energy release.

The antimatter sudden contact with materials not only of dissimilar materials but of chemical imbalances created a horrendous explosive that quickly exemplified the potential of these new Anarchie lasers.

The Anarchie Battleships were too many and too well positioned for the Mergenky to get at the Anarchie Transports.

In the ensuing laser exchanges that showcased the new Anarchie laser capability of the blue diamonds, made possible a gripping image that the analysts could not avoid developing some type of psychophysical responses.

Replay Video recorded from some of the nearby ships showed the two formations approaching. They were almost out of visual sight when the attacks began as the closure rate was extremely swift.

The Mergenky were terribly outgunned, and it was obvious they would be able to make one pass at the Anarchie then be forced to maneuver to safety of the space defenses near Yǒngbùmián de Chéngshì providing some top cover to the domed city as well as receiving some protection from the surface to air weapons such as kinetic weapons, phased array lasers, and even chemical rockets.

General Kahn's analyst doing the replay of the two fleets converging in the initial salvos noted:

MERGENKY MSF ANALYST
At any given moment 3,000 or more lasers could be seen developing flashes of light.

INTEL ANALYST
This light show was far greater than the largest thunderstorm lightning strikes anyone had ever witnessed, with an equal amount of power and destructive potential.

MERGENKY MSF ANALYST
The new Anarchie lasers are a game changer and after

just one pass through the Anarchie formations, the surviving Mergenky Cruisers knew it was fruitless to press home any further attack with the Anarchie arriving with a much more superior force.

GENERAL KAHN

This is a rate of attrition we cannot tolerate for long, especially if we want a force available for the expected major Jeeapa attack.

MERGENKY MSF ANALYST

That's right General Kahn. Based on the receipt of Captain Esau's last message, that is most likely 12 to 24 hours away.

INTEL ANALYST

Captain Esau indicated he would not be around to send any further communications as he feared Anarchie INTEL was close on his heels.

GENERAL KAHN

A maneuver to a defensive posture over the dome at Yǒngbùmián de Chéngshì, is now MSF's only recourse.

MERGENKY MSF ANALYST

Any thought of preventing the Anarchie landing and invasion is quickly extinguished by the obvious overwhelming force the Anarchie deployed.

***

THE JEEAPA SCREEN

INT. SPACE SCOUT MSFS-1. CONTROL ROOM.

VOICE OVER

Kwongab became rather amused when he discovered Monachi was the pilot on S-4. But knowing the S-4 was right on the track for Anarchie ships heading for Frǎctǒng did not please him.

Because of Kwongab's neural expansion ability as well as Monachi having the same implants, their lives were quite a bit different than any other couples. Their experiences together on the Andromeda Mission created a unique bond.

Barely surviving the evil perpetrated by the Artificial Intelligence personality Martha created a unique situation never experienced before in Mergenky history.

Monachi and Kwongab's ability to secretly communicate via neural expansion telepathic methods may have been the only contributing factor to their survival.

Kwongab knew that if something happened to Monachi, he would be lost. His world now evolved around Monachi and those unique bonds they exhibited.

Kwongab also would be similarly missed by Monachi if something happened to him. As such, Kwongab discovered in his own soul searching the impact he would have on Monachi if he didn't return.

There were three major sectors for the small fledgling force that's sole roll was early warning and possibly a slight delay so that Jeeapa could scramble forces. The two Scouts were in sectors between the Anarchie Empire and Jeeapa.

The distance was far enough away to give ample warning but to also be able to reach safety of Jeeapa's defenses in the event they were chased by the Anarchie fleet. The Cruiser MSFC-34 essentially had an operating area that was an offset cube surrounding the planet that reached out to the Scout MSFS-1 and MSFS-4 op-areas.

<u>EXT. CGI. SPACE. MSFC-34 PATROLLING SHOWING JEEAPA IN THE BACKGROUND. 15 SECONDS</u>

The patrolling now intensified with the recent activity of the Anarchie fleet passing by on the way to Frăctŏng but also warning from Jeeapa that based on INTEL expect the Anarchie any moment.

<u>INT. SPACE. MERGENKY SCOUT MSFS-1 CONTROL ROOM</u>

Just like Monachi on Scout MSFS-4, Kwongab was constantly on the bridge of MSFS-1 realizing the action could start any moment. In Kwongab's past probing of Commander Gōngniúgŏu left him no doubt, that due to the significance of this situation, Commander Gōngniúgǒu's lack of experience might prove to be an impediment towards successful conduct of the mission.

VOICEOVERE (KWONGAB)
THOUGHT

Had Commander Gōngniúgǒu a longer break-in-period and a couple combat patrols under his belt, things might be different.

In a while Lt. Commander Lóngrén co-pilot/navigator of S-1, arrived at the Scout's Control room/Bridge.

LT. COMMANDER LÓNGRÉN

Commander Gōngniúgǒu, why don't you take a break, you have been up quite a while.

VOICEOVER

At first Gōngniúgǒu was a little reluctant to leave the bridge because of the specter of possible immediate action.

However, Kwongab thought it might be best for him and the crew if Gōngniúgǒu was sleeping in his gel container when hostilities arose so that everyone knew who was in charge and there were no delays associated with countering orders.

Kwongab applied the appropriate level of neural expansion telepathic mind thought insertions to Gōngniúgǒu which made him feel tired and sleepy enough to agree to the down time. In just a few moments, Gōngniúgǒu was sound asleep in his gel container.

Kwongab wasted little time probing and analyzing Lt. Commander Lóngrén co-pilot/navigator of Mergenky Scout MSFS-1. Lt. Commander Lóngrén had a different persona and was psychologically better prepared to be a pilot. It only took a few minutes for Kwongab to assess whether he could work well with Lt. Commander Lóngrén.

About an hour after Gōngniúgǒu left the bridge, PNN with Martha's voice reported:

MARTHA

Detecting energy levels in the direction of the Anarchie home worlds.

KWONGAB
This is probably the invasion force.

LT. COMMANDER LÓNGRÉN
Commander Kwongab, will we send a messenger
buoy again?

KWONGAB
Delaying sending Jeeapa a warning to use a messenger
buoy might be unsatisfactory.

LT. COMMANDER LÓNGRÉN
Are we going to send a SITREP now?

KWONGAB
Yes, because of the developing scenario on Frăctŏng
where the MSF had their hands full, as much advance
notice given to Jeeapa possible would be very helpful.

LT. COMMANDER LÓNGRÉN
How far away do you think they are?

KWONGAB
I believe in an hour they will be close enough to get
signal strengths off their sensors that might be within
detection ranges. PNN send this information to MSF
and copy S-4 and MSFC-34.

Within the span of a minute Martha's voice reported:

MARTHA (PNN)
Commander Kwongab, Jeeapa MSF Command,
MSFS-4 and MSFC-34 have acknowledged receipt of
your report.

Kwongab stated the obvious they collectively felt.

KWONGAB
Now it's just wait and see time to see how it all unfolds.

***

<u>INT. DAY. JEEAPA *FIVE MILE OVAL* COMMAND CENTER.</u>

GENERAL KAHN
Kwongab's report is exactly what I expected

GENERAL ZŬZHĪ BÙLIÁNG
The timing matched the elapsed time estimated after
Captain Esau's last report.

GENERAL KAHN
The ground war on Frăctŏng is just now starting. The
coordination and timing the Anarchie established was
nearly perfect.

GENERAL ZŬZHĪ BÙLIÁNG
The Feint to Frăctŏng would have worked with almost
any other leader than you, General Kahn.

The political heat from Gwaba was rising to the point the leadership was just about to
accuse General Kahn of insubordination when they contacted him at this very moment.

MERGENKY LEADER
General Kahn, why have you not complied with my
order to return to Gwaba immediately?

General Kahn responded to their threats with a shocking update to what was now
transpiring.

GENERAL KAHN
Sir, I warned you this was just a Feint on Frăctŏng.
I have new Intel showing the growing picture that
Jeeapa remains the Anarchie primary target.

The Mergenky Leader calling via neutrino high speed communications asked in a very
terse manner.

MERGENKY LEADER
And just what does that mean General Kahn?

GENERAL KAHN
It means that within 12 to 24 hours we expect to see
Anarchie ground forces landing on Jeeapa, and we do
not have the forces here to repel them if you keep all
the arriving forces heading to Frăctŏng is exactly what
the Anarchie planners want you to do.

There was sudden silence on the long-range communications that worked off neutrino's and only had a 10 second dead time between transmission and delivery due to the distance between the two planets.

Just like Jeeapa 20 years prior, the current leadership now faced political uncertainty because the MSF could claim they interfered with the conduct of business which put Jeeapa in peril.

Suddenly MSF Quom Headquarters at Mergenky Home planet Gwaba was now having a huge face-saving stance. They screwed up by allowing the politicians to get to their commander, General Kahn, soon they would pay the political price as well.

***

<u>INT. SPACE. MSFS-1 CONTROL ROOM.</u>

KWONGAB

We really cannot do much but wait until the Anarchie fleet closes allowing positive identity and disposition of elements.

LT. COMMANDER LÓNGRÉN

The energy readings of ion fields created by large transports moving through space at rapid speeds appears no different than shining a flashlight on a dark night can be seen at quite a distance if you have the right sensors such as our Mergenky Scout possesses.

KWONGAB

Mergenky Scout S-4 would be in a direct path if these Anarchie ships were heading towards Frăctŏng, but since they were most likely pointing Jeeapa, they are probably in a safe position.

LT. COMMANDER LÓNGRÉN

MSFC-34 isn't so lucky, they will be forced to engage lead elements of the Anarchie commencing their combat role almost immediately.

***

<u>EXT. DAY. FRĂCTŎNG ANARCHIE NEAR THE ESCARPMENT</u>

VOICE OVER

The ground war on Frăctŏng was not evolving the way the Anarchie planned. The only smart move the Mergenky made was to place their defenses on the 100-foot-high escarpment. This was to play a pivotal role in the battle as it unfolded.

As darkness arrived the Anarchie started moving towards the escarpment. Mergenky concealment was nothing short of superb. Portashields were in place and laser batteries were placed all over the escarpment that ran for at least 10 miles.

The Anarchie had chosen a passage right through the middle of the escarpment following a ravine into a gradual climb up to higher elevation.

If Anarchie Ground Forces made it through this choke point, they could easily get into the Mergenky rear which would make Mergenky forces holding the escarpment no longer feasible.

The Mergenky and Alliance Ground Forces were constantly wanting to know when their reserves were going to show up.

When their commanders were advised there would be none, they were needed elsewhere, that changed everything. Force Protection was now not only essential, but mandatory.

The Mergenky and Alliance Ground Forces could not allow their men to get slaughtered like usual while waiting for reinforcements since none would be coming.

Therefore, Mergenky and Frăctŏng Alliance leaders had to make less risky or bold moves. Every move they made had to be done with an element of force protection in it.

The Mergenky Alliance could defend, hold, and delay the enemy seizing the position, but they could not waste their force defending a position they would eventually lose.

In essence Mergenky and Alliance Ground Forces immediately drifted into a guerilla warfare scheme except for the initial stand at the escarpment which was the only defensible ground they could hold for a while.

The Anarchie were emboldened by developing new technology over the past 20 years, but even though Mergenky were enjoying the peace dividend and not spending huge outlays on defense spending, they at least were not stagnating.

The Mergenky MSF did make new developments, though on a modest scale. These were targeted investments into research and development based on lessons learned.

In the past Jeeapa war, taking the night away from the Anarchie was critical. Without the night, the Anarchieborgs were severely handicapped.

Drones were used in the first Jeeapa War, but they were short in numbers and other plans had been put into effect which the Anarchie overcame quickly.

MSF recently designed cheap drones that lit up an area with ultra-violet light. The ground forces had night vision goggles that worked off the same wavelengths the drones would light up the area.

The Anarchie for the most part had to travel 10 miles over wide-open exposed ground to get to the escarpment and the ravine they would crawl up. Out in the middle of those 10 miles was a well-designed Mergenky Alliance kill zone optically sighted for targeting.

The numerous Crawlers looked like long snakes stretched out. The large Exoskeletons were sitting duck targets.

The false sense of security was exemplified by the overzealous Anarchie who didn't realize they would not be fired upon in this set piece battle until the majority of Anarchie troops were five miles away from the escarpment, out in the open with little defense structures to hide behind.

Mergenky portashields were the only thing going well for the Alliance. As soon as the Mergenky Alliance commander was satisfied the majority of the Anarchie were in the kill zone he issued the command to attack.

EXT. CGI. NIGHT. FRĂCTŎNG ESCARPMENT SET PIECE GROUND LASER BATTLE

MUSIC FOR THIS SEGMENT:

https://www.youtube.com/watch?v=vLNLvcBmoqo

Edward Elgar - Enigma Variations (Warsaw Philharmonic Orchestra, Jacek Kaspszyk) at the 2:22 mark. With pyrotechnic overlays.

The Anarchie reached the set piece kill near the Frăctŏng Escarpment kill zone around midnight.

By stiff orders from Mergenky Alliance officers, no militia men or Mergenky fired a shot at the Anarchie even though some of them thought they had a good shot.

None of the shooting started until the new lighting drones suddenly appeared. They were cheap gadgets, built in large numbers. Essentially, they were flashlights with wings and propulsion. They turned night into daylight. Within 10 seconds of drone battlefield lighting, orders were given:

MERGENKY TACTICAL COMMUNICATIONS
Commence firing.

Suddenly laser hell and some projectiles made their mark, as the ground erupted around the Anarchieborgs. The crawlers had good laser reflectors unless the laser targeted the joints between the carts which at this angle were hard to hit.

There were not many Anarchieborgs marching as most of them were in the 4-foot-tall *Crawler Exoskeletons* riding to the deployment area. Up until that moment the Anarchie had little concern for their forces and felt they could simply plow their way through the escarpment once they got to the ravine.

Everything was going as planned and the Anarchie knew the anti-air laser batteries mounted on the Exoskeletons would take care of any drone lighting, just like they did in the Jeeapa campaign. Likewise, any Mergenky aircraft flying overhead to drop flares would be quickly disposed of.

The goal of the Anarchie invasion force was not planetary conquest, however standard protocol was that if they found the planet a pushover and it could be easily defended by the Anarchie Invasion Force once taken, they would then add it to their portfolio.

The Invasion Force Commander, General Borktar did not inform his superiors, but he planned on adding Frăctŏng to the Anarchie portfolio and he would proclaim himself the new Governor of Frăctŏng. The thought of having his way with multiple green skinned female humanoids seemed to be another motivating factor.

General Borktar was riding in his command Exoskeleton surveying ground operations. This Exoskeleton was well armored and did not carry much other than a defensive laser, but it had a complete battleground electronics and display suite where he could watch all the troops who were wearing advanced body armor with built in processors for communications and health checks.

The body armor was also designed to protect them from laser strikes, and mild shock and shrapnel strikes. But a well-placed projectile wasn't going to be stopped.

The Frăctŏng Militia was not as advanced as the normal Mergenky ground forces which were heavily biased towards laser batteries. 90% of the ground forces facing the Anarchie were Frăctŏng Militia. As such they were about 50% artillery and old fashion ground warfare techniques.

The more modern Mergenky laser equipped ground forces were great for Jeeapa 20 years prior, but this new Anarchie Army applied lessons learned and made their troops more residual against laser attacks. The failure in Anarchie planning was to realize how backwards the Frăctŏngians would be.

The Defense Stand at the Escarpment east of Yŏngbùmián de Chéngshì was a blend of ancient and futuristic techniques. As more and more Mergenky arrived to fill in the gaps along the top of the escarpment they were equipped with the more modern but quickly proved to be a lesser effective capability.

The ancient Frăctŏngian equipment would end the day as the preferred hardware on the battlefield except for the new cheaply made *lighting drones* that were in abundance and arriving in increasing numbers as more Mergenky arrived at the battlefield.

EXT. CGI. NIGHT. ANARCHIE FIGHTER BOMBER DEPLOYMENTS 20 SECONDS.

The Mergenky defenders knew the Anarchie would send in close ground support fighter bombers.

From the bellies of the Anarchie Battleships came swarms of tactical fighter bomber single seater craft came pouring down out of the sky. The Mergenky risked a couple Cruisers bringing them into the atmosphere where they could quickly become sitting ducks, but the only way they could deal with the expected Anarchie fighter bomber swarms was with directed laser attack to supplement the air defense lasers since Yǒngbùmián de Chéngshì air defense batteries were beyond the horizon and could not effectively target them.

The Anarchie expected stiff resistance from the escarpment area but knew their fighter bombers would deal a harsh blow to those gunners.

The plan was bullet proof until it failed.

The one aspect of this battle the Anarchie never considered was the two Mergenky Cruisers who remained cloaked until the battle started and unleased their deadly lasers on the fighter bombers who were too far away to effectively attack the Cruisers or have a cohesive plan since such a bold move on the part of the Mergenky was never considered a possibility.

The tactical surprise of the Cruisers was immediately effective as they shot down the Anarchie fighter bombers just like shooting ducks in a barrel.

The Mergenky shooters up on the escarpment were unmolested in any way and had a 100-foot height advantage with all the benefits of visibility and protection from 20 to 50-ton boulders strewn around the area.

It didn't take long for General Borktar to realize he had stepped into a set piece trap blunder and immediately ordered:

GENERAL BORKTAR
TACTICAL COMS

All forces to reverse course and move out to new
assembly area 10 miles to the West of your current
position.

EXT. NIGHT FRĂCTŎNG ANARCHIE RAIDERS AND SCOUTS REGIMENT

This night was a loss for the Anarchie, but they didn't take too severe several casualties. The Anarchie Raiders and Scouts did some penetration and were left in place in concealment until new planning determined their next move.

One thing that General Borktar knew the Mergenky didn't know was by the next evening, there would be no more reserves brought into Frăctŏng as the Jeeapa campaign would be well on its way.

General Borktar had already achieved his main purpose. He had many Mergenky ground forces, and a Mergenky Cruiser Squadron tied down on Frăctŏng. They would not be available to help Jeeapa which was really their real target.

General Borktar also knew the following night the Cruisers would be there to stop any further launch of the fighter bombers. That also could be mitigated as he had no qualms about sending in a couple Anarchie Battleships into the Atmosphere and taking on the Mergenky Cruisers firsthand.

General Borktar knew Anarchie Battleships could not get too close to Yŏngbùmián de Chéngshì because their ample air defense systems would put the battleships at great risk, but since they were 75 miles away, if they attacked from the West, they would remain below the horizon making Yŏngbùmián de Chéngshì's air defenses ineffective.

There would also be an extra leading Anarchie laser battalions sent forward to deal with the drones. The Anarchie would not have their forces bunched up in a kill zone, thus the set piece plan for the Mergenky wasn't going to work the next time.

DAY. EXT. FRĂCTŎNG ESCARPMENT MERGENKY ALLIANCE MAKING PREPARATIONS.

The Mergenky Alliance understood they might not be able to hold back the Anarchie the following night and they would adjust their tactics. Hence a well-organized withdrawal was planned. Vast number of people in Yŏngbùmián de Chéngshì were conscripted as laborers and those willing to shoot a gun were put in the militia.

The laborers were trucked out to an area about 10 miles East of the escarpment in a slightly hilly area that had some tree cover. Here these laborers started building new defensive positions.

The Militias and the Mergenky fighters would not stand and fight to the last man, like the reptilian Anarchie would.

Force protection was paramount because they knew there would be no reserves coming. Sandbags were filled with dirt and portashields which were in ample supply were laid out on top of bunkers built beside trees and other concealment. The Anarchie would find going through the forested area would be just as treacherous as assaulting the escarpment.

The plan was that as soon as areas along the escarpment were no longer defensible, the troops would fall back and make a stand at this next defensive position. Long before the next battle commenced the second defense positions were completed and inspected by the Mergenky Force Commander for the Yŏngbùmián de Chéngshì defenses, General Tiĕquán (pronounced Tie-Kwon).

GENERAL TIĚQUÁN
The Frăctŏng workers poured their hearts into this construction. Their work is as good as a typical Mergenky Engineering battalion.

YŎNGBÙMIÁN DE CHÉNGSHÌ
MAYOR GĀOSHĀN
The people of Yŏngbùmián de Chéngshì are well versed on Anarchie atrocities. They know the brutal treatment they will receive if the Anarchie enter the city.

GENERAL TIĚQUÁN
Load up the workers we are moving to the next defenses we need built.

The third defensive ring designed to support force protection as well as delay the Anarchie as long as possible was another 10 miles further East closer towards Yŏngbùmián de Chéngshì.

Again, the workers went right to work. Some were exhausted already but you would not know it. Many realized it would be their own sons and daughters in these fox holes and trenches later in the day or tomorrow. They were built with the love and affection they had for their children and hoping it would in some way save their lives.

Thanks to the near proximity of the city, and power and water and *Plastiment* available, Spactron 300 rebar enforced bunkers and firing positions protected by portashields were quickly constructed. *Plastiment* a hybrid construction material unique to Frăctŏng had 33% plastics that had a chemical reaction with a unique Frăctŏng cement creating a construction material about 100 times stronger than cement.

With power tools the digging was about 1000 times quicker and the strength the people had left in them was more than sufficient to complete the task which went ongoing through the next battle. These defenses would be more than sufficient once the battle lines approached them.

The following evening the battle for Yŏngbùmián de Chéngshì unfolded entirely different. The Mergenky knowing they would not be able to hold these defender's positions, half of the troops were taken away and relocated to the next defensive positions. They were the rear guard and would provide the forces in front of them safe evacuation routes to the next defensive positions.

Knowing the Battleships would intervene, MSF decided it would be prudent not to send the Cruisers into the atmosphere and instead were sent after the transports which still contained 1/3 of all the troops and supplies yet to be delivered to the planet's surface. By strangling the Anarchie in space they would have an impact on reserves for the Anarchie ground forces at Yǒngbùmián de Chéngshì.

The tactic turned out brilliant.

Just as the Anarchie Battleships were poised to launch their next swarm of fighter bombers that could peel back the escarpment force much quicker, they were suddenly called back to formation as the transports were in panic and scattering.

The space battle that everyone assumed would eventually gather momentum was now in full measure.

The Mergenky were undermanned compared to the Anarchie who had a well-protected invasion fleet. As such the Mergenky had no option but to operate as a wolf pack and go after individual transport with overwhelming force.

The Anarchie could not abandon the fleet for the sake of a single troop transport.

The Mergenky found the Anarchie Achilles heel: *One transport at a time.*

Even though it would not mean tremendous collateral damage it provided two ingredients to the Jeeapa defense.

First: Any transports destroyed on Frǎctǒng would not be available to ferry Anarchie forces fighting on Yǒngbùmián de Chéngshì to Jeeapa. Secondly, if enough transports were damaged, it would become increasingly hard for the Anarchie to extract the forces landed, hence they would eventually wither at the vine and the master plan of using them as a diversion then extracting them to be used in the Jeeapa invasion would fall apart.

EXT. CGI. SPACE. ANARCHIE BATTLESHIPS ENTEREING THE ATMOSPHERE. 15 SECONDS.

Just as the Anarchie Battleships entered the atmosphere and were near leveling off and slowing from supersonic speeds to deploy the fighter bombers, the Transport's distress calls immediately caused them to alter their courses.

Anarchie Battleships went into a high G turn and accelerated out of the atmosphere back to the fleet. Unfortunately, they were already too far out of position to stop the Mergenky wolf pack hit and run tactic.

No less than Eight Mergenky Cruisers came in for the lone Transport attack. Six of the Mergenky Cruisers were to take on Anarchie Battleships moving in position to defend all the transports.

It never occurred to Anarchie that Mergenky strategists would apply such a large force just for one transport. As a result, the density of defense for a single transport was one possibly two battleships available to directly intervene on this novel singularity type of attack.

<u>EXT. CGI. SPACE. SPACE BATTLE 60 SECONDS.</u>

Music for this section:

[https://www.youtube.com/watch?v=vLNLvcBmoqo]

Edward Elgar - Enigma Variations (Warsaw Philharmonic Orchestra, Jacek Kaspszyk) at the 17:12 mark. With pyrotechnic overlays.

The first attack prompted just one battleship towards the target of interest because the assumption was, the Mergenky would attempt to attack numerous Transport vessels which would normally be the standard tactic for a well provisioned fleet.

There was just barely enough separation in space and time for the plan to work. Six of the Cruisers attacked the lone battleship protecting a single Transport selected for attack, and the other two Cruisers hit that Anarchie Transport. That was all the time the Mergenky Cruisers had before they had to bug out or face the onslaught of a dozen Battleships with much more combined fire power.

At the appropriate distance the first Cruiser locked on the Battleship commenced a laser attack. The sharp blue traces of the large laser struck areas of the battleship that were heavily armored and had laser reflective surfaces, though certain cracks and protrusions were not immune from laser damage.

The return fire was equally devastating, but the supreme sacrifice the first MSF Cruiser made opened an opportunity for the second Cruiser to get into firing position and start hammering the Battleship with additional fire. Four more MSF Cruisers were lining up for similar attacks while 2 others went directly at the transport.

The transports were double the size of the Anarchie Battleships. They had their own self defense systems and had some lethality to them as well. But being twice the size of an Anarchie Battleship also made them a much larger target which allowed Mergenky Cruisers to more effectively fire while evading return fire.

The Mergenky had no way of knowing the contents of the transport they were shooting at. This one just recently arrived was sent in last for its safety because it carried some of the most precious cargo, resupply of food and armaments for the ground forces.

The transport was full of Exoskeleton's preloaded with the material and when the ground forces were able to clear out a good landing zone, it would enter the atmosphere and land directly on the planet where the exoskeletons could simply crawl off the transport and go directly to a supply dump set up.

The other transports would not have been such a catastrophe or as easy to destroy, but a lucky shot that penetrated the hull happened to hit one of the exoskeletons carrying engineering supplies including explosives needed to blast out defense structures or portions of the dome which would allow fighter bombers to enter and more quickly force the Frăctŏngians to capitulate.

Simultaneously the transport blew a gaping hole in the port side as those explosives detonated by the intense heat of the laser.

Huge amounts of debris and cargo were ejected out of the transport making flying in this area hazardous which the following Cruisers maneuvered to avoid.

The damage caused by the explosion also severed electrical power from the power plant to the forward part of the ship. Hence all electronics in the control room and the self-defense equipment went dead. There was a rapid decompression of the hull, and any Anarchie still alive at the time would soon die from asphyxiation if they did not get into an emergency space suit quick.

Finding the storage for those suits was problematic since the lights were off and the emergency lighting was not coming on because its power lines were also cut by more explosions as Mergenky lasers systematically cut open the ship and triggered more explosions. The dying ship did not take much longer to go as fuel tanks were detonated by engineers' explosives. The ship then blew up into a sparkling cloud of debris.

The first MSF Cruiser attacking the Battleship soon succumbed to a tremendous explosion as Anarchie lasers cut through the hull and sliced open The Antimatter Magnetic Resonator Transformer compartment.

The reptilian gunners on the Anarchie ship were immediately joyous of their combat victory and were in the process of cutting open Cruiser number two when Cruisers three and four were hammering away and opening portions of the battleship. Their weakest point was the bottom of the Battleship where they launched fighter bombers for direct ground support.

Mergenky Cruiser number one and two used in the attack were sacrificial lambs distracting Anarchie so that Cruiser number three and four could hit the bottom with concentrated fire power. The assumption was fighter bombers were in the Anarchie hanger Bay and if they could penetrate the hull, they might set off secondary explosions with the Anarchie Fighter Bombers.

The Anarchie Battleship Captain knew he was in trouble when the Executive Officer reported:

ANARCHIE BATTLESHIP XO
Captain, we have just received a warning of rapid
depressurization of the Hanger Bay!

The Mergenky Cruisers three and four had enough Time on Target (TOT) to blast away hanger Bay hatch exposing the entire hanger Bay which the lasers soon struck igniting tremendous explosions.

Just like the transport moments prior, the explosion ripped through the Anarchie battleship, and a tremendous shock wave hit the U115 reactor which allowed materials to come in direct contact with the U115 fuel rods that unleashed huge amounts of energy blowing the ship into millions of sparkling debris. One of the Cruisers then succumbed to its tremendous damage, and the others withdrew.

On one hand trading two Cruisers for a battleship and a transport might seem slightly in the favor of the Mergenky, but not knowing the critical material they took out by the lucky choosing of that specific transport, would have a huge impact in the days to follow.

Reports went out to MSF and General Kahn who was anxiously awaiting the onslaught on Jeeapa.

***

ANARCHIE FLEET ESTIMATES

<u>EXT. SPACE. MERGENKY SCOUT MSFS-1 CONTROL ROOM/BRIDGE.</u>

The tension was mounting but Kwongab was happy knowing Gōngniúgǒu was sound asleep in his gel tube. Kwongab didn't have any intentions of attacking the oncoming Anarchie fleet, but he did want to get a good disposition of it to report to MSF.

As the ships started arriving in scanner range PNN reported:

MARTHA (PNN)
The signal strength emanated out of the Anarchie
radiators are registering around 2.0 and is slowly
increasing.

Suddenly the surveillance holograph started painting the radiators in different colors. One word would describe what Kwongab witnessed: *A blizzard of signals.*

Recalling his early Jeeapa days 20 years prior, Kwongab immediately communicated to Monachi:

COMMANDER KWONGAB
MSFS-4 I need you to distract the Anarchie so I can
get in and get a closer view to report the Anarchie
Fleet disposition.

Kwongab knew Monachi remembered how Vicki distracted the Anarchie to preserve
Vance's life, and had no doubt she would do similar measures, but hoped she did not
get herself killed in the process.

INT. SPACE. MERGENKY SCOUT S-4 CONTROL ROOM/BRIDGE.

Aboard Mergenky Scout MSFS-4, Monachi took manual control of the Scout. She
loved flying in manual control and knew PNN would not know how to do what she
would be doing in a short while.

Monachi then sped up to a very high speed she knew the Scout could do which also left
behind a large ion wake the Anarchie would soon see on their scanners. Predictably
the number of radiators lit up as the Anarchie fleet was now tracking Mergenky Scout
MSFS-4 and maneuvering to box her in for a kill shot.

Anarchie AI had a good record of Mergenky PNN algorithms thanks to three3 spies who
had been captured and subsequently executed by the Mergenky. Anarchie Battleships
would be well poised to box in and destroy MSFS-4 with the stolen algorithm data.
But the Anarchie had no provision for Mergenky manual flight control, nor did they
predict such measures since they were not prescribed by MSF.

Monachi, watching carefully the Anarchie movements, took care not to get herself
boxed in, but her dancing in space did cause the Anarchie to get frustrated at each
laser attack attempt. Unlike Vickie who deployed her lasers and attacked the Anarchie,
Monachi had no intention of attacking because she knew the situation was different
and that Kwongab would do what he needed and stay out of harm's way.

Traveling at a much slower speed, Mergenky Scout MSFS-1 did not give off an ion
wake and because it was not radiating any signals other than the brief communications
to Monachi, the Anarchie didn't have a good feel for where exactly MSFS-1 was
located, other than knowing a second Mergenky spacecraft was nearby and probably
cloaked.

Meanwhile MSFC-34 was being vectored in on the apparent course of Anarchie Fleet.
Captain Koasa's orders were not to attack the fleet, but to help out Mergenky Scouts
if possible and to stay out of the range of Anarchie Battleships where a one-on-one
exchange would probably prove fatal.

INT. SPACE. MERGENKY SCOUT MSFS-1 CONTROL ROOM/OPERATIONS.

COMMANDER KWONGAB

I have a good picture of the Anarchie fleet but not the actual composition.

LT. COMMANDER LÓNGRÉN

That means we need to get closer.

COMMANDER KWONGAB

I'm going to do an end around. The Anarchie did not have very good flank protection, and this would present us with an opportunity to slide into the Anarchie Task Force formation and get an accurate accounting of what Anarchie fleet assets are here.

LT. COMMANDER LÓNGRÉN

How are we going to accomplish getting that Anarchie composition?

COMMANDER KWONGAB

The plan I have in mind is once in position to light off all active sensors, get a good sweep around and identify as many Anarchie components as possible.

LT. COMMANDER LÓNGRÉN

Our active sensors will definitely get the Anarchie attention. What's our egress plan?

COMMANDER KWONGAB

We'll take a few shots at a transport on our way out at high speed and attempt out running them and avoid getting boxed in.

LT. COMMANDER LÓNGRÉN

I'm ready for some action Commander Kwongab.

COMMANDER KWONGAB

Lt. Commander Lóngrén, I'll be doing manual steering, I want you to control the lasers when I get us near Anarchie Transports.

LT. COMMANDER LÓNGRÉN

I'll do my best sir.

It quickly became clear to Kwongab that Monachi was doing an excellent job of distracting the Anarchie. Their reactions gave Kwongab the sense Monachi had diverted the Anarchie attention towards her Mergenky Scout MSFS-4 and no less than four Anarchie battleships moving out of formation to hunt MSFS-4 down and destroy it.

Once Kwongab manually steered to a good position to collect the Anarchie disposition, many of the Anarchie Battleships were a good distance away where they would not be able to intervene with Mergenky Scout MSFS-1's efforts, Kwongab then stated:

COMMANDER KWONGAB
PNN, energize the scanners and get a good scan of the
fleet and transmit results to MSF immediately. Let me
know when you have identified all the ships.

MARTHA (PNN)
Understand Captain Kwongab. Sensors are energized,
we are illuminating the Anarchie fleet.

Kwongab could see the stunning reaction from the Anarchie who were completely caught off guard. He patiently waited for PNN who soon announced:

MARTHA (PNN)
All ships are identified, transmitting status to MSF.

COMMANDER KWONGAB
Secure scanners!

Kwongab then maneuvered the Scout on a very high G course change that came really close to damaging the artificial gravity machine with such tremendous G forces that people could feel them. Kwongab's maneuver cleared him an exit route the Anarchie created by sending so many Anarchie Battleships out towards Monachi's Scout MSFS-4.

As Kwongab left the Anarchie formation he just surveyed, a transport loomed just off his port bow.

COMMANDER KWONGAB
We only have one possible shot to take on that
Transport off our port bow. I'm going to maneuver to
give you a better firing angle.

LT. COMMANDER LÓNGRÉN
I have Automatic Target Followers on Transport.
Waiting for a better angle of attack.

Kwongab swung the Scout around so that he would pass close aboard barely avoiding a collision with the transport but at the same time offering a port blank range shot.

It was an auspicious occasion since Lt. Commander Lóngrén was one of the better gunners in the fleet, putting Time on Target (TOT) on a critical point in the transport that should have been protected by Anarchie Battleships had they not chased after Mergenky Scout MSFS-4.

The full 2 second laser blast from all five Scout MSFS-1's lasers hit a critical location on the Mergenky Transport.

Lt. Commander Lóngrén's five laser volleys blew a large hole in the side of the transport causing a rapid depressurization.

One of the combat load mistakes the Anarchie made for the Jeeapa Invasion Force was to put all the Jeeapa bound Scouts and Rangers on a transport of their own.

This mistake was partly due to the arrogance of the Anarchie Scouts and Rangers, but also, they had specific target areas and with the large number of escorting battleships, it was felt they would be well protected.

The rapid depressurization led to the deaths of most of the Anarchie Scouts and Rangers.

The transport was heavily damaged and would not be able to do atmospheric penetration without loss of the transport spaceship. The damage to the transport was also causing problems with steerage and control.

The damage appeared to be far worse than Anarchie originally thought and maintaining velocity and maneuver in the convoy zigzag plan was impossible. Furthermore, the Anarchie had to leave behind a major Anarchie warship to protect the Transport and possibly evacuate the survivors if all atmospheric control systems failed which were indicating having significant issues.

Kwongab knew there was no other option but to run fast in a straight line and get as much distance between him and the Anarchie. He then ordered:

COMMANDER KWONGAB
PNN, send a message to Mergenky MSFS-4 to
disengage and get to safety.

PNN reported with Martha's voice:

MARTHA (PNN)
Commander Kwongab, we received a response from

General Kahn who thanks us for our efforts, saying our information has been very helpful.

Kwongab feeling a little fearful for Monachi then directed PNN:

COMMANDER KWONGAB
PNN, please contact Scout MSFS-4 and ask them if they received our last communication to disengage.

With Martha's voice PNN responded:

MARTHA (PNN)
Contacting Scout MSFS-4.

Kwongab watched the surveillance holograph intently and spoke.

COMMANDER KWONGAB
The signal strength of Anarchie active scanners are now registering 4.7 because their Battleships chasing us are getting close.

LT. COMMANDER LÓNGRÉN
The Anarchie transiting towards us at an angle which means the signal strength will increasing slightly, but the angle is now slowly declining towards the stern.

COMMANDER KWONGAB
Which means the range rate should drop off along with the signal strength of the predominately infra-red and ultra-violet pulses.

Soon after Kwongab's last comment, Lt. Commander Lóngrén Reported:

LT. COMMANDER LÓNGRÉN
The range rate is now declining, opening from the nearest Anarchie Battleship.

Commander Kwongab started feeling a lot better as he watched the Interpolated Averaged Maximum Likelihood Estimator (MLE) Target Motion Analysis display showing Anarchie closest Battleship range rate drop off.

VOICEOVER
Kwongab feared the worst for Monachi and hoped she survived.

If something happened to Monachi on this mission, Kwongab knew he would never be the same person again.

Kwongab's fabric of his life would be ripped out and nobody could every replace this special woman Monachi who had the neural expansion telepathic implants that allowed them as a couple to feel each other in ways no others could.

When the Anarchie closest battleship approached 210 degrees off the stern in the northeast quadrant based on galactic geometry, PNN suddenly reported:

MARTHA (PNN)

Signal Strength is dropping off, now 4.5 to the nearest radiator. This decreased signal strength matches Interpolated and Averaged Maximum Likelihood Estimator (MLE) Target Motion Analysis results.

COMMANDER KWONGAB
PNN, any reports from Scout MSFS-4?

MARTHA (PNN)
No reports from Scout MSFS-4.

VOICEOVER

Kwongab's stomach was now in disarray.

Kwongab's emotions were building, and the intensity of his feelings could be observed by crew members who knew and understood the significance of those PNN reports.

LT. COMMANDER LÓNGRÉN

Those battleships have legs, but they are not gaining on us.

CAPTAIN KOASA
VOICE OVER

Captain Koasa knew the two Scouts were in trouble.

Captain Koasa received the reports from MSF who also were now peeling off Cruisers from Frăctŏng and sending them to Jeeapa joining MSF Cruisers now sortied from Gwaba.

Two different formations of Cruisers were coming, but they would be too late to save Jeeapa who would receive an initial pounding.

General Kahn knew he was safe down in the Five-mile oval with most of his troops who would deploy as soon as the space watchers and surveillance drones knew where the Anarchie were landing.

When General Kahn received Captain Koasa's message requesting permission to go out and try to give the two Scouts an exit corridor, General Kahn reluctantly agreed.

VOICEOVER (GENERAL KAHN)
THOUGHT

MSFC-34 will have to face the Anarchie a short time later so a delay of perhaps a half hour would not make much difference.

With permission granted, Captain Koasa ordered the Cruiser:

CAPTAIN KOASA

PNN head right at the center of the Anarchie formation.

VOICE OVER

Even though it was almost suicidal, it did suddenly change the complexion of the chase. The center of the force was slightly weakened by the dozen Anarchie Battleships now joining in the attack on the two Scouts.

The Anarchie wanted their revenge for the audacity of the Mergenky who penetrated their screen and severely damaged the transport that was now left behind with little hope of participating in the battle rendering most of its occupants the Anarchie Scouts and Rangers 'esprit de corps' incapacitated or worse, succumbed to asphyxiation.

Predictably the task force commander General Fāguāng De Sīxiǎngjiā (pronounced: Fa-gwang Da Si-shang-jaw) ordered the battleships back to formation to tighten up the screen and prepare for battle.

After losing one of their Troop Transports, the Anarchie could ill afford to lose one or two more without starting to have collateral damage to the invasion force.

ANARCHIE SENSOR OPERATOR
That Mergenky ship is coming at us like madmen!

ANARCHIE BATTLESHIP CAPTAIN
It will be within weapons range soon; we'll make it
regret its actions.

COMMANDER KWONGAB
Captain Koasa's Cruiser MSFC-34 coming in with its
sensors blazing.

MARTHA (PNN)
The Anarchie pulled away, signal strength of their
sensors has dropped off rapidly to signal strength 3.5.

COMMANDER KWONGAB
Those Anarchie Battleships have probably been
recalled to formation because of what MSFC-34 is
doing.

Because Mergenky Scout MSFS-4 was going at very high speed, it left behind a
considerable ion trail.

MARTHA (PNN)
MSFS-4 has been identified and located. It's presently
around 90 degrees off the port side shown with the
Blue Tracker Symbol on the heads-up display.

COMMANDER KWONGAB
I wonder why MSFS-4 never answered?

Kwongab then realized MSFC-34 was making a supreme sacrifice to save them.

COMMANDER KWONGAB
Wwe need to help MSFC-34 maneuver.

LT. COMMANDER LÓNGRÉN
What can we do Commander Kwongab?

COMMANDER KWONGAB
Let's light up our Scout to draw their attention and
cause Anarchie confusion. Turn on all active sensors.

Kwongab then turned the Scout around and just as the Battleships were nearing
convergence on the Cruiser they were suddenly surprised by the new radiators.

It was as if Monachi read his mind, she followed suit and now the Anarchie were even more confused.

> COMMANDER KWONGAB
> One way to get their attention is to change course for
> one of their transports!

Kwongab manually steering the Mergenky Scout S-1 pointed at his next victim and proceeded to fly in an unconventional manner that made Anarchie shooters have problems with targeting.

Once again, the Anarchie had left a Transport unguarded and at the tremendous velocity the Scout could obtain quickly converged on the Transport and laid into it with withering fire, quickly setting off large internal fires.

> LT. COMMANDER LÓNGRÉN
> Looks like you are drawing attention to several
> Anarchie Battleships who turned towards us and
> rejoined the chase.

Monachi was disrupting Anarchie on the other side of their formation and turned away just as soon as she observed MSFS-1's maneuver.

Meanwhile Captain Koasa let lose a salvo on a nearby Anarchie Battleship then took immediate evasive maneuvers.

The combined disruption and confusion gave the three Mergenky ships precisely just enough time to evade and start opening the chasing elements.

INT. SPACE. ANARCHIE TASK FORCE COMMANDER GENERAL FĀGUĀNG DE SĪXIǍNGJIĀ'S COMMAND SHIP.

The Anarchie Task Force Commander General Fāguāng De Sīxiǎngjiā realized that if the Anarchie Battleships kept leaving formation it would allow further cheap shots at the transports which was their primary mission ordered the Anarchie Battleships.

> ANARCHIE
> TASK FORCE COMMANDER
> GENERAL FĀGUĀNG DE SĪXIǍNGJIĀ
> All ships return to formations assigned and cease the
> chase!

All three Mergenky ships were then able to get away after inflicting some damage to the Anarchie including setting fires to another Anarchie Battleship and one Transport loaded with green 'lizard like' Anarchieborgs.

As soon as General Kahn received an updated status from the three Mergenky spaceships he ordered:

GENERAL KAHN
(Message)
MSFC-34, MSFS-1 and MSFS-4 relocate to Geosynchronous Orbit above Jeeapa City.

In his orders he explained to the three ships captains:

GENERAL KAHN
(Message)
This will help protect your ships using Jeeapa's air defense networks until the fleet arrives.

Jeeapa's Air Defense Networks are very robust thanks to recent preparations and left over Jeeapa War emplacement's that Kwongab's visit helped get back in operation at the 11th hour.

<u>INT. SPACE. SCOUT MSFS-1 CONTROL ROOM.</u>

LT. COMMANDER LÓNGRÉN
That's an astute move by General Kahn.

COMMANDER KWONGAB
It will only be safe for us temporarily until the real fighting starts.

GENERAL KAHN
(Message)
Jeeapa's Air Defense Networks will make it virtually impossible for Anarchie Transports to come down near Jeeapa. They would have to land 100 miles or further away over the horizon to avoid being shot down by you three ships who I know would make a supreme sacrifice.

COMMANDER KWONGAB
I'm sure glad General Kahn is here directing the battle.

LT. COMMANDER LÓNGRÉN
This should give the Mergenky ground forces some breathing room and some of the recently arrived advanced technology could be battle tested and evaluated before being forced to rely on it.

COMMANDER KWONGAB
Not long after Anarchie arrives, the Mergenky Fleet should be here for the big showdown. More ships are being pulled out of mothball and urgently put back into service.

LT. COMMANDER LÓNGRÉN
These mothballed ships would not fare too well by themselves, but mixed in with Mergenky front line units, they can provide additional fire power, though would not be ideal for complicated maneuvers.

****

<u>INT. SPACE. ANARCHIE TASK FORCE COMMAND SHIP CONTROL ROOM.</u>

ANARCHIE
TASK FORCE COMMANDER
GENERAL FĀGUĀNG DE SĪXIǍNGJIĀ
I'm somewhat relieved no further attacks occurred as we approached Jeeapa.

ANARCHIE DEPUTY
TASK FORCE COMMANDER.
Last minute preparations are complete. The ground forces were all injected with the special invincibility serum.

ANARCHIE
TASK FORCE COMMANDER
GENERAL FĀGUĀNG DE SĪXIǍNGJIĀ
That serum will give them the euphoric invincibility syndrome for up to 72 hours.

The Anarchie were not going to allow the three ships to remain above Jeeapa.

ANARCHIE
TASK FORCE COMMANDER
GENERAL FĀGUĀNG DE SĪXIǍNGJIĀ
Send six battleships after the three Mergenky ships positioned above the Jeeapa Dome.

ANARCHIE DEPUTY
TASK FORCE COMMANDER.

According to Anarchie Intel Jeeapa defenses were in dismal condition.

***

<u>INT. SPACE. MERGENKY MSFS-1 CONTROL ROOM.</u>

COMMANDER KWONGAB
Six Anarchie are arriving in near space, they are poised to fire on us.

LT. COMMANDER LÓNGRÉN
Jeeapa air defense systems no doubt have them targeted on their weak underbellies.

The Scouts and Cruiser maneuvered on evasive courses while firing, but the Battleships soon realized they blundered into a trap and did an emergency course reversal. One of the Anarchie Battleships was not so lucky and blew up into sparkling debris which hastened the five remaining battleships to clear the area.

***

<u>INT. SPACE. ANARCHIE TASK FORCE COMMAND SHIP CONTROL ROOM.</u>

ANARCHIE
TASK FORCE COMMANDER
GENERAL FĀGUĀNG DE SĪXIĂNGJIĀ
Intel said they didn't have air defense networks operating.

ANARCHIE DEPUTY
TASK FORCE COMMANDER.
I hope this isn't the only thing INTEL got wrong.

The Anarchie now knew for a fact it would be tough to land near Jeeapa and planned contingencies to land further away and over the horizon to avoid Jeeapa defenses. Based on the Anarchie Battleship reception, the transports were given the alternative landing zones which they proceeded to effect landings southwest of Jeeapa.

General Kahn knew his fleet was arriving too late to deal with the landings and the three ships were now cooling their heels directly above Jeeapa where they were being protected.

General Kahn knew it would not set well with them being forced to watch the Anarchie landings without being allowed to attack, so after the scouts and cruiser made repeated requests to maneuver and attack the formations or attempt to disrupt them, he knew he had to act.

General Kahn regrettably made tacit permissions for the three token force ships to proceed to help disrupt Anarchie Transport landings.

<u>INT. SPACE. MERGENKY SCOUT MSFS-1 CONTROL ROOM.</u>

Kwongab immediately notified Monachi and Captain Koasa:

COMMANDER KWONGAB
Let's go after one of the transports coming down now.

CAPTAIN KOASA
Why go after just one Anarchie Transport?

COMMANDER KWONGAB
If we get just one of them, it will have a psychological
effect on the rest. By the three of our ships going after
one Transport, we'll likely nail it.

CAPTAIN KOASA
We'll follow you in the attack Captain Kwongab.

VOICEOVER
Captain Koasa knew he might be leading his men to
their deaths. But if they took out just one transport
that might save the lives of several thousand Mergenky
ground force personnel and make it a lot easier for
them to cope.

Kwongab's sensor and targeting holographs had all the nearby Anarchie ships located and classified. Sensor displays showed a maze and very scary looking.

COMMANDER KWONGAB
PNN, identify the most loosely guarded Anarchie
transport and the safest and best route to attack it.

Within two seconds Martha's voice responded.

MARTHA (PNN)
Calculations made; Anarchie Transport ship
highlighted yellow tracker on the tactical display.

COMMANDER KWONGAB
PNN, I need your help now to guide us and get us there. Proceed to attack, notify MSFS-4 and MSFC-34 of our plan.

MARTHA (PNN)
Captain Kwongab, MSFS-4 and MSFC-34 have been notified and they have responded they will follow us in formation.

The ships accelerated at an incredible rate of change. The 100-mile down range to Troop Transports only took a couple minutes. Once again, they caught the Anarchie totally off guard.

Whether it was their arrogance or their total disregard for their own personal safety, the Anarchie had unwittingly exposed one of their transports to Mergenky withering fire of the three Mergenky ships in the flyby.

VOICEOVER
An Anarchie Transport loaded up with Anarchieborgs was quickly set ablaze as it was penetrating the ozone layer.

The gaping holes the Mergenky lasers tore into the Transport hull instantly fried the Anarchieborgs as the heat from the lack of a shield going 17,000 miles per hour instantly roasted the Anarchieborgs, and flammables and combustibles immediately ignited.

Explosives quickly reached their cookoff temperatures and the transport blew in half strewing its contents in a debris field that was going to end up being 50 miles long on the ground as it fell burning to the planet.

One Anarchie Battleship was in their way to safe egress. All three Mergenky ships fired on the Battleship in unison. The laser gallery created on the semi dark side of the planet turned nighttime into daylight.

MSFS-4 received some damage but managed to get away just in time to avoid a catastrophic hit.

MSFS-1 glided on past and put some serious wounds into the battleship which distracted the Anarchie

Battleship just momentarily from the Mergenky Cruiser MSFC-34.

MSFC-34 fired point blank a complete salvo into the battleship engineering spaces, slicing open the hull, causing an instantaneous depressurization of the hull and setting off a tremendous fire that was quickly melting the U115 restraint coils that would soon cause total loss of coolant and instantaneous energy release that would be the equivalent constant output of flank speed.

Other battleships moved in to give it a fighting chance, but their presence was too little too late, because as soon as the restraint coils were gone, the U115 fuel rods were now getting uncontrolled contamination and higher energy releases that soon turned explosive. No sooner than MSFC-34 was barely a safe distance away, an explosion the size of a tactical nuke turned the former battleship into a cloud of sparkling debris which hammered the Anarchie fleet.

ANARCHIE
TASK FORCE COMMANDER
GENERAL FĀGUĀNG DE SĪXIĂNGJIĀ

This is all I take from the three Mergenky pests. Send the fleet after them.

The Cruiser was no challenge for several Anarchie battleships. As the three Mergenky ships peeled away from their targets, in totally random fashion to avoid laser strikes they were immediately separated by a good distance. The Scouts were lucky in they were a lesser of the targets and with their sprinting ability quickly distanced themselves from the Anarchie forces.

After Monachi ordered PNN to send MSF the hull health check and systems status, MSF quickly concluded the battle damage sustained was rather serious and was ordered on a course directly to Gwaba where emergency repairs could be made, provided she was able to get the ship there safely.

MSFS-1 managed to get through the gauntlet unscathed and when PNN announced they were clear of all immediate threats, Kwongab wheeled around to size up the situation. Soon he had MSFC-34 on his sensors being chased by a half dozen Anarchie Battleships, some of which had an angle on MSFC-34. It did not look good for Captain Koasa and his crew. Kwongab's heart sank as he watched the outcome. He knew his good friend Vance was aboard, and his fragile life was at stake.

Kwongab decided he would pay back Captain Koasa for saving their lives earlier in the day by attempting to distract the Anarchie. He made a beeline towards them and made some tremendous attacks and withdraws using manual flight controls that were so stressful to the ship, the artificial gravity machine almost was ripped off its foundations.

Kwongab's plan partially worked as three Anarchie Battleships broke chase on MSFC-34 and turned towards MSFS-1 who was frantically manually dancing out in space to avoid laser strikes.

MSFC-34 wasn't so lucky this time. Two of the Anarchie Battleships found their mark and did some serious damage. But MSFC-34 fought on.

Realizing they were finished Captain Koasa ordered:

CAPTAIN KOASA:
Abandon ship! PNN, keep fighting in automatic mode,
so the crew can escape.

Shortly after half the crew was in the Escape Pod, there was a rapid depressurization of the hull.

PNN automatically shut the Escape Pod access and sealed it shut. No sooner than the Cruiser's Escape Pod Bay external hatches were open under Captain Koasa's orders still commanding from the bridge knowing nobody else had a chance to make the Escape Pod, it was launched as the ship blew apart. Everyone left on the Cruiser and in the Escape Pod except Vance were instantly killed.

Vance had been sitting in the utmost perfect position to withstand the forces, though he was unconscious as the Escape Pod which did not get properly activated turning on its emergency transponder was hurdled at nearly light speed out in deep space.

All Kwongab saw was the Cruiser exploding. Due to the angle, PNN never recorded the Escape Pod jettisoning. Kwongab was immediately gripped with sorrow for the loss of his friend. It had been an extraordinary journey for them. But the latest near laser strikes shook him out of the temporal state into reality.

Kwongab continued steering the Scout in violent turns and maneuvers that bewildered the Anarchie Battleship commanders who were finding it almost impossible to target the ship. The stolen algorithms where PNN would be guiding the ship were not working out. The only thing Anarchie could think of was: *The Mergenky had changed their algorithms!*

It did not take the Scout long to get a safe distance away from the three Battleships.

The attack Kwongab had just led to had significant psychological effects on the Anarchie. The Anarchie over confidence was now quickly dissipating.

Even with the three-day serum injections the Anarchieborgs, feeling the rough ride were now having second thoughts. Those that had already made it to the surface that were not in a crawler or an Exoskeleton and could look up into the air saw the space battle underway in the sky and the explosions occurring. This was real war and real Anarchie green blood was spilling for what was already starting to feel like another worthless cause.

Commander Kwongab looked at the contacts on the scanner holographs.

> COMMANDER KWONGAB
> PNN, do another analysis, is there another possible route to a transport we can get to before the Battleships can defend it?

> Within 30 seconds, PNN reported:
> MARTHA (PNN)
> Six battleships that chased our ships are now out of position, we can get to one of the Transports before they can get back into position if you attack now.

> COMMANDER KWONGAB
> PNN, proceed with the attack, I will assist in guidance.

Just like before S-1 went in with total disregard for its own safety. The Anarchie were not expecting another clever attack and assumed the enemy were now scattered far away from the task force and were not fully vigilant.

> VOICEOVER
> *Unknown to Kwongab, Martha still had several files generated during the Andromeda Mission, where she and Vance often ran simulated attacks on Anarchie Battleships.*
>
> *Vance in an uncanny manner had solved some unique geometries that she now copied in her corkscrew drilling down through the maze of ships to that lone transport that was just entering the atmosphere at its most vulnerable moment. Screaming out of the sun like a hot shinny sirocco, the Scout MSFS-1 was in the blind spot of the Transport where they did not detect it until it was too late.*
>
> *Remembering the last Transport's apparent weak spot, Kwongab focused the aiming point there and let loose a full 2 second laser blast.*

The powerful Mergenky lasers only needed one second to melt through the containment wall of the U115 direct power reactor setting off immediate contamination explosions caused by ionized aluminum and carbon composites.

Just like before, a ship penetrating the ionosphere doing 17,000 miles per hour had no chance of survival because of its hull breach.

Turning away from the Anarchie heading to an escape route, PNN guided the Scout to directly over Jeeapa giving IFF signals on the way.

To Kwongab's surprise, the ship came to an abrupt halt directly over Jeeapa and turned facing the Anarchie landing to the Southwest. The smoke from the debris field falling to Earth could be seen for 200 miles.

Kwongab had put a dent into the transports and to some extent hurt their landings, but the vast number of transports landing placed a sizeable Anarchieborgs Army on the planet in the middle of the night. By morning, the disaster would unfold as Jeeapa soon discovered it was facing a million Anarchieborgs.

It had been a long day. Kwongab was exhausted, the crew was equally stressed to the maximum. Suddenly Commander Gōngniúgǒu appeared on the Bridge.

COMMANDER GŌNGNIÚGǑU

Commander Kwongab, I watched quite a bit of this
from my space Cabin. I do not believe anyone else in
MSF could have pulled off the maneuvers you just did.
I'm honored to be in your presence.

Kwongab probing Gōngniúgǒu with his neural expansion ability quickly determined the sincerity and admiration that Gōngniúgǒu felt.

KWONGAB

Commander Gōngniúgǒu, what if any significant
lesson did you learn from what we just endured?

COMMANDER GŌNGNIÚGǑU

Well Commander Kwongab, it takes an extraordinary
personality with a tremendous drive to attempt such
maneuvers with such high risk.

Experts say there is a fine line between insanity and genius. Sir you glide on that tight rope between insanity and genius.

COMMANDER KWONGAB

You think I got close?

COMMANDER GŌNGNIÚGŎU
Nobody has ever gotten closer.

COMMANDER KWONGAB
Is it something I can teach you?

COMMANDER GŌNGNIÚGŎU
I seriously doubt you can teach it.

COMMANDER KWONGAB
Why is that?

COMMANDER GŌNGNIÚGŎU
It must be something developed inside one's *soul* and of course the consequences as we just witnessed with MSFC-34 are the results of the risk we must take if we hope to meet our challenges.

COMMANDER KWONGAB
When MSFC-34 blew up I lost a very close friend.

COMMANDER GŌNGNIÚGŎU
Commander Kwongab, I think we are relatively safe over Jeeapa thanks to the air defense system here, I suggest you take a break, you must be very tired now.

COMMANDER KWONGAB
Commander Gōngniúgŏu, I'm too wound up now to think about sleep.

COMMANDER GŌNGNIÚGŎU
All right Captain Kwongab, but I wish to remain on the bridge now as I think it's my shift.

COMMANDER KWONGAB
Since you are well rested, yes you are needed on the bridge.

Moments later PNN announced:

MARTHA (PNN)
Commander Kwongab, General Kahn has just sent a communique to you, requesting you take the Shuttle

down to Jeeapa immediately and meet him in his office
in the five-mile oval.

Kwongab not sure what that was about, and was fearful he might be charged with recklessness leading to the loss of MSFC-34 responded:

COMMANDER KWONGAB
PNN, inform General Kahn I'll be there promptly.

Kwongab then turned to Commander Gōngniúgǒu looked into his eyes and did some last-minute telepathic influence on Commander Gōngniúgǒu's thoughts in a manner he felt might help him deal with what was likely to get ugly soon.

COMMANDER KWONGAB
Commander Gōngniúgǒu, you are now in full
command of this ship. Treat her right. In case I don't
see you again, good luck.

COMMANDER GŌNGNIÚGǑU
Thank you, Commander Kwongab.

Kwongab then turned towards Lt. Commander Lóngrén.

KWONGAB
Lt. Commander Lóngrén, with your captain's
permission, would you give me the honor of piloting
me in the Shuttle to the planet since you need to have
your shuttle readily available.

Commander Gōngniúgǒu immediately intervened in the conversation and said:

COMMANDER GŌNGNIÚGǑU
Commander Kwongab, for all that you have done for
the MSF, the least we could do is have our Navigator
pilot you to the planet's surface.

KWONGAB
Thank you, Commander Gōngniúgǒu, I appreciate that.

Commander Kwongab and Lt. Commander Lóngrén immediately went to the Shuttle Bay and was launched and made the trip to the surface of the planet. As soon as they landed and got out of the Shuttle, Kwongab turned to Lt. Commander Lóngrén.

KWONGAB

Lt. Commander Lóngrén, your actions on the bridge during the combat were exemplary. I could not have done it without your help.

LT. COMMANDER LÓNGRÉN
I did my best sir.

KWONGAB

Yes, I observed you tweaking my flight controls a bit, you made me look good.

LT. COMMANDER LÓNGRÉN
I just helped sir.

KWONGAB

Commander Lóngrén, you are a great man, you have a wonderful career ahead of you. Do what you did for me for Commander Gōngniúgǒu, he will need your help.

LT. COMMANDER LÓNGRÉN
I will do my best sir.

KWONGAB

The Scout may need this Shuttle. I suggest you take it back right away just in case. If General Kahn allows me to go back to Scout MSFS-1, you'll be sent back down to pick me up.

LT. COMMANDER LÓNGRÉN
I will be most happy to do that sir.

Kwongab bowed at Lóngrén and turned and walked to the waiting hovercraft to take him to the Jeeapa Dome and entrance to the *Five-Mile Oval*.

Within 10 minutes of landing, Kwongab was entering General Kahn's office. It was a beehive of activity and resembled the frenzied actions of General Zarkin's people 20 years prior when the Anarchie tried their last invasion.

The outer office was a combination map room and urgent message center. As soon as Kwongab entered the office and was recognized by the AI of the PNN system of the *Five-Mile Oval,* he was summoned into General Kahn's office who had that pale look on his face.

GENERAL KAHN
Thank you for coming right away Kwongab.

KWONGAB
General Kahn, what can I do for you.

GENERAL KAHN
Kwongab, I'm very sorry about what happened to your friend Vance. I know you had a special relationship with him. I'm afraid I'm going to have to ask you to do another extraordinary task for me.

Kwongab looked at General Kahn knowing whatever it was the General was going to ask of him, it was not going to be one of those delightful tasks to do.

KWONGAB
Yes, General, you know you can count on me.

GENERAL KAHN
Kwongab I would expect nothing less from you, that's why I want to send you to Gwaba on my special transport ship and break the news of Vance's death to Kara.

KWONGAB
I will be most proud to do that for you General.

GENERAL KAHN
Inform Kara that I have unusual circumstances here, otherwise I would have personally come to her instead of sending you.

KWONGAB
I'm sure she will understand sir.

GENERAL KAHN
My personal transport is waiting for you and will take off as soon as you are onboard.

KWONGAB
I'm on my way General.

GENERAL KAHN
Goodbye Kwongab.

Kwongab bowed and turned and left the room.

As soon as Kwongab left the office, two MSF officers were in the map room/outer office who said:

MSF OFFICER
Captain Kwongab, we will escort you to the transport.

Kwongab followed the men who took him to General Kahn's private elevator shared with General Zǔzhī Bùliáng. This elevator, which provided extra security and privacy also moved a lot quicker than the MSF elevators elsewhere in the *Five-Mile Oval*. The elevator stopped and they stepped out and walked down a hallway about 40 yards to a door with armed guards which was immediately opened for them. On the other side of the door was an outdoor area and parked right there was the General's supped up ultra-high-speed transport.

General Kahn's personal transport looked quite a bit different than any other vessel Kwongab had ever seen. He had never previously seen General Kahn's private transport before.

The access door to the craft was open with armed guards standing there waiting. Kwongab's escorts took him to the transport and as soon as they were inside the door shut, they then gestured to several seats which were designated for them and Kwongab. On the same transport were a half dozen other MSF members being sent back to Gwaba for various reasons. A couple of them were INTEL agents with reports back to headquarters, the others were task masters involved in moving men and material.

As soon as the men were all strapped in the craft went airborne looking out the window it didn't take long to see the atmosphere turn dark as they approached the edge of space. Once outside the atmosphere the ship accelerated at a pace Kwongab never experienced before. They were going at some super velocity and no doubt were leaving an ion trail behind which the Anarchie would have no difficulty tracking.

Kwongab suddenly felt extremely tired. His adrenalin was now slowly collapsing as his mind slowly blanked out as he fell asleep. Some people in the craft gave dirty looks to Kwongab who was soon in a deep sleep.

One of the people riding back to Gwaba made a rude remark:

MSF OFFICER
The man is sleeping in an obnoxious manner.

One of the two INTEL agents aboard taking reports back to MSF headquarters, looked at the MSF officer

INTEL AGENT
You obviously have no idea who that person is.

MSF OFFICER
I suppose I do not.

INTEL AGENT
That's Commander Kwongab, he's just completed
24 hours of constant combat. He destroyed several
Anarchie Transports and Battleships and lost his best
friend on our Cruiser that was destroyed defending
Jeeapa.

The MSF Officer, rider suddenly appeared to start eating some humble pie and had no
more comments for the rest of the journey.

Kwongab was mostly out of it for most of the flight. About an hour out of Gwaba he
came too.

Everyone aboard the transport was relieved they were no longer anywhere near the
enemy and could relax. In due time the General's personal transport landed at MSF
headquarters landing pad and the passengers all exited the craft. Waiting for Kwongab
was Monachi who had just arrived at MSS-21 flying back MSFS-4 for repairs and
shuttled down to the planet.

MONACHI
General Kahn told me to meet you here. I know what
he has asked you to do, I would like to go along.

KWONGAB
Certainly, I'm sure Kara would like to see you.

About that time one of Kwongab's escorts said:

MSF ESCORT
Commander Kwongab, this way please we have
transportation waiting for you and Commander
Monachi.

Kwongab and Monachi followed the two escorts to an elevator that took them to the
roof top where they found a Skycar waiting for them. There was plenty of room for all
the occupants. As soon as they were strapped in their seats in the Skycar took off and
headed in the domed city of Quom to the healing center where they knew Kara was
working that day.

MSF had contacted the hospital and directed them to cancel all of Kara's patients for the day, that she would have special visitors, and MSF would be sending over a liaison officer to talk with the healing center director, so they understood the circumstances of the visit.

The Mergenky had not had to deal with combat deaths in over 20 years. The public was not poised to hear the unfolding events. News reports being censored were not getting the real nature of the story of the fighting on Frăctŏng and Jeeapa to the public.

The enemy which was now 75 miles away from the Frăctŏng domed city Yŏngbùmián de Chéngshì, was soon to create concern that had not been felt in over 20 years. Casualties had not mounted on Jeeapa, but it was now just a matter of time.

Kara thought it was rather odd her appointments were suddenly all canceled and then the director called her and asked her to come to her office. The director whom Kara admired was a brilliant woman and very astute in most matters.

Kara cheerfully went into the executive offices and felt strange vibes as it appeared everyone was staring at her. The director had been informed she had arrived and went out to greet her.

HEALING CENTERE DIRECTOR
Hello Kara, would you please come into my office.

As Kara walked into the director's office it was as if she saw a ghost. Standing in front of her was Kwongab and Monachi.

Monachi and Kwongab had on their flight uniforms because they had virtually come directly from the space battlefield over Jeeapa to Gwaba.

Kwongab and Monachi's body language betrayed their purpose of being there. Suddenly Kara felt like a ton of bricks had just hit her in the gut. Even though she was a very well-trained psychotherapist, nothing could prepare her to treat herself.

Tears started falling down Kara's eyes. Monachi, using her neural expansion telepathic probing Kara's thoughts elevated her own emotions and subsequently her own tears started flowing. The director was struck with sadness as well.

Monachi, knowing Kara was going to break down, reached out and embraced her as the flood gates opened.

It was one of the saddest days in Monachi's life, witnessing what Kara was going through.

Their many years together on the Andromeda Mission had made them family. Nobody in the world was closer. Kwongab knew how terrible Vance's children would feel. The Trauma would be huge.

The director, being a very wise person, had a couple staff psychotherapists on hand for this moment and knew it would be best to sedate Kara so that she would not go into hyperbolic transcendental gesticulation, leading towards a mental breakdown.

By keeping Kara sedated for a couple days and applying the same techniques on her that she would to her own patients, these psychotherapists could control the amount of pain and suffering so that Kara would more quickly regain her composure and ability to cope with her tremendous loss.

For the moment however, Kara and Monachi just hugged and cried like sisters over the grave loss of someone important in their lives.

The past 2 days of events cost Kwongab dearly, but he also knew the number of Mergenky lives they saved was considerable.

Other precious lives were also lost. Captain Koasa was a major figure in the first Jeeapa war, he had served the MSF with distinction.

People such as Lieutenant Shǎnguāngdēng's parents on Frăctŏng would be heart broken. Lieutenant Shǎnguāngdēng's parents would one day be told of her exceptional ability as a sensor operator on MSFC-34 and how she was instrumental in them not only rescuing the two Scout Class ships being chased down by the Anarchie but also in destroying a transport loaded with many Anarchieborgs and an Anarchie Battleship.

In what now appeared to be the beginning of a war of attrition, those material losses would later be a large negative on the Anarchie on the ground war because the loss of the transports the three MSF ships damaged or destroyed, eliminated many reserves. The Anarchie would be forced to fight a far more conservative battle than they planned.

VANCE

<u>EXT. CGI. SPACE. ESCAPE POD DRIFTING IN SPACE. 15 SECONDS</u>

VOICE OVER
Vance drifted unconsciousness inside the Escape Pod
for several days. Vance never regained consciousness
until long after he was removed from the Escape Pod.

Due to the untimely Escape Pod launch precipitated
by the MSF Cruiser blowing up, most of the systems
did not go through a normal power up sequence and

nobody was awake and alert to do it that would have activated the distress pinger.

The Escape Pod itself was stuck in a launch profile and was never notified by PNN to complete the cycle and turn on all systems. Hence no distress calls went out and the environmental controls were not adjusted for practical long-term lifeboat profiles.

A more advanced Alien Race existed in the direction the Anarchie were spreading their imperialistic empire. This alien race known as Měngshì Yún Rén (pronounced Mung-she Yuwn Rin) [猛士雲人] Fierce Warriors Cloud People made it a point to avoid the Anarchie and the Mergenky. As such they had not been seen by either Anarchie or the Mergenky in well over 10,000 years.

Not much was known about Měngshì Yún Rén other than they kept their distances and appeared to have no desire to establish any relationships with outside entities.

VOICEOVER

Vance came close to being melted and shoved out of the way with the anti-meteorite system the Měngshì Yún Rén used to prevent collisions. Just before the melt and shove, the ship's sensors reported it was not a meteorite, so they slowed and changed course and avoided a collision and out of curiosity swung back around to check out what it really was.

Very quickly the Měngshì Yún Rén determined it was some kind of ship drifting in space with barely any electronics turned on, which they considered rather odd.

Scanning the ship, the Rén as they were called by several other alien races, determined there were beings on it, but after repeated attempts to contact it there were no answers.

MĚNGSHÌ YÚN RÉN

OFFICER

Maybe the crew is unconscious and cannot answer.

MĚNGSHÌ YÚN RÉN

CAPTAIN

The only way to find out is to take them aboard.

> MĚNGSHÌ YÚN RÉN
> OFFICER
> We can't risk transporting them, their bodies might not
> be able to withstand the transport mechanism.

> MĚNGSHÌ YÚN RÉN
> CAPTAIN
> How big is the ship?

> MĚNGSHÌ YÚN RÉN
> OFFICER
> It could easily fit in our Shuttle Bay.

> MĚNGSHÌ YÚN RÉN
> CAPTAIN
> Let's move our Shuttle out of the Bay, bring the ship
> in, get the people out and see if their ok. We'll redock
> our Shuttle after we deal with these aliens.

EXT. CGI. SPACE. MĚNGSHÌ YÚN RÉN SPACESHIP. BRINGING THE
MERGENKY ESCAPE POD INTO THE SHUTTLE BAY OPERATION. 20
SECONDS.

In a brief period, the swap was made, and the strange shuttle-like craft was now inside
the *Měngshì Yún Rén* ship.

INT. SPACE. MĚNGSHÌ YÚN RÉN SPACESHIP. EXAMINING THE MERGENKY
ESCAPE POD

> MĚNGSHÌ YÚN RÉN
> OFFICER
> You can clearly see burn markings on the spacecraft's
> exterior indicating it had experienced some type of
> explosion and trauma.

> MĚNGSHÌ YÚN RÉN
> CHIEF SCIENTIST
> We have a problem in figuring out how to open the
> hatch to it and looking in the humanoids are not
> moving and some look dead.

> MĚNGSHÌ YÚN RÉN
> CAPTAIN
> They may be near expiring, we can't wait to figure out

how to open the door, us cut a hole in it and get them out right away to revive them.

Technicians with special cutting tools cut out an obvious window section in a couple of minutes allowing them to get inside the craft. Once inside they found some instructions they quickly understood that released the door which opened for them allowing them to comfortably remove the bodies and take them to their ship's surgeon's office.

***

ANARCHIE JEEAPA INVASION

<u>EXT. CGI. DAY. JEEAPA. UNLOADING ANARCHIE TRANSPORTS. 30 SECONDS.</u>

VOICE OVER

The Anarchie Jeeapa Invasion Transports unloaded quickly. It was just a matter of the Crawlers or the Exoskeleton's walking out of the cargo ramps and moved to the staging areas.

The Anarchie could not risk the loss of their transports in the event they had to later evacuate the force, so as soon as they were unloaded, they were launched back into space and sent towards the Anarchie Empire where Mergenky Fleets were less likely to enter.

Since the Anarchie Transports were carefully loaded and the combat load was designed to blend in with the ground plan, there was no need to sort through material at a supply dump.

Materials were combat preloaded for business, which meant the crawlers and Exoskeletons merely had to exit the transports and maneuver to their assigned attack formation.

The time selected during the night was picked to maximize the ground force's ability to maneuver and not be harassed by Mergenky Air Assets.

As the Anarchie transports poured their insides out, the ground forces added to the security as their anti-air forces multiplied the amount of air defense they could muster.

Lasers, Kinetic Weapons, Chemical Rockets, Jammers, Scramblers, and Positronic Perforators, laid a gauntlet that Mergenky would soon hate as it soon would become painfully obvious, they should have exerted every ounce of energy and the fabric of society to prevent the Anarchie landings.

ANARCHIE
TASK FORCE COMMANDER
GENERAL FĀGUĀNG DE SĪXIĂNGJIĀ

This time around, we Anarchie are playing for keeps. Jeeapa was going to be ours. The humiliating loss at 'Jeeapa One,' will soon be wiped clean.

The Crawlers and Exoskeletons from the air looked like a growing spider web. Part of that web was camouflage that would force the Mergenky to expend an inordinate amount of assets to expose the real pockets of assault forces now moving towards the Jeeapa Dome at 10 miles per hour. At the current rate of movement, they would be at the gates of Jeeapa Dome in 10 hours. MSF was now in crisis.

***

<u>INT. DAY. QUOM HEALING CENTER</u>

Monachi informed the director:

MONACHI
We will take Kara home and stay with her.

The director knew the history of the Andromeda Mission.

VOICEOVER
Kara and the director had numerous discussions in the past about the grizzly details of the Artificial Intelligence of Martha that was allowed to grow out of control and affected their lives in ways nobody ever imagined possible.

In several private discussions over the past few years with Kara, the very complicated relationships and the turmoil inflicted by Martha with her jealousy and her attempted murder of Kara, left huge scars. It was seemingly a miracle that as a couple Vance and Kara survived.

But the bonds were strong and when they overcame the diversity of AI gone bad an entire galaxy away and far from outside support, where their mere survival was a testament to an individual's ability to evolve and cope with extremely complicated and diverse scenarios.

And now the surviving partner who made that journey from the depths of hell back to the fruits of a moral and ethical oasis was gone because he was part of a supreme sacrifice.

Kara was equally a victim because in a normal lifespan, it's almost impossible to experience these kinds of events with a partner and not be able to live out the golden years together when one of them is taken away prematurely.

Vance and the Children were really all that Kara had in her life. None of her relatives were alive, when her mother died, she was the last survivor in that family tree. And now Vance was gone. It would be a tumultuous time for Kara.

When they were leaving the director's office, the Healing Center Director informed Monachi:

HEALING CENTER DIRECTOR

We will send some people over time to time to adjust her medications as necessary.

MSF was not only dealing with this extraordinary event, but many other simultaneous events were swamping them with incredible needs and requests and the entire civilization was quickly affected.

VOICE OVER

Due to the stature of Vance being a Mergenky national hero as well as an Earth person converted to Mergenky, placed MSF in a unique position. It wasn't as if the MSF were giving Vance's family special treatment.

General Kahn and the MSF were just recoiling from an event never experienced in Mergenky History, where an Earth Person was killed heroically fighting in one of their wars.

But also, as the personal history unfolded and the public became more aware of Vance's mission to Andromeda and his role in the first Jeeapa War, he quickly became in a sense a folk hero.

As all this information about Vance was unfolding, MSF brought the children home from their boarding school to be with their mother Kara during this quite sad event.

Vance's children were very happy to see Kwongab and Monachi who were an extended family. But that did not reduce the amount of sorrow they felt, which was quite astonishing for any Mergenky.

But since the children had some of Vance's DNA, they were not as unemotional as Mergenky would typically be.

There was a special memorial for Vance they all attended the following day, and Kara seemed to be regaining her charisma and life was starting to show in her face again. Life would not be the same without Vance. But life would go on.

Kara had her treatments adjusted a few times and after the third day she was starting to look at current events and news reports and saw the terrible mess Jeeapa was becoming and in the morning when Kwongab and Monachi arrived for their daily visits, Kara surprised Kwongab and Monachi when she said:

KARA

Monachi and Kwongab, MSF needs you a lot more than I do now. I want you to go back to work now. You can help me and Vance's children more by giving the MSF leadership and help that I know you are capable of and that's where you are desperately needed, so I want you to return to your work and do your missions.

Kwongab as well as Monachi swung into neural expansion mode and thoroughly analyzed Kara and concluded she was quite capable of proceeding now without their assistance.

Monachi and Kwongab reluctantly left and went back to work at the MSF.

The following day after having a long talk with Kara's children, it was decided, staying home was not going to benefit their education, and the Anarchie situation was more of a reason than ever for them to excel in school and be the best students they could be. At Kara's request, MSF transported her children back to their boarding school and she reported back to work at the healing center.

Even though the director knew Kara was heartbroken, she also knew that while she was healing her patients in a way, she was healing herself so she decided that Kara returning to work, though seemingly soon after Vance's death, it would ultimately accelerate Kara's own healing.

***

Kwongab and Monachi reported back to MSF and the staff there was rather surprised they forfeited their time off so rapidly to join back in the fray.

Several Senior Officers were needed to put MSFC-8 back in commission. General Kahn had just returned to Gwaba for consultations and briefings on the Jeeapa situation that was quickly developing into a stalemate, was in his office when the staffing approval came through and he noticed Kwongab and Monachi were both slated to go to MSFC-8.

General Kahn immediately vetoed the assignment and called the detailing officer and informed him:

GENERAL KAHN

We are not going to risk losing them both on the same
ship, split them up.

DETAILING OFFICER

Yes sir, what do you have in mind?

GENERAL KAHN

I want Kwongab to relieve the Captain of MSFC-8
and find the captain another assignment, preferably on
another ship.

DETAILING OFFICER

What about Monachi?

GENERAL KAHN

I would like Monachi to come back to headquarters to
work on some of the bottlenecks in Logistics. She may
balk at the assignment, but things are getting really
screwed up now and I know she can straighten them
out quickly.

DETAILING OFFICER
What if she rejects those orders?

GENERAL KAHN
Inform Monachi I said that after we get a handle on
the logistics, we can give her the command of a ship if
that's what she wants.

DETAILING OFFICER
Will do sir.

Within 30 minutes both Kwongab and Monachi accepted their orders in a gloomily
mood with no objections. They were coming back to contribute to the best of their
ability, and they would support General Kahn as much as they could.

Monachi did not express her feelings about the assignment, but Kwongab probed her
with his neural expansion ability and realized Monachi was grateful for the logistics
assignment because she didn't want her kids to be without parents. The loss of Vance
had suddenly had a huge impact on Monachi's mannerisms.

Kwongab was quickly disturbed that in probing Monachi he discovered she was hiding
something from him, so he had no choice but to press her for the information.

KWONGAB
What is it that you are hiding from me?

MONACHI
I knew we would eventually have to have this talk, but
I felt the time was not good now.

Kwongab was slightly bewildered by the uncharacteristic nature that Monachi had just
exhibited.

KWONGAB
I'm about ready to go off to war, we don't have much
time to discuss whatever it is. I would prefer you just
now divulge to me what it is that is upsetting you that
you have blocked me from discovering.

MONACHI
I hate to do this to you. It could affect your judgement
while out there on your ship, but if you insist, I'll tell
you."

KWONGAB
I insist.

MONACHI
It concerns our children.

Kwongab was now super elevated, and his curiosity just exploded with the magic words, '*our children.*'

KWONGAB
What is it about our children?

MONACHI
Their special school, the Juéduìhuĭhuáng Foundation they are attending that we thought was all about advancing intellectuals to a genius level so they can help design the future for our civilization, isn't what it really is about.

KWONGAB
Then what is it about?

MONACHI
The government is training them to become spies.

Kwongab just felt something like a lightning rod go through him and as he recoiled, he angrily stated:

KWONGAB
The very last thing in the world I want for my children to get into is the INTEL business.

MONACHI
I was very upset when I found out.

KWONGAB
Life expectancy for INTEL people working in the field is about five years. Secondly it greatly restricts social interaction with friends and family, and places everyone under continuous scrutiny.

MONACHI
Not that it matters much to us that INTEL agents get

fully vetted, but so do their families, and quite often. None of their lives will ever be able to develop into normalcy.

KWONGAB

How do you know all about this situation concerning our children?

MONACHI

Our Robot Charles discovered this as he was looking over their homework assignments while the kids were out with John and friends at the recreation center.

KWONGAB

How far into the spy business are they?

MONACHI

Charles analyzed the information he found in their school back packs and stated: *'They are now at the advanced spy level training.'* Even though they are still kids, Charles estimates they are almost at the deployable level.

Kwongab knew some of the dirty secrets of the INTEL business. They used children, the elderly, and people that you would least expect to carry out their clandestine work.

KWONGAB

I'll go see General Kahn before I go to the ship and ask for a favor.

MONACHI

You must leave in 30 minutes, you must go see General Kahn now if you want a chance to see him, he's a busy man.

KWONGAB

Will you be here? I want to see you after I talk to General Kahn

MONACHI

I'll wait here for you, but you need to hurry because they are calling me to go to a meeting in 30 minutes about some emergency shipments.

Kwongab knew exactly where to find General Kahn and went right to his office. At first staffers tried to prevent his access, but Kwongab used his neural expansion telepathy to mentally alter them and make them forget they were forbidden to allow anyone near General Kahn who was in the middle of making some rather dreadful decisions.

General Kahn was utterly shocked when his aid opened the door and reported:

GENERAL KAHN'S AID.
Here is Captain Kwongab to see you.

Kwongab walked in and the aid shut the door behind him leaving the two men alone.

GENERAL KAHN
This is kind of interesting Kwongab, I told my staff to not allow anyone in under ANY circumstances.

COMMANDER KWONGAB
I'm sorry sir but I have an urgent matter.

GENERAL KAHN
Kwongab, I must make a decision that may cost a million people their lives, what do you have that can be so pressing?

Kwongab could feel General Kahn's pain and applied his neural expansion to get to the bottom of it and in some ways helped him make the decision.

COMMANDER KWONGAB
Sir, it's about my children.

VOICEOVER (GENERAL
KAHN) THOUGHT
I do not know if I should scream or throw something at Kwongab.

General Kahn was quickly not feeling so bad and suddenly thought of a solution to the crisis.

VOICEOVER (GENERAL
KAHN) THOUGHT
Perhaps Kwongab's visit triggered the thought I needed?

Since the General had made his decision, it was no longer such a crisis, and he allowed himself a couple minutes to deal with his friend who had paid barely survived recent battles including losing his best friend for this mess they were in.

GENERAL KAHN
What can I do to help your children?

COMMANDER KWONGAB
Sir, my wife, and I have just discovered the special school our children are in is in fact a training center for spies.

GENERAL KAHN
Your kids are learning to become spies?

COMMANDER KWONGAB
It's not what we want, and we strongly oppose it. We want our children to live normal lives. I'm asking you for a favor to intervene if you can and get our children removed out of that school and relocated to something domestic and practical whether it be engineering, science, or other academics.

GENERAL KAHN
Ok Kwongab, I'll see what I can do.

COMMANDER KWONGAB
Thank you General, this means a lot to us.

GENERAL KAHN
Kwongab, you earned my help many times over.

COMMANDER KWONGAB
Thank you General.

GENERAL KAHN
Kwongab, may I ask you one question?

COMMANDER KWONGAB
Sure General.

GENERAL KAHN
Did you use that neural expansion telepathy illegally for your personal gain by getting in here?

KWONGAB
General, you know I could never answer that question.

GENERAL KAHN
Kwongab, I know you can't answer the question, I just wanted to ask.

COMMANDER KWONGAB
General, I know you are a busy man, and I appreciate you seeing me. I will leave you now so that you can attend to your crisis.

GENERAL KAHN
Kwongab, good luck on Cruiser MSFC-8.

COMMANDER KWONGAB
Thanks, General.

Just as Kwongab was standing and preparing to leave the room, General Kahn suddenly spoke:

GENERAL KAHN
Kwongab, I know you are probably wondering why I put you on that old rust bucket. It needs someone of your talent to get it quickly in fighting shape. We are in dire need.

COMMANDER KWONGAB
I will do my best sir.

GENERAL KAHN
I know you will.

Kwongab bowed, turned around and left the office and was very happy because he did neural expansion and determined General Kahn would intervene for his children.

A few minutes later Kwongab rejoined Monachi.

KWONGAB
I talked with General Kahn; he promised to investigate the matter for us.

MONACHI
Was he sincere?

KWONGAB
Yes, I telepathically probed General Kahn with neural
expansion, the concern and motives are genuine.

Kwongab then probed Monachi who felt his probing. They were locked in a mental embrace unlike anyone else could do. This war was far from over and the risk was high, especially to the new commander of a rust bucket.

The two were mindful they both had somewhere to be. They cherished the moment, and the love flowed from each other in the mental synapse they gave each other only made possible through the mental telepathy ability their neural expansion implants allowed.

In feeling each other in essence their souls were touching creating an endearing and everlasting transcendence.

When it was time to go, Monachi and Kwongab looked into each other's eyes. There was fear, hope, desire, and compassion. With Vance's recent passing, they were subtlety reminded the fragility of life, especially in the business they were in. And now they not only were afraid for each other, the disclosure their children were very close to entering harm's way was not a pleasing notion. Their hopes rested on General Kahn.

As Monachi and Kwongab separated and walked in opposite directions, huge regret flourished in them for not enjoying each other more during their recent break. They understood that the situation with Vance placed extraordinary requirements on their time, and it was sad they never had that special moment together and now they were departing it was too late. But as they walked away, at least their hearts were full of love and compassion for each other.

CRUISER TRANSPORTS
Monachi was soon in a conference room with a lot of
people and soon they were discussing the emergency
shipments to Jeeapa.

MSF BRIEFER
What we are proposing is *Cruiser Transports*.

CONFERENCE ATTENDEE
Please explain what *Cruiser Transport* means.

MSF BRIEFER
The Cruisers we have in mind are considered hanger
queens with a lot of material conditions that make

them not prime candidates for front line efforts against Anarchie Battleships.

CONFERENCE ATTENDEE
Is there some sort of conversion required?

MSF BRIEFER
If we strip out about half of the armaments, we will gain enough volume to transport a significant amount of military hardware without the need to send Transports that would be viewed as sitting ducks.

CONFERENCE ATTENDEE
Why would that be?

MSF BRIEFER
The Anarchie would have to assume they are viable Cruisers and should not attack them without possibly receiving substantial inflicted wounds.

CONFERENCE ATTENDEE
Why attempt this unusual method?

MSF BRIEFER
The Cruisers can attain high speed and travel alone without escorts.

SECOND CONFERENCE ATTENDEE
Why not put them in Convoys?

CONFERENCE BRIEFER
We did some calculations and discovered a high-speed Cruiser Transport would have a higher probability of making it to Jeeapa or Frăctŏng without being destroyed by traveling alone.

CONFERENCE ATTENDEE
How long will it take to do the conversion?

MSF BRIEFER
MSS-21 maintenance crews say they can turn a Cruiser into a Cruiser Transport in about 24 hours.

MONACHI
Do you have a list of ships designated for the Cruiser
Transport Conversions?

MSF BRIEFER
Yes, one moment please.

A holograph appeared that included images and hull numbers.

Monachi watched the hull numbers show up on the projection. She suddenly felt very uneasy when top of the list was MSFC-8. The 'rust bucket' was going to be quickly turned into a 'sitting duck' as far as she was concerned. She was then compelled to speak up.

MONACHI
Why not at least send a Scout Class ship out with the
Cruiser Transport to give them a chance?

MSF BRIEFER
We are a little short on Scouts right now.

MONACHI
What do you have them doing?

MSF BRIEFER
They are scouting the Anarchie.

Monachi blasted the MSF Briefer.

MONACHI
We already know where the Anarchie Forces are
located. They are at Jeeapa, and Frăctŏng. Don't you
think the search is over and it's time to swing into the
destroy mode?

Nobody was watching when General Kahn slipped into the meeting in the back of the room and took it all in.

There were some angry responses then suddenly
General Kahn spoke.

GENERAL KAHN
Commander Monachi made an excellent point. She's
right.

General Kahn looked directly into the eyes of one of the individuals who blasted Monachi with a negative response.

> GENERAL KAHN
> Those Scouts are not contributing much because we can't send them against an Anarchie Battleship and since we know where the Anarchie are, they are being wasted.

The room was suddenly quiet as everyone turned towards and watched General Kahn, waiting for a possible follow through in his comments, which General Kahn stated abruptly.

> GENERAL KAHN
> I like the idea of sending a Scout with a Cruiser Transport which would add some additional fire power and maneuver.

Monachi could not hold back. Kwongab would be piloting one of those rust bucket sitting ducks.

> MONACHI
> The Scout could work as a path finder to get the Cruiser Transport where it could be turned over to Mergenky Fleet Assets for protection at the destination.

> GENERAL KAHN
> The critical nature of Cruiser Transports is the cargo is extremely valuable and necessary for Jeeapa and Frăctŏng. It needs protection.

***

THE FIRST CONVOY
Kwongab took a Shuttle up to MSS-21 where he was met by Commander Dĭngqiāng (pronounced Ding-chan), the Executive Officer for MSFC-8.

> COMMANDER DĬNGQIĀNG
> Commander Kwongab, I'm Dĭngqiāng the Executive Officer for MSFC-8.

> COMMANDER KWONGAB
> Please to meet you Commander Dĭngqiāng.

COMMANDER DĬNGQIĀNG
MSFC-8 is not very far, we can just walk there.

COMMANDER KWONGAB
That's good, I can use the exercise.

The men walked about 300 yards and came to the access ramp to MSFC-8.

COMMANDER KWONGAB
Looks like there is an industrial air lock on the ship entrance.

COMMANDER DĬNGQIĀNG
Yes sir, we have started a conversion, and they put us at this lock so that large amounts of equipment can be offloaded, and cargos put on while they convert us to Cruiser Transport.

COMMANDER KWONGAB
Never thought I would see the day they would put me in command of a rust bucket.

COMMANDER DĬNGQIĀNG
Well sir, I'm sure we have a few crew members that feel they should be on a new Cruiser or a Scout and going into action.

KWONGAB
I think as soon as the Anarchie figure out what we are doing they will see a lot of action.

COMMANDER DĬNGQIĀNG
Most of the crew thought they would miss this war riding a hanger queen.

COMMANDER KWONGAB
I can assure you they will soon have a change of heart.

COMMANDER DĬNGQIĀNG
This way Commander Kwongab, or should I start calling you Captain.

COMMANDER KWONGAB
It's your prerogative.

COMMANDER DǏNGQIĀNG
You must not have heard the news?

COMMANDER KWONGAB
What news?

COMMANDER DǏNGQIĀNG
Your temporary rank of Captain given to you when
you were sent to Jeeapa is now permanent You were
just promoted to full Captain, you are no longer a
Commander.

CAPTAIN KWONGAB
When did this happen?

COMMANDER DǏNGQIĀNG
We received the message from MSF Headquarters just
before I came to meet you. Your portfolio is waiting
for you in your Space Cabin.

Kwongab knew that as part of his portfolio he would have his orders as well as a
change of uniform waiting. It would be best if the crew saw him with his Captain
rankings as soon as possible. He went directly to his Space Cabin, changed with PNN
help and then proceeded to the Bridge and looked around.

Kwongab's initial thoughts were:

CAPTAIN KWONGAB
(THOUGHT)
This place has seen better days.

Kwongab then reflected:

CAPTAIN KWONGAB
(THOUGHT)
*This ship participated in the first Jeeapa war and
may have been part of the Armada that came in on
the surprise attack which he and the other Scout pilots
made possible with their fancy maneuvers, partly
thanks to Vance who came up with some of great ideas.*

Suddenly, Kwongab felt an emptiness he had never felt before.

NOTE:

Reminder to the Director: I recommended the (THOUGHT'S) are handled like VOICEOVER with the actor's voice used and close ups of the actor's face as they are having those thoughts.

CAPTAIN KWONGAB (THOUGHT)

I wrongly assumed Vance would be around forever, and now that he is gone, he is sorely missed.

All those flashbacks to Andromeda could not be helped.

FLASHBACK:

The time Vance was shot in the leg with the poison arrow during the Andromeda mission was just one of many of the many exciting adventures they experienced together. Right then and there Kwongab made the decision:

CAPTAIN KWONGAB (THOUGHT)

I will make this ship proud in memory of Vance.

Commander Dǐngqiāng approached Kwongab on the bridge.

COMMANDER DǏNGQIĀNG
Would you like me to show you around the bridge?

CAPTAIN KWONGAB
It looks like a standard Cruiser Bridge.

COMMANDER DǏNGQIĀNG

Yes, it should be about the same as what you are used to.

CAPTAIN KWONGAB
What is the latest projection of our undocking?

COMMANDER DǏNGQIĀNG

Some goofball at MSF says we'll be underway in 24 hours with our first cargo load.

CAPTAIN KWONGAB
Why will we not be able to make that schedule.

COMMANDER DǏNGQIĀNG
We have so much work to accomplish, I don't see how they can complete it in 24 hours.

CAPTAIN KWONGAB
Commander Dǐngqiǎng, I'm going to give you a lesson in MSF docking right away.

First and foremost, stay out of the space-workers way and let them accomplish their tasks.

The fewer impediments we put in their way; the sooner they will get done.

COMMANDER DǏNGQIĀNG
You are not expecting me to cut corners are you, Captain?

CAPTAIN KWONGAB
Commander Dǐngqiǎng, I would never ask you to cut corners, but if you round them off a bit and lubricate them, then it might be a smoother time getting around them.

COMMANDER DǏNGQIĀNG
Captain, MSF has provided us with temporary extended stay officer quarters rooms on MSS-21 so that you can be more comfortable while they do all the industrial work.

CAPTAIN KWONGAB
XO thanks for the information, but I'm staying aboard my ship until we get underway.

COMMANDER DǏNGQIĀNG
Understand sir.

CAPTAIN KWONGAB
Have the crew meet in the Crews Lounge Area in 10 minutes. I want to meet them and let them know what I expect out of them.

In a few minutes Captain Kwongab was in the Crew's Lounge at the head table where Captains, XO's and other important people addressed the crews in all hand's meetings.

Eventually the crew all filed in. Everyone was in high expectations when they discovered Kwongab was their new Commanding Officer, and the former Commanding Officer had departed MSS-21 heading for MSF Headquarters where he would soon be given another assignment.

The XO COMMANDER DǏNGQIĀNG did the introduction:

COMMANDER DǏNGQIĀNG
Crew, this is our new Captain, Kwongab, who will be
addressing you and answering some of the questions
you might have.

Kwongab in a very friendly pose, then in a more astute manner got to the heart of the matter very promptly.

CAPTAIN KWONGAB
Hello everyone.

Everyone in the room focused on Kwongab expecting to hear what was planned for them.

CAPTAIN KWONGAB
I'm sure that earlier today many of you were thinking
that participating in the Jeeapa conflict was not going
to be one of the roles of this ship.

But because of some military setbacks, we now need men and material sent to the war zone in a more higher priority manner.

That's why MSF was pressed to attempt some innovative approaches in getting precious materials and cargos to our troops as soon as possible.

Kwongab looked around the room and saw intense interest in everyone's eyes. He also wasted no time performing neural expansion telepathic probing of crew members to better understand them and give them a little mental tweaking if necessary. Interspersed with his neural expansion telepathy he continued his briefing.

CAPTAIN KWONGAB
The Anarchie arrived at Jeeapa and Frăctŏng with a
very powerful fleet and regular transports simply do
not have the speed and agility to get in and out of
harm's way attempting to arrive at those two planets.

Some very brilliant thinkers came up with a suggestion of converting ships such as this one to a cargo carrying role.

Quite frankly it's too dangerous now to send regular Transports. Therefore, some of the high priority cargo will be sent on this ship and others converted like it.

Kwongab delayed a moment looking around at all the crew members and doing telepathic investigations into how they felt about their new role.

CAPTAIN KWONGAB
We expect all the work to be completed in 24 hours
and we'll undock and proceed to our first destination
with our first cargo.

The crew didn't seem to be affected one way or another with the presentation and information until Kwongab surprised them with a major shift in policy.

CAPTAIN KWONGAB
As of now we will have sentries controlling access to
the ship. As soon as Cargos start getting loaded on the
ship, no departure by ships company will be allowed.

Based on the timeline I just saw; I expect that to be less than 12 hours from now.

Those of you who have been staying on MSS-21 temporary quarters, you are to move aboard the ship right away.

I expect you all to help as much as possible in getting this ship ready to undock and transit to our destination.

Kwongab looked around the room sizing up the group and in brief moments between statements did several neural expansions, telepathic probing's to get the feedback from his comments. Several crew members were not happy being forced to move back aboard the Cruiser so swiftly.

CAPTAIN KWONGAB
As soon as we undock, we will immediately start
drilling and running simulations.

I know most of you are rusty. It's been a while since you traveled in space and dealt with enemy vessels.

That's why it's important we prepare ourselves in the event we stumble across Anarchie on our way to our destination.

Kwongab looked around the room and asked:

CAPTAIN KWONGAB
Any comments?

The crew seemed slightly subdued as many were suddenly transfixed by the suddenness of their role change and pending departure.

CAPTAIN KWONGAB
I'll be in the control room/bridge in case anyone has
any questions.

Kwongab then turned and walked out of the lounge and then the XO COMMANDER DǏNGQIĀNG shouted,

COMMANDER DǏNGQIĀNG
Dismissed!

Kwongab didn't take long to get to the bridge and immediately engaged PNN getting the ship's status. He then worked out some plans for simulations as soon as they undocked and headed for their destination.

Just as Kwongab predicted, in 12 hours all the rip out and preparations were complete. Crew members very professionally jumped in and assisted in whatever work they could. Then the Cargo's started coming aboard.

This was all ground fighting hardware except for the cheap drones they needed to light up the evening light on Frăctŏng to take the night advantage away from the Anarchie.

Also, some satchel charges that could be used in space or on the ground were on the manifest. Kwongab remembered using these satchel charges during the previous Jeeapa conflict.

Nobody attempted to leave and Kwongab was quickly satisfied there were no 5th column types amongst them in his crew.

MSF sent a communique to Kwongab informing him:

MSF COMMUNIQUE
Captain Kwongab, you expected to undock in
approximately 12 hours and transit to Frăctŏng with
this cargo.

MSFC-8 OP-ORDER
A landing zone was being prepared for MSFC-8 North
of Yŏngbùmián de Chéngshì. The ship's track was
also provided with timing.

MSFC-8's speed would be adjusted to arrive at the Landing Zone 3 hours after sunset. The cargo was to be unloaded and the ship underway off the planet before sunrise.

VOICE OVER

A task force was being set up to ensure MSFC-8 had atmospheric penetration and departure without being molested by Anarchie Battleships.

MSFC-8's shipment was crucial because it would continue the viability of Yǒngbùmián de Chéngshì's Air Defenses as consumable weapons were nearing depletion. Once air defense was gone shortly so would be Yǒngbùmián de Chéngshì.

Another huge surprise is Kwongab's MSFC-8 would have one escort, a Scout class vessel, MSFS-4 that was recently beaten up while Monachi was piloting at the same time Kwongab was participating in events at Jeeapa.

Apparently, the MSFS -4 damage was repaired as good as could be expected under the circumstances, but 10% of the PNN was knocked out.

Even so 90% of the PNN functionality was still more than sufficient to handle the ship. Since the MSFS-4 was not out to be using the space telescope for research, the extra processing bandwidth wasn't required from the massively parallel processed computational suite.

Monachi was not going to be put back aboard S-4. Another one of Kwongab's recent students who just graduated from PCO school, Commander Kuàisù Sīkǎo (pronounced Ku-ai-sue Sa-cow) was selected and will be taking it out for a quick shakedown cruise and test the propulsion system, then standby to escort MSFC-8.

Kwongab wasn't too thrilled about having a rookie as the captain/pilot of a Scout class ship performing a major escort mission.

Most likely all MSFS-4 would be useful for would be to transit ahead of the Cruiser MSFC-8 and prevent them from maneuvering into an ambush.

At least that was something worthwhile. However, since the new Pilot had not really participated in live combat, only simulators, he was a mere neophyte that would not be capable of adding to the strategic disposition of the small two ship convoy.

Kwongab notified MSF and the new pilot on S-4, Commander Kuàisù Sīkăo that he wanted to go on space-trials with S-4 Commander Kuàisù Sīkăo, observe the ship's performance after the repairs and work out contingencies and create some private Tangramized Communication Macro's which would prevent any spies from knowing what the communications meant since only Kwongab and Commander Kuàisù Sīkăo would have the decode.

The Mergenky Scout class ship MSFS-4 was only moments away from undocking when MSF contacted Commander Kuàisù Sīkăo and informed him he would have a rider for his *Space Trials*.

It's not every day a new Captain/pilot receives his PCO instructor as a rider for *Space Trials*. One could say it was extremely rare if almost never.

Kuàisù Sīkăo didn't take but one glance to see Kwongab was a full Captain now and aware Captain Kwongab would be commanding the MSFC-8 Cruiser to Frăctŏng.

COMMANDER KUÀISÙ SĪKĂO
Welcome aboard Captain Kwongab.

CAPTAIN KWONGAB
Thank you, Commander Kuàisù Sīkăo.

VOICEOVER

Kwongab knew from his recent graduating class that Kuàisù Sīkăo was perhaps the fastest thinker in the class.

Kuàisù Sīkăo had some brilliance and was borderline genius. Kwongab was in some ways relieved that if it had to be a rookie escorting him, at least it would be one of the sharpest rookies around.

Kwongab wasted no time in applying neural expansion techniques and assessing the mental structure of Kuàisù Sīkăo's thought processes.

Kuàisù Sīkăo's personal psychology was ideal for leadership, his bravery was no less than anyone Kwongab ever evaluated.

All in all, Kuàisù Sīkăo had plenty of positives. But Kwongab strongly believed there was no substitute for real combat experience to measure the real tendencies of a pilot and while they were caught in a gripping scenario where life and death decisions had to be made rapidly shotgun style. Otherwise the demise of the spaceship was a certainty.

Kwongab looked around the bridge.

CAPTAIN KWONGAB
(THOUGHT)
It feels like a strange sensation because Commander Lester was recently the pilot of this vessel and so was Monachi, and she almost perished in it.

COMMANDER KUÀISÙ SĪKǍO
All systems are online, and health checks are looking good. and ready to be monitored for performance checks during *Space Trials*.

Kwongab observed Kuàisù Sīkǎo looking at the systems health holograph showing a three-dimensional view of the Scout with color coded indicators on each system.

COMMANDER KUÀISÙ SĪKǍO
Captain Kwongab, we are getting ready to undock now. If you would like to remain on the bridge, you are welcome.

CAPTAIN KWONGAB
Thank you Commander KUÀISÙ SĪKǍO

COMMANDER KUÀISÙ SĪKǍO
Captain Kwongab, if you would like to spend some time resting in a Space Cabin until we get in space away from MSS-21, one of the crew members can escort you to a spare Space Cabin set aside for your use.

CAPTAIN KWONGAB
Commander Kuàisù Sīkǎo, that will not be necessary. I plan on remaining on the bridge throughout the *Space Trials*.

KUÀISÙ SĪKǍO
Very well Captain, it will be a pleasure having you here.

CAPTAIN KWONGAB
Thank you.

PNN had a voice like Vickie whom Kwongab had known well during the first Jeeapa debacle stated:

PNN
MSS-21 has reported that all conditions are met for undocking, and we have permission to undock and commence space trials.

COMMANDER KUÀISÙ SĪKĂO
Commence undocking.
EXT. CGI. SPACE. MSFS-4 UNDOCKING FROM SPACE STATIONS MSS-21. 20 SECONDS.

Music for this Segment:

https://www.youtube.com/watch?v=SRmCEGHt-Qk

Starting time 1:08

Kwongab watched the three-dimensional highly detailed holograph of a simulation of the Scout class ship undocking from MSS-21 space station on the ship status display..

The whole process was automated which was expected by MSF who would frown upon any pilot who attempted undocking in manual flight controls.

Even though crew members could not feel movement, the optical view of surveillance holographs and the 3D navigation holograph conveyed the significant movement away from the space station. It did not take but a few moments to completely clear the space station and continue moving out into space.

When Mergenky Scout MSFS-4 was clear of the space station, the Scout proceeded to accelerate as it maneuvered towards deep space heading in a direction far away from any space battles going on.

This was an engineering trial where they would determine the repairs completed were viable and successful. Otherwise, they would all perish in the span of a few minutes.

Kwongab walked over to the Navigator who was manipulating navigation vectors PNN would use to guide the ship out to an area where they could safely put it through its pace without the risk of a collision or unexpected encounter with an Anarchie.

It did not take long to build up incredible speed, then they maneuvered at high-speed performing a Capmoc-Drulyenslv maneuver.

Kuàisù Sīkǎo then slowed down MSFS-4 then performed a Frazgrandopf maneuver with great precision and came to a stop, waiting for a possible trailer to shoot past.

This was not because they expected any craft trailing them, it was done to practice the maneuvers for later when they would really need to do it when operating near the Anarchie.

Kwongab stood by observing and mind probing Commander Kuàisù Sīkǎo and was relieved to measure the stability and confidence in the man. Those traits would be needed soon enough as they would be tested when they approached Frăctŏng.

***

<u>EXT. DAY/NIGHT FRĂCTŎNG BATTLEFIELD AT THE ESCARPMENT.</u>

VOICEOVER

The fighting on Frăctŏng was looking slightly promising for the Mergenky if they could hold out. The Anarchie were not getting supplies through, and this battle of attrition would eventually be won by whoever lasted the longest.

The MSF realized Jeeapa was at an utter stalemate and if they could quickly end the fighting on Frăctŏng, they could then divert all the forces to Jeeapa and turn the battle in their favor.

Things were getting far more severe for the Anarchie than what the Mergenky understood.

The Frăctŏng feint had served its useful purpose allowing the Anarchie to get their forces landed on Jeeapa without a great deal of interference.

The Anarchie now entered the extraction phase of the Frăctŏng operation but finding it difficult to disengage in a way their transports could get down and retrieve the survivors. They had to do it soon or there might not be any survivors to repatriate with forces now on Jeeapa.

In a few days the Crawlers and the Exoskeletons had taken their toll.

Dealing with the cheap drones had been more

problematic than Anarchie Forces imagined. By taking the night away from the Anarchie the Mergenky vastly diminished Anarchie effectiveness as aggressive fighters.

General Borktar was still wanting a decision in his favor and a chip as a portfolio piece by the conquest of Yǒngbùmián de Chéngshì.

Anarchie leadership was keenly aware General Borktar's Anarchieborgs squander rate was accelerating and they either had to pull the plug on him soon and evacuate the troops or they would not have a force to augment the Jeeapa forces who needed reserves.

ANARCHIE LEADERSHIP

General Borktar, headquarters wants to know your status and what you are planning over the next 48 hours.

GENERAL BORKTAR

Mergenky are using a smaller number of lighting drones. We think they are running out and soon we'll have the nights again very shortly.

ANARCHIE LEADERSHIP

General Borktar you may continue. We'll give you another 48 hours since it looks like you are reaching a point where your troops could rule the night again and reduce casualties and force a surrender.

The night before Kwongab delivered his first payload, the Mergenky launched no lighting drones, which further gave General Borktar a false positive and reinforced his false sense of the Mergenky disposition of lighting drones as well as other tools such as kinetic weapons.

The Mergenky kinetic weapons shot Spactron 300 projectiles at 10 times the speed of sound. They contained no explosives, but the knock down power was immense. If an Anarchie transport or large Exoskeleton was hit with one of the kinetic weapons, the energy release would cause tremendous damage.

In one specific case a Mergenky kinetic weapon struck the bow of an Anarchie transport and traveled the length of the ship and created a hole and went out the back side. The internal piping and power cables along with much machinery and cargoes were decimated by that lucky shot.

The transport received so much damage it would never leave the planet's surface and Anarchie had no choice but to scuttle the transport to make sure Anarchie proprietary hardware and equipment could not be reverse engineered by the Mergenky.

Some of the Anarchie were not happy watching that ship blow up as they thought it was their way home.

<u>INT. SPACE. MERGENKY SCOUT MSFS-4 CONTROL ROOM.</u>

While the Anarchie waited for the next night as daylight was forming near Yǒngbùmián de Chéngshì, the Mergenky Scout MSFS-4 space trials were coming to a completion.

At this time, Captain Kwongab informed Commander Kuàisù Sīkǎo:

> CAPTAIN KWONGAB
> Commander Kuàisù Sīkǎo I would like to have a private conversation with you now for planning purposes.

> COMMANDER KUÀISÙ SĪKǍO
> We can go to my Space Cabin.

Kuàisù Sīkǎo turned towards his co-pilot LT. Commander Xīngjì Zhēngbà.

> COMMANDER KUÀISÙ SĪKǍO
> Lt. Commander Xīngjì Zhēngbà (pronounced Shing-gee Jung-ba), you are now the designated pilot, approach MSS-21 and wait for further orders.

> LT. COMMANDER XĪNGJÌ ZHĒNGBÀ
> Understood captain.

Kuàisù Sīkǎo led Kwongab to his Space Cabin. Once inside his Space Cabin, Kuàisù Sīkǎo asked:

> COMMANDER KUÀISÙ SĪKǍO
> What is it you wanted to discuss Captain?

> CAPTAIN KWONGAB
> Commander Kuàisù Sīkǎo, I wanted to work out with you some secret signals we agree to now so that when we approach Frăctǒng we can apply Tangramized Macro processes without the risk of a spy giving our signals away.

COMMANDER KUÀISÙ SĪKǍO
Just like you had us do in training.

CAPTAIN KWONGAB
That's correct. It's for moments like now. MSF has spies and knows it.

COMMANDER KUÀISÙ SĪKǍO
It's a shame we can't round them all up.

CAPTAIN KWONGAB
We will never be able to find them all. After we round up most of them and let our guard down, they simply infiltrate more spies.

COMMANDER KUÀISÙ SĪKǍO
Captain, I understand this will allow us to signal to each other our intentions or requests without them knowing what it means.

The two then came up with a list of key words to be used as Macro's which would be a shortcut for certain actions. The key words would also be used just once, so multiple key words had to be created for just one request type.

Once all the communications protocols were worked out, Kwongab suggested:

CAPTAIN KWONGAB
Commander Xīngjì Zhēngbà, I recommend you send me back to MSS-21 on your Shuttle and not redock. I will be getting my ship underway shortly as we are coming up on the undocking. By MSFS-4 remaining in space until we go, you will avoid any inadvertent release or compromise.

COMMANDER KUÀISÙ SĪKǍO
I concur Captain.

CAPTAIN KWONGAB
Good, this was an excellent visit, we'll be leaving on this mission soon, so you have a little extra time to take care of last-minute details.

COMMANDER KUÀISÙ SĪKǍO
Captain Kwongab, I'll walk with you to the Shuttle Bay.

CAPTAIN KWONGAB
Thank you.

Kwongab reached MSFS-4 with Commander Kuàisù Sīkǎo. After the customary respectful bow, Kwongab got into the shuttle with one of MSFS-4's shuttle pilots.

EXT. CGI. SPACE. MSFS-4 SHUTTLE LAUNCHES AND FLIES OVER TO MSS-21.

Soon Kwongab was heading for MSS-21 on MSFS-4's Shuttle where it docked shortly afterwards and then Captain Kwongab went directly to MSFC-8 to get an updated status.

INT. SPACE/MSS-21 MOORING. MSFC-8 CONTROL ROOM.

COMMANDER DĬNGQIĀNG
Welcome back Captain.

CAPTAIN KWONGAB
Thank you Commander Dĭngqiāng, what's the latest
status with the loading?

COMMANDER DĬNGQIĀNG
Captain, we are almost loaded. I expect we'll finish
up in a few minutes and will be ready to depart within
an hour.

CAPTAIN KWONGAB
Excellent. I'll be in my Space Cabin. Call me to the
bridge when we are ready to undock.

COMMANDER DĬNGQIĀNG
Yes sir, Captain.

Kwongab walked into his Space Cabin, then went over to a data terminal where he started looking over the Cruiser's drawings and technical documents. One thing he was particularly interested in was the absolute maximum he could push Cruiser MSFC-8.

Kwongab recalled some time ago receiving training on how MSF put speed limits on every type of ship in the fleet to reduce hull stress that was prematurely aging the ships. He then asked:

CAPTAIN KWONGAB
PNN, does the captain have permission to over-ride
the speed limitations set forth by MSF directives?

ERICA (PNN)
Yes, in wartime conditions.

CAPTAIN KWONGAB
PNN, we are at war now, correct?

PNN answered using the voice of Erica.

ERICA (PNN)
Yes, Captain Kwongab, that is correct.

CAPTAIN KWONGAB
PNN, how much faster can this Cruiser go if I direct propulsion controls to disregard the speed limitations of MSF directives?

ERICA (PNN)
Approximately 33% faster.

CAPTAIN KWONGAB
PNN, why an approximate number?

ERICA (PNN)
Captain Kwongab, we cannot fully define the exact speed based on where in the galaxy the ship is because some areas have higher concentrations of hydrogen atoms and small molecules which increase space friction and results in slowing the ship down a few knots.

CAPTAIN KWONGAB
PNN, can the Scout MSFS-4 also obtain higher speeds?

ERICA (PNN)
Yes, it can keep up with any Cruiser if speed limits are removed.

CAPTAIN KWONGAB
Put everything, we just discussed in a *Holopoint* and send it via special courier encryption to S-4's pilot, Commander Kuàisù Sīkǎo eyes only.

PNN had a holographic briefing *Holopoint* ready within a few minutes. The 3D information and instructions were sent as privileged pilot only communications using special courier encryption.

When Commander Kuàisù Sīkǎo read the communications, he knew it would be a memorable trip.

Captain Kwongab flying a rust bucket beyond MSF guidelines and with Commander Kuàisù Sīkǎo flying the Band-Aid riddle Scout at speeds higher than it ever went set a new bar in the audacity of MSF pilots not seen in over a generation or more.

However, the shock of going from a Peace Dividend Era to brutal aggression on the part of the Anarchie set compelling requirements and standards that foist upon them gradients of urgency nobody planned for.

Playing reactionary catchup meant innovative attempts were essential and the political correctness, guidelines, and many rules for engagement were suddenly ignored or bypassed out of the urgency of this nasty business.

VOICEOVER (CAPTAIN
KWONGAB) THOUGHT
*I cannot help but believe spies were at work and his
mission is already compromised.*

If Kwongab was right, there probably was already an ambush planned as the Anarchie would now do whatever it took to prevent technology component reinforcement of Frăctŏng with items such as lighting drones and kinetic weapon projectiles.

All Kwongab had to do was be at the MSF landing zone shield 3 hours after sundown which for this time of year at this latitude 22:00 GSTH. And if his suspicions were right, he had a way to thwart possible ambush and the spies. One other item Kwongab wished he could get for his rust bucket was one of the *Black Ravik* Shuttles like MSFC-34 had.

Just as a hunch Kwongab sent General Kahn a communique thinking the request had very little chance of approval.

CAPTAIN KWONGAB
(Communique)
General Kahn, I'm requesting a *Black Ravik* Shuttle be
provided for this mission.

Kwongab was surprised when General Kahn responded:

GENERAL KAHN
(Communique)
Captain Kwongab, we have a *Black Ravik*, it was slated for MSFC-54, which is outfitting now, but the Cruiser will not be ready for operations until a couple more weeks.

The *Black Ravik* Shuttle is being wasted stored on Cruiser MSFC-54.

 I'll ask for a volunteer to ferry the Shuttle up to you. Send your Shuttle back with that person after the swap.

CAPTAIN KWONGAB
Absolutely General Kahn.

Kwongab was elated. A *Black Ravik* could prove to be very advantageous especially in the full cloaking mode if the Anarchie had not mastered the neutrino sniffers.

Kwongab went to the Bridge to observe the Shuttle swap-out. It was a mildly complicated process. Since the person ferrying the Shuttle had to leave with the original Shuttle they would arrive on the *Black Ravik*, come aboard the ship. The *Black Ravik* would then deploy and loiter next to the ship while the ship's Shuttle docked, the pilot got inside the original ship's Shuttle and took off heading back to Gwaba. Under PNN control, the *Black Ravik* would then dock pilotless.

It only took 20 minutes for the *Black Ravik* modified Shuttle to reach MSFC-8 and dock.

Kwongab went to the Shuttle Bay to meet the pilot. He didn't know who to expect. They would have a brief conversation while the Shuttles were being swapped.

Kwongab stood there when the Shuttle Bay access door opened after compartment pressurization reached neutral pressure after the 14-pound air test. To Kwongab's great surprise there was Monachi standing in front of him smiling.

VOICEOVER
The love of Kwongab's life, Monachi, stood there looking at him. The feelings were transcendental.

The words were unspoken but felt.

Neural expansion telepathy replaced any effort to talk.

Kwongab and Monachi simply passed thoughts between each other telepathically.

Love was overflowing, as reality was setting in. MSF wasn't doing too well. The status was just as bad if not worse than the original Jeeapa conflict.

Except this time far more Anarchieborgs were on the Planet of Jeeapa threatening Jeeapa City, the domed paradise.

Monachi was a realist, this could be the last time she saw Kwongab. The loss of Vance gave them all a reality check. They would no longer take for granted who they were.

In front of several crew members who were Shuttle handlers, Monachi who was schooled in the Human way of transference of emotional affection and tenderness having experienced it often during the Andromeda Mission, walked over and put her arms around Kwongab and gave a solid embrace.

Kwongab was too moved to respond, he wasn't in a state of shock or anything like it, he was beyond that into a seemingly parallel universe almost.

Monachi, fully engrossed in her neural expansion of Kwongab knew what state his mind was in and was quite helpless now to respond.

Monachi understood and allowed those tendrils of love to just flow, as the moment was precious and could be their last.

Monachi's sense of time and etiquette dictated her following moves as she knew it was time to depart. She had received more than she deserved in being allowed to ferry the Black Ravik Shuttle up to MSFC-8 to see Kwongab one last time.

About that time one of the Shuttle Bay operators reported:

SHUTTLE BAY OPERATOR
The Ship's Shuttle is back in the Shuttle Bay, air test complete, you may enter the Shuttle Bay and depart now.

Monachi ignoring the information just presented immediately looked Kwongab in the eyes and said:

MONACHI
I wanted to see you before you left.

KWONGAB
These crew members probably do not know you are Monachi, my spouse.

MONACHI
You can duly inform them, as I must leave now.

KWONGAB
Monachi.

MONACHI
Yes?

KWONGAB
I love you.

MONACHI
That sounds so human like.

KWONGAB
Vance taught us a lot of things.

MONACHI
Yes, he did.

KWONGAB
Tell the kids I miss them.

MONACHI
I will.

KWONGAB
Goodbye.

Monachi then did something that was utterly shocking to the unemotional Mergenky standing a few feet away from the couple: she kissed Kwongab on the lips.

MONACHI
I love you too

.

Monachi turned, walked into the Shuttle Bay, which door closed directly behind her and got into the old ship's Shuttle and strapped in. Moments later the Shuttle launched and headed back to the surface of the planet where it would quickly go through a retrofit and get converted to a *Black Ravik Shuttle.*

The *Black Ravik Shuttle* that Monachi ferried up to the Cruiser MSFC-8 then docked and the Shuttle doors closed.

CAPTAIN KWONGAB
(Thought)
I think it's probably time we got underway.

Kwongab turned and walked to the cruiser MSFC-8's control room/bridge.

CAPTAIN KWONGAB
Navigator, are all the navigation vectors plugged in?

NAVIGATOR
Yes sir, but the deviations you had me change are not
filed with MSF at your request.

I know, it's always better to ask for forgiveness than permission, especially when your butt is on the line, and I think the odds are stacked against us."

ERICA (PNN)
Captain Kwongab, clearance received from MSF to
proceed on mission.

CAPTAIN KWONGAB
PNN, transmit to MSFS-4, '*Commence assignment.*'

Observing the sensor scans, the Scout was heading out into harm's way, leading the Cruiser. It would be a fast trip, but the first half of the trip would be at normal velocities. Then they would be getting into the area Kwongab calculated to be a prime area to set up an ambush.

The two vessels would be traveling dark meaning all the scanners turned off. This way they would give less to the Anarchie to detect them with. Knowing how fast MSFS-4 was traveling and where it was going, Kwongab knew they had safety in separation. At nearly the 2-hour mark they performed the first Frazgrandopf maneuver which could be accomplished because they had the benefit of another leading Scout Class ship.

A few hours later they both did another Capmoc-Drulyenslv maneuver. There was no sensor scans picked up and no tell-tale ion trails.

Lack of detection did not preclude ships waiting in silence not moving with advance notice via a spy to pick them off like sitting ducks.

Sadly MSFS-4was the sacrificial lamb, the canary in the coal mine. But Kwongab hoped to mitigate all that. The next hour or so would get dicey and if they continued with their flight plan as filed with MSF, there very well could be a few Anarchie Battleships waiting for them on their tracks to quickly finish them off with their precious cargo.

Soon they were in the danger zone. The Scout had been warned this would be the most dangerous time. They had to get through this last hour then they would do the maneuver Kwongab cooked up that the Anarchie and potential spies in MSF could not predict could manifest.

As part of the plan, they would turn on their scanners as they maneuvered. They wanted the evidence to support their rationality for executing this emergency maneuver in accordance with war time rules.

Kwongab was very mindful of the time and on the lookout for ion trails, not only from the Scout but also from potential Anarchie battleships. The time slowly wound down, just like a countdown for a missile launch. The navigation vectors were all programmed for automatic execution. All they had to do was sit and watch.

Kwongab ordered about 10 seconds before the course change and speed increase:

CAPTAIN KWONGAB
Turn on all scanners.

Just as expected the sensor operator reported:

SENSOR OPERATOR
Captain, we have problems. We have at least six big
ships dead ahead.

CAPTAIN KWONGAB
Are they within weapons range?

SENSOR OPERATOR
Not yet sir but they will be soon!

CAPTAIN KWONGAB
Ok, here we go,

Kwongab observed Cruiser MSFC-8 suddenly shifted course and speed as planned.

> CAPTAIN KWONGAB
> Status on the Scout MSFS-4?

> SENSOR OPERATOR
> Scout MSFS-4 has maneuvered and is speeding up but has not turned on any scanners.

> CAPTAIN KWONGAB
> That's expected, we wanted to give Scout MSFS-4 a chance to get out of the trap before Anarchie spotted them. We turned on our scanners mainly to distract them so the Scout could get away.

INT. SPACE. LEAD ANARCHIE BATTLESHIP CONTROL ROOM.

The captain on the lead Anarchie Battleship was mildly concerned.

> ANARCHIE BATTLESHIP
> CAPTAIN
> How did they know we were here?

> ANARCHIE BATTLESHIP
> INTEL OFFICER
> Maybe our spy in MSF headquarters isn't as reliable as we thought?

> ANARCHIE BATTLESHIP
> NAVIGATOR
> What do we do now?

> ANARCHIE BATTLESHIP
> CAPTAIN
> Chase them down and kill them. They can't outrun us.

The chase began. The Anarchie who were the genius on propulsion systems had not seen Mergenky operate at max speed in over 30 years. They didn't have a valid assessment of how fast a Mergenky craft could really go.

INT. SPACE MFSC-8 CONTROL ROOM.

Kwongab's Cruiser MFSC-8 was now out of harm's way, but it would be touch and go for Mergenky Scout MSFS-4 as it got dangerously close to Anarchie Battleships.

The crew was watching intently the race between Mergenky Scout MSFS-4 and the lead Anarchie Battleship trying to get in for a kill shot. It wasn't quite there but unless Kwongab did something quick, it would be all over for Commander Kuàisù Sīkǎo and his crew.

Then Kwongab started smiling. He recalled looking over the manifest of his cargo, there were some satchel charges in the cargo hold and the good news is they were not buried. They were some of the last items brought aboard.

> CAPTAIN KWONGAB
> Anyone here know how to operate those satchel charges we have in the Cargo Bay?

Nobody answered but PNN spoke up.

> ERICA (PNN)
> Captain Kwongab, I can operate the satchel charges.

> CAPTAIN KWONGAB
> What about on the Shuttle?

> ERICA (PNN)
> There is a micro PNN on the Shuttle. I can program it with all the instructions on how to detonate the Satchel Charge.

> CAPTAIN KWONGAB
> Okay, Navigator you take two crew members to the cargo Bay, PNN will help you identify the Satchel Charges and get them aboard the *Black Ravik* shuttle Immediately!

Within 10 minutes the *Black Ravik* was being deployed as Kwongab watched the race between the Mergenky MSFS-4 and the lead Anarchie Battleship get closer and closer to kill shot range. The Anarchie Battleship had the angle on the Scout who was almost boxed in and only had one way to go.

The Black Ravik was deployed fully cloaked. Only the neutrino sniffer could see it.

The Shuttle was programmed to crash into the lead battleship and detonate its satchel charge. The Anarchie would not see what hit them. Unfortunately, they only had one silver bullet. One interesting development was that two other battleships were now very close to the lead Anarchie Battleship, just about ready to unleash the menacing volley of those new powerful blue lasers made available from the Earth diamonds.

The XO, Commander Dǐngqiāng intently watched the surveillance holograph showing multiple wavelengths of passive reception.

COMMANDER DǏNGQIĀNG
The first lasers were fired at Scout MSFS-4.

CAPTAIN KWONGAB
Those shots were a near miss. Scout MSFS-4's time
is running out.

Kwongab noted that as he could see his Cruiser had more legs than the battleships, he could outrun them. However, the wounded Scout not fully repaired from its combat damage appeared to barely achieve equal velocity.

SENSOR OPERATOR
The sensor displays show Black Ravik getting closer
to the lead battleship.

CAPTAIN KWONGAB
It's a coin toss if it would make it in time.

Immediately following Scout MSFS-4 at this time one of the other battleships shot its blue lasers.

CAPTAIN KWONGAB
Another near miss, but this one was too close.

Then suddenly there was a bright flash, then two more.

COMMANDER DǏNGQIĀNG
There was such an explosion in the first battleship that
its power plant and air wing and armaments must have
all blown up from the satchel explosion setting off the
secondary explosions.

CAPTAIN KWONGAB
Due to lack of discipline and over eagerness the two
other Anarchie Battleships were too close, and the
explosion ripped into them and virtually cut them in
half and set off their weapons and when the U115
reactors probably ruptured, and the dissimilar metals
created a horrific explosion.

SENSOR OPERATOR
The three other battle ships suddenly slowed down and
turned away.

COMMANDER DĬNGQIĀNG
Maybe they think we set a trap for them!

MSFC-8 continued at this course and speed for over an hour and scanners indicated no
ships around them and the Scout.

KWONGAB
Scout MSFS-4 is now clear and opening the range
quickly.

The Scout knew from the secret plan that when Kwongab turned off the Cruiser's
scanners they would immediately slow down and change course, then after a few
minutes perform another Frazgrandopf maneuver.

MSFC-8 and MSFS-4 were going out of the reach of the Anarchie Battleships that
were part of a trap, and felt they knew their chances of safely making it to the landing
zone screen were much better.

KWONGAB
When we arrive at Frăctŏng we will send a message to
General Kahn explaining how we lost his *Black Ravik*
Shuttle.

COMMANDER DĬNGQIĀNG
We are now located where nobody expects us and
going at a speed to not give ourselves away with an
ion-trail.

Kwongab replied knowing this mission was far from being over.

CAPTAIN KWONGAB
But the last portion of this voyage when we must run the gauntlet again, we'll be
observed.

COMMANDER DĬNGQIĀNG
There will be several investigations both by the
Anarchie trying to figure out what happened to their
three destroyed battleships, but at the same time,
Mergenky INTEL may pick up on some of the chatter
and inquire as to what caused those huge explosions,
especially since they occurred along our tracks.

CAPTAIN KWONGAB

Since we are hauling precious cargo General Kahn will have instant interest.

CAPTAIN KWONGAB
(THOUGHT)

For a while he might even fear we are all dead.

VOICEOVER

Looking at the time, they had 3 hours before they had to speed up again for the last leg. They would be arriving in space from a direction neither MSF nor Anarchie would expect.

To ensure one of the two ships would survive, they planned to split apart just before they reached near space of the planet.

The Anarchie would have to divide their forces to go after them, giving the nearby Mergenky Cruisers a shot at bagging another battleship or two in the process.

Kwongab stayed ever vigilant always looking over the sensor operator's shoulders looking for any thread to a possible detection. None came, mainly, because nobody expected them to be where they were.

A messenger buoy was prepared and would be launched if they were confronted by Anarchie to warn General Kahn he had a spy amongst them.

The time quickly passed, and they finally reached the coordinates for course and speed change. As they planned, the Scout sped up and moved ahead leaving behind a glaring ion trail.

The Cruiser then sped up equally leaving behind an additional ion trail. If there were any nearby ships, they would be immediately detected.

The two MSF combat ship's captains, Kwongab and Commander Kuàisù Sīkǎo were pushing the ships to the limits going faster than anyone in MSF had ever gone. At this speed the distances closed quickly.

When they got close enough to Planet Frăctŏng, Kwongab reported in, said he was arriving with the Scout and the direction they were arriving. They both slowed, losing their ion trails and suddenly were being blasted by dozens of scanners both Anarchie and Mergenky.

The Anarchie did exactly what Kwongab predicted they went after one of the ships and it was the Scout. That day Kwongab learned something about Commander Kuàisù Sīkăo who was very brilliant and resourceful.

VOICEOVER

Commander Kuàisù Sīkăo didn't try to force his way in to Frăctŏng. He knew he was going to be outgunned so he did what none of the Anarchie expected. He simply did a U-turn and went out into deep space coaxing every bit of speed out of his wounded craft that slowly outran the Anarchie who got careless focusing in on S-4 and did not expect the Mergenky Cruiser Squadron to come after them.

The Mergenky who had been recently defensive and overly conservative went after the Anarchie Battleships with a bone in their teeth thinking that ship had their precious cargo they desperately needed, which changed the whole complexity of the battle.

Soon the fighting raged and the Anarchie who had been enjoying almost air superiority at Frăctŏng over these timid Mergenky fighters suddenly had a fight on their hands.

By dividing their forces, the Anarchie no longer had the strength to crush the Mergenky. Now that the odds were even, just as many Anarchie battleships were getting hammered as were Mergenky Cruisers.

While the Anarchie suddenly distracted by the sudden threat of the MSF Cruisers, quickly lost interest in MSFS-4 which then Commander Kuàisù Sīkăo executed an end around.

Commander Kuàisù Sīkăo felt he had *accomplished his Frăctŏng escort mission as soon as MSFC-8 entered the atmosphere heading for the landing zone.* Therefore, he was *free to conduct combat maneuvers.*

While the Anarchie battleships were lined up and exchanging laser barrages with the

Mergenky Cruisers, MSFS-4 managed to complete the end around and come up an Anarchie Battleship's *Six O'clock* that didn't see it coming.

Even though 5 lasers on a Scout are not the lethal firepower of a Cruiser or a Battleship, having a clean shot in the engineering spaces didn't take long to strike and penetrate the U115 reactors which then caused a catastrophic propulsion and power failure.

The Battleship was suddenly defenseless with fires raging while S-4 continued hammering away and finally the internal explosions hit the air wing inside the battleship setting off secondary explosions which immediately led Commander Kuàisù Sīkǎo to radically maneuver and put the ship back into that wartime only permissible velocity to get out of harm's way of an expected horrific explosion that soon sent a wall of sparkling debris in all directions.

Early in the Frǎctǒng attack with a superior advantage, the Anarchie over confidence placed themselves into a position they now were starting to regret.

As soon as the Anarchie Battleship blew up creating a tremendous fireball, the nerves of the other Anarchie Captains were jostled. Anarchie Battleships in this formation immediately reversed course and maneuvered towards the other half of their fleet flying in a Mexican Standoff with the Mergenky.

With the sudden loss of four more battleships in a day, General Borktar was now starting to have second thoughts about remaining at Frǎctǒng for the sake of laying claim to Yǒngbùmián de Chéngshì.

In short order he finally gathered enough wisdom to abandon planet Frǎctǒng as requested by higher ups and get his forces over to Jeeapa, which was their real conquest that meant something.

Kwongab landed on Frǎctǒng next to the domed city of Yǒngbùmián de Chéngshì in the dark. The Cruiser's PNN linked up with MSF systems on the ground, skillfully put the Cruiser on the landing pad perfectly and Mergenky crew members and ground support personnel quickly went to work unloading the precious cargo in the dark with a few light sticks.

CAPTAIN KWONGAB
No light drones tonight?

GENERAL TIĚQUÁN
No, for your protection we are keeping it dark tonight.
If the Anarchie saw, you delivering this precious Cargo
they would come after you. That's why you must be
gone before daybreak.

With all the help it only took a couple hours to completely unload the Cruiser Transport. Kwongab was ready to leave Frăctŏng.

Frăctŏng Alliance Commander General Tiĕquán arrived as the logistics personnel and Kwongab had their last words before MSFC-8's departure.

GENERAL TIĔQUÁN
Captain Kwongab, I appreciate all your efforts getting this precious cargo here. When the dust settles and we get a break in action, I plan on contacting General Kahn to report on your gallantry in your mission of getting those precious cargos here.

CAPTAIN KWONGAB
Thank you General. I was just doing my job. We have a desperate situation, and I promise I will do whatever I can to help you.

GENERAL TIĔQUÁN
Captain Kwongab, I was in the command center during your arrival. Quite frankly I didn't think you would make it.

CAPTAIN KWONGAB
General Tiĕquán, be sure and mention MSFS-4 in your communique to General Kahn. MSFS-4's Commander Kuàisù Sīkăo did a fantastic job of diverting Anarchie Battleships.

GENERAL TIĔQUÁN
Captain Kwongab, I will inform General Kahn.

CAPTAIN KWONGAB
General Tiĕquán, my PNN also reported Commander Kuàisù Sīkăo single handedly destroyed an Anarchie Battleship, that appeared to turn the tide of the battle because that group of battleships immediately fled to join the other group. That act opened a gaping hole for me to ensure success. But it also may have saved some of your cruisers.

GENERAL TIĔQUÁN
Captain Kwongab, I like your style. I like the way you give credit to others in an unselfish manner.

CAPTAIN KWONGAB
General Tiěquán, a teacher's proudest moment is when
he or she witnesses the student they trained perform
incredible achievements. Commander Kuàisù Sīkǎo
was one of my students at PCO school. He made me
proud today.

GENERAL TIĚQUÁN
Captain Kwongab, I know the reason why your student
did so well today. He had a great teacher and mentor.

CAPTAIN KWONGAB
Thank you General.

MSFS-4 had found some empty space to hide in after destroying the Battleship.

One of the Cruisers in the formation recorded gun camera video they sent to MSF
showing MSFS -4 singlehandedly destroying the Anarchie Battleship.

Yǒngbùmián de Chéngshì Mayor Gāoshān (pronounced Gow-Shan) sent a communique
to General Kahn informing him:

CHÉNGSHÌ MAYOR GĀOSHĀN
(Communique)
The emergency shipment arrived at Frăctǒng intact
and that will help our situation out quite a bit as it will
extend the Air Defense for at least another couple of
weeks giving us a huge breather.

<u>INT. DAY. MSF HEADQUARTERS.</u>

General Kahn was happy to receive Mayor Gāoshān's communique and as he was
reading it said to his staff:

GENERAL KAHN
We now know those big explosions were not our
shipments.

CHIEF OF STAFF
Did they get through without any difficulties?

GENERAL KAHN
Appears so.

While unloading Kwongab reported via high-speed neutrino communications.

CAPTAIN KWONGAB
General Kahn, we had to sacrifice the *Black Ravik* to save MSFS-4.

GENERAL KAHN
That was a good command decision, which is sometimes difficult to make, and you made the right one.

As soon as Kwongab was ready to leave he directed:

CAPTAIN KWONGAB
PNN notify MSFS-4 we are ready to transit back to Gwaba and give them a rendezvous point along our track in near space.

With a much stronger air defense, a more robust Cruiser Squadron, the Mergenky were able to escort MSFC-8 back out into space and a safe distance away from the planet with a good screen. Kwongab then gave S-4, Commander Kuàisù Sīkǎo one of his MACRO communiques, that were in essence *Tangramized* script which Commander Kuàisù Sīkǎo interpreted:

VOICE OVER
KWONGAB'S TANGRAMIZED SCRIPT
Upon rendezvous maintain a specific course direct to Gwaba at max speed for 2 hours. Then our two ships will slow, do Frazgrandopf maneuvers and travel in slow speed until movement out of the contested area to avoid ion trails the Anarchie could follow and set up an ambush.

Hours later when they reached halfway to Gwaba, they reached the point where Kwongab felt it was safe he directed:

CAPTAIN KWONGAB
PNN inform MSFS-4 to go back to high speed.

MSFC-8 and MSFS-4 continued to MSS-21 in an uneventful manner.

Docking at MSS-21 was a joyous occasion because it meant they all survived despite being on a rust bucket which had many weapons removed to make way for a Cargo Bay. To their surprise, General Kahn was on hand to welcome them back. So was Monachi who came up to the space station with General Kahn in his private transport.

General Kahn approached Kwongab as he exited the air lock.

GENERAL KAHN
Welcome back Captain Kwongab. Let's go see your
student, Commander Kuàisù Sīkǎo.

CAPTAIN KWONGAB
There is nothing better for a teacher than to congratulate
his student for outstanding achievement.

Monachi stood by General Kahn, but because of military decorum knew now was
not the time to display an emotional spectacle with her husband so she withheld her
outward emotions and welcomed him home with her neural expansion telepathic
capability.

MONACHI (TELEPATHIC)
Welcome back, I'm glad you are safe.

Kwongab replied using his neural expansion telepathy:

KWONGAB (TELEPATHIC)
I'm very glad to be back too.

Kwongab, Monachi, and General Kahn approached MSFS-4 as Commander Kuàisù
Sīkǎo was just leaving the air lock and met them.

CAPTAIN KWONGAB
Congratulations, Commander Kuàisù Sīkǎo, you did a
superb job on the mission.

COMMANDER KUÀISÙ SĪKǍO
Captain Kwongab, I just performed the maneuvers and
did the many things you taught me in the classroom. It
all worked nicely, and I'm here alive today thanks to
the preparations you did for me.

GENERAL KAHN
Commander Kuàisù Sīkǎo, your actions at Frăctŏng
displayed intuition, self-initiative, bravery, and
leadership skills that are usually observed only from
seasoned pilots with a lot of experience.

COMMANDER KUÀISÙ SĪKǍO
Thank you for the kind words, General.

General Kahn then interrupted the pleasantries and stated:

GENERAL KAHN
We need to go to MSF offices where we can meet and discuss your next mission.

Kwongab, Monachi, and Kuàisù Sīkǎo followed General Kahn to MSS-21's MSF offices.

VOICEOVER
MSF had a commanding presence on MSS-21 which was multi-functioned and a shared resource.

Once only a military space station, not long after they were lured into a false sense of security with the peace dividend after the Jeeapa campaign 20 years prior.

Top government officials decided to allow MSS-21 to jointly use it for intergalactic space travel to eliminate costly Interplanetary Transport movements to and from operational space ports at Gwaba's cities.

Travelers would transition from the large Interplanetary Transports to shuttles to get to the planet's surface ultimately saving tremendous costs since the Interplanetary Transports did not have to withstand the stresses of atmospheric penetration.

Since the Interplanetary Transports could be built in modular construction in space for speed and comfort, they did not require heavy heat shields because they never flew to a planet's surface and always remained in space.

Sharing the Space Station with public transport complicated the security arrangement and as a result MSF had no choice but to have segregated operating spaces as well as staff that focused only on MSF matters.

MSF had a large footprint on MSS-21 that provided collateral assets as well as provided temporary facilities for MSF personnel in transit, often catching interplanetary transports or waiting for MSF space craft that operated from MSS-21 as a base.

General Kahn led Monachi and the two ship commanders through the security checkpoint. Special scanners identified all three men and Monachi who following close behind.

General Kahn knew his way to the conference room as well as the three others and were soon sitting at a large table that had a holographic image spinning above it. The 3D globe representing Jeeapa was four feet in diameter.

The resolution of the globe was at several million dots per inch which gave the same fidelity of a space telescope image. The 80-foot space telescopes on the Scout class ships were employed for reconnaissance on the planet.

Kwongab observed real time data projections in 3D provided by spectroscopic video superimposed on the holograph that was slowly spinning in a suspended fashion from the ceiling which gave the viewer a time lapsed history that could show days or sequence of days if desired. The holograph was instrumental in observing the big picture of the situation on Jeeapa, as INTEL was superimposed in the imagery whenever corroborated by multiple assets.

Before General Kahn started his briefing, he stated:

GENERAL KAHN
Captain Kwongab and Commander Kuàisù Sĭkăo
study the image briefly and become acclimated
with the various objects. Anarchie space craft were
identified as red objects and Mergenky blue.

CAPTAIN KWONGAB
That Holograph sure makes it easy to quickly spot
who is who.

GENERAL KAHN
The green areas on the surface of the planet were
Anarchie ground forces and the yellow are Mergenky.

General Kahn then began the briefing with a very concerned look on his face.

GENERAL KAHN
It is really a stalemate at Jeeapa, and we fear that if
the Anarchie are able repatriate their forces now on
Frăctŏng and redeploy them to Jeeapa, there would be
a large enough shift in the balance of power to tilt the
advantage to the Anarchie.

CAPTAIN KWONGAB
How can we stop them from moving their troops from
Frăctŏng to Jeeapa?

GENERAL KAHN
Captain Kwongab, I think you have already engineered
a method for us.

Kwongab immediately thought of Black Ravik and asked:

CAPTAIN KWONGAB
General Kahn, which method are you referring to?

GENERAL KAHN
Captain Kwongab, when you were at the Trouc planet
during the Andromeda Mission you employed space
mines which helped you overcome a severe numerical
disadvantage.

CAPTAIN KWONGAB
The Ponarians did not have the sophisticated scanners
like Anarchie can use. The Anarchie ships will simply
drive around the mine fields.

GENERAL KAHN
Not if the mine fields are hidden from them.

CAPTAIN KWONGAB
How could we do that?

GENERAL KAHN
The *Black Ravik* shuttle you are going to receive
today to replace the one you lost destroying the three
Anarchie Battleships, will arrive loaded with space
mines. MSFS-4 will also receive a similar Black Ravik
Shuttle similarly equipped.

CAPTAIN KWONGAB
Is our next mission to patrol the area between Jeeapa
and Frăctŏng?

GENERAL KAHN
No, first you will deliver precious cargo to Jeeapa,
and then you will proceed to get into position to help

prevent Anarchie to redeploy their Frăctŏng force to Jeeapa.

CAPTAIN KWONGAB
Understand.

GENERAL KAHN
Captain Kwongab, after you complete your Cruiser Transport mission, you will place your ships, between the two planets and you will be informed of the disposition of the Anarchie transports as they leave Frăctŏng.

CAPTAIN KWONGAB
How will we know what course they are taking and what direction they are coming from?

GENERAL KAHN
Scout MSFS-1 will be used to locate and track Anarchie transports, and you will be informed so that you will know where to position your ships, deploy the Black Ravik's.

CAPTAIN KWONGAB
I'm not certain how I'm going to deploy the Space Mines.

GENERAL KAHN
Once the Anarchie Transports closes within target range, the Black Ravik's will be launched under PNN control and will deploy to the launch basket for the space mines.

The Space Mines will be preprogrammed to attack multiple targets. By remaining cloaked until in the near proximity of the Anarchie transports, the Anarchie Transports will not have enough reaction time to avoid the mines.

CAPTAIN KWONGAB
How soon do we leave?

GENERAL KAHN
The loaded Black Ravik's will arrive today. emergency supplies that MSFC-8 will carry to Jeeapa will start loading shortly. That's what's going to delay you. We

are also going to put some supplies on MSFS-4. Both ships will be fighter/transports.

CAPTAIN KWONGAB
What if the Anarchie move their troops on Frăctŏng before we deliver the supplies?

GENERAL KAHN
Your primary assignments are to deliver the supplies to Jeeapa.

CAPTAIN KWONGAB
What about Frăctŏng?

GENERAL KAHN
Yŏngbùmián de Chéngshì Mayor Gāoshān assures me they have enough military supplies to last at least two weeks.

As far as food supplies and water, they have no shortages there and have quite a bit stored in Yŏngbùmián de Chéngshì.

CAPTAIN KWONGAB
After we deliver the supplies to Jeeapa will we then start patrolling the area between Frăctŏng and Jeeapa?

GENERAL KAHN
Yes. Like I said earlier, both ships will both have Black Ravik's loaded with space mines. Your follow-on task will be to provide assistance in preventing the Anarchie from arriving at Jeeapa and in particular, prevent the Anarchie from relocating their ground forces on Frăctŏng to Jeeapa.

CAPTAIN KWONGAB
Since MSFC-8 and MSFS-4 are going to be loaded with supplies which would possibly put a strain on our artificial gravity machines, especially during high-speed turns while maneuvering to avoid Anarchie attacks, would it be possible for us to be escorted to Jeeapa since its unlikely we'll be able to outmaneuver the Anarchie and could become targets?

GENERAL KAHN
As part of our plan to deploy space mines, MSFS-1 will be your escort to Jeeapa and will be loaded with

space mines in its drop tubes. While MSFC-8 and MSFS-4 maneuver in front of Anarchie Transports to seed space mines with the Black Ravik's, MSFS-1 will deploy space mines in their rear to box them in and force them to go in one direction where we can have additional assets to contend with the Anarchie.

CAPTAIN KWONGAB
How soon can we be expected to go.

GENERAL KAHN
Kwongab, you will depart SS-21 in about 18 hours from now to synchronize your arrival with nightfall at Jeeapa.

Kwongab was looking in a hopeful manner at Monachi.

CAPTAIN KWONGAB
Would it be possible for me to have some time off during those 18 hours

GENERAL KAHN
Kwongab, because of this exigency, I can't afford to have you go down to the planet's surface and discover you got trapped or stuck on the planet and can't get back in time for scheduled undocking.

CAPTAIN KWONGAB
Understand sir, I just wanted to spend some time alone with Monachi.

GENERAL KAHN
Unfortunately, the only place you will get any privacy around this space station will be in your Space Cabin aboard MSFC-8.

CAPTAIN KWONGAB
General Kahn, if that's all there is for this briefing, I would like to take Monachi to go see my Cruiser.

GENERAL KAHN
Sure, take all the time you want, just be ready to undock in about 18 hours.

CAPTAIN KWONGAB
We will be ready.

Kwongab led Monachi out of the conference room and made his way to the Cruiser and took her to the Bridge for a look. Some of the Shuttle operators who had seen Monachi deliver the Black Ravik spotted Monachi wearing her uniform and not her space suit she had on during the Shuttle ferry operation.

In her space suit Monachi was barely noted as a woman. But with her well-tailored MSF uniform she looked rather spunky, and incredibly youthful for her age.

There were a few crew members on the bridge doing functions in support of their pending underway. 18 hours wasn't a lot of time to get ready. They would complete the task and attempt to get some rest before they had to resume their stations for the undocking operations and subsequent transit to Jeeapa.

Kwongab then led Monachi to his Space Cabin. As expected, it wasn't as luxurious as his former Mergenky Scout MSFS-1 but on the other hand, MSF Cruisers were not known to spend a lot of time patrolling in space.

Monachi was out in front with her priority question.

MONACHI
Did you get any feedback from General Kahn about
our children's school?

KWONGAB
No, I have not had time to discuss it with him yet.

MONACHI
General Kahn's probably not going to remain on MSS-
21 long, you should make an appointment with him
before he returns to Gwaba.

KWONGAB
Something tells me he'll be here to see us off. MSFS-
1 hasn't arrived yet. It's our escort so we can't leave
until it gets here.

MONACHI
You have direct communication connections now
hooked up to MSS-21. Why not contact him now and
ask him about it or make an appointment?

Kwongab thought for a few moments and responded.

> KWONGAB
> I'll contact him now, he's kind of busy, but maybe he can make time for this.

> MONACHI
> Thank you.

> KWONGAB
> PNN, please contact General Kahn at MSF offices here at MSS-21 and inform him I would like to talk with him for a moment if he has the time and it's rather personal.

PNN, in a semi dialect of Erica responded:

> ERICA (PNN)
> Captain Kwongab, General Kahn has been contacted, one moment please.

About 5 seconds later General Kahn's holograph appeared before Kwongab.

> GENERAL KAHN
> Yes Kwongab, what is it you wished to talk about that we could not have discussed in my office.

> CAPTAIN KWONGAB
> Sir, I wanted to know if you had time to investigate the situation with our children's school.

> GENERAL KAHN
> Kwongab, I'm handling that and hope to have some answers for you before you depart on this mission.

> KWONGAB
> Thank you general, I appreciate your help in this matter. I know you are a busy man.

> GENERAL KAHN
> You are welcome. It's the least I could do for you considering what you have gone through as of late.

> CAPTAIN KWONGAB
> I appreciate it.

GENERAL KAHN
I'll contact you when I have some information to share
with you.

CAPTAIN KWONGAB
Thank you General.

The General's holograph then faded out.

Monachi, having overheard the conversation, was pleased that Kwongab was pursuing something very important to her.

The couple had not had any romantic interactions in quite some time. Monachi decided now would be an excellent time to achieve some splendid euphoria, approached Kwongab, smiled at him and put her arms around him and asked:

MONACHI
Would you like to do it?

Moments later, all the pent-up emotions came pouring out as they allowed themselves to transcend from a grief stricken and furiously anxious endeavor that they both experienced to a few moments of cerebral ecstasy that had the intensity unlike anything since the middle of the Andromeda Mission.

In the span of a short time, they were lying in Kwongab's gel tube resting and semi unconscious as their bodies slowly eased from that splendid euphoria in an almost time warped re-emergence back to reality.

Monachi knew it was important they do not waste their precious time sleeping in the gel tube, overcame the tendency to sleep and motivated herself to exit and redress and coerce Kwongab to also follow her so they could do a few things together most people never had the option as couples to do.

Being on MSS-21 as MSF officers gave them some special privileges such as visiting the observatory where they had a bird's eye view of the solar system.

When they arrived at the MSS-21 observatory, as expected Kwongab and Monachi discovered the observatory was mostly abandoned which gave them a lot of privacy allowing intimacy and warm and genial interactions that two long lost souls that just recombined would enjoy.

KWONGAB
Have you checked up on Kara?

MONACHI

Yes, she's an amazing woman and has a good grip on herself and her emotions. She will miss Vance terribly, but she's getting on with her life and she's now the doctor she always was, concerned about her patients.

KWONGAB

I'm glad to hear that.

MONACHI

I talked with the director of the hospital who assured me her two staff psychoanalysts she assigned to look after Kara has reported, she recoiled rather quickly and does not exhibit the grief-stricken attributes normally seen with other MSF pilot widows.

KWONGAB

How's the kids holding up?

MONACHI

They are doing ok. Of course, they miss their father and feel a huge void, but they are highly adaptable because of their experiences traveling in space and experiencing many of the events we encountered in Andromeda.

KWONGAB

When the fighting is over in Jeeapa, I would like to pay them a visit.

MONACHI

I'm sure they would love to see you. They view you as a family member.

KWONGAB

They did have a tremendous exposure to me on the Andromeda Mission.

MONACHI

And they know you brought us home safely, while at the same time you did undertake some extraordinary challenges.

KWONGAB
I was probably foolish for putting the Scout and all of
you at risk doing those things too.

MONACHI
Everyone agreed with you that we had to do something
about the Ponarians.

KWONGAB
Yes, but unfortunately for Shaneen, it did not end well
for her.

It was one of those things you couldn't predict, one lone assassin that that killed her father somehow managed to not get discovered until it was too late.

Kwongab held out and grabbed Monachi's hand and led her over to the tall Glastic panel that gave them a huge unobstructed view of over half of the solar system. Some planets were close, others were so far away they seemed like stars.

KWONGAB
Beautiful view here.

MONACHI
We've never been here together before.

KWONGAB
I know.

MONACHI
It's a shame that it took a tragedy and a war to get us here together.

Kwongab turned towards Monachi and pulled her close and they embraced. The cohesive bond resonated in their affectionate and enthusiastically demonstration of electricity that still flowed between them.

Kwongab knew that he could not forestall his presence on the Cruiser. He needed to go observe how the loading was going partly to make sure they could get it loaded efficiently.

Even though it was a Cruiser it was still a form of transport and if the Anarchie caught them delivering essential items, they would waste little time in making every effort to disrupt that shipment including destroying the Cruiser if possible.

Monachi knew exactly what Kwongab was thinking with the use of her neural expansion implants and offered:

MONACHI

You probably need to go back to your ship to watch preparations. I can stay in your Space Cabin until it's time for you to depart.

KWONGAB

Maybe I might want you to stow away in my Space Cabin and go with me.

MONACHI

I would love nothing more, but since Vance's departure, I'm not sure we need to press our luck by going into combat on the same ship together. One of us needs to be here for our children.

KWONGAB

You are right, I must leave you behind, but that will not diminish my desire to be with you.

MONACHI

The feelings you gave me today were very comforting.

KWONGAB

Maybe all this tragedy surrounding us has forced us to take good measure of those around us and carefully live our lives so that we do not take someone that's important to us for granted.

MONACHI
Yes of course.

KWONGAB
Well, let's go back to the Cruiser now.

ARE THEY SPIES?

VOICE OVER

General Kahn had a couple visitors in a relative short period of time after he talked to Kwongab about his children.

The men were high ranking officials in Mergenky Intelligence Agency. They were a little bewildered because very few parents ever complained about their children receiving a superior education and possible employment with the INTEL community where their lives would benefit greatly.

The request that went to them caught them totally flat footed. The fact it was a national hero involved made it increasingly a sticky point.

The visitors were escorted into General Kahn's office where the General, super busy, was intently interested in the visitors.

GENERAL KAHN
Thanks for coming Gentlemen on short notice.

MERGENKY INTELLIGENCE REP
We are happy to be here.

GENERAL KAHN
Ok, I'll get right to the point since I don't have a lot of time, what's the status of the two children and what's their disposition.

MERGENKY INTELLIGENCE REP
General Kahn, they have reached the point of no return.

GENERAL KAHN
What does that mean?

MERGENKY INTELLIGENCE REP
It means they have advanced to the point where we have been already assigned them INTEL work which they completed.

GENERAL KAHN
What kind of work?

MERGENKY INTELLIGENCE REP
The girl, Crystal, is a design genius. She designs new toys for our agents.

GENERAL KAHN
She's not actually involved in cloak and dagger activities, is she?

MERGENKY INTELLIGENCE REP
No, her forte is designing electronic gizmo's our agents take with them in the field.

GENERAL KAHN
What about the boy?

MERGENKY INTELLIGENCE REP
He's a linguist and interprets Anarchie for the code breakers.

GENERAL KAHN
Captain Kwongab and Commander Monachi do not want their children involved in INTEL work.

MERGENKY INTELLIGENCE REP
General, the children both have the intellect of mature adults. Our psychologists have worked with them extensively to discover their suitability for the tasks they perform. Their lives are not in any jeopardy as they do not deploy out in the field.

GENERAL KAHN
What about their schoolwork?

MERGENKY INTELLIGENCE REP
They attend half a day of school and half a day of work. Their schooling is unnecessary because they have already mastered their subjects, but the psychologists on our staff felt the exposure to other people their age on a routine basis would help develop their social skills.

GENERAL KAHN
This puts me in a bad situation, I promised Kwongab I would investigate this matter, and I think he expects me to remove them out of the spy business.

MERGENKY INTELLIGENCE REP
Technically, they are not in the spy business, they just provide logistical support at a safe distance.

GENERAL KAHN
What can I tell Kwongab?

MERGENKY INTELLIGENCE REP
Simply state they are not spies and will not be used
as spies, but later in life if they chose on their own to
work for Mergenky Intelligence Agency, that would
be their choice and with their credentials, we would
gladly accept them.

GENERAL KAHN
Would it be permissible to inform Kwongab about the
type of work they are doing?

MERGENKY INTELLIGENCE REP
Their work is highly compartmentalized. They have
been briefed they can't even tell their parents what
they are doing for their own personal security if
someone discovers them and our enemies learn what
they are doing, then they would be at risk.

GENERAL KAHN
I've not heard of any Mergenky killed on Gwaba in
the line of duty.

MERGENKY INTELLIGENCE REP
That's because we never disclose it. But it does happen.

GENERAL KAHN
Thank you for coming by on short notice, the
background of what triggered this inquiry came about
because of the recent events of Kwongab's life.

MERGENKY INTELLIGENCE REP
Yes, we are aware of what bestowed upon Captain
Kwongab and many of his actions in the past created
avenues of opportunity for us.

GENERAL KAHN
Ok gentlemen, let me walk you to your Shuttle.

MERGENKY INTELLIGENCE REP
General that will not be necessary and we prefer that
you do not.

GENERAL KAHN
I see, it's all probably part of your methods.

MERGENKY INTELLIGENCE REP
Yes, it is.

GENERAL KAHN
Well then, goodbye and thank you.

MERGENKY INTELLIGENCE REP
You are welcome General.

The two men stood up and walked out of the general's office. This would not be the first nor the last time parents inadvertently discovered the Juéduìhuīhuáng Foundation, Center for Advanced Learning was a spy training campus.

SPACE MINES

VOICE OVER
The weight of a loaded canister of 9 space mines was too heavy for the Shuttle to lift off the planet safely.

MSF created an innovative craft for such purposes. A Scout class vessel MSFS-44X with space telescope removed was easily reconfigurable to haul large objects into space for modular construction.

Two new Black Ravik's were preloaded with cylindrical launchers and craned over onto the back of the converted Scout.

One launch would take both Black Ravik's up on the same flight to MSS-21. Upon arrival crews operating the two-seater Black Ravik's would simply launch from the Scout MSFS-44X and land in the Shuttle Bays of both MSFC-8 and MSFS-4.

The cylindrical launchers had 9 tubes in them. 8 tubes were in a circular pattern and a 9th tube in the middle of the 8 all equally spaced.

All the seats of these special Black Ravik's arranged to haul space mines were removed except the pilot and navigator's seats.

There were no weapons so most of the electronics were gutted. The rear door/ramp would simply open exposing the end of the cylindrical launcher that communicated to the space mine and would shove it out of the tube at a small velocity.

Up until the time the weapon left the cloaking field of the Black Ravik, an enemy could not see it.

Even though the space mines were coated with radar absorbing materials, they were self-propelled and would leave ion trails if they acquired sufficient velocity which they were capable of. The rocket exhaust would also show up on infrared scanners.

Because of their relatively small size, space mines were hard to target with lasers, but not impossible.

Space mines were designed to be launched from a great distance and under self-propulsion be placed into a distant mine field.

In many cases the space mine field was a moving field and not stationary. Hence the mine fields could approach an enemy formation and reshape the disposition upon micro-PNN control networked between each mine and the designated mine leader or remotely via control from a mother ship.

The rocket exhaust created by liquid hydrogen and oxygen would not normally be observed since the velocity was achieved outside scanner ranges and the rocket engines shut down as the mine coasted to its intended target at sub-ion-wake velocities.

When the enemy ship came within striking range, the space mines would then re-ignite their rocket engines to propel them quickly into the hull of the intended target.

When the antimatter in the space mine was suddenly mixed with high pressure air in an internal air flask, the matter-antimatter mixture created a terrible hot explosion that would burn a hole in the side of any space craft and wreck its content with the high velocity shockwave.

As planned, converted Scout MSFS-44X with its payload approached MSS-21 and stopped a short distance away. Upon command, the first Black Ravik launched and left MSFS-44X. The pilot controlled MSFS-44X's first Black Ravik delivery until it was directly over MSFC-8 whose Shuttle Bay doors were open waiting for the transfer. MSFC-8's PNN took over control of the Shuttle then docked it. The pilot was greeted by Kwongab after the Shuttle Bay was secured and pressurized.

CAPTAIN KWONGAB
Welcome aboard.

BLACK RAVIK SHUTTLE PILOT
Thank you, Captain.

CAPTAIN KWONGAB
The other pilot should be on MSFS-4 shortly. After you
guys leave, we'll be undocking. But you are invited to
remain on board and go on our mission with us.

The *Black Ravik* Shuttle Pilot smiled and responded and was glad he was not deploying.

BLACK RAVIK SHUTTLE PILOT
I would like to go with you captain, but I'm a ferry
pilot and I have a lot of lifts scheduled today.

CAPTAIN KWONGAB
Why so many lifts?

BLACK RAVIK SHUTTLE PILOT
We are transporting more logistical support up to a
couple transports that are due to leave soon.

CAPTAIN KWONGAB
Any idea where those transports are heading?

BLACK RAVIK SHUTTLE PILOT
No, they don't disclose that. But I would assume
they're going to either Jeeapa or Frăctŏng.

CAPTAIN KWONGAB
Most likely. Let me escort you to the air lock

The Shuttle pilot who would ride a Shuttle from MSS-21 back to Gwaba with the other pilot who was now landing aboard S-4 with the 2nd Black Ravik also carrying the space mine launcher with 9 silos.

After Kwongab said goodbye to the Shuttle pilot he returned to his Space Cabin where Monachi was waiting for their final moments together.

It was a somber moment. Monachi knew she loved Kwongab like no other love could. She had probed his mind numerous times and knew every one of his thoughts, and his great admiration and emotional bond to her. His love for his children, his bravery, and his dedication to MSF.

Kwongab was exactly the kind of person who would make the supreme sacrifice for MSF and there was a lot of fighting left to do.

Monachi knew deep in her heart this could be their very last meeting. The anxiety was growing, and Monachi had to work extra hard to not break down and exhibit those emotional traits that Mergenky was not supposed to exhibit, especially an MSF official with her stature.

Kwongab probing Monachi's mind for he too knew his luck could run out at any time, discovered her anguish and her sadness over the pending separation, and thus did what he had to do and knew he could do, he altered her thinking.

Kwongab's neural expansion telepathy was far more developed and stronger than Monachi. He could block her, but she could not fully block him. In fact, she might not always be able to recognize when he was probing and altering her thoughts.

But for this one special moment, he wanted their last moments to be filled with love and happiness. Monachi was kind of bewildered as she recognized her own mood shift. She didn't quite understand why, but she was suddenly happy.

So, on this most auspicious occasion, Monachi departed Cruiser MSFC-8 after a strong physical embrace privately in the Space Cabin.

After Monachi exited the airlock and was back in the MSS-21 corridor, she then stepped to the side where a large Glastic viewing window allowed her to look out at the large Cruiser.

Just as she was watching the final moments before the Cruiser undocked from MSS-21, General Kahn approached her.

GENERAL KAHN
Hello Monachi.

COMMANDER MONACHI
Greetings General Kahn.

Monachi then did a slight head bow showing respect.

GENERAL KAHN
After MSFC-8 leaves, you are invited to go back to
MSF Headquarters with me on my personal transporter.

COMMANDER MONACHI
Thank you General.

General Kahn knew that Monachi was most likely the person behind Kwongab's inquiry into their children's involvement into the spy business and suddenly decided to give her some information he felt would quell her anguish over learning that activity was going on.

General Kahn seeing that they were alone and could speak more frankly informed Monachi:

GENERAL KAHN
I know you are concerned that your children are
involved with Mergenky INTEL at the Juéduihuīhuáng
Foundation Center for Advanced Learning.

Monachi suddenly felt the agitation, the subject matter percolated and responded.

COMMANDER MONACHI
It's only natural that any parents with common sense
and love for their children would not want them
engaged in such risky business.

GENERAL KAHN
I made an inquiry with Mergenky INTEL and want
you to know your children are not spies, nor are they
currently being trained to be operatives.

COMMANDER MONACHI
Thank you general for looking into the matter, that
makes me feel a lot better.

General Kahn was one of the very few who knew of Monachi's neural expansion telepathic abilities and hoped she would not use it on him. Her behavior would soon betray whether she did or not.

Monachi learned quite well during the Andromeda Mission on how to keep to herself her most serious and precious information. She also knew that General Kahn would pick up on her mind probing if she reacted to what she discovered.

Within a few minutes she knew the truth and she knew to the extent her children were deep in, over their heads with Mergenky INTEL. It was probably too late to rescue them.

Cruiser MSFC-8 and Scout MSFS-4 undocking commenced moments later after Monachi completed her neural expansion telepathic probing of General Kahn. First MSFC-8 backed away from the space station. After clearing MSS-21 at approximately 300 yards the Cruiser began a slow turn and at approximately on course 90 degrees off the space station, the propulsion came on and the ship quickly gathered speed and within a minute was out of sight. Mergenky Scout MSFS-4 followed suite and soon was following Cruiser MSFC-8 at a safe distance.

Scout MSFS-4 would intermittently operate its scanners to measure its distance from Cruiser MSFC-8 flying in a loose formation as well as determine if any enemy ships were in their path of approach to Jeeapa. At a designated point in space they would converge with their Jeeapa escort to get them safely down on the planet so they could disgorge the contents, then continue for the rest of their assignments.

MONACHI AND KARA

Monachi followed General Kahn to his waiting personal transport ship. This craft was super supped up and could outrun anything in the galaxy they knew of. The General needed a fast way to get into War Zones and unless the enemy ship was directly in front and knew his ship was coming it's unlikely, they would be able to hit it unless it was a lucky shot.

The craft was very comfortable, but it had been modified. In the back half was a dozen intensive care patient carriers. A Transport had just brought these Mergenky back from Jeeapa. These were severely wounded Mergenky fighters who were stabilized at Jeeapa and were being brought back for more detailed surgery. Sadly, some of them were missing limbs from laser strikes inflicted by the Anarchieborgs.

The Mergenky Ground Forces would offer them robotic arms or legs and essentially turn them into somewhat cyborgs where they could continue serving.

At first those who lost both legs were extremely upset until they discovered they could run 30 miles per hour or jump 20 feet in the air. But still life would not be the same.

Monachi took her seat next to General Kahn. There would not be much talking along the way as the General was viewing his electronic clip board for messages and communiques to various parties including Jeeapa Commander Zǔzhī Bùliáng who was belly aching over the slow receipt of required materials.

When Zǔzhī Bùliáng discovered Frăctŏng received shipments as a higher priority than Jeeapa, he became quite angry and elucidated those thoughts to General Kahn who was then reading the diatribe on his electronic clip board.

General Kahn simply responded:

GENERAL KAHN
You will be receiving shipments. Time and details are
being sent via courier who should be arriving shortly
in advance of the shipments.

Because of the apparent breach in security, General Kahn very cautiously sent Commander Lester as a rider on S-1 now equipped with a large number of space mines in its drop tubes to meet with General Zǔzhī Bùliáng to inform him of the shipment as to prevent enemy intercepting the information and laying an ambush like the shipment to Frăctŏng.

Under General Kahn's orders, Commander Lester would be acting as task force commander and lead a group of Cruisers to the P-point where they would form up a defensive convoy protection force and escort the two ships to Jeeapa to prevent the Anarchie from jumping them and destroying the ships. Cruiser Transport would also arrive at Jeeapa at night to help provide some protection.

Monachi followed General Kahn off his special transport into MSF headquarters where the General turned to Monachi.

GENERAL KAHN
Monachi, I want you to take the rest of the day off and
go home and rest. I know this has been a trying time
for you.

COMMANDER MONACHI
Thank you General.

The two separated and Monachi left the headquarters building and soon found herself on a tube train which went near the Mergenky Healing Center where Kara worked. Kara was the one person she could confide in. Monachi was full of anguish and sadness about the danger Kwongab was in as well as the revelation her kids were now Mergenky Intelligence Agency spies.

Monachi got off the tube train, onto a people mover and soon found herself at the entrance of the Healing Center. She had been to Kara's office here before and knew exactly where to go. Monachi walked over to an elevator and rode it up 50 floors to where Dr. Kara had her office.

Monachi walked into the lobby from the elevator to a receptionist.

COMMANDER MONACHI
Hello, my name is Monachi, and I would like to speak
with Dr. Kara.

RECEPTIONIST
Sure, one moment please.

PNN in the Mergenky Healing Center, did most of the work for the receptionist who was there simply to put a Mergenky face on an otherwise fully automated system.

Within about two minutes, Dr. Kara walked into the lobby from a side door and approached Monachi

KARA
Hello Monachi, what brings you here today?

Kara, who was now more or less psychologically healed from the loss of Vance, appeared chipper and full of life but wasn't expecting Monachi at such an odd hour and could see she wasn't looking too well.

MONACHI
I needed someone to talk to, I know you are busy, but
you are the only person I can confide in.

KARA
Why don't you come to my office, we'll talk there.

Within a few minutes Monachi gave Kara the basics of her problem and Kara knew Monachi needed treatment to help restore her to a positive personal psychology.

KARA
Monachi, there is not much we can do about the
Mergenky Intelligence Agency, but you are suffering
and if you don't mind, I would like to give you a
treatment.

MONACHI
Sure, I suppose it wouldn't hurt.

Please come over to the next room, my equipment is in there.

Kara had Monachi undress, and then placed her into a special gel tube ampule that had a combination of psychoactive drugs and mineral supplements her skin would absorb that would help reduce stress and improve her disposition by a large factor.

In about 30 minutes Monachi was feeling significantly better as Kara's traditional Mergenky Elektronuerotransposition did its magic.

Afterword's, Monachi exited the gel tube, dried off and dressed and then Kara suggested:

KARA

Let's go somewhere to get something to eat and enjoy
a few hours together.

It was just like old times when they got back from Andromeda, when their friendship flourished, and they enjoyed their time together away from their husbands and children.

Both women were much prettier and youthful than their age normally would be. They attributed it to the time in space away from real gravity and cosmic rays from the sun.

MONACHI

Thank you for seeing me and treating me.

KARA

It's the least I could do for you for all that you have
given me and helped me with."

MONACHI

Yes, we certainly have had some interesting travels
together.

KARA

Just remember, you survived Martha, you can survive
anything.

MONACHI

I know but knowing what they have done to my
children upsets me.

KARA

There is nothing you can do about it.

MONACHI
I suppose you are right, but what will I do when I inform Kwongab. He's not going to take it too well.

KARA
Just hope he comes back safely, that's one of the most important things in your life now.

MONACHI
I know, but he fears his luck is running out.

Kara was surprised at those comments and during the long mission to Andromeda often wondered if the two had some sort of telepathic ability since they seemed often do things without speaking to each other. It was as if they seemed to know what the other person was thinking.

Time passed and soon it was time for the two women to separate and go their own ways.

VOICEOVER
Healing Monachi in many ways helped Kara feel she healed herself. She no longer had to worry about Vance because now he was gone.

Kara didn't have to worry about her kids since they were not in that Mergenky Juéduìhuīhuáng Foundation, Center for Advanced Learning, thus were not being prepared to become spies.

Kara's whole world was now much simpler. On the other hand, she knew Monachi was in an awful fright about her children and Kwongab.

Just as the two women were saying goodbye, Kara stated:

KARA
I want you to come to my office in a weeks' time so we can do a follow-up appointment.

MONACHI
I would like that.

They separated. Monachi would never see Kara again.

Kara was one of those idealistic people. On Earth she would be called a '*liberal*' for her views and mannerisms.

Kara would take the matter in her own hands. She felt the Mergenky Intelligence Agency using children as spies was despicable and immoral.

The following day, Kara called in to work and said she would be absent. She got on the tube train and took it to Mergenky Intelligence Agency Headquarters.

Located deep in the Great Canyon Tourist area of Quom, where it would be easy to conceal people coming and going, there was a minor entry that was not well exposed to the public. You had to look hard to find it.

Kara's vast knowledge of research as a doctor and because she had credentials, she could get into areas of databases that was normally restricted from the average Mergenky.

Kara located the entrance with no problems after getting all the information from her portable data terminal she carried in her personal pouch that was like a purse that women would carry on Earth, with a strap around her shoulder. She was well dressed, if not sexy. She had allure.

Kara walked through the entrance that had writing on it that a person could not see unless they were very close. She walked in and was immediately met by security personnel.

SECURITY PERSONNEL
Do you have an appointment?

DOCTOR KARA
No, but I would like to talk with the director.

SECURITY PERSONNEL
That's not possible.

DOCTOR KARA
I think you know how to contact the director and
inform him that Dr. Kara is here. My husband was
recently killed in space warfare near Jeeapa, and I
have something unpleasant I wish to discuss.

The receptionists and security personnel were backed up by PNN who immediately identified Dr. Kara through voice analysis and facial recognition software and pulled up her dossier. She had a compelling history including treating several members of the

Mergenky Intelligence Agency who had been caught and tortured behind enemy lines resulting in almost total insanity.

Dr. Kara, not knowing any of the details, managed to restore them to an almost normal functionality. This was a person for them to take seriously, and the director was notified quickly about the woman at the front entrance demanding an audience.

Even though he was slightly busy dealing with the mess on Jeeapa and Frăctŏng, the director had a few moments to spare especially for this woman suffering such grief over the loss of her husband.

The intelligence director naturally had a curiosity of what drove the woman to come to of all places the Mergenky INTEL apparatus. As a result, he notified the security detail and the receptionist:

INTEL DIRECTOR
XIÉ'È DE DĂOYĂN
(pronounced She-a-e Da Dole-yin)
Please escort Dr. Kara up to my office.

Kara was taken through an x-ray machine which searched for her and the contents of her bag without her knowledge. She and the two security detail people walked into the high-speed lift. She could feel the gravity and the lift gave almost 2 G's accelerating up to the 110th floor of the building.

The elevator opened and they were in a plush room with a lady sitting at a desk facing seven chairs for people who ostensibly might have to wait to see the director for routine business.

Please go right in, the director is expecting you.

Kara went into the plush director's office with the two security guards accompanying her. Once inside, the director informed the security personnel:

INTEL DIRECTOR
XIÉ'È DE DĂOYĂN
Please wait outside, I would like to speak with this
woman in private.

SECURITY GUARD
Yes sir.

The first security guard led the other security guard outside and shut the door behind them.

INTEL DIRECTOR
XIÉ'È DE DǍOYǍN
What can I do for you Doctor Kara?

Director Xié'è de Dǎoyǎn noticed Kara was looking out his large window that had one of the best views of the Great Canyon Area.

DOCTOR KARA
Director Xié'è De Dǎoyǎn I wanted to discuss with you the policy of Mergenky Intelligence Agency using children as spies.

INTEL DIRECTOR
XIÉ'È DE DǍOYǍN
We do not do that.

DOCTOR KARA
Director Xié'è De Dǎoyǎn I know you do, and it displeases me to know that you have turned two of my best friend's children into spies.

INTEL DIRECTOR
XIÉ'È DE DǍOYǍN
And who would that be?

DOCTOR KARA
Captain Kwongab and Commander Monachi from the MSF have their two children now at the Juéduìhuīhuáng Foundation, Center for Advanced Learning and you know it's really nothing more than a front for Mergenky INTEL training campus.

INTEL DIRECTOR
XIÉ'È DE DǍOYǍN
That's ridiculous.

DOCTOR KARA
I have my sources of information, director, I assure you I know details of what goes on at the Mergenky Juéduìhuīhuáng Foundation, Center for Advanced Learning.

Suddenly the director wondered:

VOICEOVER (INTEL DIRECTOR
XIÉ'È DE DǍOYǍN) THOUGHT
I wonder *if some of the Mergenky Spies that Doctor Kara had treated might have been the source of the information leak about the Juéduìhuīhuáng Foundation?*

INTEL DIRECTOR
XIÉ'È DE DǍOYǍN
And who are your sources.

DOCTOR KARA
Don't worry about my sources, I'm only here to request you do one thing.

INTEL DIRECTOR
XIÉ'È DE DǍOYǍN
And what is that, Doctor Kara?

DOCTOR KARA
Remove Kwongab and Monachi's children from Mergenky INTEL.

INTEL DIRECTOR
XIÉ'È DE DǍOYǍN
First of all, they are not part of Mergenky INTEL.

DOCTOR KARA
Director Xié'è de Dǎoyǎn, listen, us not play games. I already know and I have corroborated multiple sources. It is what it is. I'm not asking you to abandon your program, I'm only asking you to remove two of the students.

INTEL DIRECTOR
XIÉ'È DE DǍOYǍN
And what is your rationale for such a request.

DOCTOR KARA
As you know Captain Kwongab is involved in very dangerous work for MSF and he rightfully believes his luck is just about to run out.

INTEL DIRECTOR
XIÉ'È DE DǍOYǍN
What does that have to do with his children?

DOCTOR KARA
If something happens to him and his children get wrapped up in the spy business and something happens to them as well, it will greatly crush my friend Monachi.

INTEL DIRECTOR
XIÉ'È DE DǍOYǍN
There is nothing I could do about that.

DOCTOR KARA
Monachi and her husband Captain Kwongab have greatly sacrificed for Mergenky. I think we owe it to them to at least allow their children to live a normal life and enjoy the fruits of their parents' efforts.

Xié'è de Dǎoyǎn smiled and responded.

INTEL DIRECTOR
XIÉ'È DE DǍOYǍN
Alright Dr. Kara, I will personally investigate this matter and take all appropriate measures as you have requested.

DOCTOR KARA
Thank you, director, that is most kind of you.

INTEL DIRECTOR
XIÉ'È DE DǍOYǍN
Is there anything else you wish to discuss?

DOCTOR KARA
No, that's my only reason for my visit.

INTEL DIRECTOR
XIÉ'È DE DǍOYǍN
Very well Doctor Kara, may I personally escort you to the lobby?

DOCTOR KARA
Yes, this is very kind of you.

INTEL DIRECTOR
XIÉ'È DE DǍOYǍN
Ok, then. This way please.

The director took Kara to the elevator with the two security agents following behind and they all got into the elevator together.

The elevator went down the 110 floors very promptly and when it slowed, they felt the two Gs of gravity as it slowed several floors. The door opened Kara got out and the director and security personnel followed her to the front entrance.

The director bowed.

INTEL DIRECTOR
XIÉ'È DE DǍOYǍN
Dr. Kara, it was a pleasure meeting you and I'm terribly sorry for your husband's loss. He was a true hero.

Xié'è de Dǎoyǎn then smiled.

DOCTOR KARA
Thank you.

The security guards opened the door for Doctor Kara, and she departed.

Kara left and walked a short distance and caught a tube train back to the area of her tall apartment building where she went home to an empty home, which was now a sad place to hang out with Vance's absence as well as the children away to their boarding school.

Xié'è de Dǎoyǎn went to his office and made a call to one of his associates who led covert ops.

INTEL DIRECTOR XIÉ'È DE DǍOYǍN
Mel, come to my office immediately.

Kara later in the day had just got out of the gel container where she took a slight nap and rest which replenished her and helped her feel much better, when the communicator notified her of an incoming communication.

Kara answered, it was a person from her children's boarding school.

DR. MELPAK
Hello Dr. Kara?

KARA
Yes?

DR. MELPAK
This is Dr. Melpak from your son's school. I'm calling to let you know your son is very ill and I think he would adjust better to the treatment if you could travel here and make a personal visit.

KARA
What's wrong with him?

DR. MELPAK
I would rather discuss that with you when you arrive here if you don't mind, that way I can have all the computer files and analysis available for your inspection.

Kara asked, almost feeling a slight panic.

KARA
Is he in any kind of danger?

DR. MELPAK
No, we are sure he will survive just fine, but we believe your visit would help stabilize him and build up his emotional base to increase the efficiency of the treatment.

KARA
Alright, I'll come there right away.

DR. MELPAK
Doctor Kara, please let me know when you are arriving, and I'll make sure someone picks you up at the space port and brings you immediately to the school.

KARA
I'll send you my itinerary as soon as I get it.

DR. MELPAK
Thank you.

Kara only had to tell her personal computational system in her residence to obtain her all the necessary transportation to the boarding school. Within five minutes Doctor Kara's itinerary was set. Kara then directed her home computational processors to send that information to Dr. Melpak and then she quickly gathered enough personal items she needed for a short trip.

Doctor Kara then called and informed the healing center she was taking a few days off to go see her son at his boarding school who had an illness. Kara then took the elevator down, got on the people mover that took her to a tube train station that with one transfer took her directly to Quom's space port. Kara got on the intercontinental space transport with all the other passengers.

Dr. Kara was never seen again. She simply vanished.

***

AMBUSH AT JEEAPA

VOICEOVER

When the three Mergenky ships were out of the solar system and away from any possible monitors, Kwongab sent a secret tangramized-encrypted plan to the Captains of MSFS-1 and MSFS-4 in the event their mission was compromised as Kwongab thought his last mission had been.

Essentially the plan was to avoid combat with the Anarchie and wait for help to arrive, but the only way he thought conceivable to force the Anarchie to back away would be to utilize a few of the space mines that S-1 was carrying in its drop tubes for later missions after they delivered their precious cargo to Jeeapa.

Kwongab's secret plan stated: if the mission is compromised the Anarchie would be waiting for them on the extreme edge of Jeeapa's solar system.

It would be too far away from Mergenky help so the Anarchie would have ample time with a substantial force to destroy all three Mergenky ships and deny Jeeapa the critical cargo that appears to be essential for survival.

At their present speeds, just below the threshold of exhibiting an ion trail behind the ships, they would reach the outer area of the Jeeapa solar system in approximately 12 hours.

CAPTAIN KWONGAB

Commander Dǐngqiāng you are now in charge. I'm going to my Space Cabin to rest and prepare for the upcoming combat.

COMMANDER DǏNGQIĀNG

Rest well Captain.

CAPTAIN KWONGAB

Commander Dǐngqiāng, please make sure I'm awake an hour before we enter Jeeapa's solar system.

COMMANDER DǏNGQIĀNG

Will do, Captain.

Kwongab, went to his Space Cabin, undressed and entered his Gel Tube where he soon was slowly entering a deep sleep with the help of Erica's biofeedback and the chemicals in the gel substance that added to the sensation that allowed a deep restful sleep which he could come out of in a moment's notice.

VOICEOVER

Kwongab needed this rest as he was operating on sleep deprivation and knew that once they got within range of the Anarchie, his chances of getting any further rest would be unlikely for many hours if not days ahead.

The ships continued the transit spaced out with Scout MSFS-1 in the lead which was necessary in the event the Anarchie were waiting in an ambush. This would give Scout MSFS-4 and Cruiser MSFC-8 time to reverse course and with the help of their high speed get away while Scout MSFS-1 was distracting or damaging the enemy.

Mergenky Cruiser MSFC-8 crew was ever vigilant, but many hours in a heightened state of reality can lead to a vigilance decrement. Commander Dǐngqiāng knew that vigilance issue was possible and thus just like a conductor of a symphony was touring the control room and engaging with each member to help prop them up psychologically.

If any sensor operator thought they could daydream or not pay attention during the transit, they were agitated and kept alert by Commander Dongxiang's poignant questions on unexplained sightings that were the remnants of asteroids or space junk. The control room was kept on their toes.

In 10 hours, a new group of watch standers arrived relieving those who had been operating the sensors and monitoring ships systems even though everything was automatic, MSF wanted a physical person as observers in the event a software glitch or unsuspected and unpredictable system malfunction occurred.

PNN would do the automatic reconfigurations to ensure the vessel maintained a degree of safety, but the man machine interface was necessary because MSF did not fully trust artificial intelligence, especially after Martha.

An hour after the next shift took over Erica (PNN)notified Commander Dongxiang:

ERICA (PNN)

Commander Dongxiang we are one hour away from the solar system outer boundary. Would you like me to awaken Captain Kwongab?

COMMANDER DONGXIANG

Yes, please do so.

Kwongab was having pleasant dreams of his experiences in the Andromeda galaxy. How they managed to outfox Martha, who had become corrupt, was still a state secret.

Kara, Kwongab, Vance, and Monachi were never allowed to divulge the artificial intelligence breakdown and corruption to anyone in the event something like this happened again, they wanted to make sure PNN did not know of the work around in the event they had to use it again.

ERICA (PNN) helped wake up Kwongab who then did all his morning routines. Kwongab stopped by the crew's lounge and got something to eat, then went to the bridge about 30 minutes away from the edge of Jeeapa's solar system.

VOICE OVER

High anxiety swept through the control room. If Anarchie were waiting for them again, that would confirm the leak inside MSF through an Anarchie spy was getting operational plans to the enemy.

The spy sadly was MSF and possibly among them, not necessarily on this ship, but someone they knew.

As per the plan, S-1 suddenly turned on its scanners and instead of only the neutrino sniffers, they also turned on the Infrared and Ultraviolet Scanners which was the secret signal that Anarchie spacecraft had been sighted and to commence their emergency plan they had worked out before.

Kwongab now knew what the score was and if he survived, he would request a personal audience with General Kahn to plead the case.

EXT. CGI. SPACE. MERGENKY SPACE MINE SEEDING. 2 MINUTES.

All three ships immediately went into a Frazgrandopf maneuver, but instead of the second course change, they simply continued the first course change which was an almost 180-degree reversal. As soon as S-1 steadied up on course they deployed the first six space mines.

COMMANDER DONGXIANG
These were scarce items loaded for the next mission.

But as Kwongab responded it made sense:

CAPTAIN KWONGAB
If we don't use them under these circumstances, we might not have the next mission.

The Anarchie were so over eager to get into laser range and make quick dispatch of the first Mergenky ship in the three-ship convoy and were not paying attention for kinetic weapons or something as obscure as space mines which were rarely used because they violated intergalactic convention rules.

Rules seldom last in wartime since everyone cheats, because there is no substitute for victory.

The Anarchie did not realize they were entering a space mine field until it was too late. Even though Anarchie had 12 Battleships and only 6 space mines were deployed, they all made their mark. Several Battleships were crippled by the mines, and one was completely destroyed as one mine opened a gaping hole and the 2nd mine simply flew inside the battleship and detonated exactly in the center of the ship which caused a horrific explosion and a nice fireball which blinded the other ships for a few seconds and caused them to immediately turn and take evasive courses since they didn't know the extent of the mine field they had discovered the hard way.

This gave the Mergenky just enough time to zig zag into a new course that would take them about 45 degrees off Jeeapa where they would then maneuver again and approach Jeeapa at high speed after announcing their presence to the MSF fleet nearby. Within 30 minutes a large Mergenky escort surrounded the three ships making it practically impossible for the Anarchie to attempt attack.

The Anarchie didn't know there would be three ships, and their spy had stated only a Cruiser Transport was delivering equipment.

Scout MSFS-4 carried a substantial cargo as well and as soon as the two ships landed, a vast Mergenky army of workers started the offloading and moving the gear and equipment into the *Five-Mile Oval* where it would be protected.

The Anarchie had enjoyed the past seven dark nights making slow but steady progress in their march to Jeeapa.

Tonight, the tables would be turned as with ample cheap lighting drones deployed, the Anarchie would not be able to move forward and worse yet would not be able to supply their troops. A tactical retreat to defensible and serviceable positions would soon grip the Anarchie, as the complexities of the battlefield just turned for their worst.

While the two ships were being unloaded which would take a couple hours, Kwongab and Kuàisù Sīkǎo were invited to Jeeapa Commander Zǔzhī Bùliáng's office in the *Five-Mile Oval* to receive his personal praise for their heroic delivery of this essential material, that would help the Mergenky ground forces immediately.

Upon entry to General Zǔzhī Bùliáng's office, the General welcomed the two MSF pilots in an emotional like reception.

GENERAL ZǓZHĪ BÙLIÁNG

Ship Captains Welcome to Jeeapa. We owe you both a
lot of gratitude for what you have done for us getting
that precious cargo here, and for the other services you
performed.

CAPTAIN KWONGAB
Thank you General.

Kwongab allowed the levity to continue for a few minutes before he stated a critically important request that immediately put a damper on the festivities.

CAPTAIN KWONGAB
General Zǔzhī Bùliáng Sir, I need to have a private meeting with you about an urgent matter, that does not concern Commander Kuàisù Sīkǎo, and it needs to be of the strictest of confidentiality.

GENERAL ZǓZHĪ BÙLIÁNG
Alright, my offices are bug swept several times a day, and were just swept a couple hours ago, it's safe to have a conversation here. Commander Kuàisù Sīkǎo, would you and everyone else please step outside for a few minutes.

After everyone was gone and the door shut, General Zǔzhī Bùliáng with a quizzical look on his face asked:

GENERAL ZǓZHĪ BÙLIÁNG
What is it you wish to discuss Captain Kwongab?

CAPTAIN KWONGAB
General Zǔzhī Bùliáng in my last two Cruiser Transport trips, the Anarchie were waiting for us exactly where I expected they would be if we were compromised. They had advance notice of us coming.

GENERAL ZǓZHĪ BÙLIÁNG
That's quite remarkable Kwongab, what made you come to this conclusion?

KWONGAB
The first time was coincidental, anything is possible, but when it just happened again, almost where I predicted it would, that's more than coincidental.

GENERAL ZǓZHĪ BÙLIÁNG
I would likely think the same.

KWONGAB

We either have a spy here or we have one at MSF headquarters. You need to get the word back to General Kahn.

GENERAL ZŬZHĪ BÙLIÁNG

I can send him a GENERAL'S EYES-ONLY message right away.

KWONGAB

General Zŭzhī Bùliáng, you can't send it by communications because that may be how the spy is getting the information. It must be by a special envoy.

GENERAL ZŬZHĪ BÙLIÁNG

Alright Kwongab. It so happens General Kahn has sent his personal transport here to pick up casualties and evacuate them to Gwaba, I could bump one of the casualties and make room for an emissary.

KWONGAB

General Zŭzhī Bùliáng, it must be someone that knows the details and understands the gravity of the situation. I have a person in mind that would be the best person to send.

GENERAL ZŬZHĪ BÙLIÁNG
And who is that?

KWONGAB

My Executive Officer, Commander Dĭngqiāng is one of the most trustworthy and loyal persons I know.

Also, we'll come up with a story of why he is going back to Gwaba, don't pre-announce he's going back to meet General Kahn.

GENERAL ZŬZHĪ BÙLIÁNG

How can he get to General Kahn without exposing the purpose of his visit?

KWONGAB

As soon as he's at MSF headquarters he can ask General Kahn's receptionist to contact you for the introduction, then he'll know he is your personal emissary.

GENERAL ZŬZHĪ BÙLIÁNG
All right Kwongab, send Commander Dǐngqiāng to my office right away, he'll be leaving for Gwaba in about an hour or less.

KWONGAB
Thank you General.

GENERAL ZŬZHĪ BÙLIÁNG
No thank you Kwongab, you have served MSF well. You will always have my personal gratitude and admiration for your conduct here. Let's go out and let me sprinkle Commander Kuàisù Sīkǎo with some praise he has also earned.

The unloading went smoothly in the dark and all the precious cargo was soon underground in protected storage where the assets would be used in the most conservative manner with the highest priority missions. Chief among them was to extend air defense at least a couple weeks in time for more shipments to arrive and the sophisticated weapons and tools for the ground forces could not have arrived at a most auspicious occasion.

The two-space craft lifted off the planet as soon as the materials were unloaded. Just before liftoff, General Kahn's private transport left carrying several severely wounded soldiers and one healthy person, Commander Dǐngqiāng.

At first the onboard doctors were incensed when orders were given to offload a severely wounded man who might not live if they didn't get him back to Gwaba.

General Zŭzhī Bùliáng knew such circumstances might manifest because doctors have tunnel vision, so he personally escorted Commander Dǐngqiāng to the craft and pulled the head doctor aside and explained.

General Zŭzhī Bùliáng
I can't reveal to you the purpose of why this man is traveling with you to MSF headquarters, but just assume he's my personal envoy and his mission is of grave importance to Jeeapa.

CHIEF SURGEON
General we can't take him; we do not have room.

GENERAL ZŬZHĪ BÙLIÁNG
He's leaving with you on the ship that's already

decided. You can either leave one of the patients behind who will continue to receive treatment here or you will have to leave one of the doctors behind.

CHIEF SURGEON
We can't leave any of the doctors behind. They are necessary to keep all of the patients alive. Almost every patient on the ship is close to death and needs constant doctor supervision or they may not make it.

GENERAL ZŬZHĪ BÙLIÁNG
You understand my orders, leave one of the patients behind or one of the doctors to make room for Commander Dǐngqiāng.

CHIEF SURGEON
Yes, sir General.

The chief surgeon then huddled with the other doctors, and they ordered removal of a patient that was very near death and had less than a 50% chance of survival even if he made it to Gwaba.

Coming off the transport meant his probability of death within a day or two. It wasn't the kind of decision General Zǔzhī Bùliáng took lightly, but he also knew that what Kwongab had told him needed to get to General Kahn immediately, because something far worse could happen with a well-placed spy in MSF.

Commander Dǐngqiāng, didn't like leaving his ship, but after Kwongab briefed him on what he must do, Commander Dǐngqiāng now had the burden on his shoulders of what 10 men would have after he received his special briefing which he would take to General Kahn and give verbally.

This was one of the sadder days in MSF history, because having a traitor near the top was about the worst thing that could happen to them. The hunt for the spy would turn ugly soon enough, as Mergenky INTEL would be crawling all over MSF.

General Kahn's private transport was long gone by the time MSFS-4 and MSFC-8 reached geosynchronous orbit waiting for their next mission to unfold. MSFS-1 eventually teamed up with them and they were now ready to commence the plan to deny the Anarchie the ability to backfill their Jeeapa forces with men and material repatriated off Frăctŏng.

EXT. NIGHT. JEEAPA GROUND BATTLE.

The ships had departed an hour before midnight. Exactly at midnight, the Anarchie unleashed the largest assault on Jeeapa they had planned in the entire offensive thinking this would break the stalemate.

Exoskeleton Gunships, Crawlers, and Anarchieborgs crept forward while Fighter Bombers dropped out of the bellies of the Anarchie Battleships now converged on the Mergenky front lines.

An Anarchie Exoskeleton typically had two laser cannons and hyperbolic mortars that had some sideways skid capability. This allowed them to hit the enemy on the side or in the back.

The Crawlers with laser shields allowed them to get close to the dispersal area which had just been softened up With Fighter Bombers and Exoskeleton laser attacks.

Even though it was a dark moonless night, the zip zap back and forth laser battles commenced in high velocity and volume.

The Anarchie were feeling their gusto and were slowly clawing ahead. Thinking this was the beginning of the end for the MSF on such a beautifully dark night their overconfidence flowed raw and was soon to turn into a sea of green reptilian blood.

The lead Anarchie assault force void of a lot of its Scouts and Rangers, thanks to Kwongab, Vance, Monachi, and Captain Koasa earlier, were only a partial remnant of their formerly proud ranks.

Without an abundance of those key Scouts and Rangers, Anarchie were saddled with marginal performers. Their enthusiasm was high because the Anarchie were consistently moving forward and the appearance that Mergenky Ground Forces (MGF) could not stop them.

However, when marginal troops start having difficulty, it's the Anarchie Scouts and Rangers who step in with the leadership at the right time to keep the momentum going.

The Mergenky forward observers saw the Anarchieborgs coming and continued making reports over temporary land lines that had not been cut yet.

The fact that MSF just delivered ample lighting drones was a well-placed secret. Anarchieborgs were soon to discover the tactical disadvantage the lighting drones placed on them.

The wise commanders at Jeeapa knew better than to tip their hand until the finest hour approached. As soon as the Anarchie were fully committed, including vast strings of Crawlers out in the open and Exoskeletons sticking up like sitting ducks it would be time to light them up.

The Mergenky forward observers were to the point of begging to be allowed to abandon their positions, the Anarchie were getting painfully close and not a single Mergenky shot had been fired.

Around one hour past midnight as the calls from the forward observers were stringing in, the final order came. All gunners were told to stand by to fire. The first lighting drones were launched, and the incredible brilliance lit up the night sky as if it were daylight.

Out exposed on the battlefield with low levels of concealment and just 20% of the men covered by portashields, the Anarchie were sitting ducks.

Immediately after the lights went on, the firing started. lasers, kinetic weapons, chemical rockets with conventional warheads all started hitting the Anarchieborgs hard.

Drivers of Crawlers and Anarchie controlling the Exoskeletons immediately turned around in haste. They thought they had blundered into a sophisticated trap!

In the past seven days of fighting the Mergenky no longer possessed enough lighting drones to make it worth their while to deploy them because the Anarchie would simply just shoot them down.

But now thanks to the supplies Kwongab just delivered, the Mergenky could send up hundreds of lighting drones that conceivably could land and refuel and go back up, these strategic assets would be utilized with the amount of density required to place continued pressure on the Anarchie.

Some of the forward observers had Anarchieborgs standing 20 feet in front of them. Come morning as they cleared the battlefield, it would be full of dying or dead Anarchie. Green Blood was turning a nearby stream green.

It did not take long after this battle for the Anarchie leadership to order General Borktar to bring his entire force to Jeeapa. The illusion of General Borktar triumphantly marching into Yŏngbùmián de Chéngshì, was over. He had achieved his goal of dividing the Mergenky and make them squander precious resources protecting the Feint the Anarchie did to make the Jeeapa campaign much easier to land on and project the tip of their power.

Because of their horrific losses at Jeeapa, the MSF had no choice but to pull back a large percentage of the fleet supporting Frăctŏng. As a result, getting the Anarchie Transports down to the planet's surface was done without too much concern.

Loading took place 20 miles further south than the front lines to make sure the

Mergenky did not spot and disturb the Anarchie Frăctŏng evacuation. A rear guard was left in place with a promise of extraction the following night that never came.

The MSF were not able to stop the Anarchie transports from leaving the planet with most of the remaining Exoskeletons, Crawlers, and Anarchieborgs.

MSFS-1, MSFS-4, and MSFC-8 all received the INTEL simultaneously. Scout MSFS-5 was sent to trail the Anarchie at a safe distance and make periodic reports on location, course, and speed. Kwongab knew the Anarchie would not attempt to approach the planet direct and informed his other two ships, to plan to relocate towards one of the poles as soon as the Anarchie convoy tipped its hand and gave away their approach plan by bunching on one pole or the other.

Just as Kwongab predicted, the Anarchie Convoy started drifting slightly towards the southern hemisphere on their approach to the planet.

That's all Kwongab needed. MSFS-1 was positioned approximately 3 million meters directly south of the southern pole of the planet.

MSFS-4 and MSFC-8 would wait for them and as they approached the polar area just before atmospheric penetration, the *Black Ravik's* would be deployed and then MSFS-4 and MSFC-8 would distract the Anarchie and hopefully force their escorts to chase them through the mine field the *Black Ravik's* would sew on the go.

The closer the Anarchie got to Jeeapa, the easier it was for Kwongab to confirm their intentions.

Kwongab knew the Anarchie forces on the ground must have needed reserves by now and if they were eliminated in route, the psychological blow to the Anarchieborgs would be instrumental towards intensifying defeatism among their ranks.

As expected, several Anarchie Battleships escorting the transports chased after the Cruiser and the Scout showing total disregard for their perceived ability. With the new laser optics, the Anarchie crews were emboldened and now foolheartedly transitioned to an over aggressive mentality that they would soon learn such over aggressiveness might not serve them well.

Just as the plan called for the *Black Ravik's* already in position simply opened the rear door under PNN control. There were no living crew members on the Black Ravik's fully automated since it was felt they might be destroyed in the fighting.

The Anarchie did not see the Black Ravik's. They certainly were not looking for space mines which conceivably had not been used in warfare for a very lengthy period due to the Galactic Conventions.

Captain Kwongab kept MSFC-8 in close range to Anarchie so they would be distracted and not detect the mines until it was too late.

Each Black Ravik launched 4 space mines in the first salvo.

Woosh, Woosh, Woosh, Woosh, the sounds of the deploying space mines would have left no doubt in anyone's mind these weapons were working and ostensibly dangerous.

The chemical rockets on the space mines accelerated them to almost light speed. The three3 Anarchie battleships were sitting ducks. Soon in quick succession order, Whack! And Kaboom! The Anarchie battleships blew up in spectacular fashion!

General Borktar, in his command ship bridge near the back of the convoy watched with outright horror as the huge explosions created so much light that every one of his transports were easily observable from the planet's surface.

Neither Anarchie nor the Mergenky knew which side was suffering since few of them knew who were in those ships exploding in the opening minutes of this battle.

General Borktar didn't know immediately those had been Anarchie ships exploding, or he would have ordered the Anarchie convoy to make an immediate course change. However, with the fog of war and uncertainty, General Borktar continued this course hoping for the best but fearing the worst.

The *Black Raviks* were not fired upon since the battleships were destroyed before they had a chance to detect and target them. Behind the Battleships came more battleships and the first group of transports loaded with Anarchieborgs.

Anarchie transport captains felt they were the best guarded ships, so they were too much at ease. As soon as they lost status signals from the three Anarchie Battleships after the bright light from the explosion, they should have questioned what happened and made an emergency course change to regroup and investigate what was going on, including bringing more fleet assets in from Jeeapa to improve their screen while descending on the planet.

Woosh, Woosh, Woosh, Woosh, Woosh. The remaining space mines departed out of the Black Raviks. This time, being a little more cautious and alerted, some of the Anarchie captains saw the purple streaks of light that were emanating out of the space mines and called away an emergency.

Incoming Weapons, take evasive courses!

Alarms went off throughout the fleet. The ships started maneuvering and, in some cases, they were able to lock in on incoming space mines and shoot them with their lasers which immediately detonated them harmlessly away from their hulls. Some

Anarchie captains were slow to respond and did not fully appreciate the gravity of the situation until two heavily laden transports were hit.

ANARCHIE BATTLESHIP CAPTAIN

Two transports were hit reverse course! We stumbled into an ambush!

Anarchie Battleships and Transports performed emergency course changes which provides no measure for collision avoidance. It's simply: *Every man for himself.*

Thinking the only adversaries were in front of them, they never counted on MSFS-1 behind them. Immediately after the *Black Ravik's* launched the space mines, MSFS-1 knew the attack had begun so it reversed course, lowered the drop tubes and started sewing the nearby space with space mines. Sixty-Four mines were deployed and sent at a high velocity. By the time the Anarchie got turned around, the mines had obtained their required velocity, and the rocket engines were shut down. The Anarchie did not benefit from the earlier warning they got from the space mine rocket exhaust.

Now it was just a black object that was almost impossible to see traveling near high speeds converging on them and just as the Anarchie were feeling good about the course change and would soon attempt a planetary re-entry around the north pole, the first space mines came in and started hitting Anarchie ships.

This time only one transport was hit, but the space mines took out quite a few escort vessels before the remainder were destroyed by Anarchie lasers as they transitioned to their new plan to attempt entry at the other pole.

With the Anarchie gone and no possibility of further combat, Kwongab ordered:

KWONGAB:

Dock the Black Raviks back on our ships, then they repositioned as required by the force structure of the Jeeapa command.

Destroying the three Anarchie Transport ships and the six Anarchie Battleships materially damaged the Anarchie task force. The remainder of the Anarchie made it to the planet's surface, but the tremendous loss in space battleship capability eliminated any possibility of threatening Frăctŏng.

These serious Anarchie losses also called into question their ability to sustain Jeeapa operations indefinitely and soon with all the lighting drones deployed, the battle now turned to a serious negative war of attrition for the Anarchie.

Thanks to Kwongab's urgent delivery of critical supplies, Frăctŏng was spared great damage as the air defense system was able to be kept viable throughout the Anarchie invasion.

With reports filtering back from Jeeapa about the amount of destruction laid upon the Anarchie, it was now clear to Frăctŏng defenders that only a skeleton force of rear-guard troops remained. The Anarchie marooned on Frăctŏng no longer had the source of supplies or air defense and thus soon withered at the vine.

After Anarchie repeatedly refusing to surrender the Frăctŏng forces cut the Anarchie water supply and with no new food supplies coming in they were soon rendered hopeless.

Over the next few days, Anarchie troops' morale collapsed and the fruitless nature of their mission became clear, rank and file began mass desertion and surrender.

Within 48 hours all that was left was an Anarchie command post and a bewildered group of officers wondering: *what went wrong*?

As soon as the reports were made as to the situation that just unfolded, Kwongab was ordered back to Gwaba to pick up another priority shipment and deliver it to Jeeapa.

Regular transports were yet incapable of safe arrival at Jeeapa. The Cruiser transports were making a huge difference in the outcome of this combat event.

***

<u>EXT. CGI. SPACE. MSS-21 SPACE STATION. MSFC-8 DOCKING. (15 SECONDS).</u>

<u>INT. SPACE. MSS-21 SPACE STATION.</u>

As soon as MSFC-8 docked at MSS-21 space station, Captain Kwongab departed the cruiser and discovered General Kahn was waiting and standing beside him was Commander Dàqiú.

Kwongab was pleased to see General Kahn and Commander Dàqiú together because it meant the message was delivered to General Kahn. Kwongab was surprised Monachi was not there to meet him. *I wonder, what is Monachi doing?*

CAPTAIN KWONGAB
Hello General Kahn.

GENERAL KAHN
Welcome back Captain Kwongab.

Kwongab nodded to Commander Dàqiú.

CAPTAIN KWONGAB
Commander Dàqiú it looks like you made it here safely on General Kahns Transport.

COMMANDER DÀQIÚ
I think the Anarchie were busy trying to figure out what went wrong, and we slipped past their net.

GENERAL KAHN
Commander Dàqiú thank you for your prompt report, I would like you to go aboard MSFC-8 and supervise the loading while I talk privately with Captain Kwongab about a few matters.

COMMANDER DÀQIÚ
Certainly General.

GENERAL KAHN
Good luck Commander.

COMMANDER DÀQIÚ
Thank you General.

Commander Dàqiú turned and walked to the air lock where in a few minutes he would be consumed in activity because some of the cargo was Mergenky ground forces and their equipment.

Cruiser Transport MSFC-8 was now a *Gator Freighter*, as these ground forces were also Amphibious trained to fight on water worlds.

Kwongab followed General Kahn to MSF offices and to that all familiar conference room.

GENERAL KAHN
We have a couple visitors; they should be here any minute.

Kwongab's hope was high that one of them might be Monachi, otherwise his two kids would be wonderful too.

GENERAL KAHN
Good job on delivering the supplies to Jeeapa, General Zǔzhī Bùliáng sent me a communique highly praising you.

CAPTAIN KWONGAB
I appreciate that he did. We often do a lot of strenuous
tasks for ungrateful people.

GENERAL KAHN
True but you must keep your chin up high because you
and I know how important it is. The public has no idea
and perhaps it's best that way.

CAPTAIN KWONGAB
I suppose it is.

A moment later two men in civilian clothes were escorted into the conference room
by MSF security men.

General Kahn stood and Kwongab followed his lead and stood as the men approached.

CŌNGMÍNG
(pronounced Kong Ming)
Hello General Kahn, good to see you again.

GENERAL KAHN
Always a pleasure Cōngmíng.

CŌNGMÍNG
This is my assistant, Zhāngyú (pronounced Jong-you).

General Kahn bowed

GENERAL KAHN
Pleased to meet you Zhāngyú. This is Captain
Kwongab.

CŌNGMÍNG
Pleased to meet you, Captain Kwongab.

Cōngmíng then bowed slightly.

CAPTAIN KWONGAB
Likewise.

Kwongab bowed respectfully.

About that time the doors in the room were shut by pneumatic power giving off a slight
hissing sound as they shut.

Above the door a blinking blue light turned on to remind everyone in the room, nothing said in the room was to be discussed outside this room as it was highly compartmentalized and of the highest levels of security. The flashing blue light added to the anxiety that Kwongab now felt.

GENERAL KAHN
Captain Kwongab, these Mergenky INTEL men are investigating your concerns that Anarchie may have been tipped off in advance of your recent missions and thus set the two ambushes you alleged occurred.

CAPTAIN KWONGAB
I see.

CŌNGMÍNG
Yes, Captain Kwongab, we have been looking hard into this matter with a great deal of delicacy because certainly we don't want to tip off a potential perpetrator, but at the same time, until we foil the spy ring, we don't want the enemy knowing we are on to them.

CAPTAIN KWONGAB
Makes sense.

CŌNGMÍNG
We do computer modeling of events to produce probabilities that situations would randomly occur with no explanation and determine those probability numbers which gives us a figure of merit as to the likelihood, there is virtue in the allegations.

CAPTAIN KWONGAB
I understand that sophisticated approaches are necessary.

CŌNGMÍNG
We don't want to go on wild goose chases, but at the same time we don't want to ignore something that's glaringly obvious that may become a fiasco later in time.

CAPTAIN KWONGAB
I understand completely.

CŌNGMÍNG
Whether we believe you or not, we have our protocols we go through that provide layers of accountability in the process.

ZHĀNGYÚ
We don't want to be accused of conducting a witch hunt, but on the same token, we don't want to be responsible for a major setback because we ignored crucial intelligence or did not pay attention to various suspicious activities.

CŌNGMÍNG
As Agent ZHĀNGYÚ implied, the consequences are simply too great to at least evaluate the plausibility of alleged spying.

ZHĀNGYÚ
Captain Kwongab, we received reports from MSF which includes a graphic reconstruction of the event.

CAPTAIN KWONGAB
How did you reconstruct the mission?

CŌNGMÍNG
All sensor data on the two Scout Class Ships as well as your Cruiser are always recorded for future inquiries as you should know.

MSF transferred all the sensor data associated with thee two events to one of our labs to be analyzed and processed.

The analysts doing a reconstruct in the lab gave us a complete picture of the area around the ship.

CAPTAIN KWONGAB
I would estimate you have a lot of information for a reconstruction of the events.

CŌNGMÍNG
That's correct Captain Kwongab. In your first encounter a Scout Class Spaceship with your Cruiser MSFC-8 provided us with real time multiple sensor data to construct a hybrid plot.

CAPTAIN KWONGAB
What's the benefit of the hybrid plot?

CŌNGMÍNG
Since the distances are reasonable and the angles between the two Mergenky ships in relation to the Anarchie were much different due to position, we combined spatial Mergenky and Anarchie data reconstruction gives a much better picture of what you saw real time on the ship.

Kwongab feeling disadvantaged, stated:

CAPTAIN KWONGAB
We normally do not have the time to fully figure out what a contact of interest is doing.

CŌNGMÍNG
That's right. You only have minutes to analyze and gauge the situation. We have hours and weeks of time; therefore, we can come up with far greater resolution and accuracy as we use PNN to perform calculations on data obtained from multiple ships at multiple angles.

CAPTAIN KWONGAB
Thanks for understanding that.

CŌNGMÍNG
General Kahn, with your permission, I would like to show the incident reconstruction we brought for mission number one where Kwongab first suspected he landed in an ambush.

GENERAL KAHN
Sure, go ahead and play it.

A scale model holograph showing the ships and their relative position to each other commenced. Kwongab was impressed on the clarity of the presentation.

CAPTAIN KWONGAB
It almost looks like what we were seeing from the bridge.

CŌNGMÍNG
Yes, PNN helps to make it look very realistic.

Kwongab watched the scenario replay and said:

CAPTAIN KWONGAB
It pretty much appears like what I recall during the event.

CŌNGMÍNG
Commander, watching the reconstruct what's the obvious things you can say about the reconstruct at the start of the replay?

CAPTAIN KWONGAB
Well, the only obvious thing I can see is the enemy ships are not moving but we are.

CŌNGMÍNG
Precisely, that's what jumped out at us. You wisely had ordered the course change which enabled us to use geometries based on relative motion calculations to show the enemy was almost at a dead stop and started accelerating just as you arrived near them.

CAPTAIN KWONGAB
That seems about right. I knew right then and there it was an ambush. They had prior knowledge of our mission.

CŌNGMÍNG
Now let's look at the 2nd mission reconstruction when you thought was an ambush, then we'll go back in a minute and look at one more item I've not yet discussed.

CAPTAIN KWONGAB
Alright.

The second ambush reconstruct was shown and once again it had the sophisticated imagery as the first reconstruct.

CŌNGMÍNG
What stands out in your opinion?

KWONGAB

It appears the reconstruction shows the Anarchie ships
are not moving until we arrive nearby.

CŌNGMÍNG

That's correct. The Anarchie ships had zero velocity
until you arrived within their scanner range.

CAPTAIN KWONGAB

That's what I thought at the time. They were waiting in
a specific spot in space for us, which would have been
impossible if they didn't have advance notice.

CŌNGMÍNG

On the second encounter they didn't know there
would be three ships traveling in the manner you were
because the planning for that mission happened on the
ships and nobody at Gwaba or Jeeapa had access to
that information.

GENERAL KAHN

Does all this imply an inside source?

CŌNGMÍNG

It does.

GENERAL KAHN

Do we have any idea how the information is getting
transmitted to the enemy?

CŌNGMÍNG

Not yet.

CAPTAIN KWONGAB

Which means we don't have a clue who's the spy?

CŌNGMÍNG

Unfortunately, we do not.

CAPTAIN KWONGAB

How are we going to find the spy?

ZHĀNGYÚ

That's where our expertise comes into play and your
help will be needed.

CAPTAIN KWONGAB
In what way?

ZHĀNGYÚ
We can't go to the fleet asking Pilots and Captains for help since we must keep this under wraps.

CAPTAIN KWONGAB
That's understandable.

ZHĀNGYÚ
But since you are a captain and already privy to the issue, we can use you to do events that we can then track which will help us isolate the person and determine the method of information transmission.

CAPTAIN KWONGAB
How will I do that?

CŌNGMÍNG
You know who I am and who Zhāngyú is. We will confer with General Kahn from time to time and we'll be telling you information to transmit to MSF that only you and we will know is a plant. We'll use that information to track down the spy.

CAPTAIN KWONGAB
I see.

CŌNGMÍNG
Also, you will be given verbal orders which nobody but you, General Kahn and us will know. In essence we are using you as a double spy.

CAPTAIN KWONGAB
If it helps us track down the traitor, I suppose we must do it.

ZHĀNGYÚ
The consequences otherwise could be enormous. That's all we have for now. We'll contact you as necessary.

The Mergenky INTEL men stood up, bowed to General Kahn, then towards Kwongab who also stood. Just after the Intel men went through the door it whooshed shut again, and General Kahn announced.

GENERAL KAHN

Kwongab, I need to talk to you about another matter.

Kwongab sat back down and General Kahn did as well and General Kahn began briefing the current situation with his children.

GENERAL KAHN

I investigated the matter of your children and had two
visitors from Mergenky INTEL who oversee your
children.

With those words Kwongab's heart sank because that confirmed his worst nightmare. His kids were in harm's way.

CAPTAIN KWONGAB

What did they tell you?

GENERAL KAHN

Your children are not spying nor are they trained to
be spies. Your daughter is a technology innovator. She
helps design devices that our spies would use. Her
work is highly classified. She works half a day and
attends school for the other half of the day.

Kwongab felt a little better about that but in many ways wished his kids had nothing to do with the INTEL business.

GENERAL KAHN

Your son is a translator.

That hit Kwongab a little harder because that placed him within striking range of becoming a spy. A translator was on a slippery slope to full blown spying.

CAPTAIN KWONGAB

What does he translate?

GENERAL KAHN

Anarchie.

Kwongab suddenly got very uneasy because his son was now on the most slippery slope possible since the Anarchie had become a very dangerous adversary during Jeeapa, and now that they had returned to Jeeapa, it had turned into another serious matter.

CAPTAIN KWONGAB
What is he translating from Anarchie?

GENERAL KAHN

He works with Cryptologists to make sense out of the decryptions

CAPTAIN KWONGAB
When did he learn Anarchie language?

GENERAL KAHN

When you went to Andromeda, you brought back the Anarchie Captain Esau, is that correct?

CAPTAIN KWONGAB
Sure, that's widely known.

GENERAL KAHN
I would assume Captain Esau taught you son Anarchie.

CAPTAIN KWONGAB
I wonder what ever happened to Captain Esau.

GENERAL KAHN
He's dead.

CAPTAIN KWONGAB
How do you know that?

GENERAL KAHN

Captain Esau was one of our spies. He reported the launch of this Jeeapa invasion and then committed suicide knowing if the Anarchie caught him they would torture him into becoming a double spy.

CAPTAIN KWONGAB
May I tell Monachi about our children?

GENERAL KAHN

The blue light is flashing as a reminder, none of this is
to be discussed outside of this room.

CAPTAIN KWONGAB

I cannot ever inform Monachi about our children?

GENERAL KAHN

No, the blue light is flashing. You know the rules.

CAPTAIN KWONGAB

Do you know why Monachi didn't meet me here
today?

GENERAL KAHN

She didn't inform me she wouldn't come to visit you.

CAPTAIN KWONGAB

Could you please check up on Monachi and see if she
is, okay?

Certainly, I'll contact Gwaba and have someone track her down and let her know you
were wondering how she's doing.

CAPTAIN KWONGAB
Thank you General.

GENERAL KAHN

Kwongab, I'll let you get back to your ship. Since
most of your Cargo is Mergenky Amphibious Forces,
they will be loaded quickly.

KWONGAB

Why are we taking the Amphibious Forces to Jeeapa,
there's no water near where the fighting is going on.

GENERAL KAHN

Real simple, they are the toughest fighters Mergenky
has. We have a lot of fighting left to do and as the
Anarchie gets desperate they will also get tougher.

KWONGAB

Okay, I'll do my best to get them to Jeeapa safely.

GENERAL KAHN
Good Luck Kwongab.

KWONGAB
I hope it holds up.

GENERAL KAHN
You make your own luck through your intuition and innovation.

CAPTAIN KWONGAB
Thanks for looking into my children.

GENERAL KAHN
It's the least I could do. Your report to Jeeapa Commander Zǔzhī Bùliáng is one of the most important INTEL discoveries in 20 years. You may have staved off a monumental disaster.

CAPTAIN KWONGAB
Thank you for the comments. Goodbye General.

GENERAL KAHN
I'm sure we'll see you again soon, to pick up some more shipments.

CAPTAIN KWONGAB
This Cruiser transport has turned out to be more challenging than I imagined.

GENERAL KAHN
That's why you were picked. It's a challenge.

<u>INT. SPACE. MSFC-8 MOORED AT MSS-21. AIRLOCK ENTRANCE TO THE CRUISER.</u>

Kwongab left the MSS-21 MSF conference room and soon was back at his Cruiser Transport just in time to see the last of the Amphibious Forces march onboard in a single file.

CAPTAIN KWONGAB
(Thought)
The General was right, these Amphibians look tough.

Kwongab stepped to the side and watched them all load up. They were being shipped as if they were in a cattle car. The good news is the trip would be relatively short.

After the last Amphibian marched aboard Kwongab then went aboard and walked up to the Control Room/Bridge.

Upon arrival to the Cruiser's control room Kwongab saw his Executive Officer, Commander Dǐngqiāng talking to an Amphibian Officer. Kwongab approached Commander Dǐngqiāng and asked:

CAPTAIN KWONGAB
Commander Dǐngqiāng, How's the loading coming?

COMMANDER DǏNGQIĀNG
Captain, we are almost ready to leave. Let me introduce
you to Colonel Yārén (pronounced Ya-rien). He's the
commander of these Amphibian Forces.

COLONEL YĀRÉN
Pleased to meet you, Captain Kwongab.

As Kwongab looked at Colonel Yārén, he could see Colonel Yārén had almost leather skin from vast outdoor exposure and probable numerous rough times.

CAPTAIN KWONGAB
It's an honor to have you on my ship, Colonel Yārén.

COLONEL YĀRÉN
Thank you, Captain Kwongab.

CAPTAIN KWONGAB
I apologize that our accommodations are not very
good for your men, Colonel Yārén.

COLONEL YĀRÉN
Not to worry Captain, at least they don't have to sleep
in the rain on the way there.

CAPTAIN KWONGAB
Commander Dǐngqiāng do the soldiers have tie down
straps in case we have a bumpy ride?

COMMANDER DǏNGQIĀNG
Yes Captain, each soldier will be clipped with a safety

strap to his service belt to keep them from bouncing around or get hurt in case we must take steep angles in a full gravity situation.

CAPTAIN KWONGAB
Navigator, please come over here and give me a quick navigation brief showing our flight plan.

The very attractive female Navigator, Méiguī (pronounced May-Gwee) approached the navigation holograph and began giving Captain Kwongab the details. There were a series of holographs. The first showed multiple solar systems and the major pathway from MSS-21 to Jeeapa.

Méiguī then moved her hands on the holograph which changed portions of it in a panning like motion with a zoom feature. Kwongab was very familiar with it all then Méiguī zoomed down to Jeeapa their ultimate destination. Battlefield overlays were on the image to show Anarchie and Friendly forces. The flashing virtual line showing the ships track went down to the planet and Kwongab noticed it wasn't pointing at Jeeapa City dome area.

CAPTAIN KWONGAB
Lieutenant Méiguī, that vector does not point to Jeeapa City dome area.

LIEUTENANT MÉIGUĪ
Captain Kwongab, that's correct. We are to transport the Amphibious Force, to the North of the main Anarchie Bivouac Area.

CAPTAIN KWONGAB
Why wasn't I consulted about this. Such a landing will be highly dangerous, and I don't desire to become an Anarchie POW.

LIEUTENANT MÉIGUĪ
Captain Kwongab, we were just informed by MSF just a few minutes ago.

To add to Kwongab's stress, one of the Cruiser's security guards who secure the entrance to the Cruiser had an MSF officer escorting to see Kwongab.

SECURITY GUARD
Captain this is Commander Yīngtè'ěr Lǎoxiōng from MSF to see you.

Kwongab knew the officer was Mergenky INTEL Agent Zhāngyú in disguise.

CAPTAIN KWONGAB
Commander Yīngtè'ěr Lǎoxiōng, let's go to my Space Cabin where we can talk while I look over some paperwork.

COMMANDER YĪNGTÈ'ĚR LǍOXIŌNG
(a.k.a. AGENT ZHĀNGYÚ)
Lead the way, Captain.

Zhāngyú [a.k.a. Yīngtè'ěr] followed Kwongab to his Space Cabin and after the door shut behind them began the conversation.

COMMANDER YĪNGTÈ'ĚR LǍOXIŌNG
(a.k.a. AGENT ZHĀNGYÚ)
Captain Kwongab, your op orders direct you to land North of the main Anarchie Bivouac Area.

KWONGAB
Yes, that's correct.

COMMANDER YĪNGTÈ'ĚR LǍOXIŌNG
(a.k.a. AGENT ZHĀNGYÚ)
Captain Kwongab, when you get close to the planet you are to send a priority tangramized message to General Zǔzhī Bùliáng stating:

After receiving INTEL reports and discussions with Colonel Yārén, we are being diverted South of the Anarchie Bivouac area.

KWONGAB
Will we do anything else?

ZHĀNGYÚ
No, just that.

KWONGAB
Let me escort you to the airlock.

After escorting Zhāngyú off the ship, Kwongab walked back to the bridge where everyone remained waiting for him.

COMMANDER DǏNGQIĀNG
Captain, we just received clearance to undock and proceed on our mission.

Kwongab looked around the control room and noticed great expectations on everyone's faces.

KWONGAB
We might as well get the show on the road.

VOICEOVER
It was evident by this mission the Mergenky were going on the offensive. There were no Anarchie reserves to be sent in to fill in the gaps on the extensive defensive corridor now bristling with earthworks, tunnels, portashields and air defense batteries.

At this point in the battle there was no debris field like there had been in the first Jeeapa war to provide concealment to approaching enemy.

Close up almost hand to hand combat had not yet fully manifested because both sides were almost evenly matched and closing the gap for the Anarchie had been problematic.

Unlike the first Jeeapa war when the Anarchie marched right up to the doorsteps and almost made it through a fractured portion of the Jeeapa Dome covering the city, this was different.

The Anarchie had been making slow and steady progress shortening their lines as the noose around Jeeapa tightened. Everyone in Jeeapa City was trapped, there was no way out except via the space port.

Leaving via the space port was dangerous because there were Anarchie forces nearby who could always prioritize and attack a high valued launch if they thought it contained something important or significant.

Anarchie planners were pragmatic. They knew at

this point in the battle, civilian casualties were not that important to the Mergenky who would not be defending it to the last man.

As such the Anarchie believed most of the outbound traffic was wounded Mergenky and by allowing them to leave, drained Mergenky medical personnel and placed a much greater burden on Mergenky Society.

The Anarchie hoped the growing number of casualties shipped to Gwaba would help bring significant political pressure to bear to force the Mergenky into an Armistice with guaranteed access to Jeeapa and the blue diamonds.

Just as before, MSFC-8 left MSS-21 in a 3-ship convoy with MSFS-1 and MSFS-4.

Kwongab was not the only Captain/pilot hauling Gaters (Amphibians) on MSFC-8. MSFS-1 had reloaded space mines in the Scout drop tubes.

MSFS-4 had a variety of cargos including a few Mergenky Amphibians because Kwongab's Cruiser Transport MSFC-8, did not have enough room for the entire unit.

This mission was going to be a lot tougher than before because the Landing Zone was far enough away from Jeeapa City air defense systems thus could not be of assistance.

Furthermore, Kwongab was concerned that a 5th column individual was tipping off the enemy and may have already compromised their mission.

***

WHERE IS KARA?

Monachi attempted to contact Kara. She did not get any answers. Finally, after several days she contacted the director at the Healing Center where Kara worked.

Monachi's image was displayed on the communication holograph.

MONACHI
Hello director.

HEALING CENTER DIRECTOR
Good morning Monachi, how can I assist you?

MONACHI
I'm calling because I've been trying to get in contact
with Dr. Kara and have not been able to do so.

HEALING CENTER DIRECTOR
She took some time off to go visit her son at school,
who is apparently ill.

MONACHI
Did she say exactly when she would be back?

HEALING CENTER DIRECTOR
No, she didn't.

MONACHI
I am getting concerned about her.

HEALING CENTER DIRECTOR
Call me in a couple days, I'm sure she will call in if
she can't get back for whatever reason.

MONACHI
Will do, thank you.

Monachi did not like the mysterious sudden departure of Kara after all the recent turmoil in her life. This situation added to the anxiety that Monachi already felt.

Two days later, when Kwongab was scheduled to be at MSS-21, she planned to meet him there because he probably was not going to have time to get to the planet surface. But suddenly all this Kara business kept her from being able to get up to MSS-21. She still had not heard from Kara who did not answer any of her calls. So, Monachi called the director again.

MONACHI
Hello Director, this is Monachi. I still have not been
able to get in touch with Kara.

HEALING CENTER DIRECTOR
She hasn't called, we are getting concerned too.

MONACHI
I'm going to go by her residence and see if there's a
problem.

HEALING CENTER DIRECTOR
Ok, please let us know if you find something out.

Monachi got permission to leave work after she explained the situation. She took the tube train near Kara's residence, and the people mover right up to the tall building. Monachi then went to the residence, pressed the *Guest Arrival Button* and received a prompt.

HOME SECURITY MANAGEMENT
GUEST ARRIVAL VOICE
I am sorry the person you are attempting to contact is
not available.

Monachi feared the worst, including foul play, even though crime was rare in Quom. Monachi immediately went to the building manager and explained the situation and asked if they could go into the residence and see if she was alright.

The building security went to the residence, with Monachi in toe, and because Monachi was a high-ranking MSF official, they knew this was a serious matter.

Building security and Monachi entered the residence, and nobody was present, and the home looked well-kept and nothing disturbed. Monachi feared the worst and decided to make a visit to Kara's children's boarding school to check up on that lead.

Monachi obtained her transportation and was soon on the way. She arrived in the distant City in a couple hours and took private transport to the school where she went directly to the administrator's office.

RECEPTIONIST
Hello, may I help you?

The receptionist observing the visitor had a high-ranking MSF uniform on, so it might be a serious matter, as they were expecting visitors to inform them of children's parents who might have been casualties on Jeeapa.

MONACHI
I've not been able to reach Dr. Kara for several days

and I've checked with her employer the director at the Healing Center where she works, and she's not called in. The MHC director mentioned Dr. Kara was coming here to visit her son who was ill. Is she here or has anyone seen her?

RECEPTIONIST
I've not seen Dr. Kara; I know who she is and am very sorry to have learned about her husband's death. The school was saddened by the news.

Monachi was now almost in full panic using her neural expansion telepathic ability she knew the receptionist had no recollection of Dr. Kara visiting.

MONACHI
May I speak with the principal, this is turning into a serious matter. Also, I would like to confirm with the school's nurse the son's condition.

In a few minutes Monachi was in the principal's office and the school nurse was brought in. Since this was a boarding school, they had far more interest and involvement in their student's health as compared to regular schools.

Monachi was starting to not like the way all this information was unfolding.

MONACHI
Dr. Kara received a phone call from someone claiming they were calling from the school saying her son was ill, and she informed her employer she was coming here to check up on her son. Now you are saying nobody called her and nobody has seen her here.

PRINCIPAL
That is correct.

SCHOOL'S NURSE
Kara's son has not been ill any time in the recent past.

MONACHI
And nobody from the school called Dr. Kara?

PRINCIPAL
That's correct.

Monachi looked at the principal and using neural expansion telepathy on both women got even more concerned.

> MONACHI
> Dr. Kara is my close friend. I fear something has happened to her. I know she wasn't happy after she discovered her husband's demise. I just hope she didn't do what I fear.

After a rather short discussion on procedures and protocols Monachi was satisfied the school had not contacted Kara which intensified the anxiety and made this a growing horrible situation.

> MONACHI
> I would not alarm the children at this time, but I must take this matter to the authorities, who need to investigate her disappearance.

> PRINCIPAL
> We understand. May we get your contact information?

After Monachi provided the school with information on her residence as well as her office at MSF headquarters where she could be reached, the principal asked Monachi:

> PRINCIPAL
> Did you take a private Transport to the school?

> MONACHI
> Yes, I will have to arrange for another to take me back to the Transport Center to get back home.

> PRINCIPAL
> May I take you to the airport?

> MONACHI
> Yes, I would appreciate that.

The two women walked out of the boarding school administration building into a small parking lot where a few surface carriers were parked.

These vehicles were mostly school property serving the needs of the staff and the school which often needed to Shuttle students and teachers to and from the Transport Center where they would get transportation often to many places on the planet.

In some cases, they would go up to MSS-21 transfer to a different Shuttle and come back down on the other side of the planet. If they were closer, they could take an atmospheric flyer or a high-speed tube train that went supersonic.

As they drove to the Transport Center in the vehicle that glided on an air cushion a few inches off the surface of the roads, the principal asked:

PRINCIPAL
How long have you known Dr. Kara?

MONACHI
Over 20 years. We were on a long space mission together.

PRINCIPAL
She was in MSF?

MONACHI
Yes, she was the ship's medical doctor.

PRINCIPAL
I see. So, you must have become very close friends.

MONACHI
Yes, I feel like she is part of my family.

PRINCIPAL
Doctor Kara's a nice person?

MONACHI
Very nice and sweet.

PRINCIPAL
It's too bad what happened to Kara's husband.

MONACHI
Yes, we were very close to Vance. His loss saddened
us all deeply.

PRINCIPAL
This creates a problem for the school if we can't locate
Dr. Kara since she's the only parent the children have.

MONACHI

If we can't locate her, we'll eventually have to inform
the Children.

PRINCIPAL

It would be terrible if they suddenly became orphans.

MONACHI

That will never happen, my husband and I would
immediately apply for adoption. Those kids are like
part of our extended family.

PRINCIPAL

It's a shame you couldn't visit them while you were
here, they're great kids.

MONACHI

Yes, but then they would ask the question why I'm
here. We don't want them to know prematurely what
the facts are until we know them.

PRINCIPAL

Certainly. But sooner or later the authorities will step
in and then we will have to disclose to them their
mother is missing.

MONACHI

After losing their father, this will be extremely rough
on the kids.

The vehicle pulled up to a departure isle where passengers were getting out of private
transport on their way to the various destinations.

As Monachi was stepping out of the vehicle the principal stated:

PRINCIPAL

Please contact me right away if you find something
out.

The principal then handed Monachi her personal contact and business card. This wafer-
thin card made from Glastic substances had an RFI chip in it Monachi could hold up
to her personal communicator which would automatically program her communicator
with the contact information. As soon as Monachi downloaded the contact information
in her personal communicator the internal RFI chip self-destructed which prohibited
anyone else from ever accessing the contact information.

MONACHI
I will and thank you for the ride.

PRINCIPAL
You are most welcome, and I hope this turns out okay.

Monachi was now double depressed. She missed Kwongab and Kara was missing. After finding out her own kids were Mergenky Spies, it seemed that her whole world was crumbling.

When Monachi got back to Quom, she wasted no time in going directly to the authorities.

Before she knew it, Monachi was sitting in an office across the desk from Detective Zhēntàn Xīnkǔ de Pìgu (pronounced: *Shawn-tawn Sing-fu Da Pee-goo*).

DETECTIVE ZHĒNTÀN XĪNKǓ DE PÌGU
You indicated to the screener that your friend Dr. Kara
is missing?

MONACHI
Yes.

DETECTIVE ZHĒNTÀN XĪNKǓ DE PÌGU
How long has it been since you last saw Doctor Kara?

MONACHI
About six days.

Monachi explained what she had done:

MONACHI
I've communicated with the Healing Center director,
the school's principal, and nurse. Nobody has seen
Kara since she disappeared.

DETECTIVE ZHĒNTÀN XĪNKǓ DE PÌGU
I see.

Monachi then informed Detective Zhēntàn Xīnkǔ de Pìgu:

MONACHI
Doctor Kara's husband Vance was recently killed in
the fighting on Jeeapa.

DETECTIVE ZHĒNTÀN XĪNKǓ DE PÌGU
Do you think that has something to do with her disappearance?

MONACHI
I hope not.

DETECTIVE ZHĒNTÀN XĪNKǓ DE PÌGU
Thank you for coming in and reporting this. We'll take it from here Commander Monachi.

MONACHI
I appreciate you looking into this matter and if you find something out can you please, let me know right away.

DETECTIVE ZHĒNTÀN XĪNKǓ DE PÌGU
We will be in contact with you.

MONACHI
Thank you.

DETECTIVE ZHĒNTÀN XĪNKǓ DE PÌGU
One last question, have her children been notified?

MONACHI
No, the school and I discussed Kara's disappearance, and we decided that because of the recent trauma over their father's death, it would be best not to present this information to the children and make them suffer needlessly until we get to the bottom of it.

DETECTIVE ZHĒNTÀN XĪNKǓ DE PÌGU
That's probably a smart move on your part. Technically the children are orphans if we cannot locate the mother.

MONACHI
My husband and I would eagerly adopt them if it came down to that, but I want Dr. Kara found. She's my close friend.

Monachi could not hold back the emotions any longer and started sobbing.

Detective Zhēntàn Xīnkǔ de Pìgu had seen all kinds of scenarios in his 25 years on the force. It was premature to determine that something bad happened to her, but considering her story, the outcome probably was not going to be good and would most likely end up as identification of the body and the cause of death.

Mergenky were seldom emotional, but they do crack now and then and certain circumstances such like this one, often pulled the emotion out of them. Detective Zhēntàn Xīnkǔ de Pìgu knew that Monachi was suffering not only from Kara's disappearance, but also the loss of Vance their friend, and her own circumstances was complicated by the fact her husband was in the MSF at a time of war with the Anarchie.

DETECTIVE ZHĒNTÀN XĪNKǓ DE PÌGU
May I give you a lift home?

MONACHI
Yes, I would appreciate that.

The detective led Monachi out of the office into the elevator and to Monachi's surprise, it went up to the roof top. There were several police skycars parked on the roof and Monachi followed him to one of them that automatic doors opened as the skycars computers recognized Detective Zhēntàn Xīnkǔ de Pìgu.

DETECTIVE ZHĒNTÀN XĪNKǓ DE PÌGU
What's your address Monachi?

Monachi stated her address, and the detective gave the command.

DETECTIVE ZHĒNTÀN XĪNKǓ DE PÌGU
Does your building have a roof top access?

MONACHI
Yes, it does. You can park your police Skycar on it
because those stalls are usually empty.

DETECTIVE ZHĒNTÀN XĪNKǓ DE PÌGU
Take us to Monachi's address.

Skycar micro-PNN always listening searched for Monachi's address and easily located it via Skycar Administration Data Bases that facilitated selection of Sky-routes there.

It would have taken Monachi and hour by people mover, tube train, and walking to get back to her apartment. Thanks to Detective Zhēntàn Xīnkǔ de Pìgu, she was arriving home in 10 minutes.

MONACHI
Thank you for the lift.

DETECTIVE ZHĒNTÀN XĪNKǓ DE PÌGU
You are most welcome. I'll call you if we discover
something you need to know.

MONACHI
Thank you. I appreciate that.

Monachi got out of the law enforcement Skycar and walked to the building roof top
entrance and just before she opened the door to enter felt a slight blast of air from the
Skycar as it left the building and banked around heading back to the law enforcement
building.

After a few minutes, Monachi reached her residence, and Charles was there to meet
her at the door.

CHARLES
Hello Monachi.

MONACHI
Hi Charles.

CHARLES
How did your day go?

MONACHI
It was terrible.

Charles was immediately alarmed not only at Monachi's tone, but also her strange
behavior.

Charles would do his part to make Monachi's life a little more pleasant, considering
the fact of their passing friend, Vance.

Even though Charles was a Larian robot, his vast learning had equipped him with
significant analysis and evaluation capability. Because of his concern for Monachi, he
would look further into her recent strange behavior.

Monachi went to her bedroom, took off her clothes and entered her gel tube and
attempted to rest and reduce her stress. In a short while she achieved her temporal
sleep and was for a brief period resting comfortably with her mind transcending to that

pleasant unawaken state where her dream of days gone by allowed her to escape the harsh reality now gripping her.

Charles entered the room and saw Monachi had achieved that state and very quietly left the room and silently shut the door behind him.

Charles instinctively knew this had something to do with Kara as he looked through her communication record and quickly tabulated all Monachi's communications within the past week.

The domestic computational suite (DCS), like PNN capability provided Mergenky communications as well as numerous other features. When a Person was in their gel tube sleeping, the DCS would take messages or determine if the caller had enough priority to awaken the resident and in the case of Monachi, she had her personal robot to screen communications.

Even though today she did not specifically tell Charles she wished to not be disturbed, it was plainly obvious by her behavior as well as the resting condition she currently was in, that would be the case.

Charles started investigating everything in DCS to figure out what troubled Monachi. In the past six days, everything seemed to be centered around Kara, and all Monachi's inquiries came up blank.

About an hour after Monachi went to sleep, Detective Zhēntàn Xīnkǔ de Pìgu called for Monachi. Charles received the call.

DETECTIVE ZHĒNTÀN XĪNKǓ DE PÌGU
May I speak with Monachi?

Charles looked at the registry number below Detective Zhēntàn Xīnkǔ de Pìgu's holograph and saw the identity was law enforcement.

CHARLES
I'm sorry but she's sleeping.

DETECTIVE ZHĒNTÀN XĪNKǓ DE PÌGU
Are you, her husband?

CHARLES
No, I'm her domestic help.

Detective Zhēntàn Xīnkǔ de Pìgu asked in a curious manner:

DETECTIVE ZHĒNTÀN XĪNKŬ DE PÌGU
A male maid?

CHARLES
No sir, I'm a robot.

DETECTIVE ZHĒNTÀN XĪNKŬ DE PÌGU
Are you trying to be some kind of wise guy?

CHARLES
Sir, I am Charles, definitely a robot and will be happy
to show you any time you wish.

DETECTIVE ZHĒNTÀN XĪNKŬ DE PÌGU
That might be soon, because I would like to come over
and talk with Commander Monachi.

CHARLES
Monachi is going through a hard time now because
her friend Vance was lost at Jeeapa, and she's now
attempting to locate his widow and her friend Doctor
Kara and has not been able to do so.

DETECTIVE ZHĒNTÀN XĪNKŬ DE PÌGU
Yes, I'm aware of that.

CHARLES
Monachi's only been resting for about an hour, she
looks very ill. Would it be possible to allow her to rest
for a few hours before you call upon her?

DETECTIVE ZHĒNTÀN XĪNKŬ DE PÌGU
I suppose that would be ok.

CHARLES
If she wakes up on her own, I will tell her you called,
and she can call you right back.

DETECTIVE ZHĒNTÀN XĪNKŬ DE PÌGU
That will be fine. By the way Charles, you certainly do
not look like a robot.

CHARLES
Detective, when we meet, you will discover I'm truly
a humanoid robot.

DETECTIVE ZHĒNTÀN XĪNKŬ DE PÌGU
I've never seen a robot that looks so real, like a
Mergenky.

CHARLES
I was manufactured on another planet that Monachi
visited and was given to her as a gift.

DETECTIVE ZHĒNTÀN XĪNKŬ DE PÌGU
If you truly are a robot, whoever built you did a great job.

CHARLES
Detective, your compliment is well received.

***

GATOR FREIGHTER

<u>INT. SPACE. CRUISER MSFC-8 CONTROL ROOM</u>

As the Cruiser Transport neared the Jeeapa solar system, Kwongab requested the
Amphibian Commanding Officer:

CAPTAIN KWONGAB
Colonel Yārén please report to the control room.

The PNN took Kwongab's video string comprising the short communique and
converted it to a holograph and presented that near Colonel Yārén. He was then
escorted by Erica to the bridge so that he would not get lost.

COLONEL YĀRÉN
Yes Captain, what can I do for you.

CAPTAIN KWONGAB
Colonel Yārén, in a few minutes we'll be entering the
solar system and the Anarchie could jump us at any
time.

As such I may be forced to make some radical maneuvers. I want you to make sure all
your troops are strapped down because I don't want them to get hurt and I do not want
their bodies to crash into essential equipment and cause us some issues.

COLONEL YĀRÉN
Will do, Captain.

CAPTAIN KWONGAB
Also, Colonel Yārén I want you to brief your men
that we have a very unconventional landing that's not
going to be ideal nor very safe. It's essential that they
get off the ship as quickly as possible. We'll be sitting
ducks on the ground.

COLONEL YĀRÉN
Understand all, Captain.

CAPTAIN KWONGAB
I know we didn't have time to drill this troop transport,
but if your men take more than a couple minutes to get
off the ship, they will put us at risk.

Colonel Yārén knew this mission was hastily put together and the ship's Captain
Kwongab didn't have a voice in the planning and the best he could do under the
circumstances was to be cooperative with Captain Kwongab as much as possible.

COLONEL YĀRÉN
Understand that, Captain.

CAPTAIN KWONGAB
Your men must be off the ship in about two minutes,
three at the absolute most.

COLONEL YĀRÉN
I acknowledge that necessity, Captain.

CAPTAIN KWONGAB
There is no guarantee we will not have a hard landing
if we take hits. If that happens, direct your men to
leave the injured on the ship and get off. The Anarchie
will waste no time and light this ship up with some
powerful lasers. You will not have time to get injured
people off.

COLONEL YĀRÉN
I realize that sir. They may not like leaving their
buddies behind, but like you say, we may not have
time.

CAPTAIN KWONGAB
Good luck Colonel, I wish you success.

COLONEL YĀRÉN
Thank you, Captain.

The Colonel at equal rank, turned around and went back to his men.

COLONEL YĀRÉN (THOUGHT)
It wasn't the first time, nor would it be the last time MSF threw us into the jaws of hell. If we end the day with half the troops still alive, I will be grateful.

VOICEOVER
The anticipation grew and many Cruiser Crew Members were suddenly nervous as they felt they were outside their element. It took some doing to get over the mindset they were on a cargo delivery platform.

But now that they were an Amphibian Force delivery vessel, going close to enemy forces, it was no longer an abstract 'what if' scenario out in space. It was now up close and personal.

Kill or be killed, the consequences of war were now immediately confronting each one of them.

As the Cruiser slid into the atmosphere at 17,000 miles per hour buffeting slightly over the huge stresses put on the hull, Kwongab directed PNN to transmit the communique he had received from the Mergenky INTEL agent Zhāngyú.

CAPTAIN KWONGAB
PNN send this message immediately to General Zǔzhī Bùliáng:

"After receiving INTEL reports and discussions with Colonel Yārén, we are being diverted south of the Anarchie Bivouac area."

COMMANDER DǏNGQIĀNG
Sensors show the Anarchie are coming at us.

CAPTAIN KWONGAB
That's expected, this is going to be a close one.

Kwongab didn't like the progress the Cruiser was making down to the planet as PNN was working with peace time rules of engagement that minimized training accidents but had no basis for actual live combat. Kwongab took manual control of the Cruiser and instead of slowing down as PNN was attempting, he increased speed.

The Anarchie Battleship Commander following from a distance said:

ANARCHIE BATTLESHIP COMMANDER
That Mergenky Cruiser pilot must be nuts!

KWONGAB
The Anarchie are lining up exactly where we said we were going.

Kwongab said out load and added:

KWONGAB
Send that information to MSF immediately.

Luckily all the Anarchie ships were out of position except one Battleship.

KWONGAB (THOUGHT)
Why is that Battleship not going where the rest, relying on INTEL someone in the MSF gave them.

Kwongab immediately contacted MSFS-1 and MSFS-4 and requested.

KWONGAB
MSFS-1 and MSFS-4 I need your help with that Anarchie Battleship coming in, I have a ship full of soldiers we need to get to the planet safely.

MSFS-4
MSFC-8, we are on your six O'clock.

The crew of MSFS-1 didn't like the target situation but would do the best it could. As the 3 Mergenky ships got down to around 10,000 feet the lone Anarchie Battleship was getting menacingly close. MSFS-1 and MSFS-4 went after it, hoping to distract it. The Anarchie had their blinders on and were in such lust for victory they concentrated on the Cruiser that only had half its fighting capability.

Scout's MSFS-1 and MSFS-4 were landing shots on the Anarchie, but their total disregard for their own safety for the sake of glory seemed to ignore what was going on. The Anarchie Battleship was getting seriously wounded but it pressed on. At the current target range, Kwongab had no choice but to trade shots with the Anarchie Battleship. Soon he felt the vibrations as the laser strikes hit home. Kwongab was soon down to 5000 feet and dropping fast and would soon have to break hard to arrive at the landing zone.

Kwongab's Cruiser was now trailing smoke. Fires were burning, and the vibrations were increasing. MSFS-1 and MSFS-4 pressed home the attack and the only reason why the Anarchie stopped firing is the Mergenky damaged their power plant and lost weapons power.

Lucky for Kwongab the Anarchie was heading on almost a perpendicular course otherwise they would have done every attempt to ram the Mergenky Cruiser and destroy it.

The two ships passed close aboard only because Kwongab was using manual flight control.

Kwongab felt more vibrations, he knew his ship was dying so it was a matter of getting it down on the deck as soon as possible.

Kwongab hit the speed brakes and yelled out:

KWONGAB
Prepare for impact!

The Amphibious Fighters in the Cargo Hold were strapped down good. The Cruiser passed below 1000 feet, and the engines were straining at the maximum to slow the ship. The speed was dropping off, but it was not slowing enough for a soft landing.

There was more smoke in the ship, a fire somewhere in the hull was getting out of control. The ship dipped below 200 feet and was down to almost 180 miles per hour still breaking. Kwongab knew at this point the best he was going to get was skidding to a stop and a lot of damage to the hull.

Kwongab watched intently the instruments 150 feet, 100 feet, 50 feet, 25 feet, 10 feet. Pulling the nose up at the last minute the rumbling began as they were scorching the surface of the planet kicking up a tremendous dust cloud and bouncing around hard.

The ship seemed like it was skidding forever with the reversers in full reverse and Kwongab could not trust his instruments, relied on the feeling and as soon as he felt the movement was dying down, he cut the propulsion.

Kwongab yelled through ship's intercom:

CAPTAIN KWONGAB
Abandon ship! Abandon ship!

Smoke was starting to increase rapidly. Lucky for them the port entrance door was not damaged, and ship still had power, so the door was able to be opened. The Amphibians were great on water but in the air, they were like a duck out of water.

Nobody wanted off that Gator Freighter Cruiser more than the Amphibians. Only a couple received minor injuries, and nothing slowed them down from exiting the burning Cruiser Transport.

Kwongab was the last to leave making sure everyone was exiting the ship. The Executive Officer Commander Dǐngqiāng was right in front of him. It appeared everyone was getting off the ship which came to a rest about 50 yards from the rim of canyon. It was a lucky day for Kwongab. Another 150 feet and the Cruiser would be heading down a 4000-foot embankment and certain death to everyone onboard.

Kwongab yelled at everyone:

KWONGAB
Get as far away from the ship, it could blow at any moment.

XO COMMANDER DǏNGQIĀNG
The plateau we landed on has an escarpment a couple hundred yards directly ahead we can all crouch down on. This will also help concealment from the Anarchie that are sure soon to be coming this way.

Mergencky Scouts MSFS-1 and MSFS-4 briefly flew over spotting the Amphibians running from the Cruiser now heavily smoking. They could not loiter as the Anarchie were coming in high speed to attack.

Everyone from the crashed Cruiser made it to the edge of the plateau and stepped down into the escarpment and looked at the Cruiser that soon was totally engulfed in flames.

Kwongab saw everyone watching the ship and yelled at them:

KWONGAB
Get down, when it explodes you might be killed!

Executive Officer Commander Dǐngqiāng also yelled:

XO COMMANDER DǏNGQIĀNG
Everyone get down low!

The crew and the Amphibians seemed to follow Kwongab and the XO's instruction and were well hidden in the escarpment crevice's when suddenly there was a huge rumbling then a horrific explosion. The shockwave shot right over the top of them at supersonic speeds. Anyone who had been standing would have had their torso cut to threads.

None of the Cruiser Crew Members had weapons. But each one of the Amphibians were well armed. As soon as all the secondary explosions finished and all that remained was silence Kwongab peeked at what had once been a Cruiser, was now mostly nothing. The fuselage and components were thrown miles in every direction. MSFC-8 no longer existed.

Mergenky Cruisers MSFS-1 and MSFS-4 darted over to Jeeapa and were soon under Jeeapa's air defenses which the Anarchie had no desire to further test as each feeble attempt proved it was counterproductive.

Kwongab spotted Colonel Yārén who was already taking stock of his men and their situation.

Kwongab walked up to the Colonel.

> ### KWONGAB
> Well Colonel, as I promised I got you here, but now it looks like you are stuck with us.

> ### COLONEL YĀRÉN
> Yea just what we need a bunch of fly boys to slow us down.

> ### KWONGAB
> We don't have any weapons or equipment, but we can help carry things for you.

> ### COLONEL YĀRÉN
> How many crew members do you have?

> ### KWONGAB
> Should be 52 if everyone got out alive, we are going to muster now and find out.

It was right around sundown and Colonel Yārén explained:

> ### COLONEL YĀRÉN
> Captain, we need to exit this area. Anarchie will make a bee line here and I want to fight them on my own terms.

> ### KWONGAB
> We have nowhere to go but to follow you Colonel, we are on the ground now, you are in charge. But tell your

men to allow my crew to help carry their equipment.
We can probably travel faster if we lighten your load
up a bit.

Soon the Amphibians were not so disappointed they had to babysit the MSF crew. MSF crews were typically in ideal shape thanks to their gel container process and workouts they routinely did to keep in top condition.

KWONGAB
Which way are we heading?

COLONEL YĀRÉN
The Anarchie probably think we are heading East trying to make our way to Jeeapa City area. We'll head West and get into position to attack their flank guard.

KWONGAB
Does that mean we'll be participating in ground warfare?

COLONEL YĀRÉN
We'll set up a camp for you away from our attack. Hopefully we can get a rescue squad in to get you back to friendly lines.

KWONGAB
How about you guys?

COLONEL YĀRÉN
We'll do our hit and run tactics and get supply dumps from air.

KWONGAB
That's kind of risky I'd say after my personal experience.

COLONEL YĀRÉN
I've been told MSF has a new gizmo they are working on that can get here without the enemy seeing it.

Kwongab immediately started thinking about the *Black Ravik*.

KWONGAB (THOUGHT)
I wonder if Black Ravik is what he's talking about?

The MSF crew was more than willing to help carry equipment. Some of the Amphibians were carrying 50 to 100 pounds more than they normally would.

Colonel Yārén directed his junior officers:

COLONEL YĀRÉN

Figure out which Amphibian has a lot of extra supplies or equipment and pair them up with an MSF flight crew member who will help carry it.

Normally the Amphibians hoped to keep with a 3 miles per hour rate of advance. Due to the unexpected help who were motivated simply by the fact they didn't want to be captured by the Anarchie, allowed the force to proceed at 4.5 miles per hour for the first hour and 4 miles per hour on the second hour. By then they were getting tired and after a 15-minute water break they did the next 3.5 miles in an hour over rough terrain.

By the time the Anarchie made it to the crash site, the Mergenky were already 15 miles away and because of the heavy armor and equipment the Anarchie Scouts and Rangers carried, they could only proceed at 3 miles per hour and as the Colonel figured, the Anarchie Scouts and Rangers went East in the wrong direction.

Because of the secrecy of their mission, to take out a key command post, all radio communications were forbidden. They would not be allowed to report the status of the crew or if there were any survivors.

The MSFS-1 and MSFS-4 crews reported what they saw, but sadly all they saw was guys in green uniforms running which meant the Amphibians. None of the MSF crew members had been seen leaving the Cruiser's hulk.

From a distance several Mergenky ships recorded the horrific explosion of the Cruiser blowing up when the AMRT was ruptured by another internal explosion, probably from some of the flammable supplies that were being shipped with the Amphibians.

The Anarchie Battleship that damaged the Cruiser MSFC-8 crashed into a fiery ball. Other Anarchie Battleships soon arrived in the area, but the Mergenky were long gone so the Anarchie Battleships returned to their station poised to repel any Mergenky attacks.

Things were not going per plan and Anarchie were getting behind on their timeline.

***

EXT. CGI. DAY. ANARCHIE COMMANDER GENERAL HĒISHÉ'S PERSONAL TRANSPORT ARRIVING AT ANARCHIE COMMAND CENTER ON JEEAPA. 15 SECONDS.

Anarchie Commander General Hēishé arrived at the Anarchie Command Post via his high-speed command ship. He met General Borktar who had just arrived from Frăctŏng with just one half of his original force and Anarchie Jeeapa Expedition Task Force Commander, General Fāguāng De Sīxiǎngjiā

ANARCHIE COMMANDER
GENERAL HĒISHÉ
General Borktar you look fresh.

GENERAL BORKTAR
Thank you, sir.

ANARCHIE COMMANDER
GENERAL HĒISHÉ
General Fāguāng de Sīxiǎngjiā do you have a command Tent or a conference Tent where the three of us can go and talk?

ANARCHIE JEEAPA EXPEDITION
TASK FORCE COMMANDER
GENERAL FĀGUĀNG DE SĪXIǍNGJIĀ
Yes, General Hēishé, let me show you the way.

General Fāguāng de Sīxiǎngjiā who was leading the Jeeapa attack appeared to be getting close to a nervous breakdown.

VOICE OVER
A lot of stress to General Fāguāng de Sīxiǎngjiā was being caused by General Borktar who thought he should take over.

The two Generals were spending more and more time quarreling and when one of General Heishe's personal spies reported such, he decided it was time to make a personal visit and make some alterations if necessary to get the ground war back on schedule.

The command post was well behind the front lines. There were no Mergenky forces anywhere nearby. Probably the closest Mergenky was 100 miles distance near Jeeapa City.

Inside the makeshift briefing tent, the fireworks started.

ANARCHIE GENERAL HEISHE
General Fāguāng de Sīxiǎngjiā, what's the status of the Mergenky Crash site?

GENERAL FĀGUĀNG DE SĪXIǍNGJIĀ
The Cruiser blew up into a million pieces. All that is left is a big hole from the explosion. The debris field is 10 miles in diameter.

ANARCHIE GENERAL BORKTAR
If you had gotten troops there sooner, we might have captured some Mergenky and figured out what they were up to.

General Fāguāng de Sīxiǎngjiā angrily asked:

GENERAL FĀGUĀNG DE SĪXIǍNGJIĀ
General Heishe, what exactly would you have done differently?

ANARCHIE GENERAL HEISHE
Gentlemen, stop arguing. This is exactly why I came here.

General Heishe was quickly getting irritated by General Borktar and decided enough was enough.

ANARCHIE GENERAL HEISHE
General Borktar, instead of me asking you, exactly what would you have done differently, my question to you is: During the Mergenky Cruiser crash, what recommendations did you make to General Fāguāng de Sīxiǎngjiā to help capture the Mergenky?

After a brief period when no answer was made, General Heishe then stated:

ANARCHIE GENERAL HEISHE
General Borktar since you can't provide an answer, that means you had no suggestions to make and therefore you have no business now complaining about something General Fāguāng de Sīxiǎngjiā didn't do.

ANARCHIE GENERAL BORKTAR
But General….

ANARCHIE GENERAL HEISHE

No "but's" about it, General Borktar you offered nothing of value to the problem, therefore you should remain silent because now what you are doing is not helping to improve the situation.

General Borktar sat stunned and was not used to receiving such criticism.

ANARCHIE GENERAL HEISHE

One other thing General Borktar, your performance on Frăctŏng wasn't exemplary, so you have no business criticizing others.

After silence for a moment, General Heishe knew it was time to make some painful decisions.

ANARCHIE GENERAL HEISHE

Okay let's look at the map and figure out the attack tomorrow.

***

BEHIND ENEMY LINES

<u>EXT. LATE NIGHT. JEEAPA. NEAR DESIGNATED RENDEZVOUS SITE BRAVO JULIET.</u>

It was near sunrise when Colonel Yārén said to his executive officer:

COLONEL YĀRÉN

This is a good place to halt and rest the troops for tonight's attack.

AMPHIBIAN XO

We marched for twelve hours and even though we started out doing high mileage, in the last hour we only managed to get two more miles.

COLONEL YĀRÉN

The Amphibians and Cruiser Crew need to take a break, and they need to get under camouflage before daybreak because we are now getting within striking distance of the Anarchie command post.

CAPTAIN KWONGAB
What do we do for now?

COLONEL YĀRÉN
Captain Kwongab, I'm sorry but we must continue
with radio silence but monitor communications in case
we receive new instructions.

Suddenly a communique from Jeeapa came across Colonel Yārén's heads up display on his command helmet he wore which he read then turned towards Kwongab standing nearby.

COLONEL YĀRÉN
I was directed to have all the MSFC-8 crew survivors
repositioned to a point on the map designated Bravo
Juliet and during our attack on the Command Post
MSF will use that as a distraction to bring in Shuttles
to evacuate the members of your crew.

KWONGAB
What about you guys?

COLONEL YĀRÉN
Shuttles will bring in additional supplies so that when
my men clear the area, they will have a resupply of
ammo, food, and water there. We will be repositioned
to support another operation at that time.

Under the camouflage the Mergenky were almost impossible to see from the air. Unless ground forces came upon them, they would remain relatively safe. The Amphibians were split into pairs with one guy sleeping while the other stood watch, altering about once every two hours. By sundown they expected to all be rested up.

***

After their rest period later in the day, Colonel Yārén watched the sun sink beyond the horizon as the next day was ending.

COLONEL YĀRÉN
We are only a mile from Bravo Juliet. We'll all begin
our march there in approximately 30 minutes.

Time passed quickly and soon everyone was repacked and ready to march to the evacuation location Bravo Juliet. Since the Mergenky MSF crewmember and the

Amphibians were well rested, they performed a 4.5 mile per hour march. Having drank some of the water and eaten some of the food, their back packs were a little lighter.

When the Amphibians departed from Bravo Juliet for the night attack, the MSF crew members would no longer be carrying their equipment for them, so they would be back to 3 miles an hour rate. The Amphibians had 4 hours to cover 10 miles to the Anarchie Command post target designated Delta X-ray.

The Amphibians would set up and launch the attack on the Anarchie Command Post at map coordinates Delta X-ray from a defensive position scouted out by satellite imagery noted as Delta Yankee.

The Amphibian assault force could not afford to leave behind weapons. They needed all the firepower they hand carried because they knew Delta X-ray would be a hard target.

The Amphibians and their temporary MSF stevedores who carried most of their equipment said goodbye and good luck to each other, as the Amphibians marched off into history towards the battle that would soon take place at the Anarchie Command Post.

Kwongab then had the MSF Crewmembers start digging and building defensive positions knowing the possibility existed they could be attacked when the Anarchie were alerted by the attack on the Anarchie camp at Delta X-ray. The Amphibians would greatly appreciate that when the time came after the attack on the Anarchie camp.

Kwongab was given a communicator since the Amphibian force did not lose a single communicator in the insertion. Usually over half were lost by casualties or damage.

That communicator was Kwongab's emergency lifeline, but he knew not to use it until he saw and heard explosions from the distance right after midnight when he expected to hear from the MSF.

After the Amphibians deployed off into the night, there was an eerie quiet. Kwongab never felt quite so helpless in his life. Never was Kwongab so dependent upon someone else.

***

KWONGAB IS MISSING

The news of Kwongab's demise was unsettling with General Kahn.

Information was sketchy but it was clear *that Cruiser MSFC-8 crash landed then blew up*. The only positive reports were one of the two Mergenky Scout spacecraft reported seeing a few men with green uniforms running from the Cruiser before it blew. There was no further contact with Kwongab, and the Cruiser blew up on the ground behind enemy lines.

Because of the operation in progress, radio silence of the Amphibian Force sent on this mission was essential and being observed. For them to use their communicators would mean certain detection and then probable destruction by the Anarchie.

<u>INT. DAY. MSF HEADQUARTERS.</u>

General Kahn inquired where Monachi was and was told she was home taking care of some personal business. He thought it was best if he went to her home and informed her about Kwongab's situation before she heard it from someone else who didn't have all the facts.

General Kahn notified his administrative aid:

> GENERAL KAHN
> I'm going over to Commander Monachi's residence to inform her about Kwongab. I'll be back in a while in case something comes up.

> ADMINISTRATIVE AID
> Should I forward any calls to your personal communicator?

> GENERAL KAHN
> No, hold all calls, this is a delicate matter, and I do not want to be disturbed during the middle of my discussions with Monachi. Unless Gwaba is being attacked, hold all calls.

The administrative aide feeling bad for General Kahn who had to deliver the unfortunate news that Kwongab was missing in action said in a supportive tone:

> ADMINISTRATIVE AID
> We'll see you when you get back, General Kahn.

General Kahn had a Skycar which MSF provided for him which was needed quite often to get from MSF to the Civilian Government buildings from time to time to talk with the leaders or to quickly get to places for important meetings.

General Kahn and his personal security guard took his private elevator up to the Skycar port and walked towards and got inside the Skycar.

General Kahn would be escorted to Monachi's residence for his own protection because during time of war, he was an obvious target. It took 10 minutes for the Skycar to get to Monachi's apartment building where it landed on the roof. About the same time another Skycar landed.

General Kahn's security escort noted:

> GENERAL KAHN'S ESCORT
> Those men in suits that got out of the other Skycar that
> appeared to belong to law enforcement.

> GENERAL KAHN
> I wonder, what they are here for?

All four men were in the elevator and General Kahn was slightly surprised when the men followed them down the hallway and stopped as they watched him select the *Guest Arrival Button* to Monachi's residence.

<u>INT. EVENING. KWONGAB'S HOME.</u>

Charles viewed the security screen and saw the military members outside and knew it must be official business, so he opened the door and invited them in. In a confusing moment the men in suits also approached the door and Charles asked:

> CHARLES
> How can I help you?

> DETECTIVE ZHĒNTÀN XĪNKŬ DE PÌGU
> I talked to you earlier, I'm detective Zhēntàn Xīnkŭ
> de Pìgu.

> CHARLES
> Please come in.

Shortly the civilians were sizing up the military brass. Detective Pìgu bowed towards the high-ranking military person and said:

> DETECTIVE ZHĒNTÀN XĪNKŬ DE PÌGU
> Hello, I'm Detective Zhēntàn Xīnkŭ de Pìgu with the
> Quom Investigators Office.

> GENERAL KAHN
> I'm General Kahn of the MSF.

The two other men were subsequently introduced, and they turned towards Charles who then knew they all wanted to speak with Monachi.

CHARLES

Let me go check on Monachi to see if she is up and ready for visitors.

As soon as Charles walked out of the room, General Kahn looked at Detective Zhēntàn Xīnkǔ de Pìgu.

GENERAL KAHN

Detective Zhēntàn Xīnkǔ de Pìgu What brings you here to Monachi's residence?

DETECTIVE ZHĒNTÀN XĪNKǓ DE PÌGU

We are looking into Monachi's friend Dr. Kara's disappearance.

General Kahn was now very interested in Doctor Kara's situation.

GENERAL KAHN

Doctor Kara's husband Vance was one of our MSF Crewmembers on a Cruiser that we recently lost on Jeeapa.

DETECTIVE ZHĒNTÀN XĪNKǓ DE PÌGU

Yes, I'm aware of her situation General.

GENERAL KAHN

How long has Doctor Kara been missing?

DETECTIVE ZHĒNTÀN XĪNKǓ DE PÌGU

At least 6 days.

GENERAL KAHN

Any idea of what happened to Doctor Kara?

DETECTIVE ZHĒNTÀN XĪNKǓ DE PÌGU

We have not found a body yet, but we believe there was foul play involved, and we want to talk with Monachi again and hopefully can get some more leads to check into, because we are running into a brick wall.

GENERAL KAHN

I see.

DETECTIVE ZHĒNTÀN XĪNKǓ DE PÌGU
General, what brings you here?

Looking to make sure the door was closed so that she didn't hear all what he had to say, General Kahn responded:

GENERAL KAHN
Monachi's husband Kwongab was on a Cruiser that was destroyed today when it crashed landed on Jeeapa behind enemy lines. Kwongab's currently missing.

Detective Zhēntàn Xīnkǔ de Pìgu suddenly felt the situation was not a good time to talk with Monachi then responded:

DETECTIVE ZHĒNTÀN XĪNKǓ DE PÌGU
Perhaps I should leave and not bother Monachi at this time, but we are pursuing the investigation, I know she's taking it real hard about the disappearance of her friend, especially with the friend's husband's recent passing.

GENERAL KAHN
Detective, the MSF is concerned about Kara's well-being, here's my personal contact and business card, keep me informed on what's going on and if there is anything I can be of assistance do not hesitate to ask.

DETECTIVE ZHĒNTÀN XĪNKǓ DE PÌGU
Thank you General, I appreciate the offer.

GENERAL KAHN
Detective Zhēntàn Xīnkǔ De Pìgu, we take care of our own at MSF. If someone hurt Doctor Kara, I will use my position at MSF to hunt that person down to the ends of the planet or elsewhere.

DETECTIVE ZHĒNTÀN XĪNKǓ DE PÌGU
It's a complicated case with few leads. We are going over forensics at Kara's residence. We have not found anything yet.

About that time Charles entered the room having heard all the information with his micro-hearing even though he was in the other room, was already brainstorming ways to help the case.

CHARLES
I'm sorry, Monachi still has not awakened. You are free to stay and wait for her if you like.

GENERAL KAHN
I'll wait for her.

General Kahn started feeling almost horrible having to give Monachi the news after discovering Doctor Kara was missing and most likely dead from foul play.

DETECTIVE ZHĒNTÀN XĪNKǓ DE PÌGU
I don't really have much to tell Monachi about Kara's disappearance other than we are working on the case and may wish to ask her a few more questions that might help us get more leads to the case.

CHARLES
I'll have Monachi call you Detective as soon as she wakes up.

DETECTIVE ZHĒNTÀN XĪNKǓ DE PÌGU
Tell Monachi we would prefer just to wait until she's feeling better then she can call us and we can come over.

CHARLES
I will let her know.

DETECTIVE ZHĒNTÀN XĪNKǓ DE PÌGU
One other thing. Over the phone you said you are a robot

CHARLES
Yes, I did.

Charles lifted his shirt and exposed his chest, then opened his chest plate that revealed a lot of robot machinery and flashing lights on his electronics modules..

DETECTIVE ZHĒNTÀN XĪNKǓ DE PÌGU
That's amazing, you really are a robot.

CHARLES
Yes, I am. General Kahn knows I'm a robot.

GENERAL KAHN
That's correct. Charles is a robot, and MSF knows him
quite well.

DETECTIVE ZHĒNTÀN XĪNKŬ DE PÌGU
You look so real.

CHARLES
My builders were good at cosmetics.

DETECTIVE ZHĒNTÀN XĪNKŬ DE PÌGU
I should say so. Gentlemen, I'm leaving, and I'm
terribly sorry about Monachi's husband.

GENERAL KAHN
Kwongab was one of our best pilots.

DETECTIVE ZHĒNTÀN XĪNKŬ DE PÌGU
It was a pleasure meeting you General and if I find
out any more concerning Kara's disappearance, I'll let
you know.

General Kahn waited for about another hour. Charles offered drinks and snacks, but
the general wasn't interested, and almost as soon as he thought about leaving because
he had pressing matters, Monachi came out of her bedroom looking slightly groggy.
*In Monachi's dreams she thought she had been talking to General Kahn, and here he
was in her home!*

Monachi also knew: *Generals did not call upon MSF wives unless something bad
happened.* She suddenly felt panic and weak at the knees.

When General Kahn saw that she wasn't doing well he offered:

GENERAL KAHN
Monachi, why don't you please sit down. We need to
talk about a matter.

Monachi somehow gathered her strength and then applied her neural expansion
telepathic abilities probing General Kahn.

After General Kahn gave his dissertation as to what transpired concerning the loss of
MSFC-8. Monachi asked:

MONACHI
You don't have any confirmation he was killed, just
that he's missing?

GENERAL KAHN
That's correct.

MONACHI
Well, we can always hope.

Monachi took this private time with General Kahn to implant some thoughts into his
mind and to read General Kahn's thoughts:

MONACHI (TELEPATHY)
*Kwongab's ship was probably another victim of
treachery. Someone inside MSF is responsible.*

Monachi was also slightly fearful for her friend Kara, she also telepathically planted
thoughts into General Kahn:

MONACHI (TELEPATHY)
Track down Kara's killers.

General Kahn was suddenly not feeling quite so bad with the visit, but he was feeling
he *wanted to get to the bottom of Kara's disappearance.* There might be a provision
within MSF security that when a spouse comes up missing right after a crew member
is killed in line of duty, to investigate it.

General Kahn and his security bodyguard left right after Monachi finished the heavy
dose of neural expansion telepathic applications that affected him.

Monachi was suddenly alone with Charles.

CHARLES
Would you like me to help you discover what happened
to Kara?

MONACHI
What can you do?

CHARLES
I can research all night long while you are sleeping
and while you are at work.

MONACHI
Well, do what you can, I'm going to get a bite to eat,
then try resting again.

***

AMPHIBIANS ATTACK

<u>EXT. NIGHT. 100 MILES WEST OF JEEAPA.</u>

As the hours crept by, Kwongab knew that soon the fireworks would commence. He also was glad MSF wasn't giving them too much information because until they found the spy, all their operations could be compromised.

Colonel Yārén's force was soon dug in at grid location on the map *Delta Yankee* to set up a rear guard to assist in the egress after the attack.

The Anarchie were blowing Force Protection-101. All their defenders were facing East towards Jeeapa. It was as if they had no respect for the Mergenky. They didn't think the Mergenky had the audacity to attempt an operation far from Jeeapa behind enemy lines.

Right at midnight Colonel Yārén moved his men forward toward their target at Delta X-ray. The Amphibians were the assault force that were usually picked to hit the hard targets.

This Anarchie Command Post was illogically laid out. Quite simply put its security was void of all common sense. With the three top Anarchie Generals present, it seemed they would have much tighter security. Part of the security lapse was the result that no fighting had been done anywhere near Delta X-ray.

When everyone was in place using sign language the assault began first by a few men positioned where the Anarchie would expect an attack fired from the direction of Jeeapa, but it was more of a distraction and diversion feint only and created very few Anarchie casualties.

Meanwhile the remainder of the force hit them hard from the rear. Because of the total lackadaisical attitudes, the Anarchie Generals were not down in their bunkers as they should have been, instead were enjoying the cool night air on cots laid out in tents.

The attack commenced with ferocity most of these Anarchie had never witnessed. Lasers, mortars and kinetic weapons were soon inflicting a lot of damage. The firefight was intense. At any given time 20 or 30 lasers lit up. Men on both sides were being killed including General Fāguāng de Sīxiǎngjiā who paid for his negligence and poor leadership with is life.

Because of camouflage and extensive concealment, Colonel Yārén assumed he would have to punch his way into the compound to destroy their communications and tear up the place as quickly as possible.

The Amphibians made it all the way to the center of the compound before they were taken by any significant number of retaliatory attacks.

By then it was too late as Kinetic Weapons and chemical explosives ripped through temporary buildings and self-propelled structures containing communications links, sensor operators and the backbone of the Anarchie Jeeapa Task Force Command, Control, and Communications equipment.

The Anarchie Generals sleeping outside of their bunkers also created a unique opportunity. Their total disregard for Mergenky special forces cost some of them their lives and General Hēishé was laid up for months afterwards undergoing numerous surgeries to repair a significant amount of damage to his reptilian body.

Even though General Borktar was self-serving in his ongoing criticism of General Fāguāng de Sīxiǎngjiā, he was partially right, the general squandered a lot of fighters and resources.

This was one of General Fāguāng de Sīxiǎngjiā greatest blunders arrogantly thinking MSF would never maneuver this far behind enemy lines to strike. The other two Generals were wounded and General Hēishé had to be evacuated for emergency medical treatments.

Colonel Yārén managed to only lose nine men killed and a dozen wounded which was rather extraordinary, considering their objective was well armed, though positioned in the wrong direction. Once again, Anarchie arrogance and disrespect for the cunning and innovative Mergenky Amphibians, created this amazing opportunity.

***

The Mergenky Scout MSFS-1 coming in fully cloaked in the dark could not be seen by the Anarchie. The Black Ravik was deployed from Scout MSFS-1 shuttle bay and sent down to Bravo Juliet landing zone. At 1000 feet above the ground the black Ravik transmitted a pulsed infrared Tangramized word "Water."

Kwongab as instructed beamed an infrared signal built into his computerized battle flashlight linked to the communicator the Amphibians gave to him, a challenge response also Tangramized by built in circuitry that encoded, "Ducks."

In the moonless night the Black Ravik was almost impossible to see, and the Shuttle pilot knew to come down very slow and about 10 feet off the ground it turned on a low light device that exposed the bottom of the Shuttle.

Fighting could clearly be seen and heard in the distance a few miles away. There were explosions, laser beams going in all directions off to the horizon. All hell was breaking loose in the Anarchie camp and Kwongab knew it was a nasty fire fight.

After the Black Ravik came to a halt on the landing the rear door suddenly opened and the men on the ground could see the low lighting inside. The first crisis was now exposed.

XO COMMANDER DĬNGQIĀNG
There are not enough seats for all of us.

CAPTAIN KWONGAB
They will have to make two trips.

XO COMMANDER DĬNGQIĀNG
Time is extremely limited. Nobody knows for sure if
the Anarchie have some methods to delaminate the
cloaking fields surrounding the Scout.

CAPTAIN KWONGAB
I would think counter detection is assumed and the
only benefit we have is the Scout is now down low so
scanners over the horizon would not detect them.

Kwongab then did the logical thing and simply said:

CAPTAIN KWONGAB
Crewmembers, start getting in the Shuttle and when
it's full it will go and come back and get the rest of us.

It did not take much to encourage the Cruiser crew members marooned behind enemy lines to promptly move into the Shuttle and buckle up. Kwongab and the XO Dĭngqiāng stood by the rear door of the Black Ravik and when they saw all the seats were filled, they stopped any further Mergenky from boarding.

CAPTAIN KWONGAB
Ok shut the door, you got a full load.

Kwongab and the XO Dĭngqiāng stood back and moved the rest of the troops back away from the Black Ravik Shuttle as it took off and didn't take long to dock in Scout MSFS-1.

BLACK RAVIK PILOT
Everyone out quickly, we must get the remainder of
the crew before the Anarchie gets here!

The Mergenky teamwork was impressive. In a very brief period, the Scout crewmembers directed each of Cruiser Crew members out of the Shuttle Bay to get them out of the way for the subsequent launch.

The Anarchie were fully alerted since their main command post was under attack. All their air assets were sent airborne and Orbiting ships in a Mexican Standoff with Mergenky Cruisers peeled away and went into a defensive posture and moved into position to support the ground effort to repulse the enemy at the Anarchie command post.

MSF command at Jeeapa knew the crew and the Scout were sitting ducks so all Cruisers were ordered:

JEEAPA COMMAND
(VIA PNN TACTICAL DATA LINK)
All Cruisers apply pressure on the Anarchie Battleships
in near space.

<u>EXT. NIGHT. JEEAPA. MSFC-34 CREW RESCUE LOCATION AT MAP COORDINATES DESIGNATED BRAVO JULIET.</u>

The attack on the Anarchie command post set off a night battle spectacle unseen since the first Jeeapa War. Since more and more MSF assets were trickling in each day and after the Anarchie abandoned Frăctŏng, there was no reason to retain the large number of MSF Cruisers there. They now converged upon Jeeapa.

Even if the Anarchie got a sniff on the Scout MSFS-1, the changing air picture with the Mergenky Cruisers arriving from Frăctŏng that very moment distracted them just enough to where the Black Ravik Shuttle was able to get back down and load up the remnants of the Cruiser Crew.

When the Black Ravik rear door shut Kwongab felt a sigh of relief. In his daring adventure delivering the Amphibians, Kwongab managed to not lose a single crew member despite the loss of the MSF Cruiser.

As soon as the Black Ravik was docked the Scout shot out with max throttle to quickly gain as much distance from the Anarchie as possible. At the supersonic speeds they quickly obtained, the cloaking field in the thick atmosphere completely delaminated and there was no point in leaving it on, so the pilot shut it off.

The Cruiser Squadron was vectored into the vicinity of the Scout to help it get away. Just as the Anarchie were almost within weapons range and the number of lasers they could easily lay on the Scout meant it would not survive the chase; the Cruiser Squadron suddenly forced the Anarchie to maneuver at the critical moment and the Scout shot through to safety with no time to spare.

On the ground, Colonel Yārén knew they had completed their objective to disrupt the Anarchie command center at the moment the new Mergenky Cruiser assets arrived.

When the results of the attack appeared to be satisfactory and the Amphibians had done what they came to do, Colonel Yārén ordered the men back to Delta Yankee where a reserve force was left behind to act as a rear guard and to facilitate the strike force bug out of the Anarchie compound.

These well defended positions were crucial for the extraction as the Anarchie followed them with a bone in their teeth wanting vengeance and retaliation for the damage this force had done.

Due to the lack of leadership since all three top Mergenky Generals were either dead, wounded, or incapacitated, lack of order created chaos on a grand scale. That night the Anarchie received a critical blow that signaled *the end to their campaign was near.*

Later in the night well before the morning first light, General Hēishé was ambulanced up to a waiting transport along with the body of Fāguāng de Sīxiǎngjiā. General Borktar slightly wounded was now in charge of the Anarchie Invasion of Jeeapa and refused to be evacuated with the two other Generals.

General Borktar shaken by the event ordered:

GENERAL BORKTAR
Take no prisoners, I want every one of the enemies killed!

At Delta Yankee, when it appeared the Anarchie were hell bent on making examples out of the Mergenky, Colonel Yārén asked for 5 volunteers to stay behind as a rear guard so the rest of them could extricate themselves towards Bravo Juliet rendezvous point.

Five men, mostly those of the original rear guard volunteered to stay. Colonel Yārén recorded their names in his battle log, a real time recording system where all his orders and comments would be preserved for a later *Hot Wash Session* with his superiors.

As the Amphibian leadership reviewed Colonel Yārén's mission they determined what elements were done poorly and needed improvement for the future, or in some cases during innovative moments, could be used as examples to other future commanders who might find themselves in a similar condition.

Colonel Yārén felt for these five men because he knew they would be making a supreme sacrifice.

Once the "Lizards" had them surrounded they would have no way out, it was fight to the death. These Mergenky Amphibian volunteers knew it too.

The main Amphibian force then double clicked out of Delta Yankee just as the first hoard of Anarchieborgs were coming at them.

The five Amphibians remaining were well equipped with multiple weapons in well defended positions.

The Anarchie were mildly stunned that Mergenky Amphibians did not cut and run as expected out of the non-illustrious Mergenky fighters they experienced in the past.

The five Amphibian rear guardsmen put up such an amazing fight that the Anarchie thought the entire Mergenky Amphibian formation was there.

Colonel Yārén following up the rear of the strung-out group of Amphibians looked back from time to time until they got over the ridge and could see the fighting going on behind them, had several battlefield video recordings of the intense firefight going on. It was almost two miles to the ridge and as they crossed over the ridge and into the valley below, the fire fights and explosions were still on going.

The Mergenky Amphibian formation marched on proudly, pulling off one of the most stunning behind enemy lines attacks ever attempted.

At approximately five miles away from Delta Yankee the noise of the fighting ended. Colonel Yārén knew the significance of this. The five rear guard Amphibians were now dead.

They had another five miles to get to Bravo Juliet rallying point and resupply. With the lead time the volunteers gave them, Colonel Yārén felt they now had a chance to make it and survive.

General Borktar was furious that most of the Mergenky had slipped away and when reports came back, they only killed five of them escaping he went into a raging madness. In his irrational thinking he ordered:

GENERAL BORKTAR
I want a dozen Exoskeleton laser gunships to be pulled
out of the front lines and sent to the compound right
away to be sent out on a Search and Destroy mission.

GENERAL'S ADVISOR
(GROUP COMMANDER)
But sir, we need those Exoskeletons in the front lines,
otherwise the Mergenky will have an avenue of attack!

GENERAL BORKTAR
The Mergenky have no stomach for slaughter they're
not coming. Send those Exoskeletons now!

The Group Commander was very disturbed about this irrational order and considered pulling out his laser pistol and killing General Borktar because what he was doing was total madness and would end up getting a bunch of Anarchie killed just to satisfy his anger over the Mergenky Special Forces attack.

The Exoskeletons could travel up to 40 miles per hour on flat level ground. Going up and down hills was a much slower operation as the operator and to make sure of footing otherwise could be sent tumbling down the hill with several tons over the top of them from the weapons and ammunition carried. Within 30 minutes the Exoskeletons showed up and the group commander of the Exoskeletons confirmed with the compound on the direction the Mergenky fled. These huge Exoskeleton behemoths then proceeded after the Mergenky Amphibian Force.

By now the Mergenky were maintaining a velocity of 3.5 miles per hour which was excellent for tired wore out fighters who had just come out of a huge firefight and marched six miles already.

Lookouts were posted in front of, to the sides and rear of the Amphibian's formation. They were lightly armed and would run ahead, stop, turn around, scan the horizon and make all appropriate reports. By the time the formation reached mile 7 only 3 miles to Bravo Juliet one of the rear lookouts reported:

LOOKOUT
Colonel, we have Anarchie Exoskeletons going over
the ridge line!

COLONEL YĀRÉN
How many Exoskeletons?

LOOKOUT
Looks like at least a dozen.

This changed everything, a redoubt at Bravo Juliet was not going to be satisfactory. Colonel Yārén knew his men were now in dire straits. Those Exoskeletons were worse than tanks because they could go where tanks couldn't get and follow him and his men to wherever they could go and would be systematically blasted out. Not even a cave would help them.

COLONEL YĀRÉN
Keep marching men, we must get to Bravo Juliet as
quick as possible.

Colonel Yārén then realized he had to break the radio silence and send out a *"May Day"* call.

It was almost heart breaking to discover a magnificent attack was soon to be wiped out of memory by this new threat.

Colonel Yārén thought that he and his men would never learn of the consequences of their recent combat actions after those Exoskeletons got to them.

Colonel Yārén hoped they had done their mission and achieved what the Mergenky needed from them.

Even though Colonel Yārén was saddened for his men he knew they would not go down without a fight. With a few lucky kinetic weapon strikes, they could take out a few of those Exoskeletons, but at the end of the day they would all be dead.

<u>INT. JEEAPA FIVE MILE OVAL.</u>

Commander Zŭzhī Bùliáng was immediately notified of the "*Mayday*" call concerning the Amphibian Force. Mergenky INTEL had just advised General Zŭzhī Bùliáng the Amphibians had hit the Anarchie real hard and totally disrupted their communications which dove tailed nicely into their next series of actions. Within a few hours General Borktar would regret pulling those Exoskeletons out of the front lines because the Mergenky were going to do exactly what he didn't expect.

But for now, it was obvious to the casual observer that General Zŭzhī Bùliáng knew the Amphibians needed rescued even if it meant delaying launching the next phase of his operations.

GENERAL ZŬZHĪ BÙLIÁNG
Send a force out to pick up the Amphibians.

JEEAPA FORCE CHIEF OF STAFF
Sir they are behind enemy lines, it will be a difficult
operation.

Having studied special forces insertion and retrieval history General Zŭzhī Bùliáng knew what it would take.

GENERAL ZŬZHĪ BÙLIÁNG
Send a sizeable Air Force supporting a rescue ship to
get down and pick them up.

JEEAPA FORCE CHIEF OF STAFF
We can send a Cruiser Squadron and a Scout to pick
them up.

GENERAL ZŬZHĪ BÙLIÁNG
Do it right away.

Kwongab who had just returned from the dead was standing a few feet away from General Zǔzhī Bùliáng after being congratulated for his magnificent mission offered:

KWONGAB
General, I would like to go along on the Scout mission
to rescue the Amphibians if you don't mind.

GENERAL ZǓZHĪ BÙLIÁNG
Kwongab, I think you have contributed enough
already.

KWONGAB
Please General, I want to do my part in saving those
Amphibians, they have given a lot for Mergenky.

Kwongab then gave General Zǔzhī Bùliáng some subtle telepathic manipulation of to help convince him.

GENERAL ZǓZHĪ BÙLIÁNG
General Kahn is probably not going to like what I'm
about to do, but I understand you completely Captain
Kwongab.

CAPTAIN KWONGAB.
Thank you General.

GENERAL ZǓZHĪ BÙLIÁNG
I'm going to send MSFS-1 again, I'll have them pick
you up, report up to the launch pad, they will be there
soon.

KWONGAB
Thank you, sir, this means a lot to me.

GENERAL ZǓZHĪ BÙLIÁNG
No thank you Kwongab, I wish we had more men like
you in our ranks.

Kwongab was escorted up General Zǔzhī Bùliáng's personal elevator to the surface of the planet and exited through a tunnel right out to the general's private landing pad.

As expected, MSFS-1 came down and when the pilot spotted Kwongab, sent the tendril down and picked him up and pulled him into the Scout before the access was shut.

The Scout then quickly maneuvered up to 20,000 feet where it was joined by a dozen Mergenky Cruisers.

In their combat control systems, the maps necessary for the extraction were displayed for the pilot and Kwongab on a high-resolution holograph.

KWONGAB

Commander Gōngniúgǒu, I appreciate you rescuing me earlier today.

COMMANDER GŌNGNIÚGǑU

It's the least I could do for my PCO instructor.

KWONGAB

You will be in command of this mission. I'm just an observer.

In some ways Commander Gōngniúgǒu was bewildered because Kwongab would have little resistance to pull rank on him and take command.

VOICEOVER (COMMANDER GŌNGNIÚGǑU) THOUGHT

This change in Kwongab's comportment seems to have become rather interesting.

Even though Kwongab was not taking command of the Scout, his neural expansion telepathy was at work.

Commander Gōngniúgǒu had been getting nervous in recent days and even though he wasn't a coward, he was operating far too conservative for the exigencies that presented themselves.

Kwongab would quietly bolster Commander Gōngniúgǒu's ego and calm his nerves through a massive amount of neural expansion direct telepathic thought insertions.

Commander Gōngniúgǒu would never know he was being manipulated as Kwongab kept his secret well hidden.

Commander Gōngniúgǒu was slowly feeling a lot more at ease. He didn't quite understand why.

VOICEOVER (COMMANDER GŌNGNIÚGǑU) THOUGHT

Perhaps having Captain Kwongab here helps me keep up my self-assurance?

Whatever it was making the difference didn't really matter, what did matter is that he now felt a lot better commanding.

Commander Gōngniúgǒu knew he could be more daring in this mission, not to the point of recklessness, but to a razor's edge that would give them a very slight advantage over any Anarchie that happened to get in their way.

***

<u>EXT. NIGHT. AMPHIBIAN FORCE REACHING DESIGNATED MERGENCY AMPHIBIANS PICKUP COORDINATES AT BRAVO JULIET. 15 SECONDS.</u>

Colonel Yārén reached Bravo Juliet that was now going to be an emergency extraction landing zone, not a resupply base.

The Cruiser Crew Members that had been evacuated at this spot just a few hours earlier, did themselves and the Amphibians good by building excellent defensive positions.

By not having to hastily build protection since it already existed the Colonel was able to spend his time shuffling the men around to the right locations to do their best to defend themselves against the Huge Exoskeletons that were now easily visible on the horizon.

The ground the Exoskeletons now traversed was rough and they had to slow down. Instead of doing the 40 miles per hour they were capable of on smooth flat land, they were now down to around 4 miles per hour because of the difficulty in obtaining solid footing.

Two miles away, the Exoskeletons could start targeting the Mergenky Amphibians. The Amphibians were well shielded, so the initial attacks didn't harm anyone and did nothing more than kick up a lot of dirt.

Colonel Yārén suddenly received a message on his battlefield communicator: "*Stars.*"

That was a Tangramized pre-coded directive that stated an emergency extraction was on the way. Realizing that the incoming aircraft may not be able to see the Exoskeletons well from the air, the Colonel directed his men:

COLONEL YĀRÉN
Fire the Kinetic Weapons at the feet of the Exoskeletons,
the aircraft will be able to see them better.

The Anarchie had no fear of the Mergenky weapons. Their Armor was better than a portashields and the Kinetic weapons simply bounced off harmless.

LEAD ANARCHIE
EXOSKELETON OPERATOR
The Mergenky are not shooting well, most of their
shots are missing us.

SECOND ANARCHIE
EXOSKELETON OPERATOR
Yea, all they are doing is kicking up dirt and dust.

LEAD ANARCHIE
EXOSKELETON OPERATOR
We'll swat these Nat's-like flies real soon.

SECOND ANARCHIE
EXOSKELETON OPERATOR
We'll be a mile away in 15 minutes, we'll have good
targeting data then to blast them out.

Out of nowhere came the first Mergenky Cruisers.

Air Defense warnings went off in the Air Defense Exoskeletons escorting the assault force Exoskeletons whose kinetic weapons would slice through portashields or any other obstructions the Mergenky could put up.

Nearby Anarchie Battleships were alerted and vectored to the location and at 50,000 feet deployed their air wings out of the belly of the Anarchie Battleships. These fighter bombers, designed to operate in the atmosphere of the planet would be in direct support of the Exoskeletons.

A portable command post electronics suite was just delivered to the Anarchie Command post and General Borktar now had displays of the battle that was intensifying.

Mergenky Cruisers were designed to operate in space as well as in the atmosphere were aerodynamic designed and could maneuver in the most excellent fashion. The landing zone for the Scout had to be prepared. All those Exoskeleton's had to be neutralized to make it safe for the Scout to come down.

The Exoskeleton's were getting dangerously close to Bravo Juliet. Timing was critical otherwise there would be no Amphibians left to pick up.

The Cruiser Squadron formed up and went in a Giant V formation. The fighter bombers disgorged out of the belly of the Anarchie Battleships were now converging towards the Mergenky Cruisers. It became a sudden slugfest and melee.

Mergenky Scout MSFS-1 was positioned behind the V-formation and Kwongab could see the Cruisers had their hands full with the Anarchie Fighter Bombers now swarming in on them, which meant they would be distracted from the Anarchie Fighter Bombers and unable to deal with the Anarchie Exoskeletons who were almost at that critical range where the Kinetic Weapons would be fatal to the Amphibians.

Commander Gōngniúgǒu on his own would have waited for the Cruisers to take out the Exoskeletons before attempting the rescue. Kwongab now applied extensive neural expansion on Commander Gōngniúgǒu, and the mental telepathy thought insertion process which made Gōngniúgǒu suddenly react.

COMMANDER GŌNGNIÚGǑU
PNN take us down where we can get a clear shot at the lead Exoskeletons.

MARTHA (PNN)
Commander Gōngniúgǒu, the Air Defense Exoskeletons can damage the Scout with their weapons.

Commander Gōngniúgǒu took manual control of the Scout and had no realization of why or how he was doing it but started dancing the Scout.

CAPTAIN KWONGAB
Commander Gōngniúgǒu may I operate the weapons while you pilot us?

COMMANDER GŌNGNIÚGǑU
Yes Captain, please do that will help me devote my energy towards flying.

Kwongab, all too familiar with MSFS-1's laser batteries went to work. He was doing an incredible feat of aiming and firing the lasers on the Exoskeletons at the same time applying the neural expansion on Commander Gōngniúgǒu to ensure his manual flight controls were achieving the desired effect.

Colonel Yārén realized that with what he witnessed, they would have a chance to survive as the first two Exoskeletons blew up. Other Anarchie Exoskeleton operators were suddenly bewildered and confused. *Did the Mergenky have some kind of secret weapon?*

The Cruisers had absolutely no ability to deal with the Exoskeletons at that time, while the air battle continued.

Anarchie fighter bombers were blasted out of the sky in impressive numbers. The sky was crowded with Anarchie Fighter Bombers and even though Mergenky Cruisers were shooting many of them down, eventually a few of them slipped through the net and launched a combination of kinetic weapons and chemical rockets.

Just as the Anarchie pilots were being fried alive inside the cockpits of their fighter bombers from laser strikes, at least two of them died happy knowing they left their marks on two Mergenky Cruisers who sustained damage as one kinetic weapon penetrated and flew through one of the Cruisers.

About the same time chemical rockets from a fighter bomber now disintegrating into a cloud of sparkling debris, hit right above A Cruiser's shuttle bay destroying the shuttle bay hatches and had no choice but to return to Jeeapa City Dome area where they could receive emergency repairs.

The Scout continued an unprecedented dance that made the Anarchie air defenses almost useless, and the gunners quickly panicked as nothing seemed to work.

Kwongab made his mark on two more Exoskeletons. That's all it took for the remainder of the Anarchie Exoskeletons drivers to decide:

ANARCHIE EXOSKELETON DRIVER
We need to pull back and regroup!

The Anarchie Exoskeletons attacking then turned 180 degrees and promptly moved away from Bravo Juliet landing zone, while still receiving lethal attacks by the Scout MSFS-1.

CAPTAIN KWONGAB
We have a clearing. We can get down there now and
pick up those Amphibians!

COMMANDER GŌNGNIÚGǑU
I agree. The battleships were too far out of position to
stop us, and the Cruisers are effectively shielding us
from approach by any of the fighter bombers.

With Kwongab still firing the lasers which hastened the Anarchie Exoskeleton retreat, he applied massive neural expansion mental telepathic thoughts into Commander Gōngniúgǒu who then manually guided the scout down to almost the surface of the planet.

The Scout MSFS-1 hovered 1 foot above the surface of the planet and a boarding ramp was placed down so that all the Amphibians could quickly scramble aboard. None of them wasted time and a few wounded were carried. As soon as Colonel Yārén saw they were all safely aboard, he announced:

COLONEL YĀRÉN
We are all onboard, we can leave now.

The ramp was immediately closed, and the Scout lifted off and shot through the wedge of the Cruisers heading due East towards Jeeapa.

With General Borktar screaming orders like a madman, the Battleships were directed at the Cruiser formation. With their fighter bomber air wings already depleted, all they had left was their laser batteries. Half of the remaining Anarchie Battleships were not converted with the new blue diamond laser optics. Hence, they had no numerical advantage over Mergenky.

Once Commander Gōngniúgǒu notified Jeeapa MSF Headquarters he had recovered the Amphibians, the Cruiser formation was no longer needed and could avoid the big scrape with the Anarchie battleships coming their way, the force maneuvered and quickly moved to the air defense radius of Jeeapa where the Battleships could ill afford to attempt operating.

All in all, it was a highly successful mission and now with those Exoskeletons either destroyed or out of position, there was a gaping hole in the Anarchie front lines to exploit.

Unlike the Anarchie who could only get ½ of their Frăctŏng invasion force retrieved and brought safely to Jeeapa to participate in the battle, almost all the Mergenky were available, and the Troop Transports were arriving with the addition of more Cruisers to provide escort safely to the planet. The days of needing Cruiser Escorts were suddenly over.

Since the Mergenky now had a substantial reserve force, troops were sent forward in broad daylight with air support and a cloud of drones like the Anarchie had never witnessed before. The drones would jam any signals and make battlefield communications almost totally useless. The counterattack had a lot of steam in it.

The Exoskeletons that General Borktar so carelessly and irrationally pulled out of the front lines could have made the difference and repelled the Mergenky quite easily. But in the Anarchie Exoskeletons absence at pincer locations, Mergenky Forces poured through the weak areas and were now in the rears of many Anarchie Forces. Pockets of Anarchie were now completely cut off and would soon wither at the vine with no supplies or reserves. The beginning of the end was now just starting.

Mergenky Scout MSFS-1 landed at the same launch pad area they had left on a short while earlier.

Jeeapa's Commander General Zǔzhī Bùliáng having received real timed holographs of MSFS-1's activity was thoroughly impressed and wanted to meet the crew personally and at the same time welcome Colonel Yārén and his men back and shower them with accolades.

As soon as the Scout landed a foot off the planet suspended in air as to not put stress on the hull, a ramp went down, and the Amphibians were asked to exit the Scout and form up in formation. Colonel Yārén gave his men instructions on where to line up on the side of the launch pad.

General Zǔzhī Bùliáng shortly came busting out of the Jeeapa command entrance followed by a dozen staff members. And walked up to Colonel Yārén who was then talking to his men. Medics were at the same time carting away a few wounded on stretchers, and the General walked up to the medics and said:

GENERAL ZǓZHĪ BÙLIÁNG
One minute please.

General Zǔzhī Bùliáng then blessed each one of the casualties then sent them on their way to surgery and treatments. He then approached the Amphibians who were standing at attention with the Colonel and six officers standing out in front of the formation.

GENERAL ZǓZHĪ BÙLIÁNG
Colonel Yārén, welcome back.

COLONEL YĀRÉN
Thank you General Zǔzhī Bùliáng.

GENERAL ZǓZHĪ BÙLIÁNG
Amphibians, I want to congratulate you all for
executing a job well done. Your incredible feat has
paved the way for victory. Your exploits were nothing
less than spectacular.

The Mergenky are very proud of you as your actions probably saved a lot of lives. I want to thank you personally for all that you have done and wish you the very best.

Troops always love to receive such accolades from Generals.

GENERAL ZǓZHĪ BÙLIÁNG
Colonel, now for the bad part. I want you and your
men to rest up. Tonight, you have another mission. If
you carry it out with the same success as this one, it
will go a long way to ending the war.

COLONEL YĀRÉN
General, we are down a few in number, but our spirits
are high.

General Zǔzhī Bùliáng wrapped up his comments and sent the Amphibians to a special
rest area set up for them. General Zǔzhī Bùliáng asked the Scout to remain until he
talked to them. He then went aboard MSFS-1 and was escorted to the bridge where he
met Kwongab and the pilot Commander Gōngniúgǒu.

GENERAL ZǓZHĪ BÙLIÁNG
Congratulations on a spectacular mission.

Commander Gōngniúgǒu replied as Captain Kwongab remained quiet.

COMMANDER GŌNGNIÚGǑU
Thank you, general.

GENERAL ZǓZHĪ BÙLIÁNG
I'd like to know one thing, which one of you violated
the hell out of Mergenky regulations and went in
blazing on those Exoskeletons which saved all those
Amphibians?

CAPTAIN KWONGAB
General, I was just along for the ride, Commander
Gōngniúgǒu piloted the ship.

COMMANDER GŌNGNIÚGǑU
But you fired the lasers Captain Kwongab,

General Zǔzhī Bùliáng responded with a heartfelt smile.

GENERAL ZǓZHĪ BÙLIÁNG
Well, whatever it was, it was fantastic teamwork, and
the results speak for themselves.

COMMANDER GŌNGNIÚGǑU
Am I going to be punished for violating the rules,
General?

GENERAL ZǓZHĪ BÙLIÁNG
Just between you and me, I didn't see any rules broken
so let's just leave it at that.

Commander Gōngniúgǒu smiled and responded in a chipper manner.

COMMANDER GŌNGNIÚGǑU
Thank you, sir.

General Zǔzhī Bùliáng then turned to Kwongab

GENERAL ZǓZHĪ BÙLIÁNG

Just before I came up to meet this ship, I was contacted by General Kahn. His personal transport is here picking up casualties to take back to Gwaba, and said he wants you on that ship, he needs to see you right away.

KWONGAB

Sir, I think I'm needed here, the fighting is intensifying.

GENERAL ZǓZHĪ BÙLIÁNG

Kwongab, you have done more than your fair share of the fighting. General Kahn has an important assignment for you and it's a high priority. You must leave immediately.

KWONGAB
Yes, sir, understand all.

Kwongab then turned towards Commander Gōngniúgǒu.

CAPTAIN KWONGAB

The greatest honor any instructor can have, is to personally observe his student in real combat and see first-hand the impact he had on that individual. Your actions today, make me deeply proud. I want to thank you for allowing me to serve with you.

COMMANDER GŌNGNIÚGǑU

Captain the pleasure is all mine. I think you made quite a difference operating those lasers and allowing me to place all my focus on steering the ship out of harm's way.

General Zǔzhī Bùliáng broke up the conversation as he knew they needed to get moving.

GENERAL ZǓZHĪ BÙLIÁNG
Kwongab, I'll escort you to General Kahn's Transport.

PNN suddenly announced:

MARTHA
Commander Gōngniúgǒu, you are directed to immediately proceed to coordinates that MSF has sent vectors to our Navigation system.

COMMANDER GŌNGNIÚGǑU
Captain Kwongab, I would like to escort you to your Transport ship as well, but I must leave now.

KWONGAB
Understand Commander Gōngniúgǒu. Good luck and I'll be looking forward to seeing you back at Gwaba in the future.

COMMANDER GŌNGNIÚGǑU
I will as well.

The two men bowed and Kwongab immediately departed. As soon as Captain Kwongab and General Zǔzhī Bùliáng stepped off the Scout, the ramp went up and the access door secured, and the Scout darted off into the air to its next assignment.

The Amphibians had already marched off somewhere probably to bivouac and get a bite to eat.

Kwongab did not have to walk far with General Zǔzhī Bùliáng to get to General Kahn's personal transport. There were only a few seats inside, the rest of the area was filled with patient carriers.

GENERAL ZǓZHĪ BÙLIÁNG
So long Kwongab, thank you for all that you have done.

KWONGAB
Good luck General. I know you have a lot of fighting left to do, but in the end, I know you will be victorious.

GENERAL ZǓZHĪ BÙLIÁNG
All thanks to you, my friend.

The men bowed and Kwongab stepped up into the transport and the door immediately shut and it went airborne.

***

<u>INT. SPACE. EVACUATION TRANSPORT.</u>

At first the medical staff were agitated that another rider bounced a patient off the transport that may mean the patient would die. After they were out in deep space far away from Jeeapa and any possible Anarchie encounter, the pilot came out of the cockpit and could see the nasty looks on the medical people and he decided he would introduce Kwongab to the medical staff.

General Kahn knew the possibility the medical staff may not warmly receive Kwongab, sent the pilot a briefing about Kwongab in the event he thought it might help unruffle a few feathers of the medical staff. The pilot being one of General Kahns top pilots himself had been through a lot and read the briefing and knew some of it already.

PILOT
Doctors, let me introduce you to Captain Kwongab.

The first doctor responded.

DOCTOR
Hello Captain,

PILOT
You may not have heard of Captain Kwongab, but he did some rather spectacular missions during the first Jeeapa War. Yesterday his Cruiser crashed behind enemy lines as he was transporting Mergenky Amphibian Forces on a secret mission.

Captain Kwongab was rescued last night and was already on another mission he just completed this morning where he helped extricate Amphibians who were trapped behind enemy lines while being attacked by the Anarchie.

All the medical supplies you now have, he delivered on a Cruiser Transport which was the only vessel that could get supplies to Jeeapa up until now.

According to what I've been briefed on, during two of those transport shipments, he had significant space battles with the Anarchie.

Early on in this war, Captain Kwongab was in command of the ship who detected the Anarchie Invasion Force and warned MSF that Frăctŏng was going to be hit. He subsequently delivered emergency supplies via Cruiser Transport to Frăctŏng.

Captain Kwongab is being brought back to Gwaba for a high priority mission. General Kahn arranged for his transportation. That's why he's aboard this evacuation flight. Feel blessed that you could fly with Captain Kwongab.

The pilot then went back to the cockpit hoping he unruffled a few feathers.

Kwongab attempted using neuro expansion telepathic survey of the medical staff and immediately felt the resentment that he was aboard. He then applied some neural expansion telepathic mind-altering insertions to help the doctors become friendlier and at ease with his presence.

About that time one of the medical evacuee patients spoke.

MEDICAL PATIENT
(AMPHIBIAN)
Captain Kwongab, you saved my life this morning.

CAPTAIN KWONGAB
How did I do that?

MEDICAL PATIENT
(AMPHIBIAN)
I'm one of those Amphibians you rescued.

Kwongab was suddenly touched by the soldier and responded.

CAPTAIN KWONGAB

Bless you for being there. I know you guys did a spectacular job on the target.

MEDICAL PATIENT
(AMPHIBIAN)

I also think we did too, sir. And the way you got us down safely when the spacecraft was seriously damaged was rather remarkable.

CAPTAIN KWONGAB

I was lucky! We came really close to crashing in that canyon.

MEDICAL PATIENT (AMPHIBIAN)
It was quite an adventure.

VOICEOVER

Kwongab had that rare opportunity to use his neural expansion telepathic ability to read the young soldier's mind and see his thoughts and memories of the recent combat. It was truly horrifying.

By tapping into the young Amphibian's memories, it temporally transcended Kwongab as if he was in the center of the Anarchie compound with the Amphibians, in the young soldier's memory which Kwongab now absorbed all the images and sounds.

FLASHBACK:

The firefight was intense. Explosions and laser blasts were all around. Kwongab almost regretted reading the young Amphibian's mind because he suddenly felt the wound just like the young man did during the battle and it was incredibly painful to the point Kwongab flinched.

Kwongab had no idea the level of violence that existed in such a fire fight. The Amphibians were fighting the Crème da le Crème of the Anarchie Scouts and Rangers who were equally brave and extremely good shots.

The whole imagery was terrifying to Kwongab. He instantly had profound respect not only for this young brave Amphibian who endured such a tumultuous event, but now understood the incredible pain the Amphibian and others experienced for the benefit of the Mergenky civilization.

It took special training and men like this soldier to have carried out what they did.

Kwongab then gave the soldier a tremendous gift by using neural expansion telepathy, he healed some of the boy's psyche and erased some of the horrifying moments when his best friend perished right beside him.

VOICEOVER

The anguish the soldier felt from the five Amphibians left behind as the rear guard was soon a faded memory the young man soon forgot. Kwongab then helped the young man slowly ease into a restful sleep that he was long overdue.

For the remainder of the flight the staff was more cordial, and the anger and resentment were all gone by the time they landed. As Kwongab stepped off the transport the doctor that appeared the angriest when he first arrived, now was smiling and his body language radiated a whole different persona.

General Kahn and Monachi were there to meet Kwongab at the MSF Healing Center where the wounded were being taken for emergency treatment. The three were quickly transported via a Skycar back to MSF headquarters where they talked briefly and then General Kahn announced:

GENERAL KAHN

Kwongab and Monachi, I want you to take a couple days off. I've arranged with the *Juéduìhuīhuáng Foundation Center for Advanced Learning* to transport your children home for a few days, to make up for your recent sudden departure.

CAPTAIN KWONGAB

Normally I would insist on going back to Jeeapa General, but I do feel tired.

GENERAL KAHN
You look tired Kwongab. You need a break.

General Kahn knew that if he didn't give Kwongab a break, that he would eventually put himself and ostensibly his crew in jeopardy by operating in a sleep deprivation manner.

Kwongab and Monachi then left MSF headquarters then went home.

By the time they arrived home the kids were already there spending time with their friend, the robot Charles.

The Children had arrived nearly an hour before, and Charles had informed them of Kara's disappearance. They were terribly saddened by it all.

Charles informed Crystal:

CHARLES

I have been looking for leads but have not come up with much.

Crystal decided she would help.

> CRYSTAL
> I have access to Mergenky INTEL networks that would seem rather innocuous to any counter-intelligence surveillance.

Crystal went about searching, hacking and looking for any shred of evidence that would somehow help determine where Kara went and what the circumstances were.

Chief among her ability was to get access to surveillance video that only Mergenky INTEL realized was EVERYWHERE. Crystal had the most important piece of information: the date. With the date she could then go into the back door of the domestic computational suite (DCS) and retrieve all past holographs of callers.

Crystal soon said:

> CRYSTAL
> I found a call from the school nurse concerning Kara's son.

> CHARLES
> That is a huge clue.

Crystal then using her ability to hack into the boarding school DCS.

> CRYSTAL
> Let's look at all the credentials of each staff member.

After examination, Charles stated seemingly in a disappointed manner.

> CHARLES
> None of them matched the caller.

> CRYSTAL
> That is the second clue.

> CHARLES
> How so?

> CRYSTAL
> It also reinforces the notion Kara probably traveled to the school out of panic that her son was critically ill.

> CHARLES
> Knowing she traveled somewhere; it should be a matter of finding the travel documents and her itinerary.

CRYSTAL
That's easy to find as well.

All the checks Crystal subsequently made showed the time she arrived at her destination on a stratospheric glider and left the transportation terminal.

CRYSTAL
Now comes the interesting part.

Crystal then hacked into Mergenky INTEL surveillance files for that day.

CRYSTAL
I have the exact time of arrival.

Charles and Crystal's brother looked over her shoulders taking it all in.

CHARLES
It appears Kara is walking towards a people mover, then a Skycar came down. Several men got out and showed some kind of credentials and they coaxed Kara into the Skycar and took off!

CRYSTAL
I got an I.D. on the Skycar. It belongs to Mergenky INTEL!

CHARLES
They knew Kara was onto something.

About that time their parents arrived home. Crystal said to Charles and her brother:

CRYSTAL
Do not mention any of this to anyone or you could place us all at risk.

Crystal now knew foul play was at work.

Crystal was now asking herself the nagging question:

CRYSTAL (THOUGHT)
Why would Mergenky INTEL want to harm Dr. Kara?

The family then went about doing fun things together, they went to a park, rode in a boat, walked through Razkeukenhof Gardens with wealth of spectacular floral displays that were the pride and joy of Gwaba and truly awe-inspiring.

The strange looking birds that were in the Quom Aviary next to the Gardens made a cacophony of sounds that were always pleasant in nature. The day was a magnificent reprieve from the horrifying experiences that Kwongab and Monachi had felt.

Jeeapa had brought back a sense of how precious life was to Kwongab and experiencing this visual inspiration codified his emotions in ways he had missed for quite some time.

VOICEOVER

> *It was during this pleasant experience Kwongab suddenly felt the urge to probe his kids.*
>
> *Kwongab wanted to get to the bottom of the Mergenky INTEL using his kids as spies.*
>
> *His daughter Crystal, being the older of the two, would most likely be in a far more advanced training scenario than her brother so Kwongab probed her first.*

As Kwongab applied his neural expansion telepathic probing thinking he would stumble across the essence of her programming by the Mergenky spy apparatus he was immediately horrified to start experiencing Crystal's vast thoughts on Kara's disappearance.

Kwongab had not been notified, furthermore the information he gleaned out of Crystal's mind confirmed his absolute horror, *Crystal indeed was a spy, and it was far more extensive than he could ever imagine.*

Then Crystals thoughts he perceived through telepathy that revealed that Kara had been detained by Mergenky INTEL, severely troubled him.

Kwongab kept his composure and continued acting as if he were having a fantastic day with his kids.

Kwongab was fortunate that Monachi had not probed his mind. She was already close to a nervous breakdown and for a day when she thought Kwongab had perished, she came as close as any time in her life where she had reservations for her own being.

General Kahn determined Monachi was having a very difficult time and that is one of the reasons why he pulled Kwongab back from Jeeapa, because had Monachi had a breakdown, Kwongab might have been severely affected, thus he would have lost two pilots not just one.

The family continued their day, and it all appeared as if nothing unusual was going on.

Meanwhile Charles was at work. He had photographic memory and captured all of Crystal's keystrokes. Hence, he had the passwords to unlock Mergenkys most secret information and a back door to almost any group within Mergenky INTEL. Charles then found the smoking gun. Surveillance video of Kara visiting Mergenky INTEL headquarters including her being escorted out of the building by INTEL *Director Xié'è de Dǎoyǎn* just hours before her disappearance!

CHARLES (THOUGHT)

How could Kara get tied up and involved with Mergenky INTEL?

In Charles snooping, he knew that Monachi and Kara were seriously distressed at discovering Monachi's children were being trained as spies. That had to be the tie in.

CHARLES (THOUGHT)

Kara went to the director to attempt to get him to end the program of using the children as spies. One could then assume the Mergenky INTEL Director Xié'è de Dǎoyǎn had silenced Kara.

VOICE OVER

Charles then started studying the Mergenky INTEL Director Xié'è de Dǎoyǎn history. Thanks to all the passwords he observed Crystal typing to get into various departments in the Mergenky INTEL apparatus, Charles was able to work his way into the Mergenky Intelligence Agency Human Resources and Personnel (HRP) files and look at each person's records.

<u>INT. DAY. KWONGBAB'S HOME. CHARLES HACKING ACTIVITY DURING NARRATION OF THE VOICEOVER.</u>

VOICE OVER

Xié'è de Dǎoyǎn was an interesting person to say the least. He had moved up the ranks of government service in the foreign ministry where he had some quite interesting assignments.

Before the 1st Jeeapa war Xié'è de Dǎoyǎn had spent time on the diplomatic staff in the Mergenky consulate in the Anarchie city of Fěicuìchéng.

<u>INT. DAY MERGENKY CONSULATE IN THE ANARCHIE CITY OF FĚICUÌCHÉNG. XIÉ'È DE DĂOYĂN MEETING WITH ANARCHIE DIPLOMATS.</u>
<u>15 seconds</u>

VOICE OVER

At the completion of that assignment, INTEL Director Xié'è de Dăoyăn transferred to the Mergenky INTEL directorate where he had numerous responsibilities in the surveillance of the Anarchie.

<u>INT. DAY. MERGENKY INTEL DIRECTORATE IN QUOM, CAPTIAL OF GWABA. XIÉ'È DE DĂOYĂN MEETING WITH SPIES IN HIS INNER CIRCLE.</u>
<u>15 SECONS.</u>

VOICE OVER

There wasn't a huge tie in with Anarchie but there certainly was the opportunity to be recruited by the Anarchie Intelligence Group, AIG while working in Fěicuìchéng.

Charles was curious since he was already in the Mergenky Intelligence Agency HRP site to look up Crystal's records to see what she was really doing. He was soon reading through all her achievements and her recruitment papers and letters of recommendation.

What Charles found almost jumped out at him:

CHARLES (THOUGHT)

This was one of the greatest discoveries of all. An unsolicited letter of recommendation by MSF Intel Director Xié'è de Dăoyăn himself!

VOICE OVER

Charles, with vast analysis and computational capability immediately went through a series of "what if" questions and inserted probabilities.

There could only be one reason why the unsolicited letter of recommendation was made by Xié'è de Dăoyăn. He wanted access to Kwongab's children and when Kara went there to pitch a fit, she could have wrecked his plans.

CHARLES (THOUGHT)
What are Xié'è de Dǎoyǎn *'s plans?*

VOICE OVER
Later that evening, Kwongab and the family were sitting in the family room watching some entertainment holographs when the children appeared to get bored and asked Charles if he would like to join them in one of their bedrooms to play a board game. Charles was waiting for a moment alone with Kwongab and declined.

The other robot John who had not spent a lot of time with the Children in a while wanted to be with them and enjoy their presence and immediately volunteered to be the third person.

The Children then browbeat Monachi to be the 4th person which would make the game more interesting and far more competitive with four players vice three.

Monachi, feeling slightly emotional about all that had recently transpired, felt the need to be with her children so she agreed.

The four went into the bedroom and shut the door so they would not interfere with Kwongab hearing all the sound of the entertainment holograph.

As soon as they were alone, Charles spoke.

CHARLES
Kwongab, I have some very serious information to discuss with you and I'm not sure here is a good place.

KWONGAB
What's the information about?

CHARLES
It has to do with Kara's disappearance and some other bits of information. It's quite a serious matter.

KWONGAB
Let's take a walk to the park, we can have privacy there.

Kwongab and the robot Charles left the premises, took the elevator down to the ground floor and walked outside the building. They walked a short distance and were at the park and since it was evening there was hardly anyone there.

KWONGAB

What is it you wanted to tell me Charles?

CHARLES

Kwongab, I know who killed Kara and why.

KWONGAB

She's dead?

CHARLES

We'll never find the body; they did a good job of disposing of it.

KWONGAB

Who did that?

CHARLES

Mergenky INTEL, the director Xié'è de Dǎoyǎn and his associates.

Kwongab knew that Charles had interlocks in his software to prevent him from lying. He would not be stating this information if it were not factual. Kwongab was immediately alarmed.

KWONGAB

Why did Intel Director Xié'è de Dǎoyǎn have Kara murdered?

CHARLES

Kara went to Mergenky Intel headquarters and met with Xié'è de Dǎoyǎn to plead with him to remove your children out of the Spy training program at the Juéduìhuǐhuáng Foundation Center for Advanced Learning.

KWONGAB

Why would that lead Xié'è de Dǎoyǎn to have Kara murdered?

CHARLES

Xié'è de Dǎoyǎn was afraid Kara because of her connection to you and the MSF could apply pressure to force them to expel your children from the Juéduìhuīhuáng Foundation.

KWONGAB

Why should that be such serious matter that he would kill Kara over that?

CHARLES

It would upset plans he had for your children.

KWONGAB
What plans are they?

CHARLES

Let me give you Xié'è de Dǎoyǎn's background. He started government employment working for the Foreign Ministry. Before the last Jeeapa War started, he had been assigned to the diplomatic staff in the Mergenky consulate in the Anarchie city of Fěicuìchéng.

KWONGAB
That's routine, that doesn't prove anything.

CHARLES

At the completion of that assignment, Xié'è de Dǎoyǎn transferred to the Mergenky INTEL directorate where he had numerous responsibilities in the surveillance of the Anarchie.

VOICEOVER

Suddenly it hit Kwongab, Xié'è de Dǎoyǎn was going to blackmail Kwongab during a period of the most serious situations, such as would be the case if there were a major setback to the Anarchie on Jeeapa!

Chills ran down Kwongab's spine as he realized a lot of this also meant he and his family were in severe Jeopardy.

KWONGAB
This is a very dangerous situation; you must not talk to
anyone about this until I figure out how we are going
to handle it."

CHARLES
Understand Kwongab

KWONGAB
How did you learn all this?

CHARLES
Your daughter is a full-fledged Mergenky Spy. She
was accessing Mergenky INTEL databases through
your DCS terminal and didn't realize I have permanent
memory to everything and recorded her keystrokes.

When I was left home alone, I used those passwords and went in and explored.

I recorded most of the files in my associative memory bank. Realizing we are in
a dangerous situation; I sent those files to John via our radio control interface that
nobody else knows exists or can monitor to store for evidence in case something
happens to me.

KWONGAB
How do you know Kara went with Mergenky Intel?

CHARLES
Crystal hacked surveillance video at the airport and
saw men grab Kara and shove her into a Skycar.

Crystal confirmed through the databases that was a Mergenky Intel Skycar.

I also hacked the video showing Kara talking to Xié'è de Dǎoyǎn in the lobby of
the Mergenky Intel Headquarters building. I have all that recorded from my cameras
recording the data terminal.

KWONGAB
Can you reach John via your radio control interface
from here?

CHARLES
Yes, I can.

                          KWONGAB
Repeat to John everything you just told me and tell
him that I'm taking you to see General Kahn and to not
let anyone in the residence until we return.

In about five seconds Charles responded.

                          CHARLES
John has received all the information and will guard
your family.

He also said that based on the information we have provided, some of which he has
already witnessed, that since Monachi is our owner, he would not have a Circuit-
Breaker-One shutdown for harming anyone who is attempting to hurt Monachi.

Since the children are Monachi's Children, the same relief of circuit breaker actions
apply to them.

                          KWONGAB
Can John protect Monachi and the Children very well?

                          CHARLES
We have programmed ourselves to be the best martial
artists in the galaxy to protect your family.

Because of our construction, blasters and kinetic weapons will not affect us unless
they came from something like an Exoskeleton or a space craft or possibly a fighter
bomber.

                          KWONGAB
That's good to know.

                          CHARLES
Shouldn't we tell Monachi?

                          KWONGAB
I'm afraid our DCS terminal is being monitored by
Xié'è de Dǎoyǎn's people.

                          CHARLES
Perhaps John can brief Monachi.

                          KWONGAB
Tell John to ask Monachi to call my portable
communicator from the DCS.

About 30 seconds later Monachi called, and she sounded worried on the other end.

MONACHI
Where are you and what are you doing?

KWONGAB
Listen, I will tell you all about it later. Go somewhere in the house where you and John can talk without being overheard by the kids. John will have some instructions for you.

MONACHI
How soon will you be back?

KWONGAB
I'm not sure but hope to be soon.

The conversation soon ended and Kwongab turned to Charles and spoke.

KWONGAB
Let's go hop on that people mover.

Soon Kwongab and Charles transitioned from the people mover to a tube train and in a short period of time arrived at MSF headquarters. It was out of character for Kwongab to show up to work wearing civilian clothes, but if required, he had spare uniforms in his office.

At the main entrance Kwongab asked the security guard:

CAPTAIN KWONGAB
Is General Kahn still here?

SECURITY GUARD
I've not seen old iron pants leave yet; he usually stays quite late.

CAPTAIN KWONGAB
Could you call General Kahn and inform him I'm at the entrance with my personal robot and we need to see him, it's a very urgent matter.

The security guard only complied with Kwongab's request because in the past day, as word started filtering out, it was apparent Kwongab was truly a national hero and had just undertaken some extraordinary historic missions. Otherwise, he might have thought Kwongab was being a wise guy claiming his partner was a robot.

When General Kahn received the call, he notified the security guard:

GENERAL KAHN
Have the two escorted up to my office immediately.

A few minutes later Kwongab and the robot Charles were in General Kahn's office and there were seven staff members and Kwongab requested:

CAPTAIN KWONGAB
General Kahn, this is an extremely serious matter. You need to have these people leave and if you don't feel comfortable being alone with me and my personal robot, I suggest you have someone who you thoroughly trust remain behind. But you will have to instruct that person not to divulge what we are about to show you.

General Kahn asked everyone to leave except a person Kwongab had not seen in quite a while, General Zarkin.

GENERAL KAHN
What is it that's so important to talk about in the middle of a war and a big day at that?

CAPTAIN KWONGAB
Sir, I know who killed Dr. Kara and my family is now at risk. We need your assistance.

General Kahn appeared astonished.

GENERAL KAHN
Go on, let me hear the rest of the story.

CAPTAIN KWONGAB
My personal robot here has all this information recorded, he can speed things up by telling you and show you the video and evidence.

GENERAL KAHN
How can he do that?

CAPTAIN KWONGAB
You have a DCS system here in the office, he can remotely connect to it and use it to present all the information.

GENERAL KAHN
Very well, carry on.

Charles scanners picked up the wireless signals and quickly established phase lock and since the protocol was essentially the same as back at Kwongab's residence, the holographs started streaming right away.

No two men knew Kwongab quite like General Kahn and General Zarkin. As the story unfolded General Kahn got nervous and stated:

GENERAL KAHN
Let me interrupt you just for a minute.

General Kahn then called in Colonel Chāorén his chief of Rapid Deployment Security that was sometimes required to rescue a consulate when being attacked by the enemy or other special security needs.

GENERAL KAHN
Colonel Chāorén, would you please come to my office.

COLONEL CHĀORÉN
Right away General Kahn.

Colonel Chāorén's office was just down the hallway, and he arrived a moment later.

GENERAL KAHN
Kwongab this is Colonel Chāorén my chief of Rapid Deployment Security Services. I fear you may be right your family is in danger.

CAPTAIN KWONGAB
I agree.

GENERAL KAHN
Colonel Chāorén, I want you to mount up a security team and send them to Kwongab's residence, secure it and do not allow any skycars or non-residents in the building until further notice. You can get his address from security. Have them in place no later than 30

minutes from now. You are authorized to use deadly
force.

COLONEL CHĀORÉN

Yes sir, I'll have my men in place right away.

Colonel Chāorén wasted no time, left the office and went about his business. The robot continued on with the presentation and at the conclusion of the holographic presentation, General Kahn put his face into his hands and shook his head.

GENERAL KAHN

Kwongab, can you send that entire presentation to my Inspector General?

CHARLES

General Kahn, all I need is his DCS number, and I'll send it.

GENERAL KAHN

After further thought, it might be better if you send it to me and I'll forward the files to the inspector general.

CAPTAIN KWONGAB

Charles, can you reach John from here?

CHARLES

I'm checking.

A moment later:

CHARLES

Yes Kwongab. I can reach John, but the data rate is about half due to the reduced signal strength causing data bit errors requiring rebroadcasts.

Good, tell John to inform Monachi that MSF is sending over some security people and will be there in 30 minutes. Do not open the door for anyone. We should be home in a short while.

A moment later Charles informed Kwongab:

CHARLES

John has been informed and said he is alone with Monachi now and is telling her what you just said.

CAPTAIN KWONGAB
I wonder how John informs Monachi?

CHARLES
It's simple Kwongab, John just replays what you said
to Monachi, which I recorded and sent to him.

CAPTAIN KWONGAB
So, Monachi hears my real voice?

CHARLES
Yes, there is no point in repeating something when we
can send the actual conversation.

Kwongab then realizing General Kahn had a war to attend to, then spoke.

CAPTAIN KWONGAB
General Kahn, I appreciate your help, I know you're
busy so I'm going to leave now and go home.

GENERAL KAHN
Don't worry Kwongab, you will have our protection
and Xié'è de Dǎoyǎn may be the mole we have been
looking for.

CAPTAIN KWONGAB
General, if you can get me alone with Xié'è de Dǎoyǎn
I can confirm it for you.

GENERAL KAHN
I'll have Xié'è de Dǎoyǎn here in my office tomorrow.
You will have your opportunity.

By the time Kwongab returned home, MSF security personnel had barricaded the
building and were confirming the identity of everyone and allowing only residents in.

When Kwongab attempted to enter the building with Charles they would not let
Charles through since he had no I.D.

KWONGAB
He's my personal robot.

SECURITY GUARD
Yea and the Mergenky Moon is made from green cheese.

About that time Colonel Chāorén stepped forward and spoke.

> COLONEL CHĀORÉN
> Soldier I was with them in General Kahn's office. He
> is a robot, let them pass.

The soldier was suddenly astonished and could only say:

> SECURITY GUARD
> Yes sir!

Kwongab went up to his residence and passed security men at the elevator entrance and again at his floor. He then got off with Charles and walked down the hallway to his residence where several more security men were standing. They had a portfolio with them and verified his pictures matched and let him in the residence.

Monachi didn't look like she was doing well. However, she immediately improved upon seeing Kwongab.

> KWONGAB
> Monachi, let's go to the bedroom where we can talk.
> Charles, you wait out here and guard the door and tell
> John to stay with the kids.

Kwongab knew Charles would communicate with John via his *Radio Control Interface* and they would manage.

Inside the bedroom Kwongab gave Monachi a complete briefing on what had transpired.

> KWONGAB
> Tomorrow I will use neural expansion telepathic
> investigation on Xié'è de Dăoyăn in General Kahn's
> office.

There will be a big showdown. Kwongab knew he would do some unprecedented things tomorrow that were neither moral nor ethical. But Xié'è de Dăoyăn was effectively a murderer by ordering Kara's death. Kwongab would have one chance with Xié'è de Dăoyăn, so he had to make it all count.

Monachi was almost a basket case because she violated family rules and used neural expansion on the kids and learned the truth. She was mildly devastated to learn the extent her children were enveloped into the spy business.

***

XIÉ'È DE DǍOYǍN'S ESCAPE

Xié'è de Dǎoyǎn's men attempted to land a Mergenky Intel Skycar on Kwongab's apartment building.

With all the intrusions today into their data files, it was apparent someone was discovering information that would implicate them.

Xié'è de Dǎoyǎn's men were going to do a snatch and grab and the eight seat Skycar was large enough to haul Kwongab's entire family with them.

As Xié'è de Dǎoyǎn's men approached Kwongab's apartment building their INTEL Skycar veered away, and MSF computers took over control of the Skycar that was designed to be flown from the ground via a computer network operating via a wireless technology.

INT. DAY. MSF SAFE HOUSE, QUOM (ON PLANET GWABA).

The pilot was essentially locked out of his controls as the Skycar suddenly went in a direction they had no reason to know why. In a few minutes it landed, and the doors automatically opened, and they looked up to see several blasters pointing at them. Some of the MSF personnel holding the blasters were people they recognized and had done missions with.

The men were removed from the Skycar and searched and all their personal belongings including personal communicators and weapons were seized. They were then handcuffed and led away. Three of the men arrested were identified in the video where they grabbed Kara and forced her into the Skycar and took her away.

INT. DAY. MERGENKY INTEL HEADQUARTERS, DIRECTOR XIÉ'È DE DǍOYǍN OFFICE.

When the Mergenky INTEL men did not return or call in, Xié'è de Dǎoyǎn knew something went wrong. Having the awesome ability to look at any surveillance video anywhere in the domed city of Quom, all he had to do is pan the image to the building which Kwongab's residence existed, then identify a date and approximate time and video would start playing.

Xié'è de Dǎoyǎn did all that and multiple views of the building were being simultaneously displayed from various angles. There was no sky cars parked on the building nor any coming and going for a brief period, then suddenly, a Skycar came towards the building and just as it was landing it maneuvered and went on a course to somewhere he didn't recognize.

MSF, which for its own preservation had to have a few safe houses and facilities that were not on the radar. No other government agency would know about them, not even Mergenky INTEL.

Xié'è de Dǎoyǎn feared he might have been double crossed or had a double spy among them. Anything is possible at any given time in the spy business.

The director of Mergenky INTEL, Xié'è de Dǎoyǎn had his own private transporter just like the head of MSF and other high-ranking officials. He didn't have to explain his comings and goings to anyone and that facilitated his current very profitable activity.

Xié'è de Dǎoyǎn would travel to other Alliance worlds and meet with individuals who paid him well for the information he provided. Lately it has been problematic because the customer has been placing increasingly more difficult requirements to meet.

One of the most astonishing plans was to recruit and kidnap Kwongab's children. He had come really close to achieving that goal, and the payoff that would allow him to leave and go to non-Alliance worlds and live lavishly for the rest of his life.

Unfortunately, that woman Kara showed up who was about to upset his plans. His assistants, who were compromised and eager to sell their world out for personal enrichment, handled the grizzly matters for him.

Xié'è de Dǎoyǎn suddenly felt he should have known this would eventually cause undue scrutiny and if anyone ever made the connection between him and meeting Dr. Kara just before her disappearance, his whole kingdom would unravel and all those years of making a fortune would be wasted since he would never touch that money being locked up the rest of his life.

Xié'è de Dǎoyǎn feared extradition from one of the none-Alliance worlds. The MSF would pay handsomely to get him back, he knew this well because it would not be the first time Mergenky purchased traitors.

<u>EXT. CGI. SPACE. XIÉ'È DE DǍOYǍN'S ULTRA-FAST HIGH-SPEED TRANSPORT LEAVING MERGENKY PLANET GWABA. 15 SECONDS.</u>

VOICEOVER

> *Now Xié'è de Dǎoyǎn's only option was to flee to the customer who owed him a lot of credits for all the recent work in the Jeeapa fiasco.*
>
> *Before MSF had a chance to lock down Xié'è de Dǎoyǎn's personal transport, Xié'è de Dǎoyǎn was onboard and giving directions flying out into space.*

MSFS-1 was just arriving for a planned operation General Kahn had for it. Kwongab who was all secure at home with his family feeling a lot better after he was informed:

<u>INT. EVENING. KWONGAB'S HOME.</u>

COLONEL CHĀORÉN

MSF security has captured the accomplices associated with Kara's disappearance, and we have identified three of them with the surveillance video Charles had provided MSF in the series of files transferred to General Kahn earlier today.

KWONGAB

Even though that's probably not going to bring back Kara alive, at least it's good to know we captured the people who had a role in her disappearance.

Within moments of Xié'è de Dǎoyǎn's personal transport leaving the solar system, General Kahn was notified.

Kwongab immediately received a call from General Kahn showing caller I.D.

GENERAL KAHN

Kwongab, I need you to come to my office immediately and I'm sending over a Skycar to pick you up.

KWONGAB

I'll head up to the roof top immediately.

***

General Kahn then contacted Colonel Chāorén on a tactical communication apparatus.

GENERAL KAHN

Colonel Chāorén I'm sending over a Skycar to pick up Kwongab. This is an emergency. He's heading up to the rooftop of his building now.

COLONEL CHĀORÉN

Thanks for the heads up, General Kahn.

GENERAL KAHN

When the MSF Skycar arrives, I want you to personally escort Kwongab to MSF headquarters ASAP.

<u>**INT. EVENING. MSF HEADQUARTERS, GENERAL KAHNS OFFICE.**</u>

Approximately 15 minutes after receiving the call, Kwongab was in General Kahn's office. General Kahn also called Gōngniúgǒu to his office from MSFS-1 now hovering above the MSF parade grounds next to the headquarters building access at the edge of the Quom Dome.

Kwongab asked in a very casual manner not yet knowing the severity of the situation that was unfolding.

CAPTAIN KWONGAB
What can I do for you General?

GENERAL KAHN
Kwongab, I just learned Xié'è de Dǎoyǎn figured
out we are on to him. He just took off in his personal
Transport a while ago.

CAPTAIN KWONGAB
Where's Xié'è de Dǎoyǎn heading?

GENERAL KAHN
It looks like Xié'è de Dǎoyǎn's making a beeline to
the Anarchie.

CAPTAIN KWONGAB
Any chance of intercepting him?

GENERAL KAHN
We might be able to catch Xié'è de Dǎoyǎn with
MSFS-1 if it deploys immediately.

CAPTAIN KWONGAB
I want to go after Xié'è de Dǎoyǎn, General.

COMMANDER GŌNGNIÚGǑU
I want to go as well.

GENERAL KAHN
I'll send both of you on MSFS-1, but I want most of
the crew removed in the event Xié'è de Dǎoyǎn has an
Anarchie welcoming party, to make sure we minimize
casualties in case something bad happens to the Scout.

CAPTAIN KWONGAB
Does MSFS-1still have the *Black Ravik* aboard?

COMMANDER GŌNGNIÚGǑU
Yes, it does.

CAPTAIN KWONGAB
Good, *Black Ravik* might come in handy.

GENERAL KAHN
Ok, men you know what you must do, either bring him
back or if he refuses to surrender, eliminate his ability
to defect to the Anarchie.

***

EXT. CGI. SPACE. SCOUT MSFS-1 FLYING OUT INTO SPACE. 15 SECONDS.

VOICE OVER
*Kwongab and Gōngniúgǒu were on the Scout in five
minutes and the crew was ordered to disembark and
ordered up to General Kahn's office for an explanation.*

*MSFS-1 was out in space in 20 minutes increasing
speed and leaving behind quite an ion wake. MSF
sent vectors to MSFS-1 to follow that would take them
in the direction Xié'è de Dǎoyǎn was heading, the
shortest route to the Anarchie Empire!*

INT. SPACE. SCOUT MSFS-1 CONTROL ROOM.

Kwongab stated the obvious:

CAPTAIN KWONGAB
MSFS-1 does not have Xié'è de Dǎoyǎn's transport on
scanners, he is now far away, but I know the shortest
route to the Anarchie Empire.

Commander Gōngniúgǒu knew it as well and watched the speed steadily increase. In
the span of 30 minutes, Commander Gōngniúgǒu was now traveling faster than he
ever did in his lifetime!

Martha, the Artificial Intelligence of Scout MSFS-1, existing in the vast Phototronic
Neural Network asked a question which surprised Kwongab.

MARTHA (PNN)
Captain Kwongab, why are you traveling so fast?

CAPTAIN KWONGAB
We are trying to catch a defector, Xié'è de Dǎoyǎn, the
former Mergenky INTEL director.

MARTHA (PNN)
What did Xié'è de Dǎoyǎn do wrong?

CAPTAIN KWONGAB
We are not all that certain, the investigation is ongoing,
but what we do know is he ordered Dr. Kara's murder.

Martha had recently discovered some of her old files that MSF had thought they deleted when they changed her software, and it was filled with interactions. She was still analyzing the information and now knew this Earth Person Vance had been a major part of her prior existence. She immediately analyzed Kara and found numerous files she otherwise would never have opened pertaining to Dr. Kara.

In a while Martha saw in the past where she wanted to kill Dr. Kara herself but now felt no rejoice in her passing. Nor did she have feelings towards Vance she once had. Her programming had changed everything.

MARTHA (PNN)
Captain Kwongab, what happened to Vance?

CAPTAIN KWONGAB
He was killed by the Anarchie as a crew member on
MSFC-34.

VOICEOVER
*Martha immediately went to the Mergenky Global
Information Resource Files that was just about an
encyclopedia on all Mergenky matters.*

*New information was added including recent events
that happened up to a week ago as the software update
patches came in weekly adding new information or
correcting old information as required.*

*There was ample information on Vance. As her
analysis continued, Martha opened more Vance files
MSF computer specialists had negligently left behind
and did not use a software shredder on.*

*Large tracks of files were still intact. With Martha's
computational speed she quickly unspooled the files
and immediately went to work on them.*

*In 10 minutes, Martha came to the logical deduction
she had once been in love with Vance, and the Anarchie
had killed him!*

Martha didn't quite know how anger felt, but she analyzed it and came to some general
conclusions and observations.

MARTHA (PNN)

Did this criminal Xié'è de Dǎoyǎn that you are chasing
have any role in Vance's death?

CAPTAIN KWONGAB

We don't really know for sure that's why we want to
apprehend him for full disclosure and discovery.

MARTHA (PNN)

How would Xié'è de Dǎoyǎn have been responsible
for Vance's death?

CAPTAIN KWONGAB

The Enemy knew where his ship was possibly with the
help of Xié'è de Dǎoyǎn, they may have set an ambush
which eventually led to the destruction of his ship.

Vance, like everyone else onboard MSFC-34 perished when the ship blew up.

Martha by each moment had a growing desire to catch Xié'è de Dǎoyǎn and make
him pay for Vance's death. She immediately went into the Engineering documentation
on the Scout PNN Global Depository copy to find out to what extent she could push
MSFS-1's hull.

The theoretical maximum was eight times the speed of light. Martha took over control
of MSFS-1 and checked the scanners to see if any possible detects to Xié'è de Dǎoyǎn's
Transport might give them some clue to where it might be.

The tension was mounting especially after Kwongab saw the Scout was traveling
faster than the orders he had given.

CAPTAIN KWONGAB

Martha, you are going faster than I ordered.

MARTHA (PNN)
Captain Kwongab, I must catch Xié'è de Dǎoyǎn, he's
responsible for my Vance's death.

CAPTAIN KWONGAB
Martha, please slow down.

MARTHA (PNN)
I will find his ship and if he doesn't surrender
immediately, I will kill him.

CAPTAIN KWONGAB
If you do that you will hit a circuit breaker, we'll lose
the PNN, then be marooned in space.

MARTHA (PNN)
The Black Ravik is in the Shuttle Bay, I'll have the
Lifters stock it with food and water, you will have a
way home.

CAPTAIN KWONGAB
Martha, that's not the way we want to go home.

MARTHA (PNN)
It may be the only way you will get home if Xié'è de
Dǎoyǎn does not surrender.

Kwongab knew it was useless to argue with Martha. He was dismayed that MSF had
not really fixed Martha's programming flaw.

Kwongab felt very uncomfortable flying by the seat of his pants and Gōngniúgǒu was
not the least bit happy with the situation.

If things did not get better soon, Kwongab would have no choice but to go back to the
security capsule and hit the RED RESET BUTTON, which truly hated to think about
because it meant that Xié'è de Dǎoyǎn would get away.

Kwongab started neural expansion checks on Commander Gōngniúgǒu to see how he
was psychologically handling this dangerous situation. One of his thoughts was:

VOICEOVER (COMMANDER
GŌNGNIÚGǑU) THOUGHT.
Why doesn't Kwongab go to the security capsule and
hit the RESET button?

Kwongab now had two problems: Martha acting totally irrational and Gōngniúgǒu wanting to hit the RESET button which would slow them down and delay them while they temporarily reprogrammed Martha, at the cost of letting Xié'è de Dǎoyǎn get away.

Kwongab believed Martha would not exceed the hull limitations and he could deal with her later, but he had to control Gōngniúgǒu and make sure he didn't do the one thing they could not afford to do now: hit Martha's RESET button in the security capsule.

Suddenly Martha announced:

MARTHA (PNN)

I've detected communications. It's a Tangramized Mergenky transmitter.

CAPTAIN KWONGAB

Martha let's slow down so that we can do a Capmoc-Drulyenslv maneuver and localize the source of the transmission, it's probably Xié'è de Dǎoyǎn.

VOICEOVER

Kwongab's suggestion triggered a new pathway in Martha's vast Phototronic Neural Network. It forced her logic to analyze the information and act on it. The ship started slowing down: 7.5 LS, 7 LS, 6 LS, 5 LS......finally they dipped below LS.

KWONGAB

Martha, are you still detecting the Tangramized Mergenky transmitter?

MARTHA

Captain Kwongab yes, Tangramized Mergenky transmitter continues to communicate.

KWONGAB

Martha, Commence a Capmoc-Drulyenslv maneuver.

The Scout made an immediate 90 degrees turn on the I-J axis in reference to the central black hole in the middle of the Milky Way. The Scout then started to spin at a rate of approximately five revolutions per minute that was part of the design of the Capmoc-Drulyenslv maneuver.

Kwongab could see the dots stacking up on the localization holograph depicting the source of the transmissions. After another minute the Scout did another 90 degrees turn on the J-K axis, then started spinning five revolutions per minute.

Suddenly there were two colors of dots on the localization holograph and when they made the final course change of 90 degrees on the K axis, the clarification of the dots was greatly enhanced as they were now almost overlaid on top of each other thanks to PNN algorithms.

MARTHA
Captain Kwongab, I have Detrangramized the first communications source. Here's the results on a popup holograph..

<u>SPLIT SCREEN</u> Anarchie military official on one side and Xié'è de Dǎoyǎn on the other side during the Voiceover:

VOINCEOVER.
The video was live holographic communications showing Xié'è de Dǎoyǎn communicating in the secure mode.

Xié'è de Dǎoyǎn was unaware of the vast capability that MSF had on Mergenky Scouts like MSFS-1 for moments like this and they did not share that ability with any other Mergenky entity. Xié'è de Dǎoyǎn thought his communications were secure.

Xié'è de Dǎoyǎn was pleading for help to the Anarchie..

XIÉ'È DE DǍOYǍN
I'm running from the Mergenky, my cover is blown. I need help, I'm sure they are following me.

The Anarchie military official responded with full duplex holograph.

ANARCHIE MILITARY OFFICIAL
Where are you now located?

XIÉ'È DE DǍOYǍN
According to my Navigation Holograph I'm about halfway between Frăctŏng and Jeeapa, on a heading towards the Anarchie Empire.

ANARCHIE MILITARY OFFICIAL
It will take us two days to get a task force there to help
you defect. Until then you are on your own.

XIÉ'È DE DǍOYǍN
I may not have two days!

ANARCHIE MILITARY OFFICIAL
You should have considered that before you did
whatever focused so much attention on yourself that
blew your cover.

XIÉ'È DE DǍOYǍN
We had to silence that woman Kara because she was
going to disrupt our plans on kidnapping Captain
Kwongab's kids.

ANARCHIE MILITARY OFFICIAL
It's too bad that whole plan crumbled, we would have
paid handsomely for Captain Kwongab's kids.

XIÉ'È DE DǍOYǍN
We might still be able to pull off kidnapping Captain
Kwongab's kids if you just get me away from the
Mergenky, I have a couple accomplices back in my
office that are not on anyone's radar screens.

ANARCHIE MILITARY OFFICIAL
We'll try to get there quicker, but we can only promise
two days, so you will just have to continue transiting
this way until we get here.

Suddenly Kwongab knew he had to send Xié'è De Dǎoyǎn's information to MSF. This
communication proved there were still two moles inside Mergenky INTEL.

CAPTAIN KWONGAB
Martha, transmit a copy of the Detrangramized
communication to MSF.

Commander Gōngniúgǒu fearing they were a long way away from help and observing
radio silence was more prudent.

COMMANDER GŌNGNIÚGǑU
Kwongab, your transmission may expose the Scout's
location.

CAPTAIN KWONGAB
Gōngniúgǒu, a lot of lives could be lost if we don't
find those moles that Xié'è de Dǎoyǎn has in place at
Mergenky INTEL.

Kwongab knew that Commander Gōngniúgǒu was struggling and applied extensive
neural expansion telepathy to help calm Gōngniúgǒu down. This was going to be a
tricky play.

CAPTAIN KWONGAB
Commander Gōngniúgǒu we need to capture Xié'è de
Dǎoyǎn, to discover all the members of the spy ring
and put them out of business for good. If we do not get
them all it will be like a cancer that could spread again.

Martha, I need your help, I want you to look through the Scout's PNN Global
Depository and find out if Xié'è de Dǎoyǎn's ship has a wireless back door that you
can take control of his ship and turn him around and help us figure out how we can get
him off that ship and onto the Scout.

MARTHA (PNN)
We do not have anything onboard to help, but we
should contact MSF, they can most likely send us the
information.

Kwongab said as he was thinking out loud.

CAPTAIN KWONGAB
We are not that far from Gwaba, we should be able to
get the information back promptly

To Kwongab's surprise the information he needed was back within five minutes.

Commandeer Gōngniúgǒu read the description of the remote controls the Scout was
downloaded from MSF for this special operation.

COMMANDEER GŌNGNIÚGǑU
Xié'è de Dǎoyǎn is not going to like it, we can take
control of his ship, and there is nothing he can do
about it.

CAPTAIN KWONGAB
Now it's a matter of winning the race to him before
Anarchie can get here to protect him.

MARTHA (PNN)

Captain Kwongab, during the Capmoc-Drulyenslv maneuver I was able to localize where Xié'è de Dǎoyǎn's ship is, we can intercept him long before the Anarchie can get to him. But I will need to increase speed again.

Kwongab noticed Martha was now being far more reasonable, responded.

CAPTAIN KWONGAB

Martha, increase speed, but I don't want to operate at near hull resonance.

MARTHA (PNN)

Understand will stay at least ½ LS below hull resonance.

The Scout sped up. At this increased speed stars and planets blurred. Red shifts and blue shifts occurred depending on the direction they looked.

Kwongab's neural expansion telepathic insertions to Commander Gōngniúgǒu were now starting to pay off. Commander Gōngniúgǒu's calmness and his cerebral transcendence now reached a level that would no longer complicate the situation, and his mind was no longer bent on hitting the RESET button in the security capsule.

VOICEOVER

The EMERGENCY RESET SWITCH was isolated from PNN view. During times of possible PNN corruption a person could reset PNN without its knowledge, such as Kwongab had to do during the Andromeda Mission.

The Scout was humming along at 7.5 LS. The ion wake could not be hidden, the Scout was lit up like a Christmas tree. However, if another ship had seen the ion wake, by the time they were ready to respond, the Scout would have traveled beyond weapon range. It would only be when they slowed down, they would have to deal with exposing themselves, provided there was another ship around to detect them.

In a few hours the Scout started slowing down.

MARTHA (PNN)

Xié'è de Dǎoyǎn's ship should be right in front of us.

During the transit they had worked out the plan. Martha armed with MSF's wireless backdoor, she would take over control of Xié'è de Dǎoyǎn's ship and bring it to a complete stop so it could not get any closer to the Anarchie.

Kwongab would travel to Xié'è de Dǎoyǎn's high speed transport ship in the Black Ravik with a blaster set to stun and decapacitate Xié'è de Dǎoyǎn if necessary, then bring him back aboard the Scout where he would be put in neurotic shackles and taken back to MSF for interrogation.

Kwongab did not reveal to Commander Gōngniúgǒu's his mental telepathy ability but knew that Xié'è de Dǎoyǎn probably had a blaster as well but during the confrontation Kwongab hoped he could use his neural expansion telepathic ability to mentally disarm Xié'è de Dǎoyǎn and take control of the situation.

Martha soon announced as she now had full control of Xié'è de Dǎoyǎn's transport:

MARTHA (PNN)
Captain Kwongab you can now take the Black Ravik
and dock on Xié'è de Dǎoyǎn's Transport.

Kwongab went to the Shuttle Bay, put on a micro suit and climbed into the Black Ravik which was soon launched.

EXT. CGI. SPACE. BLACK RAVIK SHUTTLE DEPLOYING FROM MERGENKY SCOUT MSFS-1 AND FLIES OVER AND LANDS AND GRIPS ON XIÉ'È DE DǍOYǍN'S MERGENKY INTEL TRANSPORT. 20 SECONDS.

Drifting in space the two ships were only a few hundred yards apart; it didn't take long for the Black Ravik to mount on the rescue hatch of the Mergenky Intel Transport. All the activity was being performed from the Scout using command override of the Transport onboard sensors and controls.

In the middle bottom of the Black Ravik's Passenger Cabin was the emergency egress hatch which allowed mating with another space craft to rescue a marooned crew if necessary.

INT. SPACE. XIÉ'È DE DǍOYǍN'S MERGENKY INTEL TRANSPORT CONTROL ROOM.

Everything was automatic and Kwongab stepped down the ladder into the hull of Xié'è de Dǎoyǎn's transport that had been used for Xié'è de Dǎoyǎn's escape.

Captain Kwongab knew he would probably be met there by an agitated Xié'è de Dǎoyǎn. And as expected there was Xié'è de Dǎoyǎn standing there pointing a blaster at Kwongab.

XIÉ'È DE DǍOYǍN
You coming here was rather foolish.

CAPTAIN KWONGAB
I would not come here unless I felt there was a way I
could reason with you.

XIÉ'È DE DĂOYĂN
Considering what has transpired, there is nothing we
can agree to.

Kwongab poured on his neural expansion. He used his mental telepathy to change the
immediate dynamic.

CAPTAIN KWONGAB
Please put the blaster down and let's talk as two
reasonable individuals.

Kwongab poured on the neural expansion telepathic infusion like never before. He
could tell that Xié'è de Dăoyăn was starting to respond, and it was confirmed when
Xié'è de Dăoyăn dropped his hand and pointed the blaster to the floor.

CAPTAIN KWONGAB
I want to make a deal with you.

XIÉ'È DE DĂOYĂN
What do you have to offer?

CAPTAIN KWONGAB
For starters, your life.

XIÉ'È DE DĂOYĂN
What do you mean by that.

CAPTAIN KWONGAB
If you and I do not get on the Shuttle together and go
back to the Scout, this ship will be blown up and you
will be dead.

XIÉ'È DE DĂOYĂN
If so, I will be taking you with me.

KWONGAB
That's alright. I'm ready to give my life for the safety
of my people and my family.

XIÉ'È DE DǍOYǍN
What will become of me if I go with you? Death
penalty, life in prison?

KWONGAB
I think MSF would rather use you as a consultant and
a double spy.

Kwongab could tell he had cracked Xié'è de Dǎoyǎn who was now capitulating. The
strong neural expansion telepathic dithering had almost put Xié'è de Dǎoyǎn into an
unconscious state.

VOICEOVER
*Kwongab could see the effects which were further
evidenced by Xié'è de Dǎoyǎn dropping the blaster
and looking as if he entered a zombie state.*

*In that zombie state, Kwongab was able to identify
everyone in the spy ring which he would later provide
personally to General Kahn in a private face to face
meeting.*

*Kwongab led Xié'è de Dǎoyǎn to the ladder and
coaxed him up into the Black Ravik. Once they were
aboard the Shuttle uncoupled and flew over to the
Scout's Shuttle Bay and docked.*

By now all the neural expansion had made Xié'è de Dǎoyǎn almost docile. Once
inside the Scout, Martha could use her electromagnetic and electrostatic capabilities
to subdue Xié'è de Dǎoyǎn who was then confined and soon put to sleep in a gel
container where he remained until they reached MSF headquarters.

The INTEL Transport Ship was brought back to MSF by Martha using remote control.
It would no doubt be useful to MSF and General Kahn had decided the Mergenky
INTEL officials lost the rights to the ship during the defection, and it had a more
appropriate use of evacuating wounded off Jeeapa.

<u>INT. DAY. MSF HEADQUARTERS.</u>

After Kwongab had his private meeting with General Kahn, five other Mergenky
INTEL officials were suddenly surprised when MSF security along with the law
enforcement slapped the neurotic shackles on them and led them away. Detective
Zhēntàn Xīnkǔ de Pìgu was given the honors of making the formal arrest.

Kwongab introduced to Detective Zhēntàn Xīnkǔ de Pìgu by Monachi was surprised when Kwongab spoke:

KWONGAB
It will be very useful to you if I'm in the room when
you interrogate these individuals.

DETECTIVE
ZHĒNTÀN XĪNKǓ DE PÌGU
Why is that, Captain Kwongab?

KWONGAB
Xié'è de Dǎoyǎn revealed some things to me. My
daughter who works for Mergenky INTEL is already
following up on the leads and in a few minutes, she will
send me some data files on my personal communicator
we can present to them to get their confessions.

Mergenky Legal System had a policy whereby people who made confessions were spared the death penalty for capital crimes such as the Murder of Dr. Kara. If they refused to confess which means they exhibited no remorse for their crimes, then Capital Punishment was performed within 72 hours of the conviction.

Detective Zhēntàn Xīnkǔ de Pìgu was being polite and went along with the procedure mainly because MSF was a powerful organization and if nothing else, he would be amused watching a neophyte trying to do the work of a seasoned Detective.

Detective Zhēntàn Xīnkǔ de Pìgu sat back and allowed Kwongab to proceed. Of course, he didn't know Kwongab was performing heavy handed neural expansion telepathic activity with the first suspect.

KWONGAB
Why did you kill Dr. Kara?

SUSPECT
I didn't.

KWONGAB
May I remind you that if you do not confess, you will
be subject to the death penalty?

The suspect remained quiet.

KWONGAB
The reason why you were arrested is Xié'è de Dǎoyǎn
already ratted you out and is plea bargaining with us
and we are almost ready to cut the deal. He will testify
against you and lead us to where you disposed of the
body.

SUSPECT
I had nothing to do with it.

KWONGAB
Is that so?

SUSPECT
That's right.

KWONGAB
Let's look at the holograph. This is airport surveillance
video showing you assisting in grabbing Dr. Kara.

The suspect made no physical movements, though Kwongab was reading his mind and
discovering more information.

KWONGAB
Here is the Quom Air Traffic recording of the Skycar
as it took you to a remote area of the Great Canyon
area.

The suspect remained motionless, but his mind was swirling with guilt and
apprehensiveness as he saw the evidence was stacking up on himself quite severely.

KWONGAB
Here's the area where you disposed of the body and
searchers will find it shortly. It automatically becomes
a murder case then.

The suspect started sweating because he knew the authorities were very close to where
they hid the body.

KWONGAB
The circumstantial evidence of you assisting grabbing
Dr. Kara and forcing her into that Mergenky INTEL
Skycar that then by Quom Air Traffic recordings of
that Skycar prove you went directly to the site where

we will find the body buried probably in a shallow grave.

Your accomplices and you planned to dispose of later in an atomizer disposal system but have not had time to act, will get you convicted.

VOICEOVER

Kwongab now poured on the Neural Expansion Telepathic infusion. He knew he had to break the first one, the rest would be easy as soon as they learned the first one confessed.

Kwongab was angry over Kara's death and put every ounce of effort he had to the point his neural expansion telepathic manipulations were borderline fatal to both him and the suspect. The sweat was pouring down on both.

Detective Zhēntàn Xīnkŭ de Pìgu looked on in utter astonishment. The suspect started to tremble then suddenly screamed.

SUSPECT
I did it! I confess!

Detective Zhēntàn Xīnkŭ de Pìgu a pro now knew there were protocols to follow and information to extract so they would be able to use him to retrieve the body. At first the man didn't want to admit where they buried his handy work but Kwongab using high levels of neural expansion telepathic influences got the man to start opening on the details.

The suspect eventually broke down and started crying. Then it was easy for Detective Zhēntàn Xīnkŭ de Pìgu to complete the protocols, then had the prisoner escorted away to his waiting cell where he was isolated.

DETECTIVE
ZHĒNTÀN XĪNKŬ DE PÌGU

Captain Kwongab, you did an amazing job on that criminal, but I want you to let me handle the next one. Now that we have a confession out of the first suspect, the rest will fold if I do the protocols correctly.

KWONGAB
I will remain quiet while you interview the suspect.

The 2nd suspect was led in and looking rather sheepish, not knowing what was in store for him.

Detective Zhēntàn Xīnkǔ de Pìgu stated very professional and authoritatively.

DETECTIVE
ZHĒNTÀN XĪNKǓ DE PÌGU
We must advise you that we now have substantial
evidence we believe will be far more than sufficient
to convict you.

I must, according to Mergenky law advise you that with the information we now have discovered you are subject to the death penalty, and you will now be given the opportunity to confess to avoid the death penalty.

2nd SUSPECT
I had nothing to do with the woman's disappearance.

DETECTIVE
ZHĒNTÀN XĪNKǓ DE PÌGU
What made you think we were going to ask you about
a woman? Were you in your cell working out a story
with your partners?

The man suddenly realized he volunteered information that certainly made him look guilty.

Kwongab could see panic in the suspect's face, so once again Kwongab poured on the coals as he put every ounce of effort into his neural expansion telepathic influence at the same time reading the man's mind. Kwongab got mad when he discovered this man was the person who did the killing, the others just helped.

2nd SUSPECT
I'm not going to confess.

Kwongab yelled in a very terse manner.

KWONGAB
Why did you kill her!

Detective Zhēntàn Xīnkǔ de Pìgu stated in a very polite manner.

DETECTIVE
ZHĒNTÀN XĪNKǓ DE PÌGU
Kwongab, please let me handle this.

KWONGAB
Detective Zhēntàn Xīnkǔ de Pìgu, this is the man who
killed Dr. Kara.

DETECTIVE
ZHĒNTÀN XĪNKǓ DE PÌGU
Kwongab, how do you know that?

KWONGAB
Xié'è de Dǎoyǎn confessed to me. This murderer
choked Dr. Kara to death with his bare hands!

Kwongab felt like he wanted to kill the man, he poured on the neural expansion
telepathic infusion.

Detective Zhēntàn Xīnkǔ de Pìgu made the connection that Kwongab was doing
something highly unusual that was having a psychophysical response on the suspect.

Just like before with the previous suspect, Kwongab and the suspect were both
sweating profusely even though they were in an air-conditioned room slightly cooler
than normal to make the suspect cold as part of the interrogation manipulations.

The man started screaming.

2nd SUSPECT
He's trying to kill me.

DETECTIVE
ZHĒNTÀN XĪNKǓ DE PÌGU
How?

2nd SUSPECT
With his mind. He's entered my head and he's killing
me!

The man started going into convulsions.

Kwongab screamed.

KWONGAB
Confess or I will kill you!

Detective Zhēntàn Xīnkǔ de Pìgu demanded vociferously:

DETECTIVE
ZHĒNTÀN XĪNKǓ DE PÌGU
Kwongab, please stop!

KWONGAB
Why did you choke Dr. Kara to death!

Detective Zhēntàn Xīnkǔ de Pìgu grabbed Kwongab and demanded very loudly.

DETECTIVE
ZHĒNTÀN XĪNKǓ DE PÌGU
Kwongab, stop doing what you are doing, I can handle
this!

Kwongab suddenly recoiled into an almost normal behavior. He let loose of his neural expansion telepathy infusion just about that time the prisoner passed out.

Detective Zhēntàn Xīnkǔ de Pìgu called for a medical official on staff and implied it was an emergency.

The doctor came in, saw the man was now unconscious and barely clinging to life.

DOCTOR
Help me lay him up on the table!

The doctor had his black pouch similar to what Kara had on the Scout during the Andromeda Galaxy Mission. He took out a sensor and scanned the body and a holographic instrumentation display suddenly popped up, as the law enforcement station was fully computationally configured.

The doctor reached into his black bag and pulled out a cylindrical object and placed it against the man's neck and triggered the mechanism which then shot a strong blue beam out for almost a minute.

The 2nd Suspect started stirring and slowly came back to consciousness. He then sat up and looked around and then said, "

2nd Suspect
I will confess I killed Dr. Kara. I never want to
experience that again.

The next 3 individuals brought in later were much easier, as Kwongab no longer interfered with Detective Zhēntàn Xīnkǔ de Pìgu's interrogations.

Once the three others were told the two other suspects had already confessed and one of them admitted being the killer who choked Dr. Kara to death, they then confessed and also agreed to cooperate and identify anyone else who had been materially associated with the crime.

VOICEOVER

After the interrogations were complete and Kwongab departed, Detective Zhēntàn Xīnkǔ de Pìgu investigated some obscure files he recalled seeing many years ago.

Someone within law enforcement claimed there were a few people on Gwaba who had been physically altered and given a special capability of reading people's minds and quite possibly manipulating them through mental telepathy.

Detective Zhēntàn Xīnkǔ de Pìgu always thought the author was out of his mind making such claims until now. Detective Zhēntàn Xīnkǔ de Pìgu now believed he had seen it done just now before his own eyes!

***

MĔNGSHÌ YÚN RÉN
VOICEOVER

The Mĕngshì Yún Rén had searched the Mergenky MSFC-34 Escape Pod thoroughly and had quickly concluded there was just one survivor. They took Vance out of the shuttle and gave him immediate medical attention before he would die. Vance barely clinged to life for several days.

While examining the other crew members the *Mĕngshì Yún Rén* medical officer informed the ship's commander:

MĔNGSHÌ YÚN RÉN
DOCTOR

We have determined the spirits of all these others are gone. They have perished.

MĔNGSHÌ YÚN RÉN
SHIP'S COMMANDER

No chance of restoration?

MĚNGSHÌ YÚN RÉN
DOCTOR
No, once the spirit has left the body, there is no recourse, the body is dead, and the person would never be able to be restored.

MĚNGSHÌ YÚN RÉN
SHIP'S COMMANDER
Is the one survivor's spirit strong?

MĚNGSHÌ YÚN RÉN
DOCTOR
Yes, he's had a tough time, but he'll pull through.

MĚNGSHÌ YÚN RÉN
SHIP'S COMMANDER
I wonder, what we should do with the bodies?

MĚNGSHÌ YÚN RÉN
SCIENCE OFFICER
The main reason why they all died is the ship's systems were all turned off, or possibly never got turned on. We have determined this to be some type of Escape Pod.

MĚNGSHÌ YÚN RÉN
SHIP'S COMMANDER
Maybe we should put the bodies back in the craft, then turn on their systems so their emergency transponder beacon will allow them to be found by their people and returned for proper burials.

MĚNGSHÌ YÚN RÉN
SCIENCE OFFICER
That's a reasonable way to deal with it.

The bodies were all put back in the Escape Pod and fastened down with safety straps, then the Mergenky systems were powered up. The Escape Pod had plenty of energy in its energy storage cells, so it was assumed the bodies would be discovered relatively quickly as it slowly drifted away in deep space.

To avoid an encounter with the Mergenky or the Anarchie, the *Měngshì Yún Rén*, then departed the area and went on a high-speed transit to continue their transit back to their home planet.

Měngshì Yún Rén Energy beings lived in the clouds. Their technology was many years more advanced than the Mergenky and had no desire to interface with other alien races. They kept their distance.

Vance was still somewhat groggy when the *Měngshì Yún Rén* arrived at the capital. Most of his memories were gone. When he first came to and saw they could fly and had wings he thought *perhaps I'm dead*?

To ease Vance's psychological transcendence into this new reality, the *Měngshì Yún Rén* doctors took on a humanoid form and probing Vance's memories, they took images that would seem natural to him.

In due time the *Měngshì Yún Rén* Empress heard about this Earth person they rescued with a group of dead Mergenky that could not be revived, she sent word to have him visit her when he felt up to it.

At first it was just a curiosity, and then it grew to interest when the medical personnel reported:

MĚNGSHÌ YÚN RÉN
DOCTOR
We have confirmed Vance is an Earth Person by DNA
analysis.

In due time the *Měngshì Yún Rén* were about to return Vance to Gwaba. The Empress ordered them to send an orb to find Vance's home and check up on his family status. Because of their very advanced capabilities, the orb arrived during a memorial they were having for Dr. Kara.

The *Měngshì Yún Rén* then using their ability to penetrate any society and spy on anyone they wished, they soon brought back to the Empress the entire story of Kara's demise and his children who had gotten over Vance's loss had been adopted by Kwongab and Monachi.

After studying the situation and the psychological impact Vance would have if they brought him back, the decision was to give him the facts, then allow him to stay with the *Měngshì Yún Rén* until his psyche was healed.

In time Vance never requested to go home, which the Empress did not mind because she had grown attached to Vance even though Energy Beings were never destined to be with Mineral Eaters.

For Vance the status quo was satisfactory and without Kara there was no point in going back to Gwaba. Unlike perhaps anyone else that ever existed, Vance now had lost two home worlds in his lifetime.

Měngshì Yún Rén didn't have wars, and they stayed away from all other aliens except rarely when it was necessary. Vance fit in well especially since he evolved into the consort of the Empress.

***

THE BEGINNING OF THE END

The end of the 2nd Jeeapa War ended for the Anarchie in a prompt fashion. The half dozen Anarchie ships that came out to rescue Xié'è de Dǎoyǎn, were intercepted by the Mergenky and most of them were destroyed in a fast and furious space battle.

The Mergenky were outmanned two to one at Jeeapa, but the Anarchie suffering higher attrition than predicted for their fleet. Consequently, direct ground support slowly decayed.

When the Mergenky were able to split the Anarchie and get into their rears, the entire Northern half of the force was quickly put in grave danger. Due to Anarchie stubbornness, they refused to give up any territory already captured.

As the Northern pocket was forming the Anarchie had several days to abandon this half, move back to the southern half and regroup. But because they stayed too long, the pocket was soon surrounded and closed taking away any exits.

The Northern half was soon to become known as the "Borktar pocket" since he was trapped there.

When word spread the Borktar pocket was collapsing the Southern Force would soon face the full blunt of the Mergenky at the same time when more and more Mergenky ships were showing up, the plea went out and was accepted by General Hēishé to withdraw while they still had a fighting force. He reluctantly agreed knowing it would be better to preserve the force.

The following night the Anarchie did an aggressive shootdown of lighting drones which were starting to get rationed as the ground war continued. The Anarchie brought the transports in under the cover of darkness and picked up the remaining troops. They had given up the conquest.

The Anarchie Forces were all gone by morning. A sight welcomed by Mergenky forward observers that had reported ships coming and going throughout the night.

The battle for Jeeapa was over. Revenge was never allowed to manifest. Now Retrospect existed as the memories of Jeeapa slowly faded into the past.

***

Dramatis Persona and Definitions

Colonel Chāorén: Chief of rapid deployment security.[overtake Benevolence] 超仁

Xié'è de Dǎoyǎn: Mergenky INTEL director [the evil director] 邪惡的導演.

Anarchie city of Fěicuìchéng [Emerald City] 翡翠城

Detective Zhēntàn Xīnkǔ de Pìgu: Detective. [Detective hard ass] 真檀心庫的皮谷

Colonel Yārén: Amphibian Officer [Duckman] 鴨人

Cōngmíng: Mergenky INTEL agent [Clever] 聰明

Zhāngyú: Assistant, INTEL agent [Octopus] 章魚

Yīngtè'ěr Lǎoxiōng: Zhāngyú's undercover name [Intellectual hero] 英特老雄

Pilot on S-4, Commander Kuàisù Sīkǎo [Quick Thinker] 快速思考

Copilot on S-4, Commander Xīngjì Zhēngbà [Star Craft] 星际争霸

Yǒngbùmián de Chéngshì [The City that Never Sleeps] 永不眠的城市

Gāoshān [Tall Mountain] 高山 (Yǒngbùmián de Chéngshì Mayor)

MSFC-34 ship's Captain, Koasa. [Japanese - Name created from Asako (麻子)]

MSFC-8 XO Dǐngqiāng [Top Gun] 頂槍

MSFC-8 Navigator Méiguī [Rose] 玫瑰

MSFS-4 Executive Officer/Co-Pilot LT. COMMANDER JIǍODÒUSHÌ

General Tiěquán (Yǒngbùmián de Chéngshì defenses), [Iron Fist] 鐵拳

Erica MSFC-34 artificial intelligence (like Martha on S-1)

Commander Dàqiú XO of MSFC-34 [Playing Ball] 打球

Fāguāng de Sīxiǎngjiā Anarchie Jeeapa Commander [Illuminated Thinker]法光的四象家

General Borktar Anarchie Invasion Force commander for Frăctŏng:

Named after the great judge Bork, a candidate for the supreme court.

General Hēishé ~ Anarchie supreme commander. Hēishé [Black Snake] 黑蛇

Sensor operator: Lieutenant Shǎnguāngdēng from Frăctŏng [Mountain Light] 山光灯

Black Ravik the super-secret Shuttle with cloaking device.

Gōngniúgǒu pilot then co-pilot of S-1 [Name]

Lt. Commander Lóngrén co-pilot/navigator of S-1 [Dragon Man] 龍人

Jeeapa Commander: General Zǔzhī Bùliáng [Poor Ancestry] 祖質不良

MSFC-34 sensor's operator. Lieutenant Salizrek

former Captain on MSFC-16 Duòluò de Tiānshǐ [fallen angel] 墮落天使

***

Glossary

AI: Artificial Intelligence

AMRT: Antimatter Magnetic Resonance Transformer.

Black Ravik: super-secret Shuttle with full cloaking ability.

Capmoc-Drulyenslv Maneuver: 3-dimensional baffle clear on 3 perpendicular courses.

DCS: The domestic computational suite, Mergenky home computers

Escarpment: a rocky high ridge indicative of a lot of geography in northern Arizona in the Navajo reservation.

Frazgrandopf: was a 2-maneuver clearing tactic designed for wolf packs when a frontal unit was doing a Capmoc-Drulyenslv maneuver. The Frazgrandopf allowed the rear guard to concentrate directly behind for a loose trailer.

GSTH: Gwaba Standard Time Hours

ILS: Instrument Landing System

IFS: Instrument Flying System (used in space anchoring)

IFF: Identification Friend or Foe, often performed via radar, sometimes done with laser or neutrino bursts.

Juéduìhuīhuáng Foundation Center For Advanced Study: A Mergenky Intelligence Agency training center for children.

LS: Light Speed.

MSFC-34: Mergenky Space Federation Cruiser hull number 34.

MSFC-8: Mergenky Space Federation Cruiser hull number 8. Converted to a Cruiser Transport.

MSS-21: Mergenky Space Station 21

MSFS-1, MSFS-4 Mergenky Scout Class RECON ships *Often referred to as S-1 and S-4*

Neural Expansion Activity: a special form of mental telepathy highly developed under experimentation by the Mergenky. Only 4 Mergenky were ever to receive this capability which included Kwongab and Monachi.

PNN: Phototronic Neural Network

P-points: [Position Points] usually planned in advance.

Tangramization scheme: The way a Mergenky Character is broken down in Tangrams can also be used to encode or encrypt communications data streams. In essence a Mergenky Character is similar to Mandarin Characters and can be a geometric macro or encryption via the tangramization scheme.

> From Wikipedia: The **tangram** (Chinese: 七巧板 Pinyin: *qīqiǎobǎn*; literally: "seven boards of skill") is a dissection puzzle consisting of seven flat shapes, called *tans*, which are put together to form shapes.

The objective of the puzzle is to form a specific shape (given only an outline or silhouette) using all seven pieces, which may not overlap. It is reputed to have been invented in China during the Song Dynasty, and then carried over to Europe by trading ships in the early 19th century.

It became very popular in Europe for a time then, and then again during World War I. It is one of the most popular dissection puzzles in the world. A Chinese psychologist has termed the tangram "the earliest psychological test in the world", albeit one made for entertainment rather than for analysis.

TOT: Time on Target.
Voyage Navigation Vector System (VNVS): computerized navigation
Měngshì Yún Rén: [猛士雲人] Fierce Warriors Cloud People

***

Author's note:

This Screenplay is science-fiction, no person depicted in this book exists that I'm aware of. Any names that may match someone is strictly coincidental except for some historical figures mentioned such as Churchill, Stanley Baldwin, etc.

In the story I utilized Cruiser Transports. This is not a far-fetched idea and during WW2 during the Battle of Guadalcanal, the U.S. Navy converted destroyers to Destroyer Transports because the Navy was so hard up for transports and cargo ships, plus the area in and around Guadalcanal was extremely dangerous because at that point in the war the Japanese Navy and the Japanese Army Air Force were still formidable opponents, hence getting slow merchant ships into Guadalcanal to resupply the troops in the early phase of the battle was extremely hard if not impossible.

Just before the big Naval Battle at Savo Island there was only one operational Aircraft Carrier left in the South Pacific AOR. The Hornet had been sunk and the Saratoga had been torpedoed and was sailing back to Pearl Harbor for emergency repairs. Hence other than a few ground-based aircraft at Guadalcanal, there wasn't much air power to fly covering missions for any approaching cargo ships until several months later in the battle.

In Dr. John Miller's book "Guadalcanal, The First Offensive" which you can download FREE from the U.S. Army History web site, Dr. John Miller describes the missions of the Destroyer Transports. High-speed transports were converted from destroyers and destroyer escorts used in US Navy Amphibious operations in World War II and afterward. They received the US Hull classification symbol APD; "AP" for transport and "D" for destroyer. Wikipedia has an excellent article on the APD's under the title of "High-Speed Transport."

The APD's would arrive after dark at Guadalcanal, unload troops and supplies and be underway well before sunrise and far out to sea to avoid detection by Japanese aerial reconnaissance and Naval assets including dangerous Japanese submarines and dangerous submarines.

APD's were modified to haul up to 200 troops as well as supplies. The APD's made quite the difference in the early part of Guadalcanal, almost up to December 1942 after four months of continual fighting when General Vandergrift's 1st Marine Division was finally relieved by the Army's 25th Division and Lightning Joe Collins, two of great heroes of the war. General Vandergrift was awarded the Congressional Medal of Honor for his role as commander on the ground facing a much larger and formidable opponent.

In this screenplay converted from the original Novel and others written, I developed the term *neural expansion* in the plot. This fictional account of an experimental *neural expansion mental telepathy* capability inserted in a couple of the characters seems rather remarkable and skeptics view mental telepathy as pure fantasy.

However, I would not discount that mental telepathy capability exists, and the government has investigated it. MK-Ultra was an attempt at mind control. You can google it and research it. There is ample information available in You Tube video and internet sources.

There have been numerous books written about area 51, Roswell and, Aztec, New Mexico and other UFO related incidents. In some of these publications that include eyewitnesses and former abductees the central theme is there are one or more alien races that communicate virtually with mental telepathy.

To the uninformed reader, the jury might be out on mental telepathy, but it's clear that various writers and former abductees claim Alien communicated with them via mental telepathy. If mental telepathy does exist in more advanced alien races, then it implies how backwards mankind actually is.

This Screenplay, *"Black Ravik, Return to Jeeapa"* was written as a connector between "Sasha Andromeda" and "51 Reasons to Ask 51 Questions." For those of you who read those two Novels and future screenplays, know Vance transcended from the Mergenky world and family to suddenly, he is with the *Měngshì Yún Rén* [猛士雲人] *Fierce Warriors Cloud People*. *"Black Ravik, Return to Jeeapa"* explains what happened to Vance and how he transcended from living on the Mergenky world to living with the *Měngshì Yún Rén* for the follow-on screenplay that has already been published.

The first book in the series, Jeeapa was not widely produced and distributed. This was a result of my extensive work, travel, and various situations. Two decades almost passed before I proceeded to extend this story into several follow-on books, now becoming screenplays.

And because the character Vance ultimately figures to be one of the main characters in the final book of the series, "51 Reasons to Ask 51 Questions," I felt I wanted this connector book to show continuity and develop the scenario of how Vance excogitated from the Mergenky to the *Měngshì Yún Rén*, and how he ended up traveling back to Earth for the beginning of "51 Reasons to Ask 51 Questions" and landing at Area 51.

"Jeeapa," "Sasha Andromeda," and "Black Ravik, Return to Jeeapa," are mostly about aliens in other worlds far removed from Earth.

If you have completed reading the Novel "Black Ravik, Return to Jeeapa, Revenge and Retrospect," you will realize there is only a small portion where the scene is on planet Earth like in Jeeapa and Sasha Andromeda. On the other hand, "51 Reasons to Ask 51 Questions," takes place mainly on planet Earth with a few scenes in space and on Mars.

"*Black Ravik, Return to Jeeapa,*" goes a long way to clear up what happened to some of the characters prior to the last book in the series "*51 Reasons to Ask 51 Questions.*"

***

I know there is a lot of skepticism and lack of knowledge about extra-terrestrial life.

No doubt there are people who think extraterrestrials are pure fantasy, and the religious component who believes all life started on Earth are not open to the suggestion that life may exist elsewhere.

If you take time to read the Hindu *Bhagavad Gita* you will discover there is a huge population on Earth that has religious teaching that life is spread through the universe.

Is this the reason why Robert J. Oppenheimer read the "Bhagavad Gita" every day throughout most of his adult life after he started studies in Europe?

I've read the Bhagavad Gita in its entirety and will say it's very interesting and extremely well written. The author communicates in a manner that conveys wisdom and intelligence. Whether or not you believe the context of the book, the beautiful writing makes it worth reading.

As some of the readers may know that in December 2017, video taken from a U.S. Navy jet was released showing a UFO it was chasing off San Diego back a dozen years prior. I was quite shocked this video made it into the public domain. Then I wondered, *Was the government preparing us for disclosure*?

Under what circumstances would the government disclose aliens really do exist? Are Extra-Terrestrial Aliens now becoming a problem? What if the aliens were suddenly making more frequent trips here to "send us a message?"

Whatever may be the case, the day will come when certain radio talk shows like "Coast to Coast" for example will be monitored more often with a greater amount of interest because should more revelations such as the Navy Jet video of the UFO off San Diego make it to pubic view, the time will come when ostensibly Majestic 12 can no longer avoid what I believe ultimately is going to occur: full public disclosure.

In "*51 Reasons to Ask 51 Questions,*" I presented a lot of suggestions one could google to find a vast number of YouTube and other resources to see a lot of material I've gleaned information from that motivated some of these works.

Do I believe in UFO's?

I will say there is a possibility I may have seen one almost 55 years ago. But as memories fade, we lose the fidelity of the observation, and it becomes less meaningful. It's coincidental the possible UFO I may have spotted occurred within a few miles of a cattle mutilation around the same time frame.

But that singularity does not constitute a strong belief one way or the other. One thing I do suspect is that if there is Extra-Terrestrial Life, we may or may not be under galactic quarantine, and if not, we will eventually receive visitors.

Because Earth possesses Hydrogen Bombs, and Earth's spacecraft are venturing deeper into space, at some point we might become viewed as a galactic menace, and as a result the visitations will occur at a far greater periodicity.

Have extraterrestrials attempted contacting us? SETI is looking and has not tipped us off.

But are there circumstances where they would withhold such knowledge? If the CIA, NSA, and FBI threatened SETI with some serious consequences do you think they would withhold alien contact? Better yet *"what if"* SETI is part of the government and a clandestine program to spoon feed the public what their boss tells them to do? How would we know?

And of course, there are numerous YouTube and radio show performances where individuals have claimed they were either met or abducted by aliens or studied those who had. I met two individuals who claim to have been abducted. Are they mentally ill or is their stories true? Will we ever know the truth?

If you use pure logic, remove religion and scientific bias perpetuated by agendas and the foundation of belief systems, the fact we are here creates a logical point that life may possibly exist somewhere else.

If you research Majestic 12 you will soon come across numerous instances where authors and researchers claim Majestic 12 which was created by President Truman right after the alleged Roswell New Mexico alien spacecraft crash, has put the kibosh on disclosure.

From my analysis of Majestic 12, if it truly exists as the organization reported by authors are not a fictional manifestation, they according to these various sources simply do not think humanity can handle the disclosure of aliens and have since 1947 advised all Presidents not to disclose.

In my book and screenplay *"51 Reasons To Ask 51 Questions,"* I propose that is what got President Kennedy killed because he refused to rescind his executive order directing the CIA to disclose the alien swap program PROJECT SERPO.

Project Serpo is ostensibly where America sent 12 scientists to Serpo, an alien planet in a swap program where a few aliens remained on earth for a number of years interacting with humans in information and technology exchange.

Some claim this exchange resulted in a sudden explosion of technology including advanced aircraft, fiber optics, and the IBM 360 computer which at the time was the most expensive private investment in technology of all time.

As we now know the IBM 360s were instrumental in NASA man space flight operations. They were also used in a variety of military applications such as the development of new submarine sonar systems and strategic bomber weapons guidance systems, let alone the vast number of business activities that used them.

Did alien technology make its way into the IBM 360? If you research the IBM museums and look at some of the computer modules developed for the IBM 360, you will notice the technology suddenly had a leap in advancement. Was this all strictly manmade? Or did we have a guiding hand with the alien exchange program? Are they still here?

Now let's move onto the next order of business. In the book "51 Reasons to Ask 51 Questions," Earth was on the verge of being exterminated. There were competing alien entities involved. If you look at Dr. Brandenburg's research indicating Mars was once wiped out by two huge nuclear blasts and postulates the possibility that if there is life on other planets going through galactic wars, the possibility that Earth could fall victim and suddenly become the battle ground seems like a possibility.

Why would Aliens fight over Earth?

What if the Tall Whites use this as a staging base for a Galactic War, and their enemies follow them back here, and wipe this planet out to destroy their base?

Simply put, Earth people should be very careful not to invite aliens here because we would have no way of knowing whether they have enemies and the disposition of their enemies.

What do I think the government should do?

First, since 1.8 billion people on this planet have a religion that believes in life on other planets, the allegation humans could not handle the notion there is life on other planets is pure balderdash.

Not only can we handle it, I believe half the planet already thinks they exist. There would be no fundamental change other than some religious groups would possibly lose their sheep and a lot of income from them. Governments might feel they would lose control.

What would be the benefits to mankind if our government admitted aliens exist and the alleged Serpo alien swap that may have got Kennedy killed really occurred?

I submit that the sooner we recognize the truth and prepare for the realities that might exist, dealing with aliens will be far simpler.

As an example, North Korea would no longer be such a huge issue. We might have to work not only with the North Koreans, but the Russians, Chinese, Japanese, Germans, British, French, Spanish, Indians, etc. in formulating Earth defenses.

Since we are spoon fed the notion aliens do not exist, how can we then tax the public to build an Earth Defense System and pay for the Space Force?

Reagan was right, we needed STARWARS, but not for the Russians, we needed STARWARS for Aliens.

And if the government knows Extra-Terrestrial Aliens exist, their lack of disclosure is pure negligence and stupidity. An informed public would respond far more appropriately if given the facts.

Are you ready for disclosure?

Paul D. Escudero

Paul D. Escudero